"The Wind Shift"

That was the Army's explanation for the death of 6,400 sheep near its Dugway chemical and biological warfare testing ground in Utah. This admission of a slight error in one of its innumerable experiments with death came only after eight months of innocent denials. Still later another spokesman added, "If the wind had drifted another way, it could have been a town."

It could have been a town!

A town like Tarsus, where *Vector* begins. Where an entire population is about to be destroyed. And where the fate of the nation will hang on the desperate plan of a man and woman who have been thrown together by disaster, held together by passion, and hunted down like animals by their own government. . . .

VECTOR

"Excellent, provocative suspense!"
—Publishers' Weekly

VECTOR

Henry Sutton

A DELL BOOK

Published by
DELL PUBLISHING CO., INC.
750 Third Avenue
New York, New York 10017

Reprinted by arrangement with
Bernard Geis Associates
New York, New York

Printed in the United States of America
First Dell printing—November 1971

For the Honorable Richard D. McCarthy,
with admiration,
And for Berney,
with gratitude.

For behold, the Lord saw that his people began to work in darkness, yea, work secret murders and abominations; therefore the Lord said, if they did not repent they should be destroyed from off the face of the earth.

Alma 37:22
THE BOOK OF MORMON

VECTOR

Tuesday, November 25

1:00 P.M., Mountain Standard Time:

On the black-and-white television screen, the President was speaking, his brow furrowed in seriousness. To most of the millions of Americans who were watching and listening to him, his words seemed to be good news indeed. Fine news! But to the officers in the lounge of the officers' club at Dugway, that furrowed brow appeared to be scowling, and the news seemed to be an indictment, or even a betrayal:

"Biological weapons have massive, unpredictable, and potentially uncontrollable consequences," the President was saying. "They may produce global epidemics and impair the health of future generations. I have therefore decided that the United States shall renounce the use of lethal biological agents and weapons and all other methods of biological warfare; the United States will confine its biological research to defensive measures such as immunization and safety measures; the Department of Defense has been asked to make recommendations as to the disposal of existing stocks of bacteriological weapons. In the spirit of these decisions . . ."

To Major William Robertson it was a kick in the head. Why was this happening? What had produced such an abrupt reversal in United States policy? And most of all, what would happen to his lab and to the other labs and test sites out here at the proving ground? What would happen to Dugway, an establishment very nearly as large as the entire state of Rhode Island?

The President was finished speaking. Robertson had

not heard or, anyway, had not been able to absorb any of his closing, general remarks. On the television screen, the President disappeared to be replaced by an earnest CBS commentator, who had his say, and then Andy Griffith's face took his place. Mechanically, Robertson reached for his coffee, but he had let it stand too long. It was cold and bitter. It was as if he were drinking the President's address.

And then he felt a hand on his shoulder.

"Not to worry," Deap said. "No fear, Doctor. It's hopeless but not serious."

Dr. Deap, an odd, studiedly elegant Englishman, seemed very calm for a man whose program had just been shot out from under him. But then, Robertson thought, that was the English way, wasn't it? Go down with the ship, go down with the whole damn empire with a clever Trevor Howard quip on the lips.

"What do you mean?" Robertson asked. It was out of politeness as much as anything that Robertson even bothered to ask the question. After all, what more was there to say, to explain, to elucidate? The President had made it all perfectly clear. The CBS commentator had summed it up for the slower viewers: The President had pledged that the United States would never engage in germ warfare, and had renounced all but defensive uses of chemical warfare. He had ordered existing stockpiles of bacteriological weapons destroyed, and had pledged unilaterally not to make use of any bacteriological weapons even to retaliate against an enemy attack. . . . What could be more clear?

"What do you mean?" he asked again.

"It's a gambit. That's what I mean," Deap said. "It's a ploy."

"Some gambit. Some ploy."

"You don't believe him, surely?"

"The President is not the kind of man who makes jokes," Robertson said.

"Is he not?" Deap asked, and he pulled a yellow flimsy from the inside breast pocket of his houndstooth

2

jacket. "Take a calm look at it, won't you?"

"You knew about this in advance?" Robertson asked.

"Since yesterday afternoon. I've already gone through what you're going through now. I've had the course, you see."

"What course?"

"Initial shock and then gradual recovery. It's much like the course of a fever."

"What recovery?"

"Ah, physician, heal thyself!" Deap smiled. "May I?"

"May you what?"

"Sit down?"

"Oh, yes. Of course."

He was an irritating fellow sometimes, but then he was a good scientist. One of the best they had. The only trouble, Robertson thought, was that he knew he was good and indulged himself in these absurd mannerisms.

"Now, look," Deap said, spreading the flimsy out on the table. "Read it slowly."

An oblique insult? The hell with it, if it was. Robertson looked at the flimsy and realized that it was, indeed, the text of the President's remarks.

"It's the second page that matters," Deap said.

Robertson continued, however, to scan the first page, the business about the comprehensive study of our chemical and biological defense policies. Blah blah blah, the President's Scientific Advisory Committee, blah blah, the National Security Council, blah blah . . . He turned the page.

"As to our chemical warfare program, the United States reaffirms its oft-repeated renunciation of the first use of lethal chemical weapons. . . ."

"You see?" Deap said, cheerfully, "it's the 'oft-repeated' that counts. Nothing new there."

But the next clause seemed new: ". . . extends this renunciation to the first use of incapacitating chemicals."

"What about that?" Robertson asked, pointing to the lines on the typed flimsy.

"Mace, tear gas, defoliants, and the rest are all ex-

cluded from that because they aren't 'incapacitating,' "
Deap said. "That's only the nerve gases he means, and
we will keep a second-strike capability, which is politi-
cally but not scientifically or militarily distinguishable
from a first-strike capability."

"All right," Robertson said, "but what about this?"
He pointed again, farther down on the page, to the business about renunciation of biological warfare.

"Two things," Deap said. "It's the oddness of the sciences that strikes me first. You can't unlearn anything.
Once you've discovered how to make a new kind of
plague, the knowledge is there. Always. You can't go
back, ever. And the way that works out, practically, is
that you can renounce all you like, but you can't ignore
or avoid these things. Look. 'The United States will confine its biological research to defensive measures such as
immunization and safety measures. . . .' There it is. We
do defensive research. But defense research is indistinguishable, scientifically and militarily, from offensive research. It's a political distinction. Or not even that. How
do you experiment for defense without simulating an
offense against which you're trying to defend? It's . . .
it's the same program absolutely, but with new public relations."

"And the stockpiles?"

"My dear Robertson! That's for public consumption
only. You can't stockpile biologicals. You know that.
The shelf life of these bugs is too short. It's too expensive. We haven't stockpiled biologicals ever. You keep
your cultures, because you're doing defensive research.
The same cultures we've always had. But now they are
for 'immunization and safety measures.' "

"And the Geneva Protocol?"

"In England, we've been a signatory to the Geneva
Protocol all along. And that hasn't affected Porton. Or
Medicine Hat in Canada. Or Queensland in Australia."

"Then what does it mean?" Robertson asked.

"Nothing. Or almost nothing. I expect we'll have to

4

tighten up security a little. And be even more careful. But otherwise . . . nothing."

"I don't know," Robertson said.

"Believe me," Deap said. "It's business as usual. You'll see!"

"Maybe," Robertson said.

"Meanwhile, we must carry on, mustn't we? A whiskey-soda, eh?"

"All right," Robertson said. "Don't mind if I do."

"That's the spirit!" Deap said, and he smiled at the play on words as he raised a beautifully manicured finger to signal the barman.

Friday, August 7

4:38 P.M., Mountain Daylight Time:

Thomas Edison slit the plastic sealer on the bottle of sour mash with a dirty cracked thumbnail and stretched his lean legs out in front of him. Holding the tin cup between his once wiry but now merely stringy thighs, he poured himself a generous slosh. It tasted better out of a tin cup. Always had. And Edison was a man who took his drinking seriously. Or it was even deeper than that. He believed in it. Back in '15, for instance, he'd got through a bad fever in Guadalupe on nothing but pulque. And that too had been in a tin cup. It had been a helluva thing, he remembered, to come back to the States after Villa had been assassinated to find the whole goddamn country gone crazy out of its mind with the Volstead Act and the Prohibition. He had spent two days in this crazy country, most of that time looking for a goddamn drink, before he had shipped out of Galveston bound for any civilized country in the world where the whiskey still flowed. And he had not returned until they'd repealed the Prohibition.

Oh, yes, that'd been a time. He thought the phrase, but did not speak it aloud. Only old men spluttered and sputtered and went around talking to themselves. Yeah. Well, he was old, but not that old. Sure, he looked like his skin was a couple of sizes too large for him, what with the way it hung in folds around his jaws and neck and arms. And he had the elevens up in his neck. And his teeth were bad. And his pecker was no good for anything but peeing. But he could still pee, and he didn't

6

mumble. No, sir! His hair was limp and white, but he still had it! Yes, sir. Drink to that! And he did, taking a deep drag on the sour mash and letting its warmth trickle down his guzzle. Yeah! He believed in it. Other things failed you. Damn near everything else pooped out, farted out, petered out. . . . But the warmth you got from the little brown jug there, you could depend on.

He inspected a cluster of insect bites on his wrist, scratched them in a cursory, absentminded way, stuck a finger into the cup, and spread some of the whiskey on the bites. It was cooling. Cool to the hand, warm to the throat. First-rate stuff. Never let a body down.

He looked at the bottle on the floor beside him and smiled at it. He wouldn't talk to it, because only old geezers with their wits all shot did that. But a man could smile, couldn't he? No goddamn law against smiling, was there? They hadn't repealed that yet! No, sir! You could still feel good and smile. He felt . . . good. Yes, he'd checked, and he felt pretty good. Even hungry. Probably could . . .

The thought of food put him in mind of his daughter-in-law, and he called out, "Mary! Where the hell you hidin' yourself?"

His daughter-in-law shuffled in from the kitchen. Jesus, he thought, but young Tom must have been drunk. Really skunked to . . . Or maybe she'd had a bag over her head. Hah! He tried that, once, just to see what it was like. In Manila? Yeah, maybe Manila. Or was it Singapore? Well, no matter! She'd charged more, but it'd been fun. And it was more fun to look back on, to know that you'd done that, that there was a port you'd entered. . . . Log that, mate. But this one? Jesus! She was still early in her pregnancy, but she had begun to waddle already, and the house slippers she wore exaggerated the waddle. She looked like a duck. And by the time she came to term, if she kept on at this rate, she'd deliver an elephant. Could a duck deliver an elephant? He looked at her critically, trying to see what his son had seen in this girl. Wispy, stringy thing. Skinny arms. Skinny legs.

Which meant she couldn't possibly have any kind of meat on her ass. And she whined. And she never looked you in the eye when she talked to you.

"Where's dinner?" he asked.

"It's on the stove," she said.

See? Face down, eyes down, and whining. People who go around apologizing all the damn time usually have something to apologize for. Right? Yes, sir! And then he realized what she had said.

"On the stove or in it? Thought we was having chicken. Told you this morning I felt like a nice piece of chicken."

"It's beans and bacon," she said flatly. "You forgot to kill the chicken before you left for the mine."

"No," he said, "I didn't forget. I don't kill chickens. That's women's work."

"What?" she asked, defiantly. "I'm not killing any chicken."

"Don't take no strength," he said. "I mean, if we was having veal, or beef, or horsemeat, or mule, I'd go out and I'd do the butchering for you. But a chicken don't take no strength at all. Any fool can wring a chicken's neck. Hell," he continued, "Carmencita used to butcher hogs. I told you about Carmencita, didn't I?"

"Yes," she said. "Many times."

He took another drink of the sour mash. Yes, he had told her about Carmencita, but he was hanged if he could see that she had learned anything from it. What did city women learn, anyway? Cities, he thought, were a curse. They made the men nervous and made the women weak. It had been a lucky thing, he'd long ago decided, that the army had found out that he was only fifteen and threw him out. He'd gone off to Mexico to fight with Villa, settled down there with Carmencita, lived a few years, and then come back to the States to ship out of Galveston. He'd gone around the world four times, had made a fortune in '27 in jade during the Chinese civil war, and had let those city folks lose it all for him in '29. But he'd learned what life was about. The other life, the one he would have led if the army had not caught him out couldn't have been half so interesting and he would have had to eat a peck of muleshit to get through it. The only thing that bothered him is that you couldn't tell anybody about it. Sure you could tell 'em the stories, but they just thought of you as an old fart. They refused to learn the easy way what you'd gained from wrestling with the world firsthand. He looked up at her, trying for perhaps the thousandth time to be sympathetic, to understand how strange his world must be to this young girl. But, hell, she'd have to shape up sometime.

"It ain't hard," he said, in a reasonable tone of voice. "You just catch the damn chicken, grab it by the neck, and twist. It's like opening a ketchup bottle. You can open a ketchup bottle, can't you?"

"Yes," she said, "I can open a ketchup bottle, but I won't kill a chicken."

"You'll eat one, wontcha?"

"Yes. But I won't kill one."

"All right," he said. "Tomorrow night we'll have chicken."

He got up from his chair and went over to the fireplace. He took down the ancient Sharps single-loader, checked the chamber, and went to the window. Leaning the rifle on the sill, he took a bead on a chicken and pulled the trigger. The chicken's head flew off. A real pretty, clean shot. Mary retched and ran from the room. He put the gun back up over the fireplace and went back to his drink. He listened to the sounds of her retching in the bathroom. One helluva weak sister, he thought. No toughness to her at all. Young Tom's mother, Jane— now she'd been a woman with spunk. She'd slept with a revolver under her pillow back in Port Huron when that Youngblood fella was running round loose. He remembered Youngblood—the nigger who'd escaped from the Indiana jail with Dillinger. They'd got Dillinger through his woman, in March, in Chicago. It'd taken a couple of months before they'd run Youngblood to ground in Port

Huron. It had only been half a mile down the road from where he and Jane had been living. But even after they'd caught him and killed him, she still slept with the revolver at hand. It was a kind of a habit. He'd buried her with the revolver so she'd feel comfortable.

But this one, she was taking an awful long time to shape up. He had no idea what it was that young Tom had seen in her. Maybe it hadn't been anything more than the natural horniness a man feels before going off to fight. And he could understand that. But still, there was no need to marry them—knocked-up or not. He supposed he had a dozen bastards strewn around the world somewhere. Still, it was done.

And what the hell, here she was, carrying his only legitimate grandchild, and he'd have to shape her up as best he could. A fine project for the child of the century. That's what they'd called him. They'd named him after the great inventor and there'd been a picture of him in the rotogravure section of the St. Louis *Post* because he'd been the first kid born in the twentieth century in St. Louis, Missouri. All the difference it had made in his life was that it had always been easy for him to remember his birthday—1/1/00. Long ago he had given up wondering about making it to the twenty-first century. There didn't seem to be anything worth hanging around for.

Mary came out of the bathroom, pale and shaken.

"Why did you do that?" she asked.

"Well," he said, "you wanted me to kill a chicken. Now it ain't man's work to go out and wring a chicken's neck. But shootin' birds—that's okay. So I figured out what seemed to me to be a nice compromise. I'd treat the chicken as if it were a partridge or a grouse and blast its head off. A nice shot, didn't you think?"

"I hate guns," Mary said.

"Well," he said, "in that case, next time you'll go out and wring the chicken's neck. Meanwhile," he added more gently, "there's a dead chicken out there. You'd better go out before the others gather round and peck it

10

into garbage. It wants to be plucked and cleaned now."

She looked at him for a long time without saying anything. Whether the look was one of hatred or resignation he could not tell—nor did he care very much. The point was for her to learn about chickens. Or about anything at all. Finally, she broke off her long staring, sighed, and went out the front door.

Without moving from his chair he was able to move his head and see her go into the hen yard. He watched her as she approached the dead chicken, knelt down, and started to cry. If that didn't beat all! Maybe he had been too hard on the girl, maybe she wasn't backward, but plumb crazy.

And then it happened. A thunderclap. He saw her start, and then jump up and look wildly around her. She began to scream—a high, keening, continuous scream. The chickens picked up her hysteria and started to flap, squawk, and cackle. It was the damndest thing he'd ever seen. He sighed, went to the window, and yelled out, "What the hell are you doing, Mary?"

Abruptly, she stopped screaming, turned back toward him, and called, "You shot at me! Goddamn you, you old man, you shot at me!"

"No, Mary," he said, "I didn't shoot at you. Why would I shoot at you? That was a thunderclap." And then, as if punctuating his sentence, there was another, fainter report.

With considerable satisfaction Thomas Alva Edison watched as his daughter-in-law bent down, picked up the dead chicken, and carried it into the kitchen.

Martha Pratt picked up the piece of apple that Soriah had dropped on the carpet. She thought for a moment about going on into the kitchen to wash it off. But it was too much trouble. She compromised by dusting the unattractive and already rusted chunk of apple against the side of her shorts, and then she handed it back to the baby. She snapped the Babee-Gate latch and summoned up a smile.

"Doan wanna appoo!" Soriah said, the petulance only underscored by the babyish imperfections of her speech.

"Feed it to Teddy," Martha suggested. "Teddy wanna appoo?"

Soriah studied the brownish piece of fruit and then picked it up to inflict it on the complaisant teddy bear.

"Joseph? You'll keep an eye on Soriah for me?" she asked. Or rather ordered. The questioning inflection was just politeness.

Joseph, her eldest son, looked up from his jigsaw puzzle that was spread out in front of him on a bridge table, said, "Sure," and went back to sorting out the pieces.

It was what she had expected to hear, but still pleasing, satisfying. She knew he would check on the baby, would call her if there were any emergency, would even fetch the flung appoo and return it to the small child a couple of times if necessary. She rubbed her hands against her thighs, wiping them on her denim shorts, and sighed wearily. She was a chunky woman, and she felt the heat more than most. She often envied the lean women she saw on television and in magazines, the ones who modeled for all those things, many of them sinful. She envied them not at all for their cigarettes and their coffee and their beer. And she did not even give much thought to how they were supposed to be so attractive to men. She didn't believe it anyway. With her undeniably heavy arms and legs, her short waist, her big shoulders, she had still done pretty well. She had Jared, after all. But she did envy those slender models for their comfort in the heat. She was sure that they felt it less.

She looked around the small living room and sighed again. She would tidy up later, after the children were in bed. She wanted to have the place immaculate for Jared when he came down late Friday night from Salt Lake City. She started toward the back of the house, stopped, went into the kitchen and told the two children, Hiram and Moriah, who were sitting on the kitchen floor working the crank on the Monkey Ward ice-cream freezer, "As soon as it's firm, scrape it out and put it in the freezer. And then go watch television with Peter."

So, they were all set, all five of them, and she knew she could count on fifteen minutes, time enough to take a bath before getting dinner, putting the children to bed, and getting to the housework. It was, she supposed, eccentric, but she found that doing the housework in the evening was easier. It was cooler then, and besides, the children were not underfoot. Five of them in eleven years; it worked out well enough and it was better for the children that way. Not having a full-time father, they needed her attention and her company during the day—especially during summer vacation. She did not envy Esther, her sister-wife in Salt Lake City. True, Esther had Jared all week long, from Monday to Friday, but Jared worked all week. And besides, Esther was the first wife. This was Martha's lot and she accepted it, grateful enough to have Jared for the two days of the weekend when he could come out and relax with her and the children.

She went into the bathroom, latched the door, and turned on the water in the tub, balancing the hot and the cold to get the right temperature. She started to unbutton her cotton blouse. But, no, she had to go back for her other temple garment, which was in the bedroom. She glanced at the tub and estimated the time it would take to fill. She had plenty of time. She left the bathroom, went into the master bedroom, and got a clean, pressed temple garment. She brought it back to the bathroom and put it on the hamper, in easy reach of the tub. Then, she got undressed and, using her teeth and her other hand, tied the worn ritual temple garment to her left wrist. There were women, good Mormons, up in Salt Lake City, who were not wearing their temple garments any more because of the revealing new fashions. Even more of them left their temple garments off when they put on two-piece bathing suits. She was glad that she did not have that kind of temptation here in Tarsus, and she regretted her moment of speculation earlier about the relative quality of her life and of Esther's. It

13

wasn't that she really believed in the powers of the blessed, chemiselike garment, which was supposed to be able to protect its wearer against fire and disaster. It was rather the feeling of tradition, the gesture of wearing the garment in which she wrapped herself as the soul wraps itself in faith. In Salt Lake one would need that protection even more. It must be harder, she supposed, to raise a family in the city. The Gentile spirit seemed to influence the young folks a great deal. Certainly the great Temple was there, but the very size of the city was a kind of threat to the Mormon way.

She stepped into the tub and lowered herself into the warm water. She looked at her body critically. For a thirty-three-year-old woman who had borne five children she was, she thought, in pretty good shape. She did not have the varicose veins that so many women had after many pregnancies so close together. Now that Soriah was two and was finally weaned, her breasts had returned to their normal size. They were not as firm, perhaps, as they had been eleven years before when she had first come to Jared, but they were better than Esther's.

She wondered whether Jared was looking forward to this weekend as keenly as she was. Two years, and they had not known each other's bodies in all that time. She did not think it was sinful for her to hope that she did not become pregnant again for a while. She wanted to enjoy Jared for as long as possible. She had cheated a little with Soriah, waiting an extra month before she had told Jared that she knew she was pregnant. It could have passed as an honest mistake and she saw no harm in it. Now that she had carried and borne Soriah and had nursed her for these two years, she would be able to resume her rightful place in the tenderest spot in Jared's heart. It was nothing to be vain about, and she hoped she was not vain. Still, she was the younger wife.

Almost as if to punish herself for the pride she took in her youth—she was ten years younger than Esther Pratt—she considered the idea of Jared's taking a third wife. But they could not afford it. Very few Mormons had more than two wives, anyway. The price of living, now, had gone so high. She was not altogether sorry. Besides, the eagerness with which he had received the news that Soriah was off the breast now suggested to her that Jared, too, was eager for this coming weekend. He had no need for a third wife, anyway. Not for a while yet.

She sat in the tub, her mind idly anticipating and enjoying the Friday night to come. Then she heard the peal of thunder. It was a sign. Surely, in this arid desert where thundershowers were so infrequent, the thunder and the rain had to be a heavenly sign of God's pleasure in the fertility of their marriage.

Nevertheless, she got out of the tub quickly. She dried herself, and then with a deft practiced motion slid one leg into the fresh temple garment before she untied the soiled one and dropped it from her body. Then she finished putting on the new one, sliding her arms into the straps, put on her bathrobe, and went to finish dressing. She wanted to be around and available. She did not want the children to be frightened if the thunder and lightning came any closer.

Paul Donovan eased himself onto a large, flat rock. He unslung his canteen, unscrewed the cap, and took a drink of the cool water. Then he poured a little of the water into his cupped palms and moistened his sunbaked face and the back of his neck. His skin felt like old leather. He sloshed a little more water onto the canteen cover so that the process of evaporation would keep the canteen cool. He screwed the top back on the canteen and put it down on the rock beside him.

He looked down at the minuscule pools of water the droplets had formed. For an insect, or for one of the lesser lizards of this arid scrubland, a single one of those droplets would have been a binge, a wonderful wallow in the luxury of wetness. He stared at the droplets, watching them soak quickly into the parched earth. He was a big man, big-boned and rangy, but with a surprising precision and delicacy of facial detail. His blue-gray

15

eyes were set wide apart and hooded by lids that turned downward slightly at the outsides, and the angles of his black eyebrows emphasized that downwardness. His lips were thin, and he had a tendency to purse them slightly, as he did now, looking down at the ground. Emotionally, he was a man of the same sorts of contrasts, for although he was a teacher of biology and a scientist, he could still feel the most unscientific regret that there had been no lizard, no skink, no insect that had been able to benefit from the rare luxury of his waste. But what the hell! The careful economy of the desert was not geared to such moments of human profligacy.

He ran his hand through his wavy black hair. It was damp with sweat, and his hand was damp with sweat. What was impressive here, what had struck him from his first day out here, was the fantastic frugality, even the miserliness of all the desert life. Or, even more than that, the adaptability and the tenacity of the life here. It was . . . hell, it was almost Irish. Not his kind of Irish, but the kind his parents and grandparents could remember: The people in the old country who got through the famines, and got out. But for that matter, there was something in the determined thrift out here that was supposed to be typical of the New England character, the flinty Yankee who plowed around the boulders in his fields. But the New England landscape was sybaritic opulence compared with the ecology of this desert. Back in Massachusetts, the abundance of water, the comparative richness of the soil, the variability of a nature that relented after two or three days or a week of scorching or freezing made for an easy life. Easy and soft. An outdoor type, Paul had, nevertheless, burned and baked and peeled, and he looked like a game tenderfoot who just might make it.

Resting there, he thought of the tradition of Western openness and hospitality, and considered it in the light of the stunning meagerness of the landscape that surrounded him. Even the mountains, with their ample water and thick trees, were not really hospitable. They

16

had produced in him, when he had gone through them, a feeling of desolation and loneliness because of the inhuman scale.

The cragginess of the young, Western mountains had not been at all sublime—it was the nineteenth-century romantics who thought of the mountains as being beautiful—but lonely and terrible in the way they had thought mountains to be in the Augustan Age. Paul had taken a kind of masochistic pleasure in the forbidding quality of the mountains, which had matched his dark mood. But here in the desert he found a consolation in the way in which all forms of life managed to hang on in the heat and the merciless aridity.

It fell apart if he looked at it too closely, or, worse than that, it turned into mawkishness, *Reader's Digest* sentimentality, and self-pity: *I had the blues 'cause I had no shoes 'til I met on the street a man with no feet.* That kind of nonsense. On the other hand, if he noticed it only through peripheral vision, there was a solace and an odd kind of tranquility that he could derive from the flora and fauna of this desolate valley. Eighty miles long and perhaps thirty miles wide, it looked like a huge oversight in the process of creation. Even the name, Skull Valley, was forbidding. But sitting still on this flat rock, considering the hairlets on the underside of the dry flower seeds of a cotton thorn, Paul was fascinated by the adaptability of nature. He was fascinated, too, by the emptiness here because it matched the emptiness he felt inside himself. In six months he would be thirty, the time that was supposed to be the beginning of the prime of life, and his life was a dried pod. It had been full enough until that inconceivable day the preceding February. The principal had come into the lab, had asked him to leave the class, and had brought Paul back to his office. Right away, Paul had known that there was something terribly wrong, because old Witherspoon, the principal, ordinarily an irritable son-of-a-bitch and an incurable chatterer, had been deferential and, even more ominously, quiet. And then, in the principal's office, he had seen the police sergeant. Paul had known even before the sergeant had spoken what must have happened, what the news would have to be. The details, of course, he had not been able to predict in that prescient microsecond, but then the details had not been important. The icy patch, the angle of the intersection, the position of the parked truck into which Marian's Volks had careened—none of this had been important, nor was important now. The only thing that mattered was that Marian was dead. And Paul, too, had died in that moment. True, he was still walking around, but like one of the Transylvanian walking dead, and it was curious how efficiently one of these undead could manage, continuing to meet his biology classes at Tarbox High. Even from inside his shell of indifference he had not been unaware of the irony of the fact that he was teaching biology—the study of life. In the classroom and in the lab there was continuous burgeoning. Plants bloomed, rabbits and gerbils reproduced, and in the newly discovered sexuality of his young high-school students there was an insistence on the explosiveness of the life force that was positively obscene.

Cheerless, childless, lifeless, he had nevertheless staggered through the remainder of the academic year. He had been passively acquiescent even in the business of the grant that old Witherspoon had arranged for him. Now, sitting in the middle of nowhere, he suspected that maybe Witherspoon had been right, and felt gratitude for the old man's tactful help.

Out of the corner of his eye he noticed a movement. Quietly, with practiced efficiency, he flicked the cover off his Nikon. When the camera was ready he looked around in the direction of the movement he had noticed and tried to find what it was that had attracted his attention. He sat still, scanning the scrub. It took him several seconds before he noticed the small lizard at the base of a gray sage. It was about two inches long, brownish-gray in color, and with blackish-brown spots in rows down its back. It was poised, entirely still, having already devoured whatever insect it had found—almost certainly that had been the movement that had caught Paul's eye. He snapped a picture of the lizard and advanced the film to be ready for the next picture. It was, he decided, a small tree lizard—but, no, upon closer inspection as he leaned forward, still sitting on the rock, and moving in the most gradual way so as not to alarm the tiny reptile, he noticed that it had no ear opening. It had to be a lesser, earless lizard. He stared at it for a long time, then, deliberately he looked away at the horizon and looked back at the base of the sage. It took him a fraction of a second before he could find the lizard again, so perfectly did the color of its camouflage blend with the color of the soil and the shadows cast by the bracts and branches of the sage above it.

It was then that Paul heard the clap of thunder. He looked up at the sky and saw beyond the Cedar Range a narrow wedge of cloud—a squall line along a cold front. It looked exactly like the illustration in the Van Nostrand *Earth Science* text. It did not mean necessarily that there would be much rain. Maybe a little. The rainfall out here was six inches or so a year. There had to be some moisture in the air, and as the warm air rose and reached the dew point, whatever moisture there was would condense and fall. He saw a flash of lightning and then counted the seconds until the next clap of thunder. He counted slowly, one banana, two bananas, three bananas, four bananas. The thunderclap came at sixteen seconds. The storm was only three miles away. He wondered whether the rain would fall in the valley or whether it would spend itself entirely on the Cedars. Or, for that matter, was there some system where it could fall on the Cedars, stop, fall on the Onaqui Mountains, stop, and then fall again on the Oquirrhs? The ecology of the pinion and the juniper was entirely different and they had considerably more water with which to indulge themselves.

He looked back, trying to find the earless lizard at the base of that sagebrush. It was gone. In its place, there was another, larger lizard, a leopard lizard with its distinctive brownish spots and white crossbars. It must have, in the brief time that Paul had been looking at the sky, devoured the little earless lizard. Paul was sorry to have missed it. The speed and the utter silence of the kill were admirable in the way that the operation of a deft pickpocket had to be admirable. He snapped a picture of the leopard lizard, closed up the Nikon, and got up from the rock. It was a quarter to five in the afternoon. He ought, he decided, to be getting back to Tarsus. He didn't want to hold up Mrs. Jenkins' dinner. He felt a little stiff. He yawned and stretched mightily. He threw his head back, moved it first one way, and then the other as far as it would go, getting the kinks out and feeling the tightness of the sunbaked skin at the back of his neck. Not leather, but dried out oilcloth. No wonder those cowboys wore bandanas.

Overhead, a couple of miles away, he saw the glint of a small plane.

Jim Ishida sat down at the bar and ordered a Coors. It was lousy beer. All the beer in Utah was lousy beer, that 3.2 stuff. But it was better than nothing, and the general store/bar/post office was air-conditioned. It was a good place at which to stop and cool off after a long day outside in the hot sun. Even when Rose was home, he stopped off for a beer sometimes. But now, while she was visiting their daughter in San Francisco, there was no reason at all for him to get home at any special time. There was nothing there but the television set and a dinner of cold cuts.

He was tired. His slight but athletic body felt the fatigue pouring out of the muscles. It wasn't so much a stiffness, for Ishida was in the splendid physical shape that comes with long years of outdoor work, but rather a sourness, as if the fatigue was a chemical that the muscles produced. He had put in a fifty-foot privet hedge for Dr. Deap. It seemed crazy, putting privet out there in the desert. But with enough water from the sprinkler

20

system it would thrive, and the army was nothing if not generous with scientists out on the base.

Behind the bar, Smith, beefy, pot-bellied, bull-necked, fished up a bottle of beer from the bottom of the ice-filled chest. He flipped off the top and poured it carefully into a chilled glass. He looked like an advertisement for beer. Not the kind that actually appeared in beer ads, of course, but truer. His big hands and fleshy lips looked as if they had been adapted by years of evolutionary progress to beer drinking. Just as you could tell from the beaks of birds what kinds of foods they ate, so you could tell from looking at Smith that he was a beer drinker. And he had a way of hesitating, as he did now, before yielding up the beer that suggested clearly he'd have preferred to drink it himself, with all the fluttering and moving of cheek and throat as it went down, and a satisfied gasp at the end of the first quick glass. It wasn't the kind of ad you saw anywhere, but it worked—just looking at Smith could make a man thirsty.

"How are you, Jim?" Smith asked. "How's it going?"

"Can't complain," Ishida replied.

"When does Rose get back?"

"I take my vacation in two weeks, and I'll be joining her out there. We'll both be back by the middle of September."

"Good town, Frisco."

There was a honk outside. Smith left the bar to go outside and sell some gas. Ishida had never seen the pass-through on the bar closed. It made no sense to close it anyway. Smith had to run out to sell gas, or stamps, or cheese too many times a day. As Smith said so often, he was probably the busiest man in Tarsus. Not that he accomplished all that much, of course. But the variety of businesses carried on in his place did keep him on the move. Ishida felt little sympathy for him. What the hell, it was air-conditioned in here. He went outside to sell gas, but that only made the air-conditioning all the better to come back into. And the little beads of sweat on the upper lip and around the forehead that Smith brought back from his brief sorties outside made his customers more thirsty. Smith had it pretty soft. The long hours that Ishida put in out in the broiling sun and the loneliness of the job—that was man's work. Or it would be if those crazy doctors and officers out at the base had any idea what gardens ought to be. He took a sip of his beer and let the coolness of it run down his throat. He reflected on the peculiarities of Americans.

They had locked him and his family up in an internment camp in '42 and had kept them all there until the end of the war. That had been crazy, an expression of fear and distrust of all Japanese-Americans. The only way you could get out of the internment camp was by enlisting in the army to go and fight the Germans in one of the Nisei units. They had decided at the end that they had made a mistake and offered reparations to some of them for the losses they had suffered on the forced sales of their homes and businesses. Ishida had been too young for the army and had had to stay in the camp with his family until '45. His parents had sent him to gardening school on the government money. When he'd finished school he'd found that California was full of Japanese gardeners—and even worse, Mexicans who had moved in with their lawnmowers during the war and worked for even cheaper wages than his people would work for. So he had come back to Utah, where he could wander around at will in all of that empty space that he had seen from the wrong side of the barbed wire. He had gone back to visit in San Francisco, and had met and married Rose, who was eager to get away from the close-knit Japanese community of the city, and they had made a good life for themselves out here in Utah.

The only trouble was that the people in Utah didn't know anything about gardens and were mostly unwilling to spend the money to hire a gardener. They were mostly Mormons, and the Mormons had peculiar ideas about servants—maids and gardeners—even when they had enough money to be able to afford them. So he had wound up working for the army, at Wendover, at Tooele, and at Dugway. That was crazy enough in itself. To have come from the camp down near Freedom where he had been guarded by the army to this job, a hundred miles away on another army base, this one too surrounded by barbed wire and guards. And everything he had learned at gardening school about design and use of the land was defeated by the willfulness of the designers of the army base, making their Eastern plans with their Eastern plots back in Washington. And even their Eastern plants. This was no country for privet. But with enough money and energy you could make it grow, even here. And it was their money, he supposed. Still, he felt like a fool having spent a whole day putting thirty privet plants in a line in the middle of the desert to satisfy the whim of that crazy doctor. Or maybe his wife.

"Hiya, Jim. How are you?"

Ishida looked up. It was Doc Cooley, the vet, who slid onto the stool next to his. "Fine, Doc. How are you?"

"All right, all right. How are things on the base there?" He pointed to the badge that Ishida was still wearing. It carried his name, his picture, and his thumbprint.

"Same as usual," Ishida said. "Hot."

Smith entered the barroom and went back behind the bar, rubbing his hands on his thighs. "What'll you have this afternoon, Doc?"

"One of them," Cooley said, pointing to Jim's glass.

"What about you, Jim?" Smith asked. "Another?"

"Sure," he said, watching with some amusement the reflex action of Smith's lips, as he extended them slightly as if to drink. "Why not?"

While Smith poured the beers, Cooley swiveled around on his chair. He was a slight, rumpled man, with tobacco-stained fingers, a tobacco-stained moustache, and hair that matched the color of his moustache. It was not tobacco-stained hair. Not unless he actually rolled those little cigars around his head before he smoked them. But age and the sun had approximated that ashtray- and humidor-tint. He was taller than Ishida, but slender. He was a gentle man, but his brusque manner and the sharpness of his hawk nose made him look mean. Still, he would lavish attention on the birds and rabbits that children brought to him, often for free when they could not pay. Or he would let them work it off by helping out with the feeding and cleaning of the cages for the animals in his veterinary hospital—a job most of the children would have paid money to do anyway, if they'd had it.

"What the hell is that?" Cooley asked.

Ishida turned his head and followed Cooley's stare. There was a pool table in the barroom. It was new. Ishida had never seen it before, and he had not noticed it earlier, because, coming in from the bright glare to the darkness of the bar, he had not been able to see much of anything. And then, once he had sat down at the bar, he had not looked around at all.

"A pool table," Smith said. "What does it look like?"

"Looks like a pool table," Cooley admitted.

"The Sears and Roebuck man delivered it this afternoon. Cost me nearly three hundred bucks. I figure it'll attract more of the servicemen from the bases. They get pretty tired of staying on the bases and like to wander around. Why shouldn't they wander here?"

"Is it just for the soldiers or are we allowed to use it too?" Cooley asked.

"No, no, anybody can use it," Smith said. "Long as you keep drinking. That's the whole idea of it," he explained. "Keep people in longer and help 'em work up a thirst."

"Regular little pleasure dome," Cooley said. "You gonna get yourself some women for the back room?"

"I would if it was legal. These boys have got to have some recreation. But you know me, I like to keep on the right side of the law."

"Still," Cooley said, "a pool table . . . that's got to be aiming right for the soldiers. No one here in town has got the time to play pool. You don't want to lose the balance you've got here and turn yourself into just an army hangout, do you?"

"Their money's as good as anybody's. And there are damned few places out here for them to spend it," Smith said.

"Still," Cooley went on, "those bases do funny things. Like close up suddenly."

"Well, if that happens, that happens. I've still got the grocery and the post office. And where else are you going to get your beer? Going to go all the way into Tooele for it?"

"I guess you're right," Cooley admitted, "you're sitting in the catbird seat."

Ishida had heard the discussion before. Smith loved the army because it meant money in his cash register and in his pocket. Cooley disliked them, had disliked them ever since that spring when all the sheep in the Valley had died because of that nerve-gas business. Cooley had been running from ranch to ranch trying to treat the sick sheep and getting nothing but a runaround from the army people. The sheep ranchers had come out of it all right—the army had paid fifty-five dollars a head for those sheep that had been worth maybe thirty each, tops. But Cooley hadn't given a damn about the money. He'd said it was a question of principle, and he'd become a bug on the subject.

It seemed strange to Ishida that sheep should be so important to a man. What if it had been people? And it seemed even stranger that a man of Cooley's age would be surprised that the government lied. He knew what governments were like—or this one, anyway. He'd spent four years behind barbed wire listening to a whole lot of lies.

Smith ducked out of the bar again and left the barroom to go into the general store, in one corner of which there was a cage that was the Tarsus Post Office. Ishida looked around and saw that Mrs. Jenkins was standing at the window with a package to be weighed for the mails. Even with a string of hookers in the back room it would not be a very exciting place for soldiers looking for action. Smith was crazy. But, hell, they were all crazy.

Smith was on his way back to the bar when they heard it. Ishida was sure it was just a thunderclap, and he thought of the line of new privet and the good fortune of having some rare free water fall on them their first day out there. It was a fortunate sign; maybe they would make it. But Cooley ran his hand through his rumpled gray hair and said, "There they go again, your soldier boys."

"Who?" Smith asked.

"It's those planes from Wendover. It's that sonic boom they make. Broke the glass on the framed picture I've got of my grandchildren a couple of weeks ago."

"Kind of a small price to pay, isn't it?" Smith asked.

"Pay for what?" Cooley snapped back. "I don't see what the hell they're doing out here. It's a big boondoggle."

"No, no, it's not," Smith said, in all seriousness. "I'm not just talking about a few more dollars in my pocket or what they do for the economy here. I'm talking about what these bases do for the defense of our country. These people out here are keeping us all safe. You've seen those containers out there, past Ophir, haven't you? A lot of that gas is left over from World War One."

He was, Ishida knew, referring to the South Tooele Ordnance Depot, where the mustard gas and the lewisite were stored in enormous tanks that looked like the storage yard of an oil refinery. The depot stretched on for as far as the eye could see—even from up in the hills.

"We're not going to be fighting ever again with mustard gas," Cooley grumbled. "And you know it."

Smith thought for a moment and replied, "That's because we have the stuff. That's the only reason the Germans didn't use it in World War Two, and the only reason the Koreans didn't use it, and the Vietnamese haven't used it. Because they know we've got it, and they don't want us to use it back, and use it better, on them. You've just been mad ever since the sheep business."

"Of course I've been mad," Cooley snapped. "What kind of safety is it, what kind of government is it, what kind of army is it when they lie to you? I could have saved those sheep, I could have saved seventy percent of 'em if they had told us what the hell had happened and admitted that they'd made a mistake. But no, they're too high and mighty for that. I tell you, when the military gets out of civilian control, out of our control, the country is in terrible shape."

"You think you know more than the generals? You think you know more than the people in Washington about what's to do?" Smith asked.

"I'm not saying that," Cooley said. "All I'm saying is that after people lie to you, it's hard to trust them, isn't it?"

It was going to get stickier, Ishida thought. They were both serious. While he was not close to either one, in a casual way they were both friends. They had been perfectly decent to him, and he didn't like to see people arguing over a lot of nonsense.

"It wasn't sonic boom," he said. "It was thunder. Just thunder."

The two of them looked at Ishida, then at each other and laughed. "Well," Cooley said, "nobody wins the argument this time." He finished his beer, got up, and picked a cigar out of the box at the end of the bar. He put down a dollar bill, waited for Smith to make change, and said, "Well, I've got to get over to the Reservation. There's a mare going to foal in a couple of hours and I got to tend to her."

"Take care," Smith said.

"You, too," Cooley said. "See you, Jim." He waved and went out into the late afternoon.

Ishida sat at the bar, drinking his beer. He glanced at the green rectangle of the pool-table cloth. He walked over to the pool table, put his glass down on the rim, and reached down underneath to the shelf where the balls were stored. He picked up three of them and, holding them in his hand, studied the green cloth. He placed first one, then the second, and then the third. It was the way he would have placed three rocks on a stretch of green grass that shape and it would have looked pretty good, he thought.

Hope Wilson, formerly Hope Wilson Tremaine, but née Hope Wilson, dismounted. She stroked the neck of the horse and was unable to tell whether the tremor was in the horse's neck or in her own hand.

"Easy, King, easy, big boy," she said soothingly, gratefully.

It had been the horse's alertness, and not her own that had saved them. The horse had shied—apparently for no reason at all. She had tried to urge him forward, but King had refused to move. He had stood there immovable, trembling, and had whinnied. And then she had first heard that terrible sound and seen not twenty feet ahead on the narrow jeep-trail the rattlesnake in one of the dirt ruts that jeep tires had worn into the track. It looked at first like a dusty piece of an inner tube, but then she had realized what it was, had seen the outlines of its coils and the bulletlike head beginning to extend itself. With what now seemed to her to be fantastic calmness—a calmness that was both surprising and pleasing—she had taken the snub-nosed .32 out of its special pocket on the side of the saddle. She flicked off the safety and, steadying her right hand with her left arm, which she propped on the side of King's neck, she had discharged four shots. The second shot hit the snake and sent it writhing. The third shot had missed, but the fourth shot had apparently broken its spine. She had watched it quiver, twitch for a moment, and then lie still.

Only now that the moment of danger was past did the fear she had postponed well up and engulf her. She could feel the cold sweat pouring down her skin. It was not the kind of sweat she had felt all that afternoon, the occasional pleasant prickle of rapid evaporation of perspiration in this dry heat, as she had wandered along these long-familiar trails on the old horse.

She led King past the place where the snake had lain and around a slight curve. She tethered the horse loosely to the low branch of a juniper and reached into the pocket of her plaid cotton shirt for a cigarette. It took her several tries with her lighter to get it lit because her hand was still shaking.

It was crazy. Now that she was safe, now that she had reason even to be proud of herself, for remembering long forgotten skills—she had not shot a gun in ten years—she felt awful. The stark beauty of the mountains, the sharpness and clarity of the sky—perfectly blue to the east, and with a beautifully delineated cloud in the northwest—all this beauty and clarity seemed to her to be a kind of reproach. She had not been able to give King credit for his native horse sense. There had been that moment or two when she had tried to urge him on, when she had thought of him and treated him as if he were some kind of recalcitrant machine. But he had stood his ground—in both senses of the word—and had possibly saved her life. She remembered the summer ten years before when she had seen him foaled and had helped Dr. Cooley as he tugged gently on neck and forelegs to get him born. She had been there in the barn and had witnessed that wonderful moment when the colt had struggled to his feet and stood.

And so, now, he had returned that help she had given him at the beginning. It was all so tidy, so simple, so direct—and so unlike the subtleties and complications of her life in New York.

She took a puff of her cigarette, and, with the heel of her left hand, wiped away the tears that were pouring silently down her cheeks. She was rather surprised to discover that she had been crying. They were the first tears she had been able to shed in years, and she had been trying, honestly trying, to cry for two months—or six?—it didn't matter. She had seen those other women in that absurd, ornate courthouse in Juárez, with their unctuous lawyers soothing them as they sobbed, but she had remained dry-eyed through it all, and even felt contemptuous at what seemed to her to be cheap and easy emotion. But now, now that she was crying herself, she realized what it really could be, and indeed ought to be —a natural, cathartic outpouring of emotion. It was no good to bottle it all up. She realized now that they had not been crying specifically about their divorces, about the breakup of their marriages, and about the losses of their husbands or the strangeness of Juárez and the peculiar mumbo-jumbo of the Mexican legal proceedings. They had been crying about everything.

It was, she supposed, a kind of luxury and a bit of luck to have had this simple confrontation with a rattlesnake. There was the snake, and there was the gun, and she had pulled the gun from the saddle holster and killed the snake. Nothing ambiguous about it at all. The rattlesnake was bad, one of the natural enemies of men and of horses too, and she had faced it and killed it. There was no need to be intricate and sophisticated about its symbolism—or that of the revolver, either. All of that was for back East, where they had nothing sensible to do with themselves. The unreality of life there was such that one lost track of the function of simple tools—guns, or phalli too, for that matter.

To put it in that wonderfully enlightened and clinically impersonal jargon of the therapist to whom she had gone, Keith had used his phallus for revenge. He had resented her success on the magazine, had felt his masculinity challenged by the fact that she earned more money than he did, and, feeling inadequate and insecure, had gone around proving his manhood to himself—and even, perhaps, trying to prove it to her. All those interchangeable little secretaries, copyreaders, receptionists, and stewardesses who continued to pour into New York in endless waves. Finally, and most ironically, even that proof failed him, at least as far as she was concerned. And her understanding attitude, her attempt at reassurance had only made things worse. Furious with himself for his impotence, and furious with her for her attempts at compassion, he had turned to liquor, which demanded nothing and forgave everything.

Her decision to divorce him had been difficult. She had felt that it would be kicking a man when he was down. But she had her own life to salvage and there was the hope, too—a real hope, she thought—that it might be the kind of shock he needed to help him salvage something of his own life. Together they were failing each other and failing themselves. The last year had been a shambles and a horror. Gradually, but inevitably the decision had formed itself in her mind, and two months ago she had announced it to him. He had been curiously apathetic and acquiescent, somewhat surly but agreeable. And now it was done. She had flown to Juárez for the divorce at the beginning of her vacation and now, trying to get her bearings, she had stopped off on her way back from Juárez to New York to visit Uncle William and Aunt Emily on the ranch where she had spent the summers of her childhood, years before. To come out to the health and outdoorsiness, but most of all to the security and the associations of the ranch and Tarsus, had seemed, back in New York, irresistibly appealing. Her actual visit so far had been simply boring. But now, out on the trail, riding King and handling the gun with the easy and even automatic competence of her girlhood, she was sure she had decided wisely. It had not been the tiresome ceremony in the Mexican courtroom, but the discharge of bullets from that revolver that had finally snapped the ties. The tears had not been for Keith or for the divorce, but for everything.

And, there was something reassuring about the mere fact that she was able to cry again. That it fit, the way her clothes did. These were the old riding clothes she had worn when she had come out here as a girl, and they were comfortable, if a little loose. The jeans were a little roomy, because she had lost weight in the nervous and competitive strenuousness of New York. But not so much weight as to be too small for her old britches. She had always been petite, trim, precise. . . . It had been as if her body had been merely a projection of her character, with the mental meticulousness working itself out into her clarity of figure and feature, the orderliness of her hair, which had lots of body and never blew out of place, the earnestness of her large, clear brown eyes. It had been good to find her old riding clothes neat and folded in the same drawer, and even better to find that they still fit, still looked good.

But they were sweaty now, and her face was tear-stained, and she was sure that if she bothered with a mirror she would find that even her hair was disarranged. It was good, though, to find out that she was human, could look merely human, could behave and cry like any other girl.

King whinnied. She dropped her cigarette and carefully ground it out with her boot. She untied him and remounted. She felt good. She was happy to have King's reminder that they ought to be getting back, he to his barn and she to supper. She started off along the trail, letting King set his own comfortable pace.

It was then that she heard the distant peal of thunder. She remembered the first time that she and Keith had made love, taking cover from a sudden thunderstorm in a boathouse on Lake Winnepesaukee. That she was able to remember the pleasure and the sweetness of the moment without bitterness and without pain was a fine sign. She heard a second peal of thunder, still faint but closer. She increased King's pace. She wanted to get back before the rain came.

It was a snafu, but it was not his goof. It was the people in Meteorology who had been responsible. They'd kept Dawes waiting for four days until the fronts were right, the winds were right, the air pressure was right, and then they'd given him the go-ahead. And he'd taken off in the ancient Grumman to fly their improbably precise mission on their guaranteed perfect day.

It was crazy, really. The way they'd cut back the funds on these tests recently. Ever since the end of the germ-warfare program—ho ho! All that had meant was that there weren't any funds for the Porton spray machines that went back and forth on tracks two feet off the ground. But over a half-acre at a time. They cost a half-million bucks, and there just weren't any funds. Downgrading the program and all that shit. So they did the tests the old way, spraying with planes—two old Grummans and three test pilots. Okay, they had a whole damn desert to spray in, and nothing down there but rabbits. But still, it was a risky business. As now.

It had been all right, had been fine during the takeoff and then the approach, but all of a sudden, out of nowhere, from across the peaks of the Dugway Range in the southwest, the thunderheads had appeared and they were coming toward him at a fair clip. It wasn't the thunder or even the lightning but the inversion that bothered him, the downdraft. He was supposed to be flying at four hundred feet, which was tricky business in the best of weather. But with the kind of bumpy air that was in the storm—well, it would be suicide not to climb, no matter what the instructions said.

The process of decision took perhaps twenty seconds. Or, even less than that. By the time he had made the conscious decision to climb he found that he had already pulled back on the stick, was already climbing, had been climbing for five or six seconds.

The motors of the old plane chattered with strain as the propellers bit into the air and the plane climbed steeply.

It was a tricky place to be in a storm like this. He was in a valley between two mountain ranges, and he had had to avoid the mountains to the west and to the south of his position. He maintained the climb until the altimeter read 3,000 feet above the floor of the valley. He could see the thunderhead below him and to the left and rear.

It was then that he noticed the red light glowing

above him on the instrument panel. "Jesus Christ," he thought. He grabbed the lever and closed the tank on the left wing. It had been open for the whole climb. He had gone into his third and final target, ready to dump the soup, and then the storm had hit and distracted him, taking his mind off the mission, taking his mind off everything but the fact that he was flying so low. He had had to haul ass out of there, and fast.

He leveled the plane and checked the pressure on the left tank. It was empty. He tried to estimate how many seconds the climb had taken. For all he knew, the tank had been empty before he had even begun to ascend. Certainly it had emptied itself out before he had hit a thousand feet. He hoped so, anyway. He had no idea what kind of stuff was in the tank this time—they never told you that—but none of it was good. Whatever was in it was something that had some effect on pigs. He had been able to see the pigs staked at each of the target sites, tethered to poles stuck in the brown earth, on which, in the kind of line they had used in high school to mark the playing fields, bull's-eyes and crosshatches had been inscribed.

The question was, what to enter in the log, what report to file when he got back to base. There would be an awful lot of flak if he told it the way it had been—or, not even that, the way he thought it might have been, was afraid it might have been, because, after all, he didn't *know*. The tanks might have been empty before he'd made the climb. Or, if they had been spraying while he was climbing, maybe the downdraft he had been fighting had brought the soup back to where it was supposed to be, anyway. It was all approximate. And, without being sure of what had happened, he certainly didn't want to report a failure. They didn't like that much at the base. Too many of them, and you suddenly found yourself hauling ass across the Pacific and over to the Nam.

It was dull out here in Utah, but at least it was pretty safe. And while it was distasteful to fly around killing pigs, at least they were only pigs. And Dawes liked flying. He liked the way he could feel the plane function as if it were an extension of his own body. He liked the almost sexual feeling of diving and soaring and the sweet-sick weight of the increase of Gs when he banked sharply. He'd been lucky to get this assignment in the first place, and he wasn't going to blow it. Not when it hadn't been his fault. He returned to the idea that Meteorology had fucked it up. He saw no reason for him to take the blame for their mistake. If a mistake had been made.

By the time he was ready to signal the tower for his clearance to land, Lieutenant Marvin Dawes had convinced himself that nothing had happened. His freckled boyish brow and his slate-blue eyes were clear and untroubled. It wasn't even going to be a lie, because nothing had really happened at all.

Monday, August 10

11:45 A.M., Mountain Daylight Time:

Captain Norman Lewine, M.D., stripped off his disposable plastic gloves and dropped them into the garbage can.

"Fine, just fine, Mrs. O'Neill," he said. "And the baby seems fine, too."

The woman on the examination table, whose face was barely visible to him over her swollen belly, raised her head slightly and smiled at the doctor. "I'm glad that part is over, though. I've always hated it."

"Yes, I know," he said sympathetically. "You can get dressed now. Come into my office, will you? We can talk there."

"He says he's calling from a pay phone," the nurse said through the green curtains.

"All right, all right, I'm coming," Lewine said.

He stepped outside the examining cubicle and went over to the nurses' station to take the call.

"Dr. Lewine?"

"Yes, yes, this is Dr. Lewine. Who is this speaking?"

"My name's Edison," the voice on the other end of the phone answered. "You treat my daughter-in-law, Mary."

"Yes?" Lewine prompted. "Is she in labor?" he asked, trying to remember a woman named Edison. He snapped his fingers at the nurse and made a V with his fingers for her to get him a cigar while he listened.

"No, no," Tom Edison said impatiently. "She's not

near ready for that yet. She's only four months gone. But she's sick."

"Hold on one second," Lewine said. He covered the mouthpiece and spoke to the nurse, "Get me the file on Mary Edison."

"What seems to be the trouble?" he asked Edison. "Is she bleeding?"

"No, nothing like that. She's puking."

"Well, that's not uncommon."

"No, no, it ain't the morning sickness," Edison snapped. "There's something wrong with her. She's got a fever, she's dizzy and headachy, and she's been puking all afternoon."

The nurse brought the folder and put it on the desk in front of Lewine. He read it as he listened to Edison. He saw that she was a dependent wife, that her husband was an airman in Vietnam, and that she seemed to be a perfectly healthy girl in the second trimester of a normal pregnancy. She was a primipara.

"Bring her along and I'll have a look at her."

"Well, I can't do that," Edison said. "I'm feeling kind of poorly, myself. Could barely get down here to the general store to make this call."

"Did you take her temperature?" Lewine asked.

"No, but I reckon she's got a hundred and one, mebbe a hundred and two."

"How about a neighbor? Can a neighbor bring her over so I can have a look at her?"

"I don't ask neighbors for favors. Can you send an ambulance out here to get her?"

"Well, ordinarily we don't send ambulances off the base," Lewine explained. "What about your own doctor?"

"What own doctor? I don't hold with doctors."

"Oh?"

"When I get sick I go to bed and drink whiskey until I'm better."

Lewine smiled. This one was really a character.

"Well, is there a doctor in town? You live in, ah . . ."
He looked at the file. "Tarsus, is it?"

"Yes, that's right. We got a vet, but there ain't no
doctor closer than Tooele. Tooele's forty miles away
and you folks are only thirty-four, thirty-six. Anyway,
thirty-six to the gate."

"Well, if you could get her to a doctor in Tooele, or
get a doctor in Tooele to come out and see you, you
could put in a claim for it and the army would reim-
burse you."

"No, sirree," Edison said, emphatically. "My son is in
the service and you people are responsible for Mary. I'm
not going to sit around doing paperwork and waitin' for
money. Why can't you just send an ambulance for her?"

"How many times has she vomited? Two? Three?"

"She ain't puked but twice, but she feels like hell.
Now I'll admit she's something of a whiner, and she
ain't got much grit, but she looks to me to be pretty
sick. And I know how *I* feel."

Lewine thought for a minute while he lit his cigar,
holding the wooden match below the end of the cigar so
as not to char the tobacco. Edison was an annoying old
coot, and Lewine was sorely tempted to tell him once
more what his choices were and to hang up. On the
other hand, he had the feeling that Edison in that case
would do nothing at all, would go back to wherever they
lived, go to bed, and try to have both of them wait it
out. For all Lewine knew, he would ply Mary with
whiskey, too.

But an ambulance meant papers and forms. Not only
that, there would be all kinds of questions. It was not
regulation at all to send an ambulance off the base that
way.

"Well?" Edison asked, impatiently. "Whatcha gonna
do?"

Lewine thought for another instant. Monday night
was not a bridge night. And then, he had a twinge of
guilt. Maybe the girl was really sick, and here he was,
consulting his social schedule and balancing in his mind

the possibility of a drive to Tarsus with Elinor, who might find it amusing to go and visit that semi-ghost town. They had wanted to get out into the desert all summer, but had just never gotten around to it. Here was a perfectly good excuse. It might be fun to take a drive in the late afternoon and come back in the evening when the desert was pretty and the heat was tolerable. Besides, what the hell, the little Dart was air-conditioned.

"Look," Lewine said, "I have patients coming in this afternoon. I'll come on out as soon as I'm finished. Probably I'll get there somewhere around five."

"Five o'clock will be fine," Edison said. "And, ah, thanks, Doc. Thanks a lot."

"That's okay," Lewine said. He hung up the phone, took a puff of his cigar, and shook his head.

Now that he had made the offer he felt a little silly. This was the kind of thing those goddamn doctors on television series did. Who the hell was he trying to kid? And if she really was sick, what the hell could he do for the woman if he went out there? Doctors had stopped making house calls because there wasn't much you could do in a home except pat a hand and maybe take a temperature. But he had said he would go, and he no longer had any choice about it. The old guy didn't even have a phone and had had to call from a pay station, so there was no way of changing his mind and calling the man back.

He picked up the phone again and dialed his home. While he waited for an answer, he did isometric exercises, trying to push one side of the doorway farther away. Lewine was in excellent shape for a thirty-two-year-old doctor. He took care of himself, made a point of taking care of himself. The athletic facilities that the base had to offer were extensive, and unlike most of the other doctors at the small base hospital at the Dugway Proving Ground, Lewine used them. It was partly his medical conviction that the human body ought to be taken care of properly and partly vanity—he had been a

39

fair college athlete, playing J.V. football and varsity baseball at Cornell. But it was also professional shrewdness. For an ob-gyn man to lose his semi-paternal sex appeal and good looks was to lose business.

"Elinor? Hi. How would you like to drive up in the mountains with me this afternoon after I finish up here. Do you think you can get a sitter?"

"Sure," she said. "I'd love to. The kids have been wild all day."

"I think it might be fun. You haven't come along with me to see a patient since before Jimmy was born."

"A patient?" she asked.

"It's complicated. I'll explain it this afternoon when I pick you up. About four-thirty?"

"That'll be fine," she said, "I'm sure I can get the Campbell girl. The kids like her."

"Great. See you then."

Lewine was not—and he knew he was not—the sharpest doctor in the world. He was not going to win any Nobel prizes. He had had enough trouble just getting through. Like many men he knew in the bottom quarter of the medical school class, he had decided on ob-gyn. It was mainly a simple specialty. Most of the time all you did was catch. There was a terrific kick, though, in helping a woman deliver and watching a baby get born. It was a feeling of accomplishment and had a kind of thrill to it that was like nothing else in medicine. Sure, the hours were lousy; women insisted on delivering at all hours of the day and night and—worse than that—going into labor at three in the morning and waiting until noon to deliver. But he figured that by the time he was old enough so that the hours started to bother him he would specialize in gynecology and leave the obstetrics to the younger men. He knew he didn't have the steel-trap mind and lightning intuitions that separated the really great doctors from the ordinary ones, but he had resolved early on to make up for this lack with patience and assiduousness. That was, in a way, what medicine was mostly about. How many times did you need those whiz kids, anyway? And now, having committed himself to go to see the daughter-in-law of that old coot who had called, he was not going to feel silly. Not at all. It was a goddamn good deed, and he was not going to be ashamed of it. He buzzed for his nurse, told her to get the next patient ready, and went into his office to see Mrs. O'Neill.

5:12 P.M., Mountain Daylight Time:

Lewine had driven out of the Dugway gate and across the flatness of Skull Valley. He had started to climb as the road wound up into the Onaqui Mountains, up and over toward Clover, but at the fork in the road he had taken the turnoff for Tarsus. He had climbed more steeply, and then the road had leveled out, descended a little, and then turned back toward Dugway where, nestled in a cut between two large mountains and in front of a third, the tiny half-abandoned town—now a hamlet, really—of Tarsus lay in moribund tranquility. It had once been a thriving, rowdy, prospecting town when the silver had been discovered. It had enjoyed a brief meteoric prosperity that gave out when the lode gave out. There was enough silver left to keep a few loners going. There were abandoned buildings, a boarded-up church, houses that stared with the sad eyes of broken windows, and the rural squalor of abandoned automobiles, old washing machines, and spare, rusted parts of forgotten machinery strewn around the lawns of trailers on cinder blocks and ramshackle, weathered old houses. As the road ascended it narrowed and crossed the mountain stream that ran down the cut. There the houses on either side of it improved, and there were even a few kept-up lawns. On the lawn of one of the large houses four horses grazed. The only public building that Lewine could see was a gas station, or maybe it had a general store with it, too. Anyway, there were a pair of beat-up Chevron pumps outside.

"I'll go in and find out where the hell these people live," Lewine said. "The guy didn't remember to give me directions. You wait in the car. It's cool in here."

Elinor smiled and nodded.

Lewine pulled up to one side of the pumps, got out, and went inside the weathered wooden building. There was no one in evidence, neither behind the food counter, nor the postal window, nor, as he stepped through the doorway into the barroom, did he see anyone behind the bar. But the door had not been locked and the lights were on.

"Hello!" he called out. "Anybody here?"

There was no answer.

"Hello?" he called again.

"Coming, coming," a voice called.

Lewine leaned against the bar and waited for a minute for the man to appear. It was not just a figurative or metaphorical minute, but a real minute of sixty long seconds, and Lewine drummed his fingers on the bar in annoyance. It seemed a hell of a casual way to run a business. On the other hand, the pace of life was probably pretty slow in a town like this. But then a stocky man came out from the back room and announced, "Sorry, mister, the bar is closed. If you really need gas, I'll pump it for you, but I'm not feeling too sharp. I'm just hanging around until five when I'm allowed to close the post office."

"Sorry to bother you," Lewine said. "I'm looking for the Edison house. I'm a doctor."

"The Edison house? You go back down the road and it's the third, no, the fourth one on the left. Has a beat-up old Chevy pickup on blocks in the front, with chickens living in it. You look for that; you'll find the house. You can't miss it."

"Thanks," Lewine said.

"You say you're a doctor?" Smith asked. "They got sickness there?"

"So I'm told," Lewine said.

"Mary, isn't it? Thought something was the matter. Usually she comes in around one every afternoon to see if there's a letter from her husband, young Tom. She didn't come by today."

"Oh?" Lewine said. He turned to go, and then Smith added, "Funny thing, no one's been in since eleven this morning. I've had nothing to do here all day but pump gas for a couple of out-of-towners and have a beer with the fellow drives the mail truck. But it's been a blessing because I've been feeling punk all afternoon—headache, and I'm sure I'm running a fever. And weak—Lord, it's all I can do to walk across the room."

"Ought to see a doctor, maybe," Lewine said, walking toward the door. "Take care of yourself, now," he said. "Anyway, get some rest, and if you've got a fever, a couple of aspirins can't hurt you."

"Thanks, Doc," Smith called, as the door closed.

Lewine got into the Dodge, turned the car around on the gas-station apron, and drove back down the cut to the Chevy pickup truck with the chickens and what had to be the Edison house.

5:22 P.M., Mountain Daylight Time:

Lewine told Elinor, "I shouldn't be terribly long," and smiled.

Elinor replied, "Take your time. I brought a book along to read. I remembered what it was like."

He smiled, patted her knee, and got out of the car. He grabbed his black bag from the floor of the back seat and carefully picked a path through the weeds and the chicken droppings in the front yard. He walked up the sagging front steps and twisted the old-fashioned mechanical doorbell.

"Come on in, the door's open," a male voice called. The old coot, it sounded like.

Lewine opened the door and stepped inside. The front door opened directly into the small living room in which a motley collection of decrepit furniture, mining equipment, fishing rods, hunting jackets, and boots were strewn around. The largest piece in the room was an old horsehair sofa on which Edison was lying, with a bright red woolen blanket pulled up to his chin. There were no curtains, and the torn shades were pulled down to the sills. Edison struggled to a sitting position, and tried to get up, but either could not or would not invest the effort.

"You the doctor?" he asked.

"Yes, that's right, I'm Dr. Lewine."

"She's in there, in the bedroom," Edison said, pointing.

Lewine looked around. It was a tiny house. Essentially, there were four rooms: The living room, in which Edison camped, rather than lived; the kitchen, which he could see through an open doorway; the bedroom; and, presumably, a bathroom. Or so he hoped, anyway.

"I'll take a look at you, too, when I'm finished with her," Lewine offered.

"Suit yourself," Edison mumbled.

It was less than gracious but it represented a retreat from his bravado earlier that day. It was, Lewine thought wryly, a triumph for medical science—but not much of a triumph. Edison looked terrible. Aside from the fact that he was probably seventy years old and had not shaved recently, he was terribly pale, obviously suffering from chills—he was shaking—and there was a peculiar expression on his face. Lewine had nothing to compare it with because he had not met Edison before, but the man looked terribly peculiar. His face was flat, staring and masklike. Lewine wondered whether the man had suffered from a stroke in the last six months. But he would examine him more carefully later.

He went to the bedroom, the door of which was

slightly ajar. He knocked, and then entered.

"Hello, Mary," he said. "I understand you don't feel very well. We'll see what we can do about that."

The bedroom was small and stuffy and the girl seemed diminished by the size of the old-fashioned brass bed on which she lay. Lewine took a thermometer from his bag, shook it down, and popped it into Mary's mouth. He smiled reassuringly as he reached for her wrist and took her pulse. Her pulse was normal, both in rate and strength. Her temperature, however, was 103.2. He helped her into a sitting position and took his stethoscope out of the bag as she unbuttoned the top of her cotton pajamas. He listened to her heart, and then had her cough for him as he listened to her lungs. He checked her ears, and then looked at her throat, apologizing in a perfunctory sort of way as she gagged at the tongue depressor.

"Now," he said, putting his stethoscope away and flipping the depressor into the wastebasket, "what seems to be bothering you?"

"I feel awful," Mary told him. "I've been throwing up, I have a terrible, terrible headache . . ."

"Any particular part of your head, or just general?" Lewine asked.

"In the front, just behind my eyes," she told him. "And I've . . . I've felt terribly dizzy when I've gone to the bathroom. Dizzy, and with my legs all aching."

He listened while she recited her symptoms, paying attention, but also paying attention to the peculiar expression on her face. It was the same odd look he had seen on old Edison's face. The eyes were wide, and her rate of blinking was noticeably slow. Around the eyes she looked like one of those funny South American monkeys. What was the name? Loris? Marmoset? Kinkajou? No matter. The broad margin of visible sclera, the showing of the whites of the eyes above and below the iris, gave her the effect of horrified staring.

Lewine thought for a moment. It was a fair guess that both Mary and Tom Edison were sick with the same thing. It was likely to be some kind of viral infection. In that case, there was not an awful lot he would be able to do for them. He could help relieve the symptoms. He could give Mary some Compazine for her nausea. It wouldn't do to have her vomiting strenuously and dehydrating. He could take blood samples and take them back to the lab. One of the benefits of the setup back at Dugway was that the medical facilities were superb.

"When did you start feeling this way?" Lewine asked. "When did this start bothering you?"

"Since this morning. When I got up this morning I felt all right, but I felt kind of sluggish at breakfast. It was all I could do to wash the dishes. At first I thought there might have been something wrong with the bacon. That it might have turned rancid. But if that had happened, I'd have felt better after I threw up, wouldn't I?"

"No," he said, "it doesn't look like it was the bacon. That wouldn't account for the fever. You've got quite a fever, you know. You and your father-in-law have probably picked up some virus. Now," he said, taking a syringe from his bag, "I'm going to take a little blood so I can go back to the lab and find out which virus it is. In the meantime, I've got some pills that will make you a little more comfortable. They'll cut down on the nausea, anyway." He drew the blood quickly, sealed the vial, and put it in his case. Then he rummaged through the bottom of his bag and found a sample packet of Compazine. "Have you taken any aspirin?" he asked.

She smiled faintly. "You told me not to take any medicine without first asking you."

"Well, I think you can try a couple of aspirin to bring the fever down."

He went to the kitchen, found a clean glass inverted in the dish rack, filled it with water, and brought it back to the bedroom. He gave her the pills, two aspirin and a Compazine, and told her to drink as much water as she could keep down.

"Water, juice, soda, any liquids you feel like."

"This isn't going to hurt the baby, is it?" Mary asked him.

"No, no," he said, "they're a lot tougher than you'd guess. They're parasites, you know. They'll just hang in there and take what they want. He'll be okay."

She smiled at him and lay back in the bed. "Thank you for coming," she said. "I really do appreciate it."

"That's all right, Mary," Lewine said. "I'm going to take a look at your father-in-law now. As soon as I know what the lab has to say I'll get in touch with you. Or maybe I'll be back to have another look at you."

He had no intention of coming back. There was so little one could do away from the office and the hospital and the laboratory. If she failed to improve, then he would send the ambulance and take them both into the hospital. Maybe that was what he should have done in the first place. He picked up his bag, waved at Mary, and went back into the living room.

"She'll be all right, I think. Looks to be some sort of virus."

"That's what you fellas always say," Edison grumbled from the depths of the sofa.

"That's what we always say when it's a virus," Lewine replied patiently. "Can you sit up?" Lewine asked.

The old man nodded, but Lewine extended his hands for the old man to grasp as he struggled into a sitting position.

"Let's have a look at your chest," Lewine said. Edison slipped the straps of the coveralls down over his shoulders, unbuttoned the top four buttons of his union suit and slipped out of the arms, and then, tired by the exertion, leaned back against the sofa. Lewine examined him. His respiration was irregular, but ventilation seemed adequate. The heart rate was relatively slow. The face and supraclavicular areas were flushed. He took a reading on the sphygmomanometer, worried suddenly that it was not just any virus, but poliomyelitis. But, no, there was no hypertension. His blood pressure, like Mary's, was normal. So polio was extremely unlikely. It was the expression on Edison's face. It was that same peculiar wide-eyed horror-show face that he had observed in Mary. It looked like the faces one saw associated with chronic Parkinsonism. Edison looked to be the sicker of the two.

"Have you been vomiting?" he asked.

"Felt queasy, but haven't actually had to puke."

He looked at Edison's throat. It was not inflamed or red. He checked his ears. They, too, seemed normal.

"You know, Doc, I figured I was pretty sick when I couldn't get any whiskey down. The idea was too much. I guess maybe I need some of that penicillin."

"No, that doesn't work on viruses," Lewine told him.

"Thought it was supposed to be some kind of damn miracle drug."

"It is," Lewine said, "but it only does certain kinds of miracles. All I can give you right now is some aspirin to make you more comfortable. As soon as I have a report from the lab I'll be able to do something more for you. I hope so, anyway." He took a blood sample from Edison's sinewy old arm. "If you and Mary aren't any better by tomorrow, you have somebody call me and we'll send an ambulance out for both of you."

"Have to be sicker than I am now for you to get me into a hospital. At my age, a man goes to a hospital mostly to die. And I ain't ready for that yet. But I'll get word to you if she's no better."

Lewine helped him get his arms back through the arms of the union suit and rearranged the blanket. He went out to the kitchen again, washed his hands and dried them on the same clean, faded flour-sack towel he had used before, and brought Edison a glass of water. The first sips would be good for the aspirin; drinking the rest would do him good, too.

"You keep drinking fluids, too," Lewine said. "But not whiskey. That will only make you feel worse."

He put the second ampul of blood in his case and snapped the catches closed.

"If you'll reach me that leather jacket on the back of that chair, there, and let me know how much it is . . ." Edison began.

"No, no," Lewine said. "I came out here to see Mary. Looking at you was helpful for my diagnosis: To help me figure out what's the matter with her."

"You sure?" Edison asked suspiciously.

"Yes, I'm sure," Lewine said.

"Well, thanks, Doc. Much obliged."

Lewine picked up his bag and went outside and back to the car. Clearly it was a virus of some kind, and Lewine was concerned but not particularly alarmed. It would have been helpful if they had come into the base. He had made a mistake coming over here. He had not been able to do very much and now that he had begun, it was going to be difficult to continue, what with Edison not even having a telephone. But, wait, he thought, he could drive back to that combination gas station and general store and see what the name was on the sign. He could call there if necessary and probably get a message to Edison.

He got into the coolness of the air-conditioned car—he had left the engine running so that Elinor would be comfortable. She closed her book, looked up at him, and said, "Where to, now, Norm?"

"I just want to check the name of that gas station so I can get a message to the Edisons if I have to."

"Were they really sick? Was it worth coming out here?"

"Oh, they were sick enough," Lewine said. "But I'm sure they'll be all right."

He started the car and turned it around to go back toward the center of Tarsus.

It was the striking facial look they had both had; that wide-eyed stare and the dull, flat expression. Otherwise, it would have been easy to dismiss the fever, the vomiting, the weakness, the headaches as some kind of flu, some simple virus attack that was likely to disappear even before the laboratory came back with a particular diagnosis of the breed of virus. Well, all he could do was wait for the lab.

He drove up the road and onto the apron of the filling station. He saw the sign over the door: Smith's Service Station, William T. Smith, Prop. It would be easy enough to find, he was sure. Only then did he realize, seeing the sign next to it—U.S. Post Office, Tarsus, Utah—that he hadn't needed to come up here; he could simply have looked up the number of the Tarsus post office. He felt a little silly, but then Elinor said, "No, wait a minute. I have to use the bathroom."

Lewine nodded. She got out of the car and walked around the apron to the ladies' room. Lewine sat in the car looking around, thinking about the Edisons. It was tough for them both to be sick at the same time—especially in a remote, sleepy little hamlet like Tarsus. It was the quietest town he had ever seen. Here it was, a few minutes after five, and there was no sign of life whatever. No children playing, no men coming home from work. It was very odd.

He was considerably reassured, then, to notice in his rear-view mirror the figure of a young boy walking down the grassy edge of the road toward the store. So there was life here, after all. Maybe they were all just smarter than he thought; staying inside in the heat of the day and coming out only when it had gotten cool. The boy continued down along the road and crossed the apron of the filling station in the direction of the store entrance. Suddenly he stopped, stood still for a moment, and then vomited in the way that children do, in helpless paroxysms. An adult would have knelt down or at least bent over. But the young boy seemed to be surprised by his own vomit. Lewine got out of the car and went around to see if he could help the child, who was now sitting on the ground, a couple of steps away from the pool of vomitus on the asphalt.

"Are you all right?" Lewine asked, knowing it was a foolish question. "I'm a doctor."

"Yes, sir, I'm okay. I just whoopsed."

50

"I can see that," Lewine said, pulling a small pack of Kleenex out of his pocket and offering it to the child. The youngster accepted it and wiped his mouth and the place on his knee where he had spattered himself. Lewine helped him to his feet.

"I was just on my way to the store," the boy explained. "My mother doesn't feel so good. She sent me down to get TV dinners I could make for the other kids."

Lewine stood there watching as the boy went into the store. Whether the boy would find Smith well enough to serve him, or whether Smith simply left the store open when he was sick so the townspeople could help themselves and settle up later, Lewine did not know. The problem flittered across the surface of his mind and he grasped at it, and then realized that he would prefer to deal with such a simple practical problem than to consider the other one—the more frightening one that had begun to loom up in the back of his mind. The kid was sick. The kid's mother was sick. He'd said so. Smith, in the store, was feeling and looking terrible. Both of the Edisons were sick. His first reaction had been entirely correct. This was a peculiarly quiet town. Too damn quiet—as they always said in the movies just before the Indians attacked.

Elinor came out of the ladies' room and returned to the car. "Norm?" she asked.

"Just a minute," he said. He had decided to wait for the boy and offer him a ride home. How long could it take? A minute? Two minutes. There wasn't a house in town that was out of hailing distance.

But then, when the boy came out of the store, he was accompanied by a rangy youngish man with wavy black hair. The boy was holding a bag.

"How are you feeling, son? Can I give you a ride home?"

"No thank you, sir," he said.

The man who had come out of the store with the youngster looked at Lewine, who suddenly realized how odd this must appear. "The boy threw up a minute ago," Lewine explained. "I'm a doctor. Dr. Norman Lewine. I thought he might not feel up to walking home in this heat."

"Paul Donovan," the man said, his cautious expression relaxing into a smile and his hand extending for Lewine to shake, which he did. "I'll drop him home; it's on my way. You here to see Smith?"

"No," Lewine said.

" 'Cause he's pretty sick. The store's just open in case anyone needs anything. There's a sign saying just to help yourself. Which I did," he said, opening his palm and displaying a bottle of Empirin. "Must have got too much sun out in the desert today. My head is splitting and I feel punchy. But I can get the boy home. He's one of the Pratt kids. He's just a couple of houses up and it's on my way. Nice to have met you, Doctor."

"My pleasure," Lewine mumbled, but his mind was not on the conversation at all. Abruptly he turned, went back to the car, got in, and sat down. Every damn one of them. He had not seen or heard of a single healthy person in all of Tarsus. He put the car in gear, pulled off the apron, and started down the road, going slowly, still hoping to find a gaggle of children somewhere on a lawn, playing ball, running, shouting—anything, any sign of normal life in an American town. Women chatting. A man washing his car. But there was nothing. It was even more frightening and menacing than the desolation of those total ghost towns like Mercur where, all human population having departed, there was at least the rhythm of life of birds, jackrabbits, and lizards.

6:05 P.M., Mountain Daylight Time:

The boy held the brown paper bag with the TV dinners in it, and Paul held the boy. He was a tough little kid. He'd staggered a couple of times, and Paul had offered

52

to carry him. But of course he'd refused. And then he'd staggered once more and fallen. And Paul had picked him up and was carrying him.

"I'm okay. I can walk, sir."

"You'll just fall down again. You're a little wobbly there."

"We all are."

Paul was considering that, putting it together with other bits of information—the illnesses of the Edisons and of Smith—when Hope Wilson appeared.

"What happened? Is he all right?"

"Well, he's sick," Paul replied. "He threw up and he couldn't walk without falling down."

"I thought . . . I saw you carrying him and, somehow, I was sure he'd been hit by a car. And . . ."

"No, no car," Paul said.

"Thank God," she said. She smiled in relief, or perhaps out of nervousness. It struck Paul that the circumstances of their meeting a few days before had been fantastically inauspicious. It was bad enough that they were the only single man and woman of appropriate age, and it was further complicated by their personal situations—he being a widower and she being recently divorced. But the transparent eagerness of Mrs. Jenkins' introduction had been deadly. Paul had been put off by the obviousness of his landlady's hopefulness, and the way in which the other townspeople in the general store had beamed at them. Hope had been put off by it too; to begin with embarrassment as the only shared experience they had in common was not—would not have been—much of an inducement to a further meeting. Even now, Paul felt himself very much aware of his physical size, the big hands and feet feeling like smoked hams. It was reminiscent of adolescence, when he had shot up at fourteen and had felt like a storybook giant for a few years. He smiled back, hoping that it did not look like the smile of a giant about to devour the poor lady's cow in one gulp, or the lady herself.

Hope reached out and took the paper sack of TV dinners from Joseph Pratt. The boy allowed her to take the bag and relaxed in Paul's arms, so that he was easier to carry.

"Thanks," Paul said.

"He's heavy enough without these," Hope answered.

They walked along for a few moments. Mostly it was just to make conversation that Paul said, "They're all sick, it seems." He shifted the burden of the boy's weight a little.

"Oh?" she asked. "That's odd. So are my aunt and uncle. It must be some sort of bug going around."

"I imagine," he agreed. He considered telling her about the Edisons and about Smith, but he was somehow afraid of seeming to be an alarmist. He did not want to appear to be talking for effect. Besides, the effort of carrying Joseph was beginning to tell upon him. The kid was heavy.

They walked on in silence until they reached the Pratt house. Paul put Joseph down, steadying him.

"You okay?" he asked. "You can make it from here?"

"Yes, sir. Thank you."

"Okay, then."

Hope gave him the sack of TV dinners. They watched as the youngster walked up to the front door and went inside. No wave, no sign, nothing.

"I was sure he had been hurt," Hope explained, "because they keep to themselves so. It isn't like them to accept help from strangers. Unless they're desperate."

"Why? What do you mean?"

Hope explained to Paul about how the Pratts were Mormons and how their arrangement did not quite fit into the laws of the United States. "She's a sister-wife," Hope concluded.

"I see," Paul said.

It would have been good to continue the discussion. Paul would have liked to hear more about Mormons, or, indeed, about anything. It would have been fine to go for a cup of coffee somewhere, or . . . But Paul's head had begun to ache. The exertion of carrying the Pratt boy had been too much for him. His head was really bad. The pain was behind one eye and sharp, white, throbbing . . .

"I . . . I have to get back," he said. "Excuse me."

"Certainly," she said. But he was sure that she thought he must be some kind of antisocial freak. He'd messed it up all right. Or his head had messed it up for him. He walked as carefully as he could, trying not to jar his head. It was the right heel that did it, sending the small tremor of impact up to trigger a new stab of pain. But at least it diverted him from the humiliation of the brusque, awkward termination of their talk.

It wasn't that Hope Wilson was all that important. But one ought to be able to manage things a little better, he told himself. This was just . . . kid stuff.

6:30 P.M., Mountain Daylight Time:

Lewine had listened to Elinor's babble about what a lovely idea it had been to go for a drive together, to get away from the kids and the base, to get out and see a little of the desert and the mountains, knowing all the while that she was going on in this way because the excursion had been disappointing and dull. He had listened and had agreed with her that they must try it again, pick out places to go, maybe try to follow the old Pony Express trail that passed just south of Dugway. . . .

And then it had hit him. Dugway. The connection had been there all the time, and he had been unwilling to make it. But there had to be other explanations. It would not do just to jump at the most melodramatic conclusion. It could be other things. It could be some new kind of flu, or something in the water or in the food. Still, there it was, the sign on the main road pointing toward Dugway Proving Ground.

Lewine had not thought about Dugway much. Sure,

he worked there, but as an obstetrician and gynecologist whose concerns were with women and babies. Dugway was just a military installation, the function of which was . . . But he had only the vaguest idea. It had been the experimental station for the chemical- and biological-warfare programs, but the President had announced that that was all over with. Or the biological warfare part of it was. There would be only defensive research now. And for that, Lewine would have assumed the Fort Detrick labs would be more than sufficient. Still, Dugway was going on, had not been closed down. There were enough military and civilian personnel still working there to require his services and the services of a whole staff of doctors and dentists and teachers. Beyond that twelve-mile limit around the town itself, out in the empty expanse of desert that made up most of the huge base, he hadn't the faintest idea of what they were doing. Had not really wanted to know.

Consciously, he had not yet accepted it, not at all, but there his foot was down on the floor, pressing the accelerator as far as it would go. The Dart began to vibrate as the needle climbed above eighty. They were out of the mountains and crossing the floor of Skull Valley. Elinor looked at him as if to speak, to criticize the speed, but seeing his face she changed her mind and remained silent. As did he. He did not speak again, until he pulled the car up in front of Bill Robertson's house.

"You go on home," he said. "I want to stop to talk with Bill for a moment. I'll see you later."

"There's nothing wrong, is there?"

"I hope not. I . . . just don't know."

She nodded and drove away. He went up the walk to the front door of the snug Tudor-style house in which the Robertsons lived and rang the bell. Laura Robertson opened the door.

"Norm!" she said in surprise. "This isn't a bridge night, is it? You and Bill aren't playing tonight?"

"No, it's not a bridge night. I came over to see Bill about something else. A problem . . ."

"Oh, all right. Come on in," she said. "Can I get you anything? A beer?"

"No, no thanks," Lewine answered, stepping into the coolness of the air-conditioned living room.

The room was the same shape as his own living room. All the houses had been put up at the same time in a large, semicircular tract design modeled on the English New Towns. There were variations, of course—some of the houses were bigger than others. They were assigned not on the basis of children and the need for extra bedrooms, but on rank. Bill Robertson, a major, had a dining room, not just a dining area, and a fourth bedroom. The living room was strictly government issue and unrelieved by personal decoration, but he knew Bill and Laura had a fishing shack up in Idaho that they thought of as home and through which they satisfied their nest-building instincts.

The living room was busy. In one corner, Jean, the Robertson's nine-year-old daughter, was watching television, and across the room, near the fireplace, Bill was playing chess with Tommy, his fourteen-year-old son.

"Hi, Norm. How's it going?" Bill said, looking up from the chessboard. "Laura give you a beer?"

"No, I don't want one, thanks. I've got to talk to you."

"Can it wait until I've dealt with Tommy's rook? He's getting to be quite a threat."

Lewine was tempted to be polite, to wait for Bill Robertson to make his move and . . . But that was crazy.

"No, Bill," he said quietly. "I don't think it can wait."

Robertson looked up in some surprise and then got up from the chessboard. "Later on, Tom," he said. "I'll get back to the game as soon as I can." He crossed the room to where Lewine was standing and said, "Let's talk in the kitchen. It's quieter there."

Major William Robertson led the way into the small but efficient kitchen where Laura was finishing the dinner dishes.

"Well, Norm," Bill asked, "what's up?"

Lewine hesitated, looking at Laura and trying to decide whether or not to speak in her presence. He had brought Elinor with him to Tarsus, but then, he had not discussed with her what he had found and certainly he had not told her—and would not tell her—what he feared. He was trying to think of a tactful way of suggesting that they go outside to talk when Bill, reading his hesitation correctly, dealt with the problem himself, saying to Laura, "You've had a tough day, dear. Why don't you go out and relax in front of the TV and I'll help you with what's left of the dishes later?"

Laura looked at him in surprise, looked at Norman, and then realized what her husband had meant. "Oh, sure," she said. "Thanks. I'd love to get off my feet for a while."

As soon as she had left the room, Bill motioned to a kitchen chair and the two men sat down.

"What's the problem?"

"I don't know," Lewine said. "I'm still hoping that there isn't a problem and that I'm just imagining things. But I'm worried. This afternoon I went out to a little town about thirty-five or forty miles from here across the Valley. You know where Tarsus is?"

"I've never been there, but I know where it is. It's off the road to Clover, isn't it?"

"Yes, that's right. It's a little town, I don't know exactly how many people still live there. Probably fifty to a hundred. Old prospecting town that's dying out. I went out there today to see a patient . . ."

Robertson's eyebrows lifted slightly.

"It's too complicated to explain why I did that, and it doesn't really matter. If I'm right, it was maybe lucky that I did. The thing that bothers me is that everybody in the town seems to be sick."

"Everybody?" Robertson queried.

"Everybody I saw. My young pregnant patient and her father-in-law, who's seventy, maybe. And a middle-aged storekeeper, a boy about twelve, and a youngish man about twenty-eight or thirty, an athletic type. And, oh yes, the mother of that boy. The kid said she was sick, too. There wasn't a single person outside. There wasn't a sign of movement in the whole town. It was spooky, and only gradually did I realize that they all had to be sick."

"Symptoms?" Robertson asked.

Lewine recounted the symptoms: The fever, the headaches, the vomiting, the slow heart rate, and, in the case of the Edisons, the peculiar facial expression.

"Facial expression?" Robertson asked, leaning forward slightly. "What kind of facial expression?"

"Well, it looked sort of like Parkinson's. That masklike look and the wide eyes."

"You bring specimens?"

"I've got blood samples from both of the Edisons. I was going to drop them off at the lab, but on the way over I decided to come and talk to you first. You're the epidemiologist around here."

From the way Robertson sat, from the way he tapped a front tooth with the nail of his index finger, suggesting that he was engrossed by the problem, Lewine took a kind of comfort. He had not been imagining things. It was a problem worth coming to Robertson with.

Finally Robertson spoke. "Well, Norm, it could be bad. It could be really bad. I hope it isn't, but . . ." He paused, passed his hand over his crew cut, and continued. "I'll tell you what. Instead of taking the samples over to your lab in the hospital, why don't we take them over to my lab? We've got an evening shift of technicians and some pretty sophisticated equipment."

"Sure," Lewine said. He hesitated for a moment, then asked the question that had been weighing on his mind ever since he had left Tarsus. "You think it could be something from here?"

Robertson was a doctor, but he was not connected with the base hospital. He was in epidemiology and was a part of the research staff of the Dugway Proving Ground.

"There isn't any flu in the area," Lewine continued,

"and it's a pretty stable population they've got there in Tarsus, so there wouldn't be many newcomers bringing stuff in. And what bothers me is the diversity of age and sex of the people I saw or heard about. I've thought of the water or the food, but then I thought that I don't really know much about these things and I ought to come and talk to you."

Robertson had already got up from the chair. "I'm glad you did," he said.

"I couldn't help wondering whether it's something from here," Lewine said. "But . . . could it be? I mean, are we—are you—playing with anything that could affect people out there?"

"The only thing to do is to go and find out," Robertson said. "I've got to get out of these," he added, pointing to his T-shirt and Bermuda shorts. "Then we'll go on over to the lab." He took a step toward the kitchen doorway and then stopped and turned back. "You haven't mentioned this to anyone, have you? I mean, Elinor?"

"I took her with me," Lewine said. "It was, I thought, going to be a nice drive through the desert in the evening. She was there but she never got out of the car. Wait, oh, yes, she went to the bathroom at the gas station. But I don't think she noticed anything. And I certainly didn't tell her anything."

Robertson thought for a moment. "Good," he said. "Don't."

He went off to change. Lewine had meant to repeat his question about what experiments they were still doing and whether one of them could have caused the sickness in Tarsus. . . . But, now that he thought of it, he realized that with what Robertson had just said, the question was already at least partially answered.

6:42 P.M., Mountain Daylight Time:

They had taken Robertson's car and Robertson was driving. As soon as he had got into uniform they had driven away from the house and onto the road that led to the interior of the base past the second checkpoint, beyond which Lewine had never gone before. Robertson had slowed the car, stopped, and taken Lewine into the bare guardhouse where two MPs, armed with M-16s, looked out at the two lanes of the road that passed on either side of their post. Behind the gray steel desk at which a third MP sat, there was an electrical panel that operated the automatic gates that barred the road. Lewine looked around curiously and stood there waiting while Robertson spoke on the phone to the officer of the day, informing him that he was taking a visitor to the laboratory. After a moment Robertson handed the phone to one of the MPs, who accepted it and spoke to the O. D. "Yes, sir," he said, and hung up.

"It's okay," he said to the second MP, the one at the desk. "But you'll have to sign for him, sir," he said to Robertson.

Robertson took from his pocket a green metal square on a chain and hung it around his neck. Lewine had never seen one of them before. It was about the size of a picture postcard. Laminated on the metal were two pictures of Robertson, full-face and profile, and his thumbprint. One of the MPs asked Lewine to come with him over to the desk. From a drawer the MP at the desk produced a blank metal tag the same size as Robertson's, also on a chain. This, however, was red and was stamped with the word "VISITOR." The MP looked at Lewine's orange identification pin—a round badge perhaps two inches across that Lewine wore on his lapel. Everyone on the Dugway Proving Ground over the age of ten wore one of these I. D. badges. The

MP copied a series of numbers from Lewine's orange badge onto a form and then handed him the red plaque. "Please wear this, sir, until you give it back to me when you leave," he said. Lewine hung the chain about his neck.

Robertson signed a paper on a clipboard which the MP then asked Lewine also to sign, snapped a picture of him with one of those check-cashing cameras, and then said, "All right, sir, if you'll get into your car, I'll open the gate."

"Thank you," Robertson said, and he led the way back out to the red Mustang.

The steel gate lifted slowly and Robertson put the car in gear. The car passed under the gate, and then, with impressive rapidity and a loud clang, the gate descended, blocking the entrance once more.

Robertson drove another half-mile and then turned off the main road to a side road marked only with a sign that proclaimed, "Building No. 4." The building was along the side road. Lewine looked ahead and saw a low, white, one-story concrete structure. It was a drab-looking building, but impressive, sitting there in the middle of nowhere surrounded by arc lights on tall poles. There was a small parking area and Bill pulled into the slot marked with his name, "Robertson, Maj. W." They got out of the car and Robertson led the way to the entrance of Building Number 4. Robertson opened the door and Lewine followed him, surprised that they left a building like this unlocked. Inside the entrance was nothing but a small lobby with a soldier sitting at a desk under an overhead light with a green conical shade. But behind him there was a second door. It was a gray steel slab with neither keyhole nor handle. The soldier immediately came to attention and saluted. Major Robertson returned the salute and took the green plaque from around his neck. He handed it to the guard who glanced at it, glanced again at the major, and said, "I have been informed by the duty officer that you are bringing a visitor."

Robertson said, "Yes, that's right."

"Yes, sir."

Lewine expected that the guard would then return the green plaque to Robertson. Instead, he turned around and inserted it into a horizontal slot in the gray steel door. Inside the door a scanning machine read the code on the plaque, which activated the mechanism that unlocked the door. With a hiss of air the door sprang open about eight inches and then rolled silently open the rest of the way. The guard returned Robertson's identification to him, and then the two men walked through the door. As soon as they were inside, Robertson pressed a button that closed the door behind them.

Robertson led the way down a green corridor lit at regular intervals by recessed fluorescent fixtures. He stopped at a door marked only with a number and opened it. "Come on in," he said to Lewine. "This is where I hang out. I've got a couple of technicians in here running some hourly tests on a batch of rats. But I can pull them off that and have one of them check the samples."

Lewine fished the ampuls out of his pocket and handed them over to Robertson. The door from the corridor had led not directly into the lab but into a small office that had a large glass window looking into the laboratory area. There was also a door leading from the office into the lab area, and this one Robertson opened with a key. He left Lewine sitting in his office and went into the lab, closing the door behind him. Lewine could see him talking with a slender, red-haired, white-coated lab technician. It took Lewine a moment before he recognized her. She had been beaten in the quarter finals of the women's singles tennis tournament a month before. She was married to some lieutenant, but he couldn't remember the name. He would not have supposed that she worked here; he had not known that she worked at all. He had supposed that she was just another army wife.

Robertson spoke with her a moment and then returned to the small office in which Lewine was sitting.

"It'll take fifteen or twenty minutes," he said.

They sat for a few moments, looking at each other. Finally Lewine asked, "Do you have any idea what you're looking for?"

"Well," Robertson answered, "I know what I'm hoping not to find."

Lewine waited, but Robertson said nothing further. The first rule of security was the "need to know." And if the findings were negative on whatever it was that Robertson feared, there would be no need for Lewine to know what it was that they were fooling around with in these labs. Which suited him fine. But he could not help wondering what sorts of experiments they were running here, now that their research efforts were limited to defensive research.

"I . . . I don't mean to pry, and you don't have to answer if you don't think you should," Lewine began, "but I can't help wondering what kinds of work you're doing here. I mean, now that it's all defensive. Immunization and control?"

"That's right," Robertson said. "But it's more complicated than that. If we were attacked by some enemy that wanted to use a biological weapon, the likelihood is that the enemy would use some disease that made it attractive as a weapon—with a high kill rate, a low secondary communicability, and adaptability to a reliable delivery system. All that kind of thing. And so we have to keep looking for new biological weapons, new diseases, new strains of old diseases so we know what we'd be likely to have to defend against."

"But is it likely? I mean, is any major power going to use biological weapons?"

"No, no major power. The major powers have nuclear weapons, which somehow or other are acceptable. It'd be a minor power—some small country with a lunatic as its leader. These things are fairly cheap to make. Nuclear weapons are expensive."

"You said a low secondary communicability," Lewine observed. "Why low?"

"You want a clean disease," Robertson explained. "You want something where you can send your own people in after a time so that you can take over. You can have your troops inoculated, of course, but that means there's a defense. The ideal weapon is one for which there is no known inoculation, one that wipes out most of the people you've exposed to it, but that stops there, doesn't spread any further. . . . That's what we've been working on."

"I see," Lewine said. So, it was the same old set of semi-exotic diseases, diseases you boned up on for an exam in medical school and then forgot about because the chances were very slim that you'd ever actually see them: Psittacosis, anthrax, tularemia, and the more classic killers, such as typhus, plague, cholera. But none of them seemed to fit the situation he'd seen in Tarsus.

"You didn't notice any nuchal rigidity, did you?" Robertson asked abruptly.

"What?"

"Stiff neck."

"I know what it is," Lewine replied with a note of good-natured sarcasm. "I was just trying to think. No. Of course, I wasn't looking for it, but nobody complained of it. General achiness was as specific as any of them got."

"Good," Robertson said.

Nuchal rigidity? Lewine thought. It had to do, then, with the central nervous system. Meningitis? An encephalidity? He wanted to ask, but even more he wanted not to. He looked across the small room at the man sitting behind the desk. Crewcut, amiable, suntanned, with an incredibly engaging smile at moments of triumph at the bridge table. And this is what his friend spent his time doing?

"You fellows have some terrific set of toys," Lewine said, trying to maintain some degree of civilized lightness about it.

"They're not toys," Robertson answered with dead earnestness.

There was nothing light, nothing civilized about it.

7:30 P.M., Mountain Daylight Time:

The red-headed lab technician came into the office and handed Robertson a piece of paper. She did not speak but stood waiting for him to read the report. She acknowledged Lewine's presence with a crisp nod and then stood behind Robertson's chair and waited for him to speak.

"Thank you, Jane," he said. It was obviously a dismissal. To be absolutely certain, she asked, "Will there be anything further?"

"No, that'll be all, thanks. You can get back to the rats now."

She nodded, said, "Yes, Doctor," and returned to the lab.

Robertson waited until the door was closed and only then did he look at Lewine, shake his head slowly, and say, "We may be in for trouble."

"Oh?" Lewine asked.

Robertson took a deep breath, let it out slowly, and rubbed the side of his nose with his forefinger. "You're in this so deep, we may as well go all the way," he said. "What we've got here is one of the arboviruses. And we've been running some tests on one or two of them out here. It's possible—it's always possible—that one of them could have got away from us. But we don't know that. It could be another strain. It could be a spontaneous infection that has nothing to do with us. In fifteen minutes, the results are pretty crude."

"What diseases are we talking about?" Lewine asked. "These are encephalidities, aren't they?"

"That's right," Robertson answered. "But the question is, which one. It's just possible that there's an outbreak here of Western equine encephalitis, or St. Louis encephalitis, but the micron measurement of these viruses isn't really right for either of them. There's Murray Valley encephalitis, but the likelihood of Australian mosquitoes flying around in Utah is pretty slim. Or it could be West Nile fever, but that doesn't seem likely either."

"And the bugs you've been playing with?"

"There are two of them. About two years ago we did a series of experiments with Venezuelan equine encephalitis. Developed a vaccine for it, actually. And it was that vaccine that helped us contain an epidemic in Ecuador in the summer of '69. But some of that got out into the wild horses that run around here. . . . We thought we'd got it all, but maybe it's sprung up again. The only natural locus of the disease in the States is in south Florida. But there have been cases out here in Utah for the past two years. Spotty, though. Nothing like this."

"And the other?" Lewine asked. "You said there were two of them."

"The other's the one I'm afraid of," Robertson said. "There's no vaccine for this one. And no treatment. That's why we've been working with it."

"All right," Lewine asked, "what is it?"

"Japanese encephalitis. We've been doing some experiments with an aerosol delivery system, using pigs— they're the natural reservoir anyway, and the weight is right for these tests."

"So what do we do?" Lewine asked.

Robertson picked up the phone. "I think we call General Wyatt and check on operations for the last ten days. With any luck, he'll be able to tell us we're way off base. And then all we'll have is a simple medical emergency."

7:35 P.M., Mountain Daylight Time:

Brigadier General Thomas F. Wyatt hung up the telephone in the small alcove behind the coatroom in the officers' club. He stood there thoughtfully for a moment chewing his lower lip and then he walked back into the card room and beckoned to his aide with a crook of the finger. His aide, Captain Roy Phipps, who was playing bridge, held up the cards in one hand and raised his eyebrows. Wyatt shook his head almost imperceptibly, like a pitcher shaking off an unacceptable signal from a catcher. Phipps immediately put his cards down, excused himself from the other officers with whom he was playing, and followed the general, who had already started to leave the club.

Wyatt was one of those solid, stolid men whose bulk managed somehow to convey enormous energy. It was not just the military carriage and briskness of movement, but the habit he had of extending his chin and with it describing the top arc of a circle in order to drive home a point, while at the same time freeing his thick muscular neck from the constriction of his tight, tailored collar. By the time Phipps had caught up with General Wyatt at the entrance of the officers' club, the general's Oldsmobile was already pulling up to the front door. Wyatt did not wait for the driver to open the door; he hardly waited for the car to come to a complete stop. He opened the back door himself and dove into the automobile. Phipps scrambled in after him. The car was already in gear and moving before Phipps had time to close the back door.

"What's up, sir?" Phipps asked, puffing slightly.

"It's too early to say yet," Wyatt answered. "Maybe nothing. On the other hand, maybe this time it's really hit the fan. Soon as we get to the office I want to see every flight report for flights from the base in the last two weeks."

"Yes, sir," Phipps said. "Choppers, too?"

"Everything. And on any of the test flights, I want a cross-check with Weather on the conditions they were flying through. Wind currents, speed, the whole works."

"That may take a little while," Phipps began.

"I want it yesterday," Wyatt answered. "You've got

ten minutes from the time we get to the office. This could make that Ralph Powell business look like a picnic."

"Ralph Powell, sir?"

Wyatt did not answer. He was thinking about the flap back in '59 when he'd been a colonel stationed at Fort Detrick in Maryland. That had been before the formation of the Army Materiel Command, when he'd been with what they still called the Army Chemical Corps. Powell, a twenty-two-year-old enlisted laboratory technician and the world's stupidest son-of-a-bitch, had awakened one morning feeling a little bit ill and with slight chills. He'd gone to work, but his fever had continued and had become worse. Finally he had gone to the Fort Detrick hospital, where it turned out that he had a full-blown case of pneumonic plague. The kicker had been his off-duty job—life guarding at the Fort Detrick swimming pool. All those wives and kids and guests. It could have been just like the Black Death. Just like? Hell, that's what the Black Death had been. Exactly. They'd managed to hush it up, delaying reports to the Public Health Service and keeping it out of the press. Khrushchev had been touring the country at the time, and if that news had gotten out, Khrushchev would have been banging both shoes at the same time.

There had been other flaps, too, during the course of Wyatt's years working with CBW—but none had been so potentially serious as that, so threatening to the entirety of the program. Oh, there had been incidents where mistakes had been made, where accidents had happened, where lab people had been careless. And there had been deaths. But very few of them had involved the general public. The public was just so damn tender-minded about weaponry of any kind. Nuclear, chemical, biological, they didn't seem to understand the nature of the threat to the very survival of their country. The outcry back in '68 over those damn sheep! Most of those sob-sister liberals had never even seen a sheep, but they had sure made it rough for McDonald. Poor guy

69

had retired early, and because of sixty-four hundred sheep. Napoleon—or maybe it was Wellington—anyway, one of them had said it takes the lives of ten thousand soldiers to train one general. Wyatt wondered with what contempt and scorn Wellington and Napoleon would have considered the situation in which sixty-four hundred sheep could ruin the career of a first-class man and a well-trained general.

The car stopped in front of GHQ. This time Phipps got out with unaccustomed alacrity. The general followed. The two men walked briskly up the three steps and into the surrealist white glare of fluorescent lighting and the slightly astringent chemical smell of the air-conditioned General Headquarters Building.

There was something reassuring about the briskness of the procedure. All the saluting, the coming to attention of the guards, the efficient sound of heels on the marbleized floors, and the wonderful orderliness of steel filing cabinets and steel desks . . . it all suggested and embodied the enormous capability of the army. Seen out of scale and unrelated to the real world, it could be illusory and delusionary—Wyatt's tour at the Pentagon had reduced all reality to a series of office routines—but here the balance between administrative procedure and actual accomplishment and experience was nicely maintained. The thing was not to get ruffled, to remember that there was no catastrophe, however enormous, for which there was not a contingency plan ready.

7:50 P.M., Mountain Daylight Time:

"I really don't understand, sir. There's a town over there with real people in it, and those people are sick. We ought to do something."

Lewine had surprised even himself by his vehemence. For the first five minutes that he and Robertson had been sitting in the general's office he had been quiet, almost relieved that the decisions, the responsibilities were out of his hands now. But listening to Robertson and the general talking about it cautiously, calmly, abstractly, and with an infuriating and frustrating deliberateness had finally made him sufficiently angry to speak up. It wasn't a question of legal responsibility. It had nothing to do with the ways in which Robertson and the general were talking about it. The clarity, the simplicity of the situation was there. The army was playing with some kind of encephalitis. Those people had contracted some kind of encephalitis. The likelihood was that it had been the army's fault, but whether its fault or no, the facilities clearly were here. The medical capability was here, and, too, the machinery necessary to cope with mass disaster.

"I mean," he said, taking a slightly different tack, "it would take less than an hour to set up a field hospital in Tarsus."

"No," General Wyatt said. "We can't do that. Not yet. It would be an admission of our responsibility, and I'm not yet sure we are responsible."

Lewine looked at Bill Robertson, expecting that he would come to his aid, would support him, would know how to deal with the general. But Robertson remained silent.

"At least let me call the hospital in Tooele and alert them. They could send in civilian help. It wouldn't be so effective as what we've got, but it's better than nothing."

The general looked at Robertson, and then Bill turned to Lewine and said, "Look, Norm, I'm a doctor, too. And I'm just as concerned as you are about these people. But this is a very tricky situation, and the forty-five minutes it's going to take to check this out isn't going to matter a hell of a lot one way or another. We can't go off half-cocked on a thing like this. It's too serious."

"But there are lives at stake," Lewine countered.

"There are lives at stake either way," Wyatt said. "It's a matter of weighing one risk against another. Look, son," he said in a kindly way, "I've been in this army for a long time now, and I've seen some pretty unpleasant things, but one of the things I've learned is that you can't do anything effective until all the information is in."

There was nothing more that Lewine could do. He was outnumbered and he was outranked, and, for all he knew, maybe they were right as well. Their combined experience—Robertson's and the general's—certainly had to count for something. He was a civilian obstetrician dressed up in an army suit. These people were the experts.

There was a rap at the general's door and Captain Phipps entered carrying a blue-green military file which he handed to the general. "The pilots' reports are on top; the weather reports are that second sheaf, sir," he said.

"Thank you, Roy," the general said. He leaned forward in his chair and began riffling through the yellow flimsies that were the file copies of the pilots' logs. "Everything seems to be okay with these four," he said, "and these are the relevant flights. Maybe we can get some clue from Meteorology." He put the four logs down on the pull shelf of his desk and picked up the long green sheets from Weather. He looked through slowly, turning the pages thoughtfully and stopping from time to time to refer to the flimsies. Attached to the last green weather sheet was an additional smaller piece of pink paper that had been stapled on. General Wyatt read the attached pink sheet which said: "Provo Weather STA reports thunderhead occluded front 3,000 feet. Now shown on DGWY RDR. Confirmed 4:28 PM MDT."

He looked up, considering for a moment how he should put it. He did not want further to excite the already excitable Lewine. Not that there was anything Lewine could do, but that kind of hysteria was not helpful. Indeed, it could be contagious. "It's too early to say yet, but we might have something here. There was a test flight Friday afternoon. The pilot's report makes no mention of this thundershower that we had the report on from Provo. It's just possible that the winds might have done something odd and carried some of the soup off target."

"Well, sir, do you want me to mobilize the field hospital?"

"Not yet," Wyatt said to Robertson. "I think I'd better have a talk with that pilot. Phipps," he said.

"Yes, sir?" said Phipps, rising to his feet.

"Find . . ." the general looked at the flimsy. "Find Lieutenant Marvin Dawes for me, would you?"

"Right away, sir," Phipps said, and he left the room.

"What would the incubation period be on the virus that you were using?" Lewine asked.

"About seventy-two hours," Robertson said, his face glum.

"Well, that's it. It's got to be," Lewine said. He had deliberately fought for restraint in his tone and expression. The look on Robertson's face was enough to tell him that the numerical balance of the argument had already shifted.

"I'm afraid Dr. Lewine may be right, sir," Robertson said.

"Maybe," Wyatt said.

"But wouldn't he have mentioned it in his report?" Robertson asked, clutching at the last straw.

"Sometimes the pilots tell us what they think we want to hear," the general said. "That's why I want to see this Dawes. To make absolutely sure."

"Well, I'm sure," Lewine said. "That's what it's got to be."

"It's my responsibility, Captain," Wyatt snapped. "If I go off on a thing like this without all the facts, it could be damaging to our entire program here. In fact, it could be fatal. And I happen to think that the work we do here is damned important. The only thing that keeps an enemy from using this kind of weaponry against us is their knowledge that we have the capability of retaliation. These programs have already been cut back; we're working on a pauper's budget now. Another mess could mean another cutback and another cutback might be just the kind of encouragement that Moscow or Peiping or Hanoi have been waiting for."

"I'm not disagreeing with you, sir," Lewine said. "All I'm trying to say is that there are sick people in that town, and they need help."

"I am quite aware of that, Captain," the general replied. "You've made your position abundantly clear."

They sat in silence for a moment. Then the phone rang. The general picked it up, listened for a moment, and then said, "Oh, for Christ's sake! Well, then go get him. Send a helicopter and a couple of MPs. I want him here in half an hour at the outside."

The general hung up the phone and sighed. "Wouldn't you know," he said. "He's off at the Chicken Coop."

"The Chicken Coop?" Lewine asked. "What's that?"

For the first time in some minutes Robertson smiled. "A whorehouse just over the Nevada line," he replied.

8:30 P.M., Mountain Daylight Time:

Marvin Dawes sat at the bar in the Chicken Coop drinking his third gin and Bitter Orange. He liked to stretch his evening out and keep the anticipation going for as long as possible, and Mama Cash ran a nice, comfortable, well-stocked bar.

The place had once been a legitimate roadhouse, but when the new interstate highway had been put through and the traffic had been diverted from the road, the old roadhouse had closed its doors and quietly died, only to be reborn a few years later as a well-run, discreet little whorehouse. The name, the Chicken Coop, was left over from the establishment's earlier respectable life as a roadhouse, which had originally been part of somebody's poultry farm. The location was ideal, about a forty-five-minute drive from Dugway. (True, you had to go about seventy, but there was no traffic to worry about.) There was also a fair amount of trade with the boys from the university and businessmen who welcomed its seclusion away from the main road. No one could notice their cars in the parking lot except other patrons, and they were not likely to be very talkative.

There were six girls, all of them fairly young and fairly good-looking. There were also a bartender, a couple of maids, and an old Negro who played the piano, all of whom were supervised by Mama Cash. She claimed to have had the name first, before that fat singer came along with a similar name. She was sometimes called "Mama Gash," but not to her face.

Dawes was listening to the piano player's rendition of "Beale Street Blues," and he was aware in a dim way of the racket of a chopper. The noise was entirely familiar because he had been living and working with helicopters for the last eleven months. It took him a while, then, before he realized that here, at the Chicken Coop, it was out of place.

"I wonder what the hell that is," the bartender said.

"Somebody needs a new carburetor," Mama Cash suggested, and then, thinking of a joke, added, "or maybe a valve job."

"No," Dawes said, "it's a 'copter."

"A helicopter? Out here?" Mama Cash asked. "The brass must be getting pretty horny."

Dawes smiled at the idea of General Wyatt running out of the helicopter, through the door and the bar, and up the stairs. Hell, if he was in that much of a hurry, maybe he'd have taken his pants off in the helicopter.

He was sitting there at the bar, nursing his drink and enjoying the idea of that tight-assed brass bastard in that much of a rush, when he realized that Mama Cash was not smiling. It wasn't a joke; there really was a helicopter out there. The noise had grown louder and louder and then, subsiding slightly, it had persisted at what seemed to be terribly close range. Could the thing have possibly landed? Here? The door opened and two MPs came in. They walked directly up to Mama Cash and asked, "Is there a Lieutenant Dawes here, ma'am?"

Mama Cash relaxed. While the place had never been put off limits, it was her constant fear that some incident, or some administrative whim, would cut her income, and that of her girls. Of course she wanted to cooperate with the authorities.

"Over there," she said, nodding in Dawes's direction.

"Lieutenant Dawes, sir?"

Dawes slid off the bar stool and faced the two MPs. "Yes?" he said.

"We have orders to bring you to General Wyatt. If you'll come with us, sir?"

So, it had been Wyatt after all. But it was no joke. He peeled off four singles and put them down on the bar. He looked at the half-filled glass and longed to take a last sip of it. He'd need it. But no, the MPs were looking at him. He picked up his hat and followed them outside.

On the lawn the chopper waited. They had not even turned the engine off. The MPs stood by as he ducked under the rotors and got in the cabin. They jumped in after him and immediately the chopper lifted off.

8:45 P.M., Mountain Daylight Time:

Mortimer Deap sat in the third maroon Naugahyde upholstered chair in front of General Wyatt's desk. He stretched his long legs out in front of him, lit a fresh Senior Service from the butt of the old one, cleared his throat, and asked, "Well, aren't there checks on these things? I mean, Good Lord! There's no amount of planning that one can do that will compensate for the fact that these fly-boys of yours don't seem to know what they're doing. What did he think he was spraying in there? Bug repellent for the vicar's garden party? This is supposed to be—what is your quaint phrase, here?—zero defects."

All Wyatt said was, "I've just heard from the MPs. They've picked the pilot up. He'll be here in ten or fifteen minutes and we can question him when he gets here. The thing before us now is to consider what to do."

Robertson had imagined how Deap would handle the situation, and indeed he had turned out to have been right. Robertson worked with Deap. In fact, he worked under Deap. Dr. Mortimer Deap, one of the leading aerobiologists in the Western world, was the head of the biology section of the scientific installation at Dugway Proving Ground. He was brilliant, there was no doubt about that, but Robertson detested him. Deap was in the game for the power. It was not only the ultimate power of life and death that Deap enjoyed playing with in the flashy way that a carnival juggler plays with flaming torches. It was the "perks" of the power, the delicious trappings of status that the United States offered to scientists who were working in certain classified areas—rocketry, CBW, nuclear weapons. They were the aristocrats of the scientific establishment, with limousines, helicopters, equipment, technicians, labs, red-carpet treatment from the entire military-industrial complex, and, not least important, most generous salaries. Deap was a brain-drain scientist, having trained at Cambridge and having worked at Porton Downs before coming to the United States, first to work at Fort Detrick in Maryland and then to take over the biological section at Dugway. He was, Robertson had to admit, a competent, no, a more than competent scientist. His great knack, though, was scientific administration. He had come into General Wyatt's office, relaxed, in a gray lounge suit, had sprawled with a studied intellectual nonchalance in the general's chair, and had quite casually and deftly maneuvered the responsibility for what had happened directly onto Wyatt's shoulders. It was not unlike the situation in the chess game he had been playing earlier with Tommy, the best defense being an attack.

For his own part, Robertson felt comfortable in his dislike for and disapproval of Deap. The relationship was perfect as far as Robertson was concerned, for it allowed him to thrust on Deap's shoulders the responsibility for what they were all doing. He had heard, shortly after the President's announcement that the United States was disavowing all of its biological warfare program, that Deap was going to move to the Canadian installation of Medicine Hat in Alberta. But the announcement had been nearly meaningless, Deap had been persuaded to remain at Dugway, and Robertson had felt—surprisingly—relief. He would be able to continue shunting the responsibility to Deap and to maintain his own carefully balanced position that his own part in the program was entirely within the legitimate concerns of an epidemiologist. The question was whether, if this kind of information was going to be gathered, one believed in knowing it and learning from it or not. Look at Ecuador, and the hundreds of lives that their work had saved.

Sure, it was a position—perhaps even a reasonable position—to suggest that technology and scientific knowhow had outstripped man's moral capacity for control. But Robertson didn't believe that. Either you were for knowledge or against it. And with nothing better to believe in, he believed in knowledge. The "fallout" from these experiments into his field was considerable, and so long as none of these weapons was actually used, it would all be clear profit.

Deap symbolized for Robertson the boundaries of a healthy kind of involvement. So long as he did not begin to share what he suspected was Deap's sick pride in the power of the weaponry, the power of his bugs, and the outward shows of that power that the society afforded him, then he, Robertson, was still okay.

"Well," Deap drawled, "if it's as you say, we shall be in for a peck of trouble. And we shall have to move both quickly and cautiously. The town, you say, is entirely isolated?"

"Yes, that's right," the general said.

"That's a bit of luck. The population," Deap said, pursing his lips and forming a tent with his fingertips, "is eighty-four?"

"Correct," Wyatt said.

"The long shot would be . . . I don't know, in some ways it's the riskiest thing, and in some ways the safest, but it does strike me that we might at least consider doing nothing at all."

"What?" Lewine asked.

"I know it sounds quite heartless, but, you see, there's really very little that we can do, anyway. Let's assume that we do send in a field hospital, doctors and technicians and the rest of it. They're not going to be able to cure anybody. We're still going to lose between thirty and forty percent, depending on how the winds took the spray. You see, it's rather a concentrated dose we had in there."

"But what about the lab tests?" Robertson asked. "What about the autopsies? The Public Health people?"

"Yes, precisely," Deap said. "There's the risk. Of course, it's difficult to know if they're likely to spot it as our disease. They might identify it as an encephalidity and blame it on the wrong bug."

"They might," Wyatt said, "if Tarsus weren't thirty-six miles from Dugway."

"Too right, I'm afraid."

"Especially after that business with the sheep," Wyatt added. "We can't afford another black eye like that."

"I wish," Deap said, "it were anywhere as simple as that. There is a difference this time. This time, you know, it's people. Upon reflection," Deap continued, "I'm inclined to side with the Major here, and even with Captain Lewine, although for slightly different reasons than those which prompted their so generous impulses. It seems to me that if we were to send in our own people—doctors, nurses, hospital, the whole kit—we should be avoiding having the townspeople bring in private help. At least we keep it all in the family, don't you see?"

"I'll give Dr. Jebba a call, then?" Wyatt said uncertainly. "Shouldn't we get him over here and brief him?"

"Quite," Dr. Deap agreed. "Whatever we decide, it might be well to be prepared should we decide, finally, to move. Which ought to be soon. In theory, the town ought to be safe, now, but we don't know all that much about how this virus works, do we, Bill?"

He turned to Robertson with a slick smile, and then added, "It might be well to break out the Porton suits. Jebba can draw those from the lab."

The general picked up the phone and instructed the switchboard to find Dr. Jebba and have him report to the general's office immediately.

As he put the phone down there was a knock at the door. Phipps crossed the room and opened it. The two MPs entered, flanking Lieutenant Dawes. They saluted, and Dawes approached the general's desk and came to attention.

"Thank you, boys," Wyatt said. "That'll be all."

The MPs saluted again, executed a crisp about-face, and left the room.

The general stared at Dawes for a long moment. Then, slowly and deliberately, he picked up the yellow flimsy from his desk, and in a dangerously quiet voice asked him, "Is there something you left out of this report, Dawes?"

"Left out of the report, sir? What do you mean, sir?"

The general got up from his chair and, with an abrupt, agile motion, kicked his wastebasket across the room. "Did you hear that, Dawes? Did you notice anything, Dawes?"

"Yes, sir. You just kicked your wastebasket, sir."

"Your hearing is all right then. And you can see?"

"Yes, sir."

"Well, if you can see and hear when I kick a little piss-ant wastebasket across my office, how can you miss a whole goddamn mother-fucking thunderstorm?"

"I guess I left that out of my report, sir."

General Wyatt turned and looked at Dawes. Robertson was surprised that the poor son-of-a-bitch didn't melt.

"You guess?" Wyatt asked.

"I left the thunderstorm out of my report, sir."

Wyatt sat down. "What else did you leave out of your report? Where were you when it hit? Had you finished your spraying?"

"Well, I don't know, sir," Dawes answered.

"Look, Lieutenant, last time I just kicked the wastebasket around the office. Next time it'll be you. What happened on that damn flight?"

"Well, I finished the first two shots, sir, and I was coming in on the approach for the third. I started the approach and I started the spray pattern, and then the downdraft hit me and I had to climb. I mean, it was all I could do not to smack that plane into the ground."

"What about the warning lights on the tanks?" Deap asked. "Were they still lit when you started to climb?"

"I noticed that they were on, sir, at the end of the climb."

"At what altitude?" the general asked.

"Three thousand feet, sir. As soon as I noticed the light was on I closed the tank. It couldn't have been open for more than ten seconds. Probably less than that."

"Ten seconds at three thousand feet," Deap said. He was silent for a moment, calculating while the others waited, or, for all Robertson knew, pretending to calculate and enjoying their attention and the suspense. Either way, he brought the moment to a close by announcing, "Well, that's it."

But Wyatt brought his attention back to Dawes. "You are confined to quarters, Lieutenant, and you are to consider yourself under arrest. You are to speak to no one. Not a word, to anyone, about anything. Do you understand that?"

"Yes, sir."

"Dismissed," Wyatt snapped.

Dawes about-faced and marched out of the general's office.

"A piece of luck, that," Deap observed.

"Rotten luck," Wyatt said.

"Oh, it could have been worse. Think what would have happened had the wind been going the other way. Ten seconds with that pressure and that concentration? We could have wiped out Salt Lake City."

"You're joking . . ." Lewine began, but immediately he broke off. It was not a joke. It was straight, serious —deadly serious. "My God!" he said, softly.

Wyatt's buzzer sounded and the general picked up the phone. He listened for a moment and then snapped, "Well, send him in." He hung up. "Dr. Jebba's here."

Jebba, a swarthy, diminutive, rather swaggering type, was the commander of the base hospital. He entered the general's office as if he were performing on a drill field. Wyatt offered him a chair and briefly, but with admirable clarity, explained the nature of the emergency that had arisen: The infection of the town of Tarsus with Japanese encephalitis through pilot error on one of Dr. Deap's tests. He ordered Jebba to get a portable field hospital and caravan ready to leave for Tarsus as soon as possible. Robertson would take it out—he was an epidemiologist. Jebba would run things from home base. "It shouldn't take more than half an hour to get it all moving. Check with me before you move out, though. By then I'll have clearance from General Norland."

"Yes, sir," Jebba said.

"Is there anything particular you should tell Dr. Jebba?" Wyatt asked Deap.

"Well, as the General said, it'll all be red alert. Contagion suits for all. You won't be needing surgeons much but you'd better take one for safety's sake. And you'll want a neurologist. But I should think most important you'd want to have Dr. Auerbach."

"The psychiatrist?" Jebba asked.

"Oh, Lord, yes," Deap answered. "One of the seque-lae, you know, is mental involvement. In a few days half of the people in Tarsus are likely to be madder than hatters."

Wyatt ordered Robertson to go along with the field hospital, and then, almost as an afterthought said, "Lewine, you've already been there. Probably you ought to go back with them."

"Yes, sir," Lewine answered.

The four men left the general's office. Lewine had been unable to decide whether he wanted to go or wanted not to go. In a way, the general's order was a relief, avoiding the necessity of having to choose.

After the men had left the office, Wyatt took off his jacket and loosened his tie. He picked up his phone and ordered, "Get me General Norland on the scrambler." He drummed his fingers on the desk while he waited the forty-five seconds or so for the connection to be made to the general's headquarters in Provo. Norland was the army commander of the military area which included Utah, Nevada, Arizona, and New Mexico. It took an-other minute to get through the Provo switchboard and into General Norland's house.

"Norland speaking."

"Mike? It's Bud. I'm scrambling." He flicked the switch on the base of his phone which would turn his words into an electronic jumble that the corresponding device on Norland's phone would decipher and turn back into a more or less reasonable facsimile of his speech. Anyone listening in between the two phones would get nothing but Donald Duck squawks. At either end the words came through as if through a poor con-nection on an otherwise working telephone.

Rapidly, clearly, unemotionally, Wyatt explained to Norland what had happened and what the consensus of the meeting had been, adding at the end that he sup-ported the view that they should send in a field hospital and do what they could, both to keep a lid on the town and also to help the people who lived there. "But, it's a civilian involvement and I thought I'd better check with you before I give the order."

He waited for a moment while Norland considered and digested what he had said.

"I don't see that we have much choice, Bud. Yes, go on and send in the field hospital. I'll be down at Dugway in the morning by 0600. Call me back as soon as you've got some word from your medical people on what shape the town's in. I'll wait until I've heard that report before I pass it along to Washington."

"Right," Wyatt said.

"Oh, and Bud?"

"Yes?"

"Let me know right away if you've got any deaths."

Tuesday, August 11

12 Midnight, Mountain Daylight Time:

There was a picture Paul Donovan remembered. It was not in the textbook that he had been using to teach from, but in another, older, textbook that he had used as a student years ago. The picture was of the human musculature and it looked like a man whose skin had been peeled away so that each muscle was shown and numbered in a vivid red. Paul could feel every one of those muscles and it was almost as if they had been branded with the appropriate numbers from the old diagram. It was a hell of an audiovisual aid. Or not actually audiovisual, but sensory, tactile. A peculiar way to teach. Clear and forceful, but very painful. He could feel the ache from every muscle with a clarity and intensity that was actually interesting.

He lay in bed looking up at the wash of moonlight on the ceiling. When he concentrated and, with great effort, brought his mind into focus, he knew perfectly well that it was just moonlight. But unless he kept control, his mind had a tendency to slip out of focus so that the wash of pale light became the light of a surgical amphitheater, the light of a wrestling ring—any light that was associated with and appropriate to the pervasive pain that he felt.

He had been sleeping. It had been a fevered, fitful, dream-tossed sleep. And he was, now, only half-awake. But his conscious—or really half-conscious—thoughts were very nearly as silly and giddy as the dreams that had flickered and flared and faded throughout his periods of sleeping. He remembered from when he was a small boy an "Amos 'n' Andy" program where the King-fish was selling some kind of insurance that would pay if you had a dream of falling and hit. One of the great features of the policy was that the payments began not at the moment of the hit, but at the moment of the beginning of the fall. It had been very elaborate, and, while he couldn't remember the details, he remembered that it had been very funny. Had the Kingfish been in the room at that moment, Paul would probably have bought a policy.

He had no idea how long he had been sleeping or what time it was and, in a trivial way, he was curious about how much was left of this most unpleasant night. He thought of turning on the light to look at the clock, but the effort that would have involved seemed enormous. What difference did it make? What time did he want it to be? If he could assume that a change of pajamas and a drink of water would help him to sleep better for the rest of the night, to sleep deeply enough so that he was unaware of all of those muscles and the throbbing of his head and the dryness of his throat and the sandiness of his eyes—if he could assume that, then he supposed that he would like for it to be about ten-thirty or eleven, with eight or nine or ten hours left in which to enjoy the oblivion of sleep and in which there was at least the chance of some improvement. Probably he had one of those twenty-four-hour virus things, and he knew from experience that the best way of beating them was to sleep through them. But, on the other hand, if the night was going to be like this all the way through, he supposed that he would like for it to be four or five in the morning. Sickness always seemed worse, more frightening, more ominous in the small hours of the morning.

It was not curiosity about the time, but the other inci-dental thought that prompted him actually to move. The idea of a clean, dry pair of pajamas, and, even more than that, a glass of water seemed to him so attractive

86

as to be worth the enormous effort that would be required to get them. And, as long as he was getting up, he might as well do it with the light on and know what time it was. He rolled over, extended his arm, and pulled the little chain on the night-table lamp. It was as if he were swimming through molasses or tar. His muscles were so tender and sore. The light was on, but it was still dark. And then he realized that his eyes were tightly closed. He opened his eyes, blinked, and then closed them again. The small lamp—a sixty-watt bulb behind a pleated parchment shade—was as blinding as a Klieg light. It felt as though the light waves hitting his retina were barbed. But the only thing to do—if he wanted the glass of water and the dry pajamas—was to bull it through, endure this new additional discomfort for a few moments for the sake of the prospect of greater comfort later. That was being mature, wasn't it? Putting off present pleasures for larger, more important ones that were deferred? He opened his eyes again, and squinting as if in the glare of the desert sun itself, heaved himself up to a sitting position. He glanced at the Travelarm on the night table. It was five after twelve. Disappointing, in that this had not been one of the times he had picked for either scenario. But it made very little difference. There was still plenty of time in which to sleep if he could get back to sleep, and, besides, it was late enough so that he could take another couple of aspirin.

Aspirin. Of course. Now it was not just a matter of adjusting his comfort but of getting some medicine. Aspirin would be good for the muscles. There was a kind of moral imperative in medication that tipped the scale just enough to force him to stand and, with great difficulty, feeling extremely light-headed and heavy-footed, cross the room to the bird's-eye maple dresser where he found another pair of light cotton pajamas. He took off the pajamas he was wearing and kicked them into a corner of the room. Then, with greater difficulty, leaning against the dresser for support, he put on the fresh pajamas. He was so giddy and weak that he almost fell down stepping into the trousers of the pajamas. This was really a pretty fair touch of flu, he thought. He left the bedroom, crossed the small hall, and went into the bathroom where he found a couple of aspirin, popped them into his mouth, and drank a glass of water. Then he refilled the glass and drained it a second time. The peculiar thing was that even after two glasses of water his mouth still felt dry, his lips were parched and cracking, and his tongue felt coated, almost woolly. He put the glass back on the ledge of the sink, and then leaned against the sink, supporting himself with the heels of his palms. He felt a sudden chill, so severe that it caused his teeth to chatter. The chattering of the teeth was not so bad but the quiver in his arms and legs, the quiver that was caused by the chill, hurt terribly because those muscles had been sore and tender to start with.

He made his way from the bathroom back to the bedroom. He went inside, got his flannel robe from the closet, and went to close the window. The effort that operation took was so great that he had to sit down in the chair next to the window to rest for a moment before negotiating the eight or ten feet across the room back to the bed. He sat in the chair, shivering, listening to and feeling the chatter of his teeth. He needed some hot broth or maybe a cup of tea. Where the hell was Marian, he wondered? She could get it for him—but then he remembered.

And that was more frightening than the chills, the fever, the aches. That he was so disoriented as to forget what had happened to Marian, that he was so sick as to feel actual annoyance with her for not being there to help him . . . Jesus!

Almost as if to punish himself and expiate for the hideous lapse in which he had caught himself, he got up and marched himself out of the bedroom, down the hall, and into Mrs. Jenkins' kitchen to make the chicken broth or the tea or whatever for himself. It would be a matter of boiling water and throwing whatever he found first into the cup.

He turned the kitchen light on, and again closed his eyes against the painful brightness. After a moment he forced himself to open them to the smallest squint that would allow him to see. He went to the stove for the kettle and took it over to the sink. By holding the kettle at an angle he could get the spigot to reach to the opening in the kettle without disturbing all the dirty dishes that were piled up in the sink.

And then he opened his eyes wider and looked at the dishes and then looked around the kitchen. It was very peculiar. Mrs. Jenkins was fanatically neat and tidy. It was not like her to leave the kitchen in this state of disorder and mess. It was very strange indeed. He could not believe that her show of orderliness and neatness was just for his benefit and when she did not have guests or boarders around she reverted to a slovenliness of the kind that he saw here. It made no sense.

He turned off the faucet and put the kettle on the stove. Then returning to the problem of the messy kitchen, he remembered back to that time that seemed ages ago but was in fact only the preceding afternoon when he had learned the Pratt boy was sick, and Smith, at the general store was sick, too. Yes, and that doctor had said the Edisons were sick. Whatever this was, there was a lot of it going around.

He had taken the Pratt boy home and then had come back here as quickly as possible, coming in the front door and . . . had he actually seen her? He tried to remember. No, he had only called to her, telling her that he wasn't feeling well, and had gone straight upstairs to bed. She had answered him from the kitchen, had been in this room at the time, but he hadn't actually seen her. He wondered whether she wasn't sick, too. That would explain the messiness of the kitchen. Of course!

He was aware of the terrible slowness of his mental processes. The activity of thinking seemed to be almost as slow and painful as physical activity.

He left the kitchen and walked down the hall to Mrs. Jenkins' bedroom. The door was closed and he knocked, softly at first and then louder. He waited for a moment, and then he called, "Mrs. Jenkins? Mrs. Jenkins, are you all right? Are you in there?" There was no answer. Feeling both worried and foolish at the same time, he opened the door tentatively and stuck his head into her bedroom. The room was not at all disarranged, and the bed was made. Mrs. Jenkins was not there.

He stood in the doorway, stupidly, trying to think, trying to invent some plausible scenario that would account for the neat empty bedroom and the messy kitchen.

After a long dull moment it came to him. Of course. He was considerably relieved by the idea—which was perfectly plausible—that she had left the house to go and help take care of one of the neighbors who had been stricken by whatever this sickness was. Maybe the Edisons, or the Pratts, or one of the other people in the town whom he had seen but whose names he did not know. It was a small town and Mrs. Jenkins was a kindly, generous old lady. It was perfectly reasonable for her to have done this. And she would not have disturbed him just to tell him that she was going out. . . .

He closed the door, feeling a little better now that he had worked out what must have happened. He went back to the kitchen, found a clean cup and a tea bag, and sat down in one of the hardbacked wooden chairs to wait for the kettle to announce with its eerie whistle that the water had come to a boil. He shifted uncomfortably in the chair. The tenderness of his back, buttocks, and thighs protested against the unyielding angularity of the wooden chair.

The kettle started to whistle and Paul got up and poured the boiling water into the teacup. He would now have to wait for the tea to brew, and he looked back at the wooden chair. No, he was not up to it. He thought of the long trek into his bedroom, and rejected that idea. He would have to dispose of the tea bag that way. The trouble with bagged tea, Marian had always said, was that you had to dispose of that tea bag—like a dead mouse. He had never worried about tea bags before, but after her remark they had always seemed to him to be like dead mice. He stood there, dumbly looking into his teacup waiting for the tea to brew, and then he figured out a plan. He could go into the living room, wait for the tea to brew, put the bag in the saucer while he drank the tea, and then, on the way back through the kitchen, on his way to the bedroom, leave the cup and the tea bag in the kitchen. Besides, the chairs in the living room were soft and upholstered and if he did not turn the lights on but just used the indirect light that fell into the living room from the hall, it would be easier on his eyes. The light was terrible on his eyes.

He threw a couple of lumps of sugar into the brewing tea, found a spoon, and left the kitchen. He went into the living room, set the teacup on a small side table, and then sat down in one of the large wing chairs near the fireplace. He sat there in the chair waiting for the tea to be strong enough to drink and thinking of Marian. She had suffused his life in the way the tea was now suffusing the water in the cup. The fact that he had all but called out to her before, and the fastidiousness about tea bags that he had acquired from her, seemed to be such odd memorials. But, in a way, they were the ones that mattered. It was in the small details of life that memory lived. He felt rather good actually, realizing that she was still alive to him in these ways. The sad thing would be when these kinds of memories faded to only the featureless, abstract sense of loss.

And then, he noticed. He stared at the shape on the floor, and it took him several seconds to realize that it could not possibly be a shadow or some trick of his delicate vision. Once the realization of what it had to be had struck him with its full force, he leapt from the chair, and, temporarily unmindful of his giddiness and fragility, he hurried across the room and knelt down beside the still figure of Mrs. Jenkins.

It was more difficult than he would have supposed to feel for her pulse, because, in the excitement of the moment, his own heart was beating wildly and his own breathing was rapid and shallow; he could hear his own heartbeat in his ears. But, after a brief moment, he was sure that he could feel with his fingertips the beating of the pulse in her pitifully delicate, almost birdlike wrist.

The realization that she was alive was sufficiently calming for him so that his heartbeat and his breathing subsided to normal—or whatever was normal for whatever he had. He put his ear to her chest and listened to her breathing. Yes, she was alive. He rubbed her wrists and patted her face, but he could not bring her around to consciousness. He did not know what had happened to her, whether it was the same thing he had or something else—heart attack? a stroke? a fall? He thought of moving her to the couch and then decided that it would be better to leave her where she was and try to get help.

Paul got to his feet and steadied himself against the doorframe. He felt the same kind of dizziness one sometimes feels getting up suddenly after having spent too long sitting in a chair reading. But that was unimportant. She was a hell of a lot sicker than he was.

Where to get help? The delicious remoteness of Tarsus, with only three telephones in the entire town, no longer seemed to be so idyllic. He would have to go down to Smith's general store, bang on the door to rouse Smith, and use the telephone there. Or, no, wait, there was a better idea than that. He could go down the road a little further to Dr. Cooley's. Cooley had a phone, too, and, being a vet, he might be able to provide some help while they waited for a doctor to come from Tooele or wherever. First aid and maybe even a little better than that.

He went to the closet in the front hall and grabbed the first coat that came to hand. He went back to the living room, tucked it gently around Mrs. Jenkins, and then went back to the front door and left the house.

His rented pickup truck—sturdy enough to maneuver

on the dirt trails of the mountains and out along the rough country of the desert—was out in front. The keys were tucked in the visor. He started the motor, put the truck into gear, backed up, turned, and drove into the road. The pedal felt strange under his bare feet. He supposed he should have gone back for shoes, but then he was not going to be out for long. It was cold and quiet in Tarsus. It got cold in the mountains and in the desert at night no matter how hot it had been during the day.

Paul's teeth chattered and he felt the tremors of the chills against his chest and upper arms. It was not, thank heaven, a very long ride. He had to go only about a quarter of a mile to get to Doc Cooley's place.

He went down the cut, past a few ramshackle houses and then past a few abandoned buildings, the old mining office, the empty, sagging church, the abandoned saloon, and the old burnt-out elementary school. A little farther down the road there were a few more trailers, and then, where the cut began to widen, he saw Cooley's house. He was pleased to see that Cooley's lights were still on. It would be faster if he did not have to rouse the vet from sleep. He pulled the truck off the road and cut the motor. He sat there for a moment, trying to fight down a new and stronger wave of chills. His teeth were chattering uncontrollably. He heard the sound of the dogs in Cooley's pens, howling, baying, he supposed, at the moon. The chattering of his teeth seemed incredibly loud. By an act of will he clenched his teeth together and only then did he realize that the sound had not been and was not of his own making. There was another rumble, outside, growing louder every moment. Paul turned around, looked out of the back window of the truck, and saw, coming up the road, into the cut and into Tarsus, a series of headlights. There looked to be more than a dozen vehicles of different sizes. Paul squinted, unbelieving, at the painful glare of the headlights. It took him a moment to adjust to the brightness before he could make out the outline of the vehicles. There were jeeps, trucks, and—ambulances! He sat there for a moment, stupid, trying to put it together, and then, as a film coming into focus in one of those arty modern movies it became clear to him. The whole town was sick, somebody had sent for help, and here it was. It was a great feeling to know that they were not alone in Tarsus and that help had arrived.

He got out of the pickup truck and, feeling a little self-conscious in his bare feet and pajamas and bath-robe, walked across the slightly damp grass as quickly as he could, getting to the road at about the same time as the lead jeep. He waved his arms to flag it down. The jeep stopped, and two figures jumped out.

Paul had assumed that the people in the convoy were soldiers. The trucks were army trucks, the jeeps were army jeeps, and, from the side of the road, he could see that the ambulances were olive green army ambulances. But the figures who had climbed out of the jeep were space men. He shook his head to clear it, rubbed his eyes, and looked again. They were still space men. They were, anyway, entirely encased in a uniform or a cos-tume of a kind that he had never seen before. The first thing he noticed—indeed he was fascinated by them—were the peculiar face masks, oblate glass goggles and, just below them, where the nose and mouth would be, a strange length of curved tubing. Below these odd heads, which looked like nothing so much as enormous enlarge-ments of the heads of insects with the proboscis arrange-ments, the bodies were entirely encased. There were gloves and large gauntlets on the hands and improbably whimsical boots made of the same cloth as the rest of the suits. They looked like the boots that artists of the nineteenth century put on their representations of elves, with the slightly curved toes and the strange flared put-tees. There were no insignia, no sign of rank, no army name tags, but the men were armed with .45s strapped low over the suits.

"What . . . who are you?" Paul asked.

"U.S. Army Field Hospital, Fifteenth Battalion Army

Materiel Corps," one of the figures replied. His voice sounded as though it were coming from an echo chamber.

"Thank God you're here," Paul said, relieved. He was about to explain that he had come down to Doc Cooley's to get help for his landlady when, from the second jeep of the convoy, three more figures in these peculiar suits approached.

"What the hell's going on, Wilson? Why have we stopped?" one of the approaching men asked.

"Civilian resident, sir," the man to whom Paul had been speaking replied.

The three figures from the second jeep approached. Paul turned to them and was about to speak, but his teeth were chattering again. As he took a deep breath to try to get control of the muscles in his jaws, one of the figures addressed him.

"I saw you this afternoon, didn't I? Outside of the gas station? You were helping that youngster get home?"

"There was a boy," Paul began. "Yes."

"I'm Dr. Lewine," the figure said. "Don't be put off by our sanitary suits. We're here to help. Are you sick?"

"Yes," Paul said, "I am, but not so sick as my landlady. I was on my way to get help for her at Dr. Cooley's."

"Dr. Cooley?"

"The vet," Paul replied. "He's got a phone."

"We'll take care of her," Lewine said. "Which house is it?"

"If I might suggest, sir," one of the figures from the lead jeep said, addressing not Lewine, but the man next to him, "if this man will come and direct us to the house, we can get the rest of the convoy moving again and start setting up the tent."

"Very good, Wilson. We'll take him in our jeep with us."

"Yes, sir."

The two men jumped back into the lead jeep and

drove slowly up the road into the center of Tarsus. Paul followed the other three men into the second jeep, staggering as he climbed aboard.

"You look pretty sick yourself," one of the men with Lewine remarked.

"Some fever and chills," Paul said. "But I'm conscious and I can walk around. I found Mrs. Jenkins passed out on the floor in the living room."

"We'll take care of her. And you."

The jeep started moving and behind it the convoy resumed its rumbling progress.

Paul was seized by another wave of chills, and this time he did not feel so much obliged to fight them. Help had come miraculously out of nowhere. He did some quick figuring, counting the houses.

"It's the seventh house on the left," he said.

"What?" Lewine asked. "What did you say?"

Paul supposed that the chattering of his teeth was worse than he had imagined. He repeated, speaking slowly and as loudly as he could, "The seventh, no, the sixth house on the left." But he could hardly hear his own words himself. There was a wild chattering. . . .

But it was not the chills. It was another noise, a rackety beating. Paul looked up and saw, above the jeep, above the town, hovering with its light shining down as if it were another, artificial moon, a helicopter. When they came to help, they really laid it on, he thought. It was a comforting, reassuring thought. His quest having been successful, and more than successful, Paul was able to relax, and as he did so, right there in the jeep he slipped into a tranquil doze.

1:30 A.M., Mountain Daylight Time:

Major General Michael B. Norland awoke from the catnap he had been taking in the reclining chair in his office. He caught the phone on its first ring and came immediately to full alertness.

"Norland here," he snapped.

"It's Bud," the voice on the other end of the line said. "Scrambling."

"Right." Norland pushed the button that activated the scrambler, waited an instant, and then said, "Shoot. What have you got?"

"It's not good," Wyatt told him. "The first quick look has turned up two dead—an old man and a three-year-old child—thirty critical and no one unaffected."

"You got a head count?"

"Eighty-six counted so far."

"Good Lord!" Norland exclaimed.

"The field hospital's set up, but it doesn't look good. The trouble with this damn thing is there's no treatment for it. Not a damn thing the medics can do except keep them comfortable and try to get the fever down."

"Any outside contact we know about?" Norland asked. "Any civilian doctors?"

"No, nothing yet. There's no doctor in town and there are only three phones."

"Interesting," Norland said. "It'd give us a little more time if something were to happen to the phone line."

"Right," Wyatt said. "No sweat."

"And how about the roads?"

"There's only one," Wyatt explained, "and we're watching it. But there's nobody well enough to leave."

"Shit, it isn't people leaving that I'm worried about now. It's people coming in."

"Right," Wyatt said. "I'll take care of it."

"I'll call Washington and then I'll hop over to Dugway. I should be there in half an hour. I'll see you then."

"Right," Wyatt said. He paused and then said, "Mike?"

"Yeah?"

"It's a helluva phone call you've got to make. I just wanted to say . . . I'm sorry."

"Well, it could be worse," Norland said. "Remember that admiral—what was his name, Kimmel? He had to call Washington from Pearl Harbor!"

"That's what I meant," Wyatt said. "I'm sorry."

"Thanks," Norland said, and hung up.

He bellowed for coffee and reached into the desk for the red phone—the direct line to the War Room in the Pentagon. He sat there for a moment looking at the phone. At the other end of it was not simply Washington, the Pentagon, the duty officer, but, ultimately, General Edward Eastlake, Chief of Staff of the U.S. Army and, in the opinion of Michael Norland, the biggest brass-lined asshole in the army. He was, Norland knew, a clever bastard. You don't get to be Chief of Staff of the Army without being shrewd. The trouble was that most of the shrewdness worked not for the army or for the country but for the advancement of his own career, for his own protection and for his own glory. Who else could return from eighteen months of disaster in Vietnam to become the public's darling and the army's boss?

But, hell, it always worked that way. Eisenhower had not been half the general that MacArthur was, even if MacArthur had been a little mad. Norland had been attached to MacArthur's headquarters in the early days of Korea and had witnessed the landing at Inchon, one of the most daring and most successful military operations of the twentieth century. It hadn't been a battle so much as a work of art. You could forgive a man a lot for that kind of brilliance in the field. But to make it big in the army you needed not so much military brilliance as political savvy. You had to know how to tack and trim, how to protect your flank personally. Eastlake sat behind the rule book the way the French sat behind the Maginot Line. It hadn't worked for the French but Eastlake still sat there, high and dry, safe and sound. It would be interesting, Norland supposed, to watch Eastlake ride this one out—interesting and brutal. He'd ride it out on Wyatt's ass, and on Norland's own.

The orderly brought in the pot of coffee, poured a cup

for Norland, and retired. Norland took a sip of the coffee, which he took straight and black, and sighed. There were more important things than a military career. He picked up the phone and a moment later he heard the voice of the duty officer in the Pentagon War Room.

2:30 A.M., Mountain Daylight Time:

It didn't make any sense. But then, after all, it didn't have to make any sense. It was an order. And that's all there was to it. You did what they told you to do no matter how strange or even stupid it sounded. You didn't have to think; you weren't supposed to think. All you had to do was what they told you to do. And so the sergeant had brought the squad out to the position on the road that the major had marked on the map and, after the two half-ton trucks had passed and gone around the curve in the road, the sergeant had sent the lineman up the pole to cut the wires. That had been easy enough, and had taken no time at all. The sergeant and the men sat in and around the jeep waiting for the big rig and the foam truck from the Ordnance Depot. The men were quiet; they had been awakened to go out and do this hare-brained job, and as they waited they dozed, leaning against the tires or the jeep. Others smoked, as incurious about this detail as about any other. If they were impatient for the arrival of the truck, it was an impatience only to be finished with the job so they could get back to the base, back to the barracks, and back to bed.

And then they saw the lights of the jeep and the big trailer rig approaching. They heard the grinding of the gears and watched the headlights increase in size as they came nearer. The truck stopped as the sergeant had been told it would and the driver and his helper got out of the truck and got into the jeep, which turned around and went off in the opposite direction. As the jeep drove away, the foam machine pulled up and came to a stop perhaps fifty yards down the road from the truck. The sergeant gave the order and the men spread out to block off the road and, even more important, to stand clear themselves. The sergeant got into the truck. The keys were in the ignition—as he had been told they would be. He started the rig up and moved it forward, shifting up the gears until he had acquired the right speed. Then, when the truck was up to speed, he opened the door on the driver's side, cut the wheel sharply, and braked. He could feel the rig totter and sway, and, just before it went over, he jumped clear and rolled.

It was tricky, but no trickier than a parachute jump. The impact was about the same, and the technique for dealing with it was almost identical. He rolled on the ground several times and then bounced back up. He turned and watched as the truck settled on its side, jackknifed perfectly across the road. If that was what they wanted, that was what they had got.

He motioned for the foam truck to come up and watched as it approached and then sprayed foam over the gas tanks of the overturned cab. He went back to the jeep and he and the three other men got in to return to the base. The sergeant looked behind him. He could see the truck straddled across the road, the white foam shining faintly in the fading light of moonset. The night was still again, as still as if the sound of whining rubber and twisting metal had never broken it. Crazy, the sergeant thought.

It was not until the red tail light of the jeep had disappeared around the curve in the mountain road that three other figures in their Porton CBW suits came from the newly blocked-off area—from Tarsus—to set up the barricade and the red warning lights around the truck. When the barricades were up and the lanterns were lit, the soldiers removed their suits and reported by walkie-talkie to field headquarters in Tarsus that the installation was complete. They got the M-16s from the jeep around the curve and began their long hours on guard duty.

4:30 A.M., Eastern Daylight Time:

General Eastlake watched with a carefully concealed disgust as Charlie Renchler, Undersecretary of Defense, poured himself his third bourbon and carelessly sloshed water into it from the crystal pitcher on the table in front of them. The drink that Renchler had made for Eastlake stood untouched beside him. Every so often Eastlake picked it up, held it, and wiggled it to make noises with the ice cubes, but then as if through preoccupation and concern with the problem at hand, he seemed always to forget that he was holding the drink and put it back on the table untouched.

"Jesus Christ!" Renchler said for perhaps the fifteenth time. "You don't think we should call him?"

"That's up to you, sir," Eastlake answered.

"Aw, shit," Renchler said. "That's not what I want to know. What do *you* think? What would *you* do?

"It's hard to say," Eastlake feinted. "It's a difficult decision to make. But I guess if it were my decision to make, I'd wait a couple of hours until we had a little bit more to go on and a little bit more to suggest. We could call a meeting for six and then, by seven-thirty we'd have not only the raw report to make but some kind of suggestion. Maybe a whole series of them."

"But my God, man, there's a whole damn town out there, dying! The President ought to be told. Right now. Don't you think?" he added, almost plaintively.

"If you think so, sir," Eastlake replied. It was, Eastlake recognized, a tricky moment. If he pushed Renchler too hard or didn't push hard enough, Renchler would pick up the phone and call the President. And that was not what Eastlake wanted. The point was to call a meeting, to spread around as widely as possible and as thinly as possible the responsibility for any decision that was made, and at the same time to keep in his hands the

101

reins of control. A call to the President would be a gesture that would drop those reins immediately. The name of the game was following orders, but you had to make sure that you got the orders that you wanted to follow.

Eastlake had been sitting in Renchler's apartment in Potomac Towers for half an hour, leading the man around, going over the same ground, and watching the pudgy politician sweat like an out-of-shape middleweight.

The call had come in from Norland, out in Utah, and immediately Eastlake had begun to calculate. Ordinarily, it would be a matter to discuss with the Secretary of Defense, Jonathan Colebrooke, but Colebrooke was in Vietnam and was not scheduled to return for another ten days. So it was Renchler, the Undersecretary, in some ways an unknown quantity, but in others a weaker, easier man to have to deal with. Eastlake had played back the tape of the telephone conversation he had had with Norland and had very rapidly figured out what would be the best thing for him—a meeting. It was a stroke of luck that both he and Renchler lived in the same new, plush high-rise apartment building overlooking the Potomac. Eastlake had considered the choices. He could get into uniform or, no, it would be even better for him to appear at Renchler's door in pajamas and a bathrobe. The urgency would be unmistakable, and the likelihood was that Renchler would be thrown just a little bit off balance, which suited Eastlake fine. So he had gone into the bedroom, found a suitable maroon silk dressing gown, picked up the phone, and had called Renchler's special number.

"Mr. Secretary," he had said, "a matter of great importance has come up. I must speak with you immediately. I wonder if it would be all right if I came right up."

Renchler, groggy, thick-voiced—almost certainly Eastlake's call had awakened him—had grunted affirmatively and Eastlake had hung up the phone, called the War Room to say where he could be reached, and then gone up the service elevator five flights to Renchler's spacious duplex. Renchler had answered the servants' entrance door in a scruffy white terry shower robe, which he still wore. It kept falling open. He was wearing nothing under it. The nakedness seemed appropriate, for, after Eastlake had told the Undersecretary what had happened in Tarsus, Renchler had replied with helplessness, nakedness, and a vulnerability that had shown only too clearly. But, then, what could anyone have expected of a competent Connecticut lieutenant governor who had delivered the state for the party in the last election and found himself now in water over his head?

Eastlake had spent the last half hour indirectly dissuading Renchler from calling Vietnam. He had gone over all the obvious arguments: There was no line of communication all the way to Vietnam that would be really secure; there was nothing that Secretary Colebrooke could do that Renchler couldn't do here; and he had appealed, subtly, and then not so subtly, to Renchler's pride. But, still, Renchler continued to wiggle like a tired but not yet exhausted game fish. If he could not hand the problem over to Colebrooke, then he wanted to hand it on up to the President—and this would not have suited Eastlake at all. Not yet, anyway. The point was to find enough people to stand between what had happened and himself, to filter responsibility, and the best way to do that would be to have some proposals for the President from other people who were nominally under Eastlake. The trick was to stay loose so that you could shift the blame if you had to, but take the credit if you could. There was always the possibility that things could work themselves out. You wanted to be prepared in case you stumbled into success.

What made it tough was that the ante was so high. Which was why Renchler was sweating. The disaster was bad enough in itself. A town was infected and the army was responsible. That was certainly enough. But to complicate things, there was the President's public disavowal of germ warfare. He would look bad if this got out. He would look like a liar! His political opponents would have a field day. It would all be unfair, of course. All Presidents lie, have to lie for the good of the nation. It was part of the job. But when they got caught out, the opposition turned it into something dirty—as if they'd been cheating at cards. And there was nothing a President could do but take it and smile. Or lie again, and claim not to have known a thing about what was going on—as Eisenhower had done with the U-2. The only trouble was that they turned around and took it out on the men who had slipped up.

So, for Eastlake, it was a matter mostly of being out of the target area when the President turned to vent the rage that he would feel. The trick was to point the President at someone else—someone like Renchler if possible. Someone like Norland, if necessary.

"If you remember, Mr. Secretary," he began, "six months ago, when that Cuban captain defected and brought the MIG-17 in under our radar defenses in Florida, somebody woke the President and he was furious. The President told Secretary Colebrooke to deal with it, making it very clear that, unlike LBJ, he did not want to be awakened except for a real emergency. Not potential, but *real*. But if you feel, sir," he went on smoothly, "that this warrants waking the President, then perhaps we ought to call him."

"What's going to happen," Renchler asked, "if he wakes up in the morning and hears about it on the radio?"

"He won't," Eastlake replied. "There's no danger of that. There was a truck accident and the town is inaccessible. The phone wires are down and the road is blocked."

"What?" Renchler asked. "Funny coincidence, that."

"It's not inconvenient, sir," Eastlake admitted. He had not been sure how to play that card. It looked good now, but later it could be a great embarrassment. The thing was to accept credit for it, but to keep on file the fact that it had not been his decision or his order that had blocked the road and cut the phone lines. Risky business, that. Norland could answer for it, or maybe Wyatt if it backfired.

"Well, how much time do we have, then?" Renchler asked.

"The President gets up at seven-thirty. If we were to meet at six we'd have enough time in which to prepare some preliminary suggestions and to get some further reports from Tarsus. Nothing's going to happen in Tarsus in the next couple of hours."

"I suppose there's no harm in it. Sure," he said, "let's have the meeting. Whom do we want?" he asked, crossing the room to the small antique desk in the corner. He pulled out several drawers, looking for a piece of paper, and finally picked up an envelope, turned it over, and came back to sit down across from Eastlake.

"Public Health Service?" Renchler suggested. "Schleiman and McGrady?" Those were the Presidential assistants for military affairs and for domestic affairs.

"And," Eastlake suggested, "maybe we ought to bring in the Defense Intelligence Agency?"

"Fine," Renchler said. "We'll set it for six."

General Eastlake treated himself to his first and only sip of the whiskey Renchler had poured for him so long before and then bade good morning to the Undersecretary. He went back down the service elevator to his own apartment to shower and get into uniform.

5:00 A.M., Mountain Daylight Time:

It was amazing, Dr. Bartlett thought, how easy it was to maneuver in these suits. He had thought, during the few drills back at the base, that it would be awkward and clumsy to deal with patients while wearing the gloves and mask, the oversized boots, and the great clumsy gauntlets that reached nearly to the elbow. Possible, of course, but awkward. What he had not reckoned on was the weird feeling of crisis that real emergency brought out, so that in actual practice one had more important things to think about. Two or three minutes would go by when he was entirely unaware that he was dressed in anything other than his regulation white coat. There had been, of course, the wisecracks and the funny remarks in the convoy as they had approached the town and had donned the suits issued to them by the lieutenant, who had then gone around very solemnly to check the closings and to confirm the filtration of the masks with crushed ampuls of spirits of ammonia.

Dr. Bartlett had seen ten patients in two hours. That worked out to one patient every twelve minutes, but they were all the same. The capacity of the field hospital was thirty beds, and very quickly Major Robertson had decided that the best way to proceed was to have the medics bring in only the comatose, the aged, the very young, and those with fevers over 104. The less severely afflicted townspeople were being seen by other doctors who were making rounds in the town.

He straightened up from his tenth patient and gave his orders to the nurse. "Wet sheets, and replace the I.V. bottle when it's empty." The I.V. contained glucose and an anticonvulsant.

The patient, an elderly woman, breathed slowly and stertorously. She would not be able to take much more of this, Bartlett thought. The disease itself was bad enough, but not having a history on any of these patients complicated further the problem of treatment and increased the frustration that Bartlett felt. All he knew about this woman was that her name was Jenkins—and he was not even sure of that. The medics tried to identify these people, but one of the men who had been brought into the field hospital had been identified as "Statler" on the basis of a towel in the man's bathroom.

Dr. Bartlett took a deep breath. He had become used to the hollow sound of his breath coming into the filter, which was rather like the sound of breathing through a

106

snorkel. He reached up, however, to mop his brow and then remembered that he was wearing the Porton suit. The suits were porous, so that one could sweat through them, but they were still warm, and when he was not actively engaged in a problem he was increasingly conscious of the weight of the suit. Or perhaps it was fatigue that was making itself felt. He had had only an hour's sleep before he had been awakened by the MP and called to assemble for this emergency field hospital sortie. He, and the others, had not been told that it was not a practice maneuver until they were halfway to the town.

He listened to the sound of the generator making its muffled clatter in the background and underscoring the dramatic silence of the ward itself, of the patients locked in deadly struggle with this exotic virus. Bartlett felt sorry for them, but he felt sorry for himself too. He was tired and very much wanted a cup of coffee. But the effort and the time involved in going to the Clean Tent, demasking in the halfway chamber, scrubbing, and going all the way inside seemed more than the coffee was worth. He decided that he would go another hour. Or he would let his body decide. Sooner or later he would have to take a leak and that would be time enough to pick up the coffee as well.

And then he heard it. A series of wild, terrified screams. Bartlett hurried toward the direction from which the screams had come, and he and two medics converged at the bed of a well-nourished Caucasian male. This one, Smith, had been brought in from the general store, comatose, with twitching musculature of the face and thorax and with a fever of 103.9. Bartlett was surprised that he had come around and become conscious so quickly. Bartlett's surprise, however, turned to dismay when he saw Smith struggling to a sitting position and heard him cry out, over and over again, "Get away from me! Get away! Get away!"

"It's all right, sir," Bartlett said. "We're here to help you."

The man in the bed struggled to his feet and called out desperately, "Help! Help! Giant insects are here! God, they're huge—and they're going to eat my organs!"

The two medics tried to take his arms and get him back into bed, but he shook them off savagely and staggered down the center aisle of the tent. "Somebody, help!" the sick man called out.

A third medic intercepted Smith's progress. "Get away! Get away!" Smith cried as the medic seized him, and then the words gave way to a shriek of pure terror and utter hopelessness. The two medics caught up with the one who was holding the patient and the three of them half-carried, half-dragged him back to the bed from which he had escaped.

Bartlett approached to try to talk to the patient again.

"It must be the masks, sir," one of the medics suggested.

"Is that what's bothering you?" Bartlett asked the patient. "These masks? They're simply a way to prevent us from catching your disease so that we can stay well and take care of you."

"You can't fool me," he said. "You're a bug! They're all bugs!" he called out. "They eat human brains and they can talk!"

The three medics were still holding the thrashing figure. Bartlett noticed that the patient had ripped the I.V. out of his arm. He thought for a moment and then ordered a straitjacket. It was either that or heavy sedation, and the choice was an unpleasant one, indeed. Sedation, in a way, seemed more humane, but it would mask too many of the symptoms and could conceivably upset the precarious balance of an already sorely tried system. They were working in the dark with this, and they could not afford to take any further chances.

"When you've got the straitjacket on, call me and I'll start the I.V. again in the leg."

7:10 A.M., Eastern Daylight Time:

It didn't matter, in the end, whether you were right or wrong. It was nice to be right, of course. It didn't necessarily mean anything, didn't necessarily translate into prestige, power, influence, or fame. Indeed, if a man was right but handled himself wrong, it could be disastrous for his career. And a man could be wrong, dead wrong, and come out of it smelling like a rose. Back in Kennedy's administration, they all had been wrong about the Bay of Pigs, but they had all been wrong together. And the way it had worked out, it had been as if an instructor at the Point had come in, not to the classroom but to the world itself, and had announced: "You yahoos all flubbed it. But I mean really flubbed it. And I'm not going to count the quiz scores this time. We're going to do it over, and this time you men had better come through. . . ."

Well, not quite, maybe. There had been a lot of dead bodies and a lot of men in Cuban prisons. But somehow, in Washington, and in the mind and heart of the country, it had been as if that little exercise had not counted. No grades. It was inhumane, maybe, but that was the nature of the business. The question was simple: Either you believe in yourself or you don't. And if you do believe in yourself, do think that you can help, that your training and your experience and your intelligence can be of help to the country; then you've got to think of your career, have got to keep that going, keep it moving along, because there will be another problem on another day, and one of those problems will need you.

That was how Eastlake saw it. And as he looked around the large conference room on the third floor of the Pentagon, he was trying to gauge the sense of the group, trying to see how they would react, and trying to

109

weigh their opinions as accurately as possible. And he believed that this was, indeed, the only way to play it. You take these things too seriously, too personally, and you're no damned good to anyone. On the battlefield, if an officer loses his head and starts to think and to feel and to react to the dying and the dead (and the dying are always worse because they make noise and you can hear them), he's no damned good any more, and there will only be more dying and more dead. Twice as many. A hundred times as many. Emotional involvement is counterproductive.

You treat a battle—or an incident like this one—as if it were an exercise, as if it were some abstract problem, and you do more good for the people who are really involved than all the emotional involvement in the world could ever accomplish. Jesus, but he wished that Dr. Maxwell would shut up. He'd been going on for far too long about the humanitarian aspects of the situation, and it wasn't helping anyone at all. The humanitarian aspects of the situation were obvious enough. And he was delaying the real business of the meeting. It was a delay that could be costly.

And then Eastlake tried to sneak up on the problem again, thinking of it merely as a problem. And figure how he'd play it if it were really up to him to decide. Open or shut? Either way it was a lousy can of worms. He didn't like either alternative. And the problem was complicated by the President's public statement, which was a factor in any decision they'd make. Unfairly, but undeniably, it was a factor.

Strictly speaking, what they had been doing was well within the President's guidelines. It was defensive research—or as defensive as any of this research could be. But to explain that to reporters and get it across to the public was another thing altogether. They'd make it look as though the President had been trying to double-talk the country and the world into a false sense of security. And that wasn't strictly true. The President had disavowed the use of germ warfare, even as a retaliatory weapon. It sounded good, and for all Eastlake knew the President had meant it. Why not? If you could go in and bomb any country in the world into a cinder inside two hours, then you could afford to disavow germ warfare. And the research, then, was defensive: Ways to cope with a germ attack.

Still, to come out with it now and announce what had happened didn't seem right to Eastlake. It was to give up without even trying to maneuver for position. It was breaking at the first pressure. It was . . . well, it was premature. They didn't even know, yet, exactly how bad it was. And most of all, it felt wrong. Deep in the gut, it felt wrong.

Of course, on the other side, the risk of keeping it quiet for too long was clear enough. If it got out through the wrong channels, if it leaked inadvertently, they'd all look even worse. The point was to keep control as long as possible, then pick the right moment.

Okay, but getting the others to go along with that was still another problem. Not extraordinarily difficult, but tricky enough to deserve some thought. The annoying part of it was that the meeting was not strictly military, and you couldn't just look at a man's collar and see immediately what his opinion was worth and how it weighed. Here it was one of those democratic meetings. But not simply democratic, either. It was more like a stockholders' meeting—where you didn't know exactly how many shares which guys were voting. Renchler had a good block of stock, but less, probably, than Schleiman, the Adviser to the President on Military Affairs. And Schleiman had less than McGrady, who'd got the man into the White House in the first place. Those two and Colonel English, the Defense Intelligence Agency man. Eastlake could not go far wrong if he managed to keep those three. If, of course, they all sided together.

Finally, it would hang on Colonel English. It was already clear enough that English would prefer to hush it up and pretend nothing had ever happened—if that could be managed. Permanently, if one could get away with it. Eastlake was not sure they could manage it permanently, but for the moment he would side with English, to keep control of the situation for a while, a few days or even a few weeks. And that meant letting English make the pitch about how there was no reason at this time to bring all the damned doves down on their necks. Not yet. And he would let English deal with the fear they all shared, of somebody's blowing the whistle and of the stink that would cause. . . .

He wished Dr. Maxwell would shut his damned face. He'd already admitted there was no cure, no real treatment. So all this talk about public health considerations was just horse-frockies. The trouble was, Eastlake knew, that the goddamn doctor enjoyed talking to the meeting, enjoyed having generals and admirals and undersecretaries paying attention to him. Paying attention? Enduring. Waiting him out.

5:15 A.M., Mountain Daylight Time:

Norman Lewine was exhausted. He had not slept for twenty-four hours, and for the past twelve he had been working under great stress. He was groggy now, working on reserves of energy. He had not been this tired since his days as an intern. In the last calm hour that he could remember, the hour in which the field-hospital convoy had been assembled and mobilized, he had read some of the literature Bill Robertson had given him on Japanese B encephalitis. It had been perfectly clear, but he had not been prepared for the confusion and the depression of finding an entire town sick, dying, and illustrating the laconic clinical descriptions in the literature:

> In epidemic form the disease carries a high mortality. The onset is of three general types: gradual, hyperacute, and characteristic acute. The case with a gradual onset is apparently the most benign of the

three, usually resulting in only mild headaches and low-grade fever followed by complete recovery. Hyperacute onset cases are described as producing acute psychoses and epileptiform seizures with profound central nervous system involvement and frequently early death. The "characteristic acute" course results in headaches, chills, fevers, anorexia, weakness, fatigue, nausea and vomiting, diarrhea, photophobia, visual disturbances, deep and superficial reflex changes, appearance of pathologic reflexes, incontinence, cerebellar signs, delirium, confusion, coma and other cerebral manifestations, basal ganglia signs, convulsions and mental deterioration . . .*

That was all bad enough. But, as Robertson had explained, this was not a natural epidemic carried by the *Culex tritaeniorhynchus,* the small mosquito in the eastern Orient. This was a clinically enhanced epidemic that had come about as a result of an error in an experiment in acrobiology—which meant that the aerosol spray in the plane had held a particularly virulent and concentrated dosage of the virus with all the particles regularly sized at five microns for maximum pneumonic infection.

So it was the description from the medical journal intensified by the circumstances of the experiment and then made hideously vivid by the terrible scenes of suffering Lewine had witnessed helplessly during the morning hours. The projectile vomiting of an eleven-month-old boy, the loss of speech control in a forty-five-year-old woman, and the terrified look she had given him that had been almost mercifully cut short as she had lost consciousness were imprinted on Lewine's mind. The kinds of help he had been able to give were merely secondary—as with the healthy, fifty-five-year-old man

* "JAPANESE B ENCEPHALITIS; *Symptom Dynamics in an Organic Psychosis*" by William F. Fry, Jr., M.D., and Arnold Tobin, M.D.; *Psychiatric Quarterly,* January 1967, pp. 91 ff.

who had suddenly been rendered as helpless as a new-born infant and had crawled half a mile down the cut from his cabin. The trip had taken him a couple of hours and he had arrived with his forearms, thighs, and belly lacerated and bleeding.

Perhaps the most disheartening and discouraging cases that Lewine had had occasion to see had been the two Edisons. It had been only the morning before that that first call had come in from the cranky old man. Lifetimes ago, it had seemed (and lifetimes had ended). Edison, for one. He had found the old man already dead and Mary hysterical, describing Edison's convulsions and painracked death. And Lewine had hardly instructed the medics to remove the body when Mary herself had gone into convulsions and begun to miscarry. The medics had had to throw Edison off the stretcher, and, as quickly as possible, take Mary to the field hospital where she had miscarried. Lewine had given her an anticonvulsant and a shot of Demerol. They were prepping her now for the dilation and curettage.

It was a simple enough procedure ordinarily. It would be complicated now, however, not only by Mary's illness but by the strange conditions under which he would have to work. The procedure would be carried on with Mary entirely encased in a giant version of a premie incubator. In the incubator she would be wheeled into the operating tent, and, standing in the tent, which would be sterile, Lewine would have to stick his hands and arms through the gloves that were attached to the wall of the operating table enclosure and, looking through a Plexiglas window, perform the D and C almost as if Mary were a piece of radioactive cobalt that he was manipulating from behind the protection of a lead shield. The device, which had been originally developed at Porton and refined at Fort Detrick, had been designed for battlefield and field-hospital surgery on a prone patient. There had not been any provision made for obstetrical work. It had taken the sanitary squad the better part of an hour to rig the table with the stirrups inside the operating table enclosure, and, now that the device had been adapted to the present need, Lewine was still apprehensive—more apprehensive than ever. The manipulation of the curette would be hampered not by the gloves, which were standard surgical gloves, but by the enclosures for the upper arm, which would in certain ways restrict his arm movements and arm angles. In a way, open-heart surgery would have been easier. At least heart surgeons can see what they're doing.

Lewine was in the scrub room ready to go into the operating tent through the connecting corridor made of the treated olive cloth. He scrubbed methodically and, in a way that he had not done since his senior year in medical school, went over the moves of this ordinarily simple procedure. He was as ready as he ever would be. The amphetamine he had taken forty-five minutes ago had begun to take effect, his head was beginning to clear, and he was beginning to feel a kind of confidence and even eagerness to get on with it. He knew that it was only a chemical confidence, but it buoyed him nonetheless. He turned from the sink at the noise of the ripping of the Velcro closure of the outer flap of the double door of the tent. He waited a moment, heard the ripping of the Velcro on the inner flap, and then saw Bill Robertson enter the scrub room.

"Come to watch?" he asked. "Are things under control?"

"No. I came in to tell you that we've been on the horn to Deap. Deap has been in touch with Detrick. We don't have to use these contagion suits any more. And your patient won't have to be in the tank when you work on her. We're going to run medical checks on everybody twice a day, but Deap doesn't think there's anything to worry about."

"Thanks for letting me know," Lewine said.

"How are you holding up?" Robertson asked.

"I get by with a little help from my friends," Lewine replied.

They both laughed.

"Me too," Robertson admitted.

Lewine was now able to have the sterile nurse glove him in the ordinary way. He went into the operating room and watched the O. R. nurses remove Mary from the tank and drape her with sterile towels. Lewine was pleased and relieved to be able to work on her in the normal way. The only trouble was that now that she was out of that strange sci-fi contraption it all seemed no more real, no more believable, no more plausible than before. There she was, an unconscious vulnerable human being, but it was utterly fantastic.

The thing about nightmares, though, is that you cannot merely will yourself to wake from them. You are condemned to acting out your worst dreams as if they were real, even though sometimes a small voice tells you that you are dreaming. That small voice was now speaking to Lewine.

The only trouble was he knew it was lying.

7:25 A.M., Eastern Daylight Time:

Eastlake had to admire the way Colonel English had worked it. It was not for nothing that these DIA men enjoyed their reputation for terrifying effectiveness. Hell, compared to the DIA, the CIA boys were right out of Nancy Drew and the Bobbsey Twins. Or a nice prep-school football squad, compared to a tough bunch of pro maulers.

English had sat there, doodling on his yellow pad, paying attention but saying nothing. He had been waiting for the momentum of the meeting to slow, falter, and finally stop as the group realized how little they could do, how limited and how discouraging their options were. Dr. Maxwell and Admiral Pennybaker were inclined toward making a public announcement about what had happened to Tarsus. Schleiman and Dr. Landis—who had come down from Fort Detrick just outside

116

Baltimore—were inclined toward trying to keep it secret. Trying—for neither of them had any real conviction that it could actually be done. For a while, yes, but not for long. Eastlake had wavered between the two positions, and had been unhappy with both. He had inclined against whichever side was speaking at the moment, and that was not a good sign at all.

And then Colonel English had come up with two suggestions. Not one, which would have been too obvious, and would have revealed the strategy of holding back until the right moment and then popping with the idea. But two! And the fact that there were two ideas threw it right back to the group, allowed them to pick and choose, did not make them feel that they were being manipulated and maneuvered.

The suggestions were both crazy. Really, they were the most ding-a-ling ideas Eastlake had ever heard, outside of television programs and movies. In fact, there was an affinity between Colonel English's suggestions and the products of those Hollywood imaginations with which even generals and admirals and presidential advisers—and presidents, too, for that matter—relaxed after a hard day of real crises. That was the style, all right. It was flamboyant and direct and . . . But it was absurd. What kind of a nut would believe that an agent from Castro's Cuba had released a virus in Tarsus just to embarrass the United States? To embarrass and to scare.

"But why Tarsus?" Pennybaker was asking.

"It happened to *be* Tarsus . . ." English started to reply.

"I know that," Pennybaker snapped. "I know it's Tarsus we have to account for. But why would a Cuban go all the way to Utah with his bottle of germs?"

"Because that's where Dugway happens to be. Because the Cubans can deny that they had anything to do with it."

"Well of course they can deny it. They didn't have anything to do with it."

"But if it is our word against theirs, which do you

117

think the American public and the world will believe?"

"It's immoral," Renchler said, quietly. Eastlake was surprised to hear Renchler put it just that way. For a hack politician, he was taking a damned high tone. Or maybe he believed it.

"Yes, sir, it is," English agreed. And Eastlake had to admire that move, too. The man was damned good.

"But it would work. And the alternatives are . . . unpleasant. Can we afford to save our own souls and hurt the nation?"

Pushing it a little, perhaps, Eastlake thought. But probably right to do so. And then he popped the other idea.

"Or, we could simply start a little fire. It'd be a disaster. All we'd be doing would be changing the kind of disaster."

"What about the people of Tarsus?"

"Take them away. Hospitalize them. How many will be left, anyway? Left alive . . . and sane?"

Colonel English looked directly at Renchler, as if somehow he expected Renchler to answer him. It was a piercing gaze that he had, a function, Eastlake realized, of the contrast between the jet black hair and the light blue eyes. And Renchler squirmed. . . . As, of course, he was supposed to do. The strategy was clear now. The idea of burning the town was not a serious suggestion. Its function was only to put an extreme position from which the meeting could retreat to the other idea—about blaming the Cubans—which would seem relatively cautious and even reasonable.

And for a while Eastlake thought it would work. Renchler was vigorous in his objections, as were Maxwell and Pennybaker. And even Dr. Landis was shaking his head. So they weren't going to burn the town down. It was McGrady who spoke what they were all thinking, saying, "No, we won't do that." Not *can't*, but *won't*.

But then Schleiman spoke out against the other suggestion, the Cuban dodge. "It is too risky," he said, speaking not so much with an accent as with a surprising softness in which the consonants were cushioned and the vowels draped with velvet. He ran his fingers through his limp, blond hair. "It would be difficult to restrain and to channel. There are any number of scenarios—all quite plausible—that could begin with such a gesture and end in war with Cuba. And after the missile crisis of some years ago, I should have thought we'd have learned a certain caution. . . ."

"Then we announce it," Pennybaker said. He had only five months to go before his retirement. He could afford to say what he thought. He could, Eastlake realized, afford to think in a way none of the others could. In a way that he, himself, did not often think. . . .

But he closed the door on that kind of self-doubt. This was not the time for it.

"We may be obliged to do that," Schleiman said. "If the time comes. . . ."

"If? If? What do you mean?" Dr. Maxwell asked.

"This afternoon, or tomorrow morning, or in three days or in ten. . . . I don't see what we have to lose by waiting. Or what we gain by acting immediately. The town is presently sealed off?"

"Absolutely," Eastlake said. It had been Norland's decision, but a correct decision. And so the number and person of the pronoun were adjusted slightly. "We saw to that at once."

"Splendid," Schleiman said. "I think what we ought to do is to follow the situation with greatest attention."

"But we haven't decided what to do," Renchler objected. "Have we?"

Schleiman smiled. "No, of course not. I was merely making my proposal for the consideration of the meeting. I suggest that we inform the President what has happened, and that we tell him that we are following the developments . . . that there is no necessity for immediate action. Certainly not for the next few hours. Perhaps not for several days."

"But the town . . ." Dr. Maxwell began.

"Is receiving the best medical attention we have," Dr.

Landis replied. Not sharply. There was a gentleness, even a tranquility in Landis' tone, indicating more clearly than any formal vote, that there was, finally, a consensus.

Not that anything had been definitely decided. But there was a posture, an attitude. Flexible, still, but at least with the beginnings of a direction.

It would be interesting to see how things worked out. With luck, nothing would happen. But sooner or later something was almost certainly going to break. And then it would be very interesting indeed to see Colonel English come back with his schemes. And Pennybaker try to stop him. And Schleiman and McGrady and Renchler —and the President—sweat.

Eastlake knew that he would sweat, too, but he was not distressed by that prospect. He felt the way one feels after the first couple of games of tennis, beginning to warm up, feeling the muscles work and the timing establish itself. And, because so far he was doing well, he felt pretty good.

9:40 A.M., Mountain Daylight Time:

Paul awoke with a dull headache and with the disappointment at not having shaken the headache during his night of dreamless sleep. He lay in bed, his eyes still closed but his mind functioning, and he took stock of how he felt. The realization that he had a headache— that he still had a headache—triggered his recollection of the night before. He remembered the chills, the fever, the aches and pains, the agony of light. The room was stuffy. He remembered closing the window against the chill of the desert night . . . and he remembered going into the front of the house, and Mrs. Jenkins, lying on the living room floor.

He opened his eyes. The room was not that bright—

his bedroom was on the west side of the house—but his eyes felt as though he were out in the desert glare. It was not so painful as it had been the night before, but still it was uncomfortable. Partly to find out whether his condition had improved and partly prompted by his recollection of Mrs. Jenkins, he sat up on the edge of the bed. It wasn't good. He felt an achiness all over his body of the kind that comes with a tough workout after a long summer of laziness and beer drinking. He had played soccer in college, and during the first week of fall training he had felt like this all the time. And the recollection of his days on the soccer team made him think of a hot shower, which was the only remedy he knew for this kind of general soreness. He felt as if he had been mauled by a Korean wrestler.

But the chills and the fever seemed to be gone and he was relieved to find that when he got to his feet he did not have that hollow, precarious feeling of being on the edge of a fall.

He went into the bathroom, took a hot shower, shaved, and then, beginning to feel human again, he took a couple of aspirins. The next step, he supposed, would be a good breakfast but the idea of eating repelled him. A cup of coffee, and maybe a slice of dry toast, but that was all he could stand to think about.

He felt well enough, however, to see about Mrs. Jenkins and find out what was happening. . . . He remembered, now, in the dark distorted night the appearance of that army convoy. It was not just Mrs. Jenkins; it was most of the town. They'd had to bring a field hospital in. That would be where to go and find out what the hell was going on.

He went back to the bedroom, put on a pair of Levi's and a light polo shirt. The boots looked to be too much trouble, so he slipped into a pair of sneakers. He grabbed his sunglasses from the dresser and put them on. With the sunglasses his eyes felt no discomfort at all. The shower had helped, and, while the aspirin had not yet begun to take effect, the act of taking the aspirin had been in itself therapeutic. He could look forward to a diminution of pain.

The rightness of the morning penetrated the protection of the sunglasses and made Paul squint as he walked down the steps from Mrs. Jenkins' house and out into the road. It was already hot, not with the heat that the town would feel later on in the afternoon, but still with an impressive force. The coolness of the morning was gone, and there was, now, a fresh vigor to the morning in its prime. It was a time of day that Paul had learned to enjoy even in the brief time he had spent here. There was an energy to the dry heat, and an irresistible optimism in the brightness and the clarity of the air.

Paul looked down the cut. There was nothing there. He turned around and looked up the road in the direction of Smith's general store, and there he saw signs of activity. There were jeeps and trucks parked, and, even more impressive, there were the discernible peaks of large olive green military tents.

He walked up the road in the direction of the tents, and the enormity of what had happened to Tarsus bore in upon him as he approached the tents and saw for the first time, in the clear light of day, the scale of the army's contingent. He, himself, did not feel too bad. It was as if he had been up all night, the way he sometimes used to do back in college when he had put off studying for exams or writing term papers. There was a kind of light-headedness and a kittenish weakness. And, of course, there was the headache, duller now since he had taken the aspirin and put on the sunglasses, but still with him. He had been unable to generalize from his own condition and that of Mrs. Jenkins to any notion of what the town had experienced. But the complex of tents and the welter of trucks, jeeps, and equipment made it clear that the crisis here at Tarsus was serious and widespread.

As he approached the closest of the tents a soldier—

no longer dressed in the weird outfit of the previous night, but now wearing an ordinary uniform—challenged Paul.

"Hold it right there, buddy."

Paul froze. He was not at all frightened. It was, he was sure, simply a matter of an overzealous and under-intelligent soldier carrying out what he thought his orders were.

"Who are you, and where did you come from?" the soldier asked.

Paul gave the soldier his name and explained that he was a temporary resident of the town, and had come from Mrs. Jenkins' house to inquire about her.

"You're from here, and you're not sick?" the soldier asked.

"Not very," Paul replied. "I can walk around—that is, if that's permitted." He flicked his eyes downward from the soldier's face to the M-16 the soldier was pointing at him.

"I'm just following orders," the soldier explained. "Let's go see the Major."

The request was clearly an order, but Paul did not mind. The major—or whoever was in charge—was the man he had wanted to see anyway.

Paul was surprised to realize that he was grinning. It was all too silly. Or perhaps his light-headedness made it appear so. But, no, it was pure foolishness. That the army had come was undoubtedly a good thing. Clearly, they had the organization and the resources to come in and deal with disaster. It was always units of the army that got called out for floods and hurricanes—things like that. But the trouble was that they had no finesse. They had to play soldier even when the situation did not call for it.

"That way," the soldier said, and indicated with a nod of his head a small tent next to the large hospital tent. The soldier stood aside and allowed Paul to precede him. Politeness? Or part of the drill? He wondered whether the rifle was still pointed in his direction, but, perversely, he did not want to turn around and give the soldier even that satisfaction.

He had reached the tent. "In here?" he asked.

"In there," the soldier said.

Paul went up the step and into the tent. It was smaller than the others that had been erected during the night, and its size, shape, and construction—with the wooden platform and the center pole—reminded him of the tents they had used as bunks when he had been in Scout camp, years ago. There were three tables set up as desks, half a dozen folding chairs, filing cabinets, and, in one corner, a field radio. There were two privates typing at one of the large tables, and then, at the table at the base of the U, a major with a sheaf of papers in front of him. The major looked up as Paul entered and smiled.

"Good morning. You're Donovan, aren't you? Feeling a little better, I see. It's all right, Rogers," the major said, dismissing the soldier behind Paul. "Carry on."

The soldier left and the major invited Paul to sit down.

"I'm Major Robertson," he said, introducing himself. "We met in the jeep last night."

"Good morning," Paul said. "I came to find out how Mrs. Jenkins is doing. And everybody else," he added. "I mean, what's happened? What's happening?" Paul looked at the major, waiting for answers, and observed the rumpled uniform, the dark circles under the eyes, the half-moons of sweat under the armpits of his jacket.

"I'm afraid she's still in coma. She's not a young woman, you know. We're doing everything we can for her." The signs of the major's fatigue only underscored the courtesy of his reply.

"Of course," Paul said.

"What makes it rough is that we don't have medical histories on most of these people and we don't know very much about this disease, whatever it is."

"I wish I could help you," Paul said, "but I'm just

124

here for a few weeks. On a grant. Mrs. Jenkins rented me a room. I think I remember that she took some kind of pills for her heart."

"Good to know. Thank you," Robertson said, pulling a yellow pad in front of him and making a note.

"What's happening?" Paul repeated. "Is everyone sick? What is it that they've—we've—got?"

"We're not quite sure what it is. It's probably a virus, but we haven't narrowed it down yet."

"Is that the reason for the strange suits last night?" Paul asked.

"That's right," Robertson said.

"But you're not wearing them now," Paul observed.

Robertson merely nodded. "Mr. Donovan, you could help us a lot if you would give me a complete medical history and answer a few questions. You're one of the very few who are ambulatory."

"Of course," Paul replied. "I'd be glad to."

Robertson folded over the page of the yellow pad on which he had made a note of Mrs. Jenkins' heart condition and wrote "Paul Donovan" in a large, forceful hand at the top of the clean page. "We'll have a look at you as soon as I've got the history. By the way," he explained, "I'm a doctor, even though I'm stuck behind this desk, running the show."

The questions were the usual ones that Paul had been asked so many times: Childhood diseases, family medical history, allergies, immunizations. At the end of it, the major asked casually, "And what was it that brought you to Tarsus?"

Paul explained about the grant and how he was collecting specimens and photographs in the mountains and in the desert. The major looked up, and, surprisingly, expressed an interest in Paul's work. Paul was struck by the disparity between the brusqueness of the guard he had first encountered and the charm of this obviously exhausted man who wanted to know about—indeed, seemed genuinely interested in—Paul's work with ecological adaptation. Paul tried to be as brief as he could, so as not to task the major's patience, but the major acted as if he had all the time in the world and a real interest in ecology. Robertson expressed approval of Paul's work, and even a thoughtful approval.

"It's a fine thing," he said. "The only way we're going to attract youngsters into the sciences is if we've got imaginative teaching of a kind that gets them into the stuff early. It can't all be textbooks and the dissection of those damn crayfish. I think it's wonderful. What kinds of specimens did you pick up last week?" he asked.

Paul had by this time lost track of the fact that the whole town was sick and that the major had probably been up all night. Beguiled by the major's expression of interest, he rambled on, listing specimens and photographs and, incidentally, mentioning when and where he had been as he had collected them.

"When was the last time you were out?" the major asked.

"Monday," Paul replied. "That's when I started to feel sick. I had to come back early."

"And before that?"

"I've been out every day," Paul told him. "There's so much stuff out there, I've tried to get out early and not come back until six or so. Dinner time."

"I see," said Robertson. "Then you missed that rainstorm the other day. When was it . . . Friday?"

"Yes," Paul said. "I think it was Friday. And I did miss it. I was out taking pictures of some lizards and I saw the thunderheads in the sky."

"Where was that?" Robertson asked.

"In Skull Valley. About ten miles north of the road that goes out to Dugway."

"Well," the major said, getting to his feet. "You've been very helpful, Mr. Donovan. And very interesting. I'd like you to go next door to see Dr. Bartlett and have him check you over. And I think he'll want you to come back tonight. Just for a quick routine look—blood pressure and that sort of thing. We're keeping a close eye on everyone."

Paul stood up and said, "Sure. I still feel a little rocky, but much better than last night." He turned as if to leave and then swivelled around to face Robertson. "Major?"

"Yes?"

"I can walk around, can't I? Without sentries poking guns in my face?"

"Of course," Robertson said. "When Dr. Bartlett's finished, ask one of the medics to print you a name tag and then no one will bother you."

"Name tag?" Paul asked. "But what for?"

"Well," Robertson answered. "We don't quite know what this is, and we don't want to risk its spreading any further. Just temporarily we've quarantined the town. Those men are out there to maintain the quarantine."

At the time, it seemed quite reasonable.

10:30 A.M., Mountain Daylight Time:

Paul came out of the field-hospital tent with his new green name tag attached to the pocket of his polo shirt. The doctor who had examined him, Dr. Bartlett, had been as exhausted as Robertson, but after the examination was over he too had displayed a kind of affability and pleasure in Paul's good fortune. Paul could not help but feel, himself, that he had been lucky. On the other hand, the glimpse he had had beyond the partition, of the thirty beds arranged in rows in the enormous tent, some of them surrounded by oxygen tents, others with I.V. bottles hanging from poles over them, made him feel guilty. It was, he knew, unreasonable. But there it was, a feeling of profound depression as he saw with his own eyes what the extent of the sickness was. And it was not a very great step from depression to this irrational feeling of guilt. Why had he been spared? And the guilt in turn gave way to a kind of fear. Would he continue to be spared? He was, after all, a visitor to Tarsus. Perhaps this had been brewing before he had arrived. Perhaps he would come down with it later. . . .

But that had not been the impression he had got from either of the doctors. He had asked Bartlett directly, and, while the answer had seemed guarded and vague, and while the doctor had disclaimed any certainty about the nature of the disease or its progress, there still had been something more than a formal reassurance in Dr. Bartlett's suggestion that Paul was likely to have avoided any serious involvement with the disease. He had gone so far as to suggest that if Paul continued to improve over the next two or three days, he would very probably come out of it all right.

And from this cautious optimism, or optimistic caution, Paul shuttled back again to the feeling of guilt and bewilderment. When Paul saw Hope Wilson emerging from the headquarters tent, therefore, he greeted her with the kind of enthusiasm that two people from the same town feel when they meet each other halfway around the world in some strange place. She too had been here, and apparently she too had eluded the infection.

"Miss Wilson!"

"Mr. Donovan!"

And, instantly, Paul could tell from her tone that she felt the same relief at seeing him up and around.

"God, it's good to see you," he said. I mean . . . ah . . . that is . . . It's good to see anybody."

He stopped in confusion. That was not what he had meant to say at all. Or, if it was, then it had come out wrong. Again he was bumbling, and he felt awkward and gangling. He remembered their previous meeting and how difficult it had been for him to talk to her then. Of course, he had been sick, and had been occupied with the Pratt boy. . . . But still, the memory of that last time and the bad beginnings of this conversation made his ears feel tingly and flushed. And it was not the sickness at all. It was Hope, herself. It was peculiar, for he hardly knew the girl, and he didn't feel much about her one way or the other. It was what song writers used to call "chemistry"—an idea that had never impressed him very much as a biologist.

"I know what you mean," she said with a smile. "I felt the same thing exactly when I saw you. Isn't it terrible? Have you been sick at all?" she asked.

"A little," Paul said. "It's not knowing what it is that's the worst part of it, though."

"Well," she answered, "it's not good, not knowing. But there are worse things than that. It's . . . it's just terrible."

"Your aunt and uncle?" Paul asked, looking toward the hospital tent.

"Yes," she answered. "They're in there."

"I'm sorry," he said, quietly. "I came over to see how Mrs. Jenkins was. She's in a coma."

"It's . . . it's frightening."

"But you're all right?"

"I seem to be okay. At least so far. But what about you?"

"I was sick last night, and I feel a little weak this morning, but not bad. Certainly not like any of them. Look," he continued after a moment, "have you had coffee? Dr. Bartlett told me there is a field kitchen serving food. You know about the army and disasters; no matter what happens they've got coffee and doughnuts."

"I'd love a cup of coffee."

Paul led the way to the dining tent that had been erected near the field hospital in the small temporary town that the army had thrown up in the center of Tarsus. He had to admire the efficiency of the army's operation, but the rows of wooden sawhorse tables and benches were depressing. Particularly now when there were very few people in the tent. Paul and Hope got their coffee from a large urn. While they were putting in sugar and Pream, Paul looked around once more and said to Hope, "You don't want to drink it here, do you?"

She looked around, wrinkled her nose, and said, "No, not really."

"Let's take it outside under a tree," Paul suggested.

"Fine," she said.

They walked outside and carried their cups to the large lawn across from the hospital. "The Petersons live here," she said. "I saw them in the hospital, too."

There were some old-fashioned wrought-iron benches under the water birch tree, but Hope and Paul ignored them and sat down on the grass. They sipped their coffee in silence for a few moments and then, abruptly, she started talking. "I can understand their being sick, but my uncle. . . . He's just gone out of his mind."

"What do you mean?" Paul asked.

"It's horrible. Just horrible. He keeps saying he's dead. He lay there all night, not moving, just crying and saying over and over again that he was dead. Not that he was going to die, or was afraid he was going to die. He really thought he was dead. And he wasn't in a delirium, because when I'd try to reassure him and say he was alive, he'd tell me I was sweet to say so, but he knew he was dead."

"I don't know," Paul said. "Maybe it's the fever."

"Maybe," she said, but she didn't sound convinced. "Dr. Bartlett couldn't explain it at all."

"And your aunt?" Paul asked gently.

"She's not so sick as he is. And her mind seems perfectly clear. What scares me, though, is that she's got asthma, and this sickness may make it much worse. That's why they moved out here twenty years ago. Because her asthma was so bad. They bought the sheep ranch out in the valley and built themselves a house here in town."

"Well," Paul said, trying to find something encouraging to say, "I'm sure the army people will do everything they can."

"They've got her in an oxygen tent, and they've given her adrenalin. I guess we're lucky," she added, "I mean,

130

the way they got here so fast with all this equipment and all these people to help."

"Yes," Paul said, "they came in like the cavalry in the last reel of a Western. I found Mrs. Jenkins lying on the living room floor last night, and I went out to get help. I went to Dr. Cooley's place, to phone for a doctor, and there they were, in those crazy suits."

"Suits? What suits?"

"Those contagion suits with the masks and the gloves. They looked really strange, almost like spacemen."

"That's funny," Hope said.

"What do you mean?"

"They're not wearing them this morning."

"No, they're not."

"Well," she said slowly, frowning thoughtfully, "if they don't know what the disease is, if they haven't figured out exactly what everybody's got, why would they take off their suits. Aren't they afraid of catching it too? I mean, we're all supposed to be quarantined here because we're so contagious. Could they have been inoculated?"

"No," Paul said, "that doesn't make sense. Not if they don't know what the disease is. You know, I asked Major Robertson about the suits, and then we talked about other things, but now that I remember, he never answered my question."

"I think they know more than they're telling us. But" —she turned to face Paul directly—"what wouldn't they tell us? What could be so terrible that they're afraid to let us know?"

There was no panic in her voice, Paul noted, only a toughminded curiosity and an admirable quickness. He had missed the inconsistencies—or were they evasions? —in the conversation he had had with the major.

She crumpled the now empty paper coffee cup.

"That doesn't make sense," Paul said, after a long pause. "Who could they be trying to protect? So far as I know, everybody in town is sick except for you and me.

Why wouldn't they give us straight answers? Why would they hold things back?"

"I don't know. It's hard, sometimes, to get straight answers out of doctors, especially strange ones. And I guess army doctors must be particularly close-mouthed."

"I suppose that must be it," Paul said. "But Dr. Bartlett and the Major seemed open enough."

"Yes," Hope said, with just a touch of hesitation. "But they aren't the same as Dr. Grierson would be."

"Who's he?"

"My aunt's doctor in Salt Lake City. A specialist."

"Did you call him?"

"I tried to," she answered, "but our phone was out of order, and I didn't want to leave them alone in the house. And then the army came. But I could call now. I mean, doctors are exempt from quarantines, aren't they? They'd let him in."

"I should think so," Paul said. "They've got to treat sick people."

"I could ask him to come over here and have a look at her, and then he could answer some of our questions. I've known him since I was a child and . . . and I trust him."

"Fine." Paul got to his feet and reached out to help her up. "Let's go down to the store and you can call him from there."

They crossed the street and went into the general store. The army had taken over the barroom and had turned it into an enlisted man's club for the off-duty soldiers and medics. It was not at all rowdy, but there was a normal, cheerful buzz of conversation and even laughter. It struck Paul suddenly and forcibly how quiet it was outside in the town. The hum of the generator and the bird songs were the only sounds he had heard. No children calling back and forth, no barking of dogs, no clatter of gears as cars and trucks turned off the main road and came up the cut. It was as if the entire town had been holding its breath. But here in Smith's store there was breathing again.

It did not stop, but modulated into a quieter and more attentive key when Paul and Hope entered. The men looked up from their pool game, their cards, or their beers at the two of them—townspeople who were walking around. Or, no, it wasn't just that. There was a whistle—at which Hope reddened slightly—that defined the quality of their attention. She was walking slightly in front of Paul and he observed the tightness of the wheat jeans over her buttocks and thighs. The whistle, while not Paul's own style, was a reasonable reaction to Hope. She was, he realized, a damn good-looking girl.

There was a pay phone on the wall. Hope stopped and looked at Paul. "Have you got a dime?" she asked. "I don't have any money with me."

"I think so," he said. As he felt in his pockets for change, one of the soldiers detached himself from the bar and came over. "I'm sorry, miss," he said. "That phone is out of order."

"This one's out of order, too?"

"Too?" the soldier echoed. "I don't know about any others."

"Our phone is out of order," she explained.

"Oh?" the soldier said. "I'm sure they'll be fixed soon. We've reported this one to the Major."

"Why don't we try Cooley's?" Paul suggested to Hope. "I don't know whether he's in the hospital or sick at home, but I don't think he would have locked his house. I'm sure he wouldn't mind."

They left the general store and went back out into the quiet, hot, bright day. Paul had taken his sunglasses off in the dimness of the store and the glare of the sunlight was an assault. He winced visibly and Hope stared at him.

"Are you all right?" she asked.

"Yes, yes," he said. "It's just that my eyes are very sensitive." He put the sunglasses back on, and they walked down the cut toward Dr. Cooley's place.

Their pace was slow, but after only a couple of hundred yards Paul began to feel heaviness and fatigue, as if he had been walking for miles. It was not the heat. He had got used to that even in the short time he had been out here in Utah. It had to be an aftereffect of the night before. The illness, whatever it was, had not left him entirely untouched. He remembered with considerable relief that he had left his truck at Cooley's. They would be able to drive back.

But as they approached the house he could see that the truck was gone. For a moment he was worried, but then he realized that this was not the city and that nobody would have stolen the truck. The army people must have just moved it into town. Orderly of them, but, at the moment, a nuisance. He would have to walk back, now, and that would be uphill.

Dr. Cooley's place, a sprawling structure of white clapboard, was part residence and part veterinary office. There were two front doors, one to the house and the other, marked with the black and white "Carleton M. Cooley, D.V.M." shingle, led to the clinic. And it was that door that Hope and Paul used. It wouldn't have felt right just to wander into the house itself.

Not that it would have made much difference. It was as unnaturally quiet here as in the rest of the town.

Hope called out, "Dr. Cooley? Anybody home? Hello!"

"I guess he's sick, too," Paul offered.

"I didn't think there'd be any answer," Hope explained, "but . . ."

"I know," Paul said. "It would have been somehow bad manners if you hadn't called out."

They were standing in a paneled waiting room that smelled faintly of disinfectant. There were maple benches and chairs, and a table with back issues of *Dog World* and fliers from pet-food companies stacked on it. Beyond the waiting room was Cooley's office—really nothing more than a passageway between the waiting room and the dispensary into which he had managed to fit a battered desk, a chair, and filing cabinets. Paul stood in the doorway while Hope picked up the phone.

He watched as she stood there, flicking the button with her forefinger, obviously trying to get a dial tone. He knew it was no good. After only a few seconds he was certain that this phone, too, would not work. But he was reluctant to intrude on Hope's continuing effort. She stood there, flicking the button, more slowly now, and, without much real hope herself. And then, before she hung up, she turned and looked at Paul.

"The line must be down," he said.

"Yes, of course," she answered, and she put the receiver back in its cradle.

It was very irksome and disappointing. Paul watched her light another cigarette and it was not difficult to read into the savagery with which she shook out the match her frustration at not being able to reach the doctor in Salt Lake City.

"I guess we should have asked at the field headquarters. They could have told us that the line was down. It would have saved us the trip."

"I guess so," Hope said.

And then, knowing that that was not enough, and wanting somehow to smooth the frown in that tired face, Paul thought for a moment and then brightened. "Look," he said. "They can do it for us. They've got a field radio or telephone or whatever it is. They've got to have some communication with the outside. We'll go see Major What's-his-name."

"Robertson," she said.

"Yes. He'll get through to your doctor for you."

"Yes, of course," she said. "I'm so tired I'm not thinking straight."

"Neither am I," he admitted with a smile.

The smile was in answer to hers, and what they were exchanging, Paul felt, was the reassurance and the sad companionship that the first two losers in a spelling bee share with each other. The moment was broken, however, by an abrupt exclamation—half shout, half cry—from outside. "Shee-it!" they heard.

Hope laughed, and instantly her amusement turned to

excited pleasure. "It must be Dr. Cooley! He must be okay. I guess he's out in back with the dogs."

"The dogs? What dogs?" Paul asked.

"He's a vet, you know," Hope said. "And he has a whole lot of dogs himself."

Paul frowned. "Of course," he said. "Sure."

But the frown did not dissipate. He had not heard any barking as they had approached the house. They had been inside and had tried to make the telephone call—it must have been three or four minutes—and there had been no sound they had not made themselves.

Hope, however, had already begun to move toward the door. There was nothing for Paul to do but follow her. They went back out through the waiting room and outside and then around the house toward the rear, where the shout had come from. As she turned the corner she stopped short. Paul nearly bumped into her, and . . .

It was not Cooley, but a soldier, a sergeant. The sergeant was standing beside a large hole and there was a pick and shovel leaning against an overturned feed box close by.

"Yeah? What do you want?" the sergeant snapped. "You got no business here."

"We came to see Dr. Cooley," Hope replied, politely but coldly.

"He ain't here," the sergeant replied. "Now get away."

"What are you doing?" Paul asked. "What . . . what is that hole?"

"What do you think it is?" the sergeant growled. "What's it look like? It's a hole. Be glad it ain't your grave."

Paul took a step toward him, not knowing precisely why. Later, when he went over it in his mind, he realized he had had suddenly an irrational fear that the sergeant was digging a grave for Doc Cooley. But it was all so fast. He took the step or two forward toward the

136

sergeant, and then, as fast as he could, he turned and grabbed Hope, held her, and tried to shield her eyes from what he had already seen. But it was too late. She had already glimpsed what the sergeant's anger had been trying to conceal—the bloodied bodies of six headless dogs. Hope gasped and then gagged. Paul tightened his grasp and, ineffectually patting her back, tried to soothe her. "Take it easy," he said.

He turned back to the sergeant and asked, "What the hell have you done to those dogs?"

"I ain't done nothin', mister," the sergeant said defiantly. "I wouldn't do a thing like that to a dog. Jesus fucking Christ! Look at it! They did it!"

"They?" Paul prompted.

"Those goddamn science guys, and the doctors. Cut their freaking heads off. And then they told me to dig a hole and bury 'em. I wish it was them I was burying. No good sons-of-bitches."

Then, he caught himself. "Sorry, ma'am." And then, looking at Paul again, he said, "You better take the lady on away from here."

With his arm still around Hope's shoulder he led her back around the house and onto the road. Slowly they began to make their way up the hill toward the center of Tarsus.

11:15 A.M., Mountain Daylight Time:

It was a bad time. It could last, Major Robertson knew, only fifteen or twenty minutes—the time it would take for the Nembutal to overcome the effects of the metamphetamine he had taken to stay alert during the long night and into the morning. Now, in the interval between the two chemicals, there was nothing to do but wait and try not to think. The feeling of depression and utter worthlessness was a function of the pills. Even if he had been engaged in other kinds of work, curing

137

cancer or heart disease or the common cold, the side effects of the pills were such that there would be this radical doubt and depression. And he knew this. But that knowledge was cold comfort as he lay in bed in this absurd frilly bedroom of the house he was using to bunk down in, a house owned by some people named Peterson, both of whom lay critically ill in a tent two hundred yards away.

The surroundings, then, conspired with the chemicals. And, even though he knew better, he felt that a terrible indictment came from the framed photographs on the dressing table, from the silly Degas print on the wall, from the plastic case on top of the night table—a case he recognized as a receptacle for false teeth. There was something unbearably intimate about false teeth.

He tried to reason with himself. Nobody had intended this, nobody had wanted it. It was an accident, like any other. People went out and got killed in cars, in planes, in boats, and left behind them photographs and false teeth. It happened all the time. And neither the descendants of Henry Ford nor the descendants of the Wright Brothers felt any particular guilt because of it.

At six that morning, when Dr. Deap and General Wyatt had paid their visit, Robertson had resented their briskness and impersonal professionalism. Especially that of Deap, who seemed more interested in the research data that would come out of this disaster than in the disaster itself. But now, in this ridiculous bedroom, he envied Deap that professionalism and that detachment. It would have been a help getting through this twenty minutes.

But, no, that wasn't right. And it wasn't just the depression from the pills, either. A man was not human if he was not moved by the death of children, by the obliteration of all that wonderful possibility, by the blasting of innocence. It was terrible, it was objectively terrible, and a man had to be warped not to see it and be moved by it. There were three children dead already, and Robertson was certain that by the time he woke up from this desperately needed rest there would be four or five—perhaps as many as seven—more.

He took several deep breaths, deliberately trying to hyperventilate to make himself drowsy and to speed up the effects of the sleeping pill. There was a soft knock at the door. He welcomed any distraction.

"Come in," he said.

The door opened. It was Corporal Marston. "I'm sorry to disturb you, sir."

"It's all right. What is it?"

"Miss Wilson and that Donovan fellow. They've come to the headquarters tent. They know all the phones are out, and they want to use the field radio to get through to a doctor in Salt Lake City. Miss Wilson's aunt has a specialist there. They were very insistent. I didn't know what to tell them."

Robertson thought for a moment—perhaps a long moment, for Corporal Marston nudged him with a diffident "Sir?"

"I'm thinking," the major snapped.

"Yes, sir."

This one was tricky, he realized. It was important to keep those two from becoming suspicious. He didn't want to have to detail men to keep those two under guard—not unless it was necessary. The point was now to play for time. "Tell them I'm asleep. Tell them I'm the only person who can authorize civilian use of the radio, and that I've been up all night, and am asleep. Uh, you can tell them they can try when I come on duty in six hours."

"Yes, sir," the corporal said.

"And, Corporal?"

"Yes, sir?"

"As soon as they've stopped arguing with you and have left, pass the word on to Captain Phipps. General Wyatt ought to be told."

"Yes, sir," Marston said, and closed the door.

He lay there, considering the decision he had just made. Yes, he had acted properly. Even if he had been up and in the office, this would have been a matter for the general to decide, either by himself or even in consultation with the bigger brass.

He felt the beginning of the sweet languor of the Nembutal finally starting to take effect. He took another couple of deep breaths, and then, most gratefully, felt himself falling asleep.

2:00 P.M., Eastern Daylight Time:

The three men studied the series of photographs on Schleiman's desk, aerial shots of Tarsus taken only an hour earlier from one of the Dugway helicopters. The photographs showed the approach road, the way the town sat in the cul-de-sac cut, the location of the overturned truck on the approach road—everything. It looked good, Eastlake thought. Better than any of them had any right to expect or even hope. A no-place place, a dying town even before this "incident"—as Colonel English kept calling it—and as isolated as any hamlet one could dream up as a military problem for undergraduates to chew on. An old mining town with the mines no longer producing ore of a high enough grade to interest anyone but the lone scrabbling operators who didn't have the strength or the sense to move on. It sat in that little fold in the mountain range like an old ticket stub left in the pocket of a suit to dissolve into pocket fuzz. It was an incredible stroke of luck that, if such a thing had to happen at all, it had chosen Tarsus to happen in.

But Colonel English was unhappy. Despite the reports from General Wyatt and General Norland, despite the evidence of the photographs spread out on Schleiman's imitation Regency desk in the West Wing office, despite the good news that there was no news, that after nearly twenty-four hours, there was not a whisper in the media, Colonel English was displeased. Not, of course, that anyone could be actually delighted with the nasty business before them. But its handling, thus far, had been good. Very good. Eastlake felt up about it. And he more than half suspected that Colonel English was unhappy because nobody had yet come around to support the new position—his and the Defense Intelligence Agency's—that the Cubans should be blamed.

Eastlake was not at all certain that this was so, but the suspicion was there, and he was annoyed by it. This was not the time for that kind of personal involvement. The situation had deteriorated considerably since the meeting earlier that day, and the stakes were higher now. The death count was higher; the report about the four healthy people in Tarsus had come in, and, in its way, health was even more dangerous than sickness; and the news with which Carl Schleiman had opened this "informal" discussion was most menacing of all.

He had made a little joke of it. Or, at least, there had been a kind of chuckle at the end. But there was a sourness to the humor of the remark which Eastlake did not find to his taste. Not at all. "I've discussed the matter with the President," Schleiman had said, "and I am instructed to report that I have not discussed the matter with the President. He knows nothing about it whatever. He said that when he learns what he has learned, he will be shocked and saddened. And very angry!" And then there had been that laugh, short and savage, revoltingly knowing. . . . There was all the contempt and all the experience of a Dietrich snort. And, in his way, Schleiman was a kind of Dietrich butch, Eastlake thought. Schleiman's whole career could be summed up, anyway, with "See what the boys in the back room will have, and tell them I'm having the same. . . ."

So, the President did not know, preferred not to be known to know, preferred to wait it out while the rest of them sweated. All right. That's just what he, Eastlake, would have assumed, because that's what he'd have done if the positions had been reversed and he'd been the President.

On the other hand, to be fair about it, if he'd been the President, he'd have taken the advice of the Joint Chiefs back in the fall, and would never have gone out on a limb with the announcement that germ warfare was over and done with. Recommend that the Senate ratify the Geneva Agreements about chemical and biological warfare—perhaps. (Even that would have been tricky, though: Defoliants are chemicals, Mace is a chemical, tear gas is a chemical, and they are all potentially lethal.) But to push it as far as the President had? It was just asking to be caught out later. And the momentary gain in calming the doves and the demonstrators wasn't worth the risk of a big loss later—when something like this happened.

Democracy was okay. Eastlake believed in it. The trouble was that it always turned into public relations, into a salesman's game, and the politicians were the salesmen. And so these crazy, grandstand bits of business were a part of the pitch. If anything went wrong, there would be someone to blame for the mess— Schleiman, Admiral Pennybaker, or himself. Or any combination. With maybe Norland and Wyatt as a side order, their heads served up like cole slaw or pickled tomatoes.

But not Colonel English. Not the DIA or the CIA or the "sensitive" agencies. Which explained why they could afford to be such wild men, coming up with all sorts of far-out ideas. They would not have to eat the mess afterwards. Not administratively, anyway, and not officially. Sure, a few personnel shifts might come if something went drastically wrong. But the agency would not suffer. So the agency thinking could be entirely free. Creative irresponsibility. Good thing or not, Eastlake wondered. Well, that depended on how he and Pennybaker and Schleiman and the President put those wild ideas to use, and when, and with what success. . . .

But Colonel English was worried now, and what worried him was precisely the cautiousness that seemed to hold everyone else in its grip. Nobody had done anything, not a damned thing, since the field hospital had been mobilized and sent in there. And there would have to be some further action or the situation would blow sky high! That's what he was saying, with all that earnestness and conviction. But Cuba? It was a risk, and too great for what was at stake.

"It isn't those four healthy people that worry me," English went on. "It's the rest of the world. Those people have families and friends. Somebody has got to try to get into that town, and the overturned truck there isn't going to work for very much longer. It just won't. Somebody will complain, will call the newspaper or the radio station . . . and then . . ."

"And then we'll announce the quarantine."

"That's a step down the wrong road. It cuts off the other options. And it's suspicious. The town is just too close to Dugway! You won't need Jack Anderson to guess. Any moron could figure it out!"

And English's idea, fantastic as it was, would not be guessed even by those professional wild men. Leon Uris, Fletcher Knebel, Richard Condon, and all those other paranoids wouldn't have the nerve, even together, to dream up such a thing. Oh, to dream it up, but to believe that it was true? That the government had actually done such a thing. . . . No! And that was the strength of the plan. It didn't even have to be Castro's government they blamed, but some Castro admirer, a fanatic, a sympathizer. That was the new wrinkle since this morning.

The great virtue of the plan was that it managed to incorporate the President's announcement about germ warfare and actually to turn the announcement into an asset. If the President has gone on television and told the public that we are no longer involved in germ warfare except for defensive research, then obviously, it can't be the United States that caused the Tarsus epidemic. Simple logic directs attention elsewhere. Cuba is close, and will do. And a Castro sympathizer. . . . Castro could deny it all he liked, but even he wouldn't be sure that it wasn't true.

Nevertheless, Schleiman was not yet willing to go with it. And that could mean—although it didn't necessarily mean—that the President himself had disapproved the plan.

"General?"

"I think we wait," Eastlake said after a pause that was not for effect but a real hesitation. He had actually flirted with . . . well, not endorsing Colonel English's plan, but with an "I don't know," which would have left the door open for another pitch. "I think we've got another twelve hours. Maybe twenty-four. And I think we can keep the town shut up for longer than Colonel English thinks. Not indefinitely, but for a while yet."

He looked at the pictures again.

"All right," Schleiman said. "So far, I agree. But then what? Eventually . . ."

He did not finish the sentence. He did not have to.

"I don't know," Eastlake said. And, surprised that, having resisted the sentence, it had come to his lips just the same, he rolled with it further. "I think we might keep the DIA proposals in mind in case it should come to that. It doesn't hurt to be prepared."

"I was about to suggest that I might fly out there myself, and have a look," English said, quietly.

Eastlake and Schleiman looked at each other. Neither of them said yes. Perhaps each was waiting for the other to say no. But neither did. Nobody said anything. And so it was decided.

It doesn't hurt to be prepared, Eastlake thought again. When it came time to decide, it would still be their decision to make. Theirs and the President's. So, what harm?

But even outside, in the limousine, on the way back to the Pentagon, he found that he was still asking the question, over and over: What harm? What harm?

2:30 P.M., Mountain Daylight Time:

Paul scraped the last bit of congealed egg from the plate and put it in the sink along with the other dishes. There was something reassuring and even mindlessly pleasant in the performance of this simple domestic chore. The idea of Mrs. Jenkins discovering that he had cleaned up the kitchen, and the pleasure that she would take from it, sooner or later, gave Paul a familiar kind of feeling. He had occasionally surprised Marian by sneaking in to wash the dishes while she was having a nap after dinner.

With something to do, with work for his hands and the small forefront of his mind, the nervousness and the apprehension he had felt earlier seemed to recede. Surely he and Hope had been imagining things. He had left her at her house exhausted, frustrated, nearly in tears, almost three hours ago, and he had returned to fall himself into a heavy, almost drugged kind of slumber.

Now, the headache was only a shadow of itself. As he pulled the plug out of the sink and drained the last of the soapy water, his mind returned to the problem of the phone call, but now it seemed much less of a problem. What they had to face was simply the inertia of all bureaucracies, all organizations. Surely he knew this well enough from his work in a high school. How much more elaborate, and therefore how much worse would the army have to be? He was confident that the major, who looked like a sensible man, and who had been reasonable enough in conversation, would cut through some of this red tape so that Hope could get in touch with Dr. Grierson.

He sprayed the dishes in the rack with hot water, squeezed out the dish cloth and hung it over the faucet, took a dish towel, and carefully dried the glassware. Then, feeling quite satisfied and even a little smug, he stepped on the garbage-pail pedal, twisted the top of the plastic liner inside the pail, and took the large garbage bag out the back door. It was not heavy, there was not much exertion involved. He felt, nevertheless, as if he had been carrying a hundred-pound sack of flour. Even this slight effort caused him to break out in a heavy sweat. He came back into the kitchen, put a new garbage bag in the can and sat down on a kitchen chair. His aspirin was in the bedroom, and he didn't feel up to going back to get them. He took two of Mrs. Jenkins' Bufferin from her medicine tray on the windowsill near the sink and washed them down with a Coke. He was partly dehydrated—his lips felt dry and he had been sweating a lot—and he needed the energy of the sugar and caffeine and whatever else was in Cokes.

The Coca-Cola left him feeling a little bloated, but otherwise more comfortable than he had been before. The sweat had dried, and he was less tired than he had been. It was simply a matter of finding small remedies for small problems. The truck, for instance. He would go and find the truck so that these minor excursions around Tarsus were not so tiring. Not only did he feel himself somewhat reassured, he realized that he was taking a certain pleasure in the anticipation of being able to share this mood with Hope, who needed it surely more than he. After all, her aunt and uncle were sick and she was deeply concerned as well as exhausted.

In a way he found it interesting to examine his feelings about Hope. The eagerness, which was very real, for the moment when he could see her and reassure her, was surprising and something of a novelty. He had, of course, known momentary lust since Marian's death, but the couple of occasions when he had succumbed to it and taken one of the willing girls home after a party had been disappointingly hygienic, and there had been the sad feeling that both of them were participating in some charade. But this feeling of interest, protectiveness, and tenderness was startling and exhilarating. Even being tough-minded about it and discounting the effects of his low-grade fever and the effect of the disaster which was, some anthropologist had explained, a psychological prompting to procreation, he was still left with an irreducible core of interest in Hope which was not limited to—although it certainly did not exclude—the very extraordinary molding of those tight wheat jeans. Well, he thought, he would see what happened.

He got up, put the Coke bottle under the sink, and left the house. He walked up the road to the center of town, Smith's general store and the military complex that had grown up around it, to look for his truck, but he was unable to find it anywhere on the apron among the military vehicles drawn up in more or less orderly rows. He thought of going to ask one of the soldiers but then hesitated. They would only refer it to the major, and he was not yet on duty. Or, no, he was exaggerating again. They would have put it out of the way somewhere. He would look further. They had enough to do, he was sure, without worrying about his truck.

He walked around past the outdoor entrances to the restrooms to the small lot behind Smith's. Among the hulks of abandoned cars, the empty kerosene barrels, and the remains of an ancient school bus he saw his truck. It was with considerable relief and a kind of buoyancy that he hurried toward it. The windows had been rolled up, and a blast of hot air hit him as he opened the door to the cab. The keys? Were in the ignition where he had left them. He rolled down the window on the driver's side and eased himself into the ovenlike interior. He turned the ignition key and depressed the accelerator. The starter whined . . . and whined and whined. Nothing happened. The motor refused to catch.

Paul was annoyed, but only annoyed. And even that was mostly because of the heat in the cab of the truck. He checked the gas gauge, but it showed the tank three-quarters full. He pumped the accelerator pedal several times. The carburetor was set for a thin mix because of the altitude. He tried the starter again, but again nothing happened. He turned the ignition off and got out of the cab. His intention was only to wait outside where it was less stifling. He assumed that somehow he must have flooded the carburetor. But, as long as he was out of the truck, he thought he would go and look under the hood.

He did not know much about automobile engines, but there were certain obvious things he knew to look for. There were even bizarre things that absolute innocence could recognize: He remembered reading a newspaper story about a man in Florida who had found a boa constrictor wrapped around his gas line. He opened the hood, looked for a moment at the engine, and tried to decide what it was that seemed strange. And then he realized—it had taken him a moment because of the heat, because of his headache, and because it was not the kind of thing one expects to find—that the distributor cap was gone. Had been removed.

It came flooding back upon him now, the idea of conspiracy, the idea that the army was shamelessly manipulating and maneuvering them all. But why? What could possibly be their reason, their purpose? They had come in on an errand of mercy to help a stricken town. What possible excuse was there for this kind of high-handedness?

"All right, buddy! Back off, real slow!"

Paul looked up and saw, in the angle between the fender and the raised hood, the center portion of a uniform from which there protruded, pointing directly at him, the barrel of an automatic rifle.

This was getting to be tiresome, he thought. What the hell! He'd already gone through this. There was nothing to do, no possible choice except to obey the soldier's orders. But then, even as he started to do what the soldier had told him, he realized that he'd been bent over the engine of the truck. The soldier could not have been able to see either his face or his name tag. Not that there was any excuse for such brusqueness. . . .

Deliberately he fought down his anger. These guys

were only carrying out orders. It was the soldier's tone and weapon that had started the adrenalin flowing. But it made a kind of sense. It was not implausible. He took the two steps backward and really forced himself to smile pleasantly. He pointed to his name tag and said, "It's all right, soldier. I belong here. This is my truck."

He took a deep breath, because now that he'd figured it out . . .

"This area is off limits," the soldier barked.

"But it's my truck," Paul repeated.

"Mister, I don't care whether it's your truck or your mother's truck. This area is off limits. Now beat it!"

The whole thing was stupid, but it would do no good to argue, Paul realized. Anyway, not with the soldier. The thing to do was to take it up with the major. The explanation was—had to be—that orders had been distorted as they had trickled down the chain of command. That had led to this otherwise inexplicable foolishness, this rudeness, these mindless demonstrations of menace. . . .

In order to make his complaint to the major in the most specific terms, he realized it would be useful to know the soldier's name. And, as that question arose in his mind, it struck him, ominously, that the soldier was not wearing a name tag over the pocket of his blouse.

"I'm not going to argue with you, soldier," he said. "I'm leaving. But what's your name? When I take it up with the Major later, I'm sure he'll want to know."

"He knows my name," the soldier answered. "Now, move on."

Paul was still flushed with anger and frustration when, a few minutes later, he knocked on Hope's door.

"Paul?" she called out.

"Yeah!"

"Come on in. I'm in the kitchen."

He opened the door and walked through the substantial comfort of Hope's aunt and uncle's house. She was sitting at the table of the large, modern kitchen, eating

149

a sandwich and drinking a cup of coffee. As he entered, she smiled. He tried to return the smile but managed only a savage rictus.

"What's the matter, Paul?" she asked.

And he told her—about the truck, about the encounter with the soldier, and even about the absence of the name tag and the soldier's refusal to identify himself. His anger was slightly diminished by the time he had finished telling her the story, and he realized that he felt the first faint twinges of guilt. After all, he had come over here to cheer her up. And what was he doing if not requiring of her exactly that kind of reassurance. But perhaps the time for polite reassurance was gone. In any event, Hope's reply confirmed his own worst fears. She was worried herself.

"What bothers me," she said, her coffee cup frozen in the air a couple of inches from her lips, "is that nobody knows about us."

"What do you mean?" Paul asked.

"I turned on the television set at noon to catch the news. You'd think that a thing like this would make the news programs, wouldn't you? I mean, the local ones from Salt Lake City. They did three minutes on the opening of a boat pond in one of the Salt Lake City parks. And then I tried the radio. Usually they tell you the most trivial thing that happens in the tiniest town in the area, but there wasn't one word about Tarsus. Don't you think that's odd?" she asked earnestly.

"Odd? It's spooky!"

"What can we do?" she asked.

"You know this town," he said. "I've only been here a few weeks. If someone wanted to get out unnoticed, is there any way?"

"Let me think," Hope said. "I used to explore a lot as a child, but I haven't been back here for ten years. If you got out, what would you do?"

"I don't know," Paul said. "I suppose—well, I'd try to get to a telephone. They can't come in here this way and just seal us up. I'll be damned if I can figure out why they'd want to do it. And I don't even much care. They just have no right to do this."

"The road, I'm sure, they've got blocked," Hope said. "I mean, if what you think is true—and I'm afraid it is. The only other way is up through the mountains, but that's a tough climb and it would be thirty miles at least that way before you'd get to the first phone." She paused for a moment, and then suddenly her face brightened. "Wait!" she said, "I know. There are the old silver mines. There's one of them that's a tunnel all the way through one of the mountains to the other side. If you could get into that, into the Tarsus entrance without being seen, they probably wouldn't know about the mouth on the other side. That'd take you out near the road that goes to Tooele. You could hitch from there."

"This is all so damn silly," he said.

"I know," she said, "but . . . what else is there?"

"I don't know," Paul said.

"Do you want me to show you where the mouth of the mine tunnel is?" she asked.

"I don't know. Maybe Major Robertson will be able to clear all this up."

"Maybe," Hope said. "Shall we wait, then, and . . ."

"Who are we kidding? What can the Major possibly say?"

"I don't know. But there has to be some explanation for all this."

"An explanation, maybe," Paul said grimly. "But an excuse?"

"No," she said. "No excuse."

"Why don't we . . . why don't we go for a walk?" Paul suggested. "Often I find that walking clears the head."

"All right."

They looked at each other across the table. Hope had put her empty coffee cup down, and now, for a moment, they stared at each other, realizing that the first step had been taken.

3:10 P.M., Mountain Daylight Time:

The opening of the mine tunnel was half-concealed behind brush. It was fifty yards in back of the abandoned, partially burnt-down church. Or, as Hope explained, the church had been erected in front of the mine entrance when women had moved into town, in order to preserve the sanctity of the Sabbath. Any miner wanting to go and work the mine on Sunday would have had to slink past the church and the evangelical fervor and pious wrath of the old-fashioned minister who had once lived in Tarsus.

It had been easier to get down to the mouth of the mine than Paul had expected—or feared. He had assumed, back at the house, that the safest way to cover the half mile down to the opening of the mine tunnel would have been to go behind the houses, sneaking as furtively as possible as far down as possible, and keeping out of sight of the soldiers. Hope, however, had calmly led the way out the front door and walked down the center of the road. Paul, nervous, fearing that a third challenge and third report to the major would be dangerous and might result in his being more closely watched or even confined, had been worried by the frontality of Hope's approach. But he had not given her sufficient credit for shrewdness. As they had passed the old schoolhouse in which most of the soldiers were billeted, Hope had simply taken his hand. The two of them, walking hand in hand and looking like lovers, had passed the lounging soldiers as neatly and as invisibly as anything Lamont Cranston had ever managed.

They had come down the cut and, after they had passed a slight curve in the road and were out of sight, Hope had abruptly dropped his hand and darted off the road and into the high grass and scrub brush on the floor of the cut. He had followed, glancing quickly behind him. There had been no one to see them, but even if there had been he realized that Hope's simple, economical gesture for the benefit of the soldiers would have provided sufficient excuse for their sudden disappearance from the landscape.

She had led the way through the thick clumps of white squaw-current, holding the branches as they snapped back so they would not hit Paul in the face. His head was throbbing again and he was bathed in sweat. The perspiration was not in itself alarming, for the sun was high and the day was hot. A certain amount of sweat would have been normal. But the throbbing of his head and the disproportionate fatigue he felt reminded him once more that he was still convalescent. The mine tunnel and the easy walk to the road could be managed, even with the headache and the weakness, bad as they were. Or, for that matter, even with worse discomfort, if it should come to that.

"We should have brought a flashlight," Hope said as they approached the dim mouth of the tunnel. "But I was afraid it would look too suspicious. If you do go through . . . or when you do, I'll carry a purse. Then you'll be able to take a few things with you."

They had entered the square timbered porch of the tunnel and for perhaps ten feet the indirect afternoon light showed the timber props of the walls and ceiling and the rusty narrow track for the hand carts that led back into the mine.

Paul felt in his pocket and produced a pack of matches. Leading the way and striking matches, he explored a little deeper into the tunnel, but the matches gave very little light and their eyes were not yet accustomed to the gloom of the tunnel.

They waited for three or four minutes, giving their pupils time to dilate and adjust, and as they waited Hope told him about the tunnel, the great boom in Tarsus years and years before when the first strike had been made, the investment of money and labor, and the disappointment as the mine's yield had fallen off to a slightly lower grade of ore than was profitable. But most important, she told him where the tunnel opened out at the other end.

"Does anybody still work the mine?" Paul asked.

"From time to time, people will come down and scratch at it, working it on weekends. There's still silver ore here, but it costs a lot to take it to a smelter. It isn't worth running trains. They truck it, though. A farm truck full of ore will fetch a hundred dollars or so. They still come, but there isn't anything to worry about. Nobody's healthy enough to do it . . . except you and me."

"I'm not sure how long I'd be good for," Paul said, only half joking.

It had become a charade, almost a game. The darkness of the tunnel and the coolness of the earth underneath the mountain made the realities outside in Tarsus seem terribly remote and almost imaginary. Or, if that was real, then this was imaginary, the two of them in a half-abandoned tunnel plotting a possible escape. But even a game has its own organization, its own thrust, its own logic. When their eyes could discern even without matches the barely perceptible outlines of timbers at arm's length, Paul lit a match. Now they were able to see with some clarity for two or three feet. Slowly he led the way holding the match high for a few yards. Then, as the match burned down close to his fingers, he shook it out and lit another, and then a third.

It was during the fourth match that they found it.

"Damn!" she said.

Paul lit yet another match and explored the ruin. Timbers shattered, earth fallen from the walls and roof of the tunnel, and the passage blocked.

"There's no way to get through a thing like that, I suppose," Paul said.

"There is," she said, "but you need machinery, you need a crew, and new timbers. It could take days even with all that. These old timbers rot out after a while, I guess. My aunt and uncle always warned me not to play here when I was a child. They were worried then. I'm sorry," she added, as if the cave-in had been somehow her fault.

"I am too," Paul said. "Let's get on back."

Hope led the way this time only because the tunnel was narrow and she was closer to the mouth.

"Wait a minute," Paul said. "Here, take the matches."

But, as he thrust them forward, either he missed her grasp or she missed his, and the matches fell to the floor of the tunnel. For a moment they groped, trying to find them, but gave it up. It was not that far back to the entrance and they were going toward the light.

"We don't need them," Hope said. "We'll be out of here in a couple of minutes," and she resumed her progress.

Suddenly she stumbled and fell. Paul had to catch himself in order not to fall on top of her.

"Damn!" Hope exclaimed. "I got my foot caught in the loose rock."

"Is it still caught?" he asked.

"No, no, it's free, but I think I've twisted my ankle."

He helped her to her feet and said, "Here, lean on me."

Half-leaning, half-hopping, making progress now very slowly, they made their way to the mouth of the tunnel, where, in the shade of the timbered porch, Hope sat down and examined her left ankle.

"How bad is it?" Paul asked.

"It hurts," she said. "I can stand on it, but it hurts."

"Well, if you can stand on it it's certainly not broken. Probably not even sprained. You just pulled something or strained it. Why don't we rest for a while and then we'll take it slow going back."

"That was dumb of me," she said with some annoyance. She reached in her pocket for a cigarette and then started to laugh. Caught between the cellophane and the pack itself there was a book of matches. "I just didn't think. I forgot I had matches with me, too. Now I feel even dumber. Paul?" she asked, a new tone in her voice. "What's that?"

Paul looked where she was pointing. There was a crumpled wrapper of a pack of Pall Mall Gold 100s. "An empty cigarette pack," he said.

"Yes," she said, "but how did it get here?"

"I don't know. Weekend miners must have dropped it."

"Let me see it a minute."

Paul handed it to her. It was dry and fairly clean.

"Look here," she said. "There's no state tax stamp. These are from a PX."

They both looked back toward the interior of the mine. There was nothing they could see, but there was nothing that they had to see. It was all as clear as daylight. It had not been an accidental cave-in.

"Wait a minute," Paul said. "It isn't necessarily that way. It could have been . . . it could have been some soldier on guard duty, taking a break and sitting down in the shade of the timbers."

"Do you think so?" she asked.

"I don't know. I just don't know."

Hope lit her cigarette and they sat there brooding, waiting for her ankle to feel a little better before starting back. It was very quiet. During the heat of the day even the birds subsided. Paul fancied that he could almost make out the distant muffled throb of the army's generators. Or maybe he was imagining that. At this distance it was so subliminal it could have been pure imagination, the sound of grass growing that farmers sometimes claimed to be able to hear.

But then, breaking the stillness sharply, cutting it like a bayonet blade, there was a shout, "Halt or I'll shoot!" And then the short, almost toylike pop of rifle fire.

The funny thing was that the scream that followed, coming from a fair distance, sounded like the scream of a child's game, high, shrill, and intense. Paul nevertheless scrambled to his feet and immediately pulled Hope back into the darkness of the mine shaft. There was nothing ambiguous about rifle fire, and there was something of a relief, even, in not having to invent reasonable explanations for inexplicable behavior any longer. They hid in the tunnel and peered out cautiously. Paul's intention had been only to seek shelter, hide, and wait until the coast was clear. Twenty minutes? Half an hour? He had no idea. It would be a matter of feel. He had not expected to be able to see what they did see— two soldiers carrying a stretcher on which a third man lay. All Paul and Hope could tell at that distance was that the figure on the stretcher was male and civilian. It was not until they heard his agonized screams that Hope exclaimed, "Oh my God! It's Jim Ishida."

The cries continued. Paul was able to make out only phrases that the intermittent breeze carried and then cut off: ". . . born in this country . . . nothing to do with Pearl Harbor . . . as American as you are . . ." And then, after a few more unintelligible exclamations, an improbable, pathetic, desperate rendition, off-key, of "God Bless America."

"What the hell is that all about?" Paul asked, *sotto voce*.

"He was in one of those internment camps in World War Two," Hope explained. "Maybe he thinks he's back there."

"Jesus!"

From their hiding place inside the mouth of the tunnel they saw the stretcher bearers pass. Ishida lay on the stretcher, still singing, more quietly now, almost crooning the anthem. Just behind him, following closely, was the sergeant they had seen this morning. He was pointing an automatic rifle at his helpless prisoner.

"Oh my God!" Hope said.

Paul looked at her, and, without any words, the shock, the concern, the meaning of the exclamation shifted, broadening out from Jim Ishida and extending to the two of them there in the tunnel, and to all of Tarsus.

3:50 P.M., Mountain Daylight Time:

Hope rolled up the left leg of her jeans and gingerly removed her sneaker. She put her foot, ankle deep, into the chilly water of the small mountain stream that came down through the Tarsus cut. Sitting a few feet away from her, leaning against the trunk of a large cottonwood, Paul felt a great sense of triumph. They were, after all that worry—hell, admit it, even fear—safe. There was nothing more plausible than two people sitting beside a mountain stream. It was the kind of thing one expected. Movie directors and screenwriters, not knowing what else to do, put their actors and actresses at the shores of lakes or oceans or streams. And, besides, the business of soaking Hope's ankle to keep down the swelling was a perfectly sensible excuse.

It was a new kind of experience for Paul. He had, of course, seen the movies and read the books, and he had supposed, as everyone supposes, that danger and fear were what those authors described, a series of sharp, vivid incidents nicely counterpointed and strenuously external. What he had not known, what he had been unable to imagine, was this other kind of fear. The fear in which nothing at all happens and in which every moment is an unpunctuated matrix of dreadful possibilities. There was nothing to fight against, nothing to manipulate. Their goal had been simply getting from the mouth of the tunnel to the bank of the stream—a journey of perhaps a hundred and fifty yards. Their progress had not been, after all, all that difficult. Hope's ankle was strained, but she had been able to hobble on it, leaning on Paul. The ankle had not been their main worry at all. What they had waded through was the recollection of the silly, childlike popping noise of those shots, the dreadful sight of Ishida and his terrible raving, and Paul's previous encounters with the soldiers. The clarity of the blue sky, the brightness of the sun, the greenness of the leaves, and the openness of the mountains that ran on to the north from primary to pastel colors were totally inappropriate to this kind of furtive animal fear. And yet this was the way animals lived, scurrying beneath the daytime hawks and the nighttime owls.

"How is the ankle?" Paul asked.

"Not too bad," Hope answered. "The water helps."

"Good. It's not sprained. It couldn't be."

"No, I wouldn't have been able to walk on it. Even this far." And then, without pause, without even turning to face him, she asked, "What are we going to do?"

And that was not really the question, Paul knew. The question was how were they going to do it—and which one of them?

"How far is it?" Paul asked.

"How far is what? After what we just saw," she went on, moving her foot back and forth in the water, "I'm not so sure that it's simply a matter of getting around the bench—the foothill, I mean—to the road. They mean business, and we don't know where they've got their people spotted."

"Then where?" he asked.

"I don't know," she said. "I guess the thing to do would be to go north for about twelve miles, keeping in the mountains away from the roads, away from places where they'd expect somebody to go."

"What's there?" he asked. "I mean, in fifteen miles?"

"The outskirts of Tooele."

"And then what?"

"I don't know," she said, "but you'd be in a town. Not a big town, not a place where you could just lose yourself, but still there'd be a kind of safety there. They can't send squads of soldiers with rifles marching around in the middle of a town shooting at people."

"But what could one do in Tooele?" he asked. "I mean," he went on, "once I got there, whom would I call?"

"Anyone," she said.

Paul picked up a blade of grass and twisted it around his finger. As he thought of telling the story to officials, to newspapermen, to anyone who would listen, it struck him with chilling force that the story would sound utterly fantastic. Who would believe him? There were all kinds of people who called up police stations, newspapers, television stations, to complain that they were being killed by television rays, that there were UFOs in their backyard, that the Russians were poisoning the drinking water . . . They called them, he remembered, fifty-fifties—because they were only half there. The police took down the complaints, said soothing words, and promptly forgot about them. There was no evidence he could bring. There was no way of proving anything.

"Just anyone?" he asked. "You think just anyone would believe me?"

"You're right," she said. "But wait! Dan Tucker, of course! He's an editor on the Salt Lake City *Tribune*. He and my uncle have gone hunting every fall for years, and I've known him ever since I was a child. *He'd* believe me."

"You," Paul said, "but not me."

"Then I'm the one who has to go," she said. "Besides, you're sick, and I know the country."

"What about your ankle?"

"An Ace bandage and high boots," she replied. "That's all it needs."

"No, it's not that easy. Fifteen miles in the mountains? When was the last time you walked fifteen miles, even in New York City?"

"When was the last time you walked fifteen miles?" she countered defiantly.

"Last Wednesday. I'm used to it. I spend a lot of time outdoors. I walk miles on field trips with my students."

"I'm not fragile, Paul," she said.

"You're not bulletproof, either," he replied, speaking softly. Incredibly, bizarrely, it was not a joke.

"And you are?" she asked.

"No, but. . . ." There was nothing to say.

"We could go together," Hope suggested.

"No," he said.

"Don't say no so quickly. We could help each other. With my ankle and your weakness we need each other. We could help each other get through. And we'd double our chances."

"Or cut them in half," Paul said.

"What do you mean?" she asked.

"Let's assume," he said, "that I go alone, and that I don't make it. In four or five days you could try. Your ankle will be stronger by then, and your chances would be better. They can't keep this up indefinitely. It may get better, easier . . ."

And then he realized that this was the wrong tack. She wanted to share in the danger. And thinking of what she wanted to hear, he seized upon the other possibility which seemed frighteningly real.

". . . or it might get worse. And somebody ought to be here. I mean, somebody who's healthy, who's sane. It wants a reliable witness."

She had no answer. Paul pushed his advantage, "You have connections here. Your aunt and your uncle live here. They'd have to believe you. If I do get through, you'll be here to back up what I've said. And if I don't make it, when your chance comes, you'll be a believable witness."

"Well, who would you call?" she asked.

"I'm not sure. I have a friend . . . a doctor in Boston. He'd believe me."

"But what about the Major?" Hope asked. "We've got to show up for our appointment, to ask to use the phone."

"You really think he's going to let us do that?" Paul asked.

"Of course not. But I think it'd be suspicious if we didn't ask, didn't show up. We even have to get a little angry about it, when he refuses."

"I guess you're right," Paul said.

Hope looked at him, smiled with a hint of playfulness

that was just a glimpse of what she would have been like at another place, in another time, and asked, "We don't have to decide anything now, but you won't *mind* if I have them tape my ankle?"

"No," he said, "I won't mind."

He waited for her to work her sneaker back onto her foot and then he helped her up. She leaned on him, but less heavily than before, as they made their way up the cut toward the field hospital and the military tents.

4:10 P.M., Mountain Daylight Time:

It had been messy, but no set of procedures was foolproof. Mrs. Jenkins had convulsed, and the convulsions had been so powerful, so strong, that, weak as she was, she had half-fallen, half-thrown herself out of the bed. Of course, she should have had bed rails. But of the thirty beds in the field hospital only twelve had come equipped with bed rails—military emergency medical procedures were designed more for wounds than for large populations of delirious or convulsed patients.

Mrs. Jenkins, then, had fallen out of the bed, and Martha Pratt, in the next bed, had screamed and had called for help. And they should have come. Right away, someone, someone should have investigated. But there had been calls, cries, screams, mutterings, ravings all night. Even horror, after a while, develops its own routines. The moans and cries, most of them meaningless, had become a part of that routine. The doctors, and the nurses too, had been paying attention to the silent ones, the critical ones, locked in their struggles with death, and crying out in silent ways—with the mercury of the thermometer, the slow labored breathing, the weakening pulse. The audible screams were comparatively unimportant—a part of the pathology, the mental involvement, for which, in the long run, Major Robertson had assured him, the prognosis was good. In an odd way, then, the cries, the screams, the groans, were signs of health.

It had not been until the routine half-hourly check that they had discovered not only Mrs. Jenkins dead on the floor, but Martha, sitting beside her, the head of the dead woman cradled in her lap.

That was bad enough. What broke Lewine up, however, what really got to him, was the knowledge that this woman, sitting on the floor and patting the dead head as if it were a child's, had lost four of her five children in the past twenty-four hours. And, of course, she didn't know this. No one had told her. She was not well enough, not up to hearing such things. Not yet.

But was anyone ever up to hearing such things? Was anyone ever up to witnessing such things as he witnessed now? It had taken the help of two nurses to pull Mrs. Jenkins' corpse from Martha Pratt's clutching maternal grasp. Over and over she had kept calling, "My baby, my baby, give me back my baby, where are my babies?"

They had got her back into bed. He had given her a shot of pentobarbital and had sat down beside the bed to wait with her a while until she drifted off into a drugged sleep.

"It's all right, Martha," he lied. "It's going to be all right." He touched her hand and then reached around and felt her pulse. It was stronger than it had been. Her physical condition was improving. She was—physically at least—over the worst of it. What she had yet to face, no doctor could make easier.

Lewine was startled and even appalled when she spoke to him, not deliriously, not raving, but in a calm —indeed wooden—tone: "She's dead."

"Yes, I'm afraid so," Lewine said. "But she was an old woman, and she'd had a full life." He looked at Martha and watched as she nodded her head, apparently agreeing with him. He was not at all prepared for her next remark:

" 'And as they begin to grow ye shall clear away the branches which bring forth bitter fruit, according to the

163

strength of the good and the size thereof, and ye shall not clear away the bad thereof all at once lest the roots thereof be too strong for the graft, and the graft thereof shall perish and I lose the trees of my vineyard.' "

"What? What did you say?" he asked. It was partly her diction, thick-tongued and mushy. This was perhaps a result of the injection, but it was also a side effect, Major Robertson had warned him, of the disease.

" 'And the bad shall be cast away, yea even out of all the land of my vineyard, for behold only this once will I prune my vineyard. . . .' "

He could not remember where that was from, and was not entirely clear what she was talking about. Again, surprising him, she sat up and with her eyes shining—from the fever? from the excitement?—and with her finger extended (betraying the tremor the medical literature had described) she explained, herself, what she had meant.

"Wickedness! The Lord is stamping out wickedness! Truly there must be much wickedness."

"In Tarsus?" Lewine asked.

He did not want to get into a discussion with her. Certainly he did not want to argue. But she seemed so eager to make herself understood that he felt compelled to make the effort.

"The Gentiles," she said.

And then she returned to her allegorizing, or quoting from whatever it was.

" 'And we will pluck from the trees those branches which are ripened that must perish and cast them into the fire. . . .' "

Lewine had not got past the business about Gentiles. What Jews were there in Tarsus? But, no, that wasn't it. She wasn't blaming the Jews. She was blaming the . . . but of course, she was a Mormon. All non-Mormons were Gentiles.

And, having unraveled that small problem, the larger problem of what she was trying to say suddenly unraveled itself. It was some kind of religious fervor, a classical symptom of paranoia, and there was nothing for him to do but sit there, appear to listen, appear to agree, and extend whatever signs he could of the real sympathy he felt.

She lay back on the bed and continued to talk, but the thickness of her speech, compounded by the drug-induced drowsiness, soon reduced all her utterances to indistinguishable mumbles. He listened, not to what she was saying, but to the slowing rate of her utterances, the breaking up of sentences into phrases and phrases into disjointed words.

He had intended to wait for the blessed remission of silence and until unconsciousness had taken her, but he was interrupted in his vigil by an orderly.

"There are a couple of people in the office, sir."

"People?" he asked. "You mean soldiers?"

"No, sir, civilians. Two of those well ones."

Wearily Lewine got to his feet, glanced down at the nearly sleeping woman, then turned and marched himself out of the main body of the tent and into the screened-off duty office in the corner.

A young woman and Paul Donovan were waiting when Lewine pulled back the heavy curtain that separated the office area from the rest of the tent. Lewine looked immediately at the girl's name tag and recognized her as one of those on the Well List. He recognized Paul Donovan instantly, even without looking at the tag. He had seen Donovan the night before.

"Mr. Donovan! Hello, there. Glad to see you looking a little better."

Donovan thanked him and introduced the young woman, Hope Wilson.

"How do you do?" Lewine said. "It's nice to see some more healthy people here in Tarsus."

"Oh? More?" she asked. "How many of us are there?"

Lewine paused to consider the question, decided that there could be no possible harm in answering it—they'd be seeing one another around town anyway—and said,

"Four, and you make five. Mr. Donovan here is one of our question marks." He turned to Paul and asked, "How have you been feeling today?"

"Well enough, thanks."

Lewine fell back on one of those old bedside manner chestnuts about how pretty nurses always help a man feel better. He was feeling better himself being able to reclassify Donovan and put him on the Well List.

"Now what can I do for you?" he asked.

The girl wanted to know about her aunt and uncle, Mrs. and Mr. James. Lewine told them that he thought they were holding their own, but admitted that nobody knew very much about the disease and its prognosis. To Paul's question about Mrs. Jenkins he was, unfortunately, able to give a straight answer. "I'm sorry," he said. "She died a little while ago."

"I'm sorry to hear that," Donovan said. "She was a kindly woman."

"She was getting on. And she wasn't quite strong enough to fight it," Lewine replied. It wasn't much consolation, but he didn't have much consolation to offer.

"You have no idea what it is?" Donovan asked.

"Not a clue," Lewine replied. "It's a virus of some kind, but there are hundreds of viruses. And it takes a long time to narrow it down to the right one. We've got the labs working around the clock. And we hope to have an answer any time now. But in the meantime, all we can do is try to treat the symptoms and wait." He looked at Donovan and then at the Wilson girl. They seemed to be swallowing it all right.

"Is there anything else?" he asked.

"Yes," Donovan answered. "We were taking a walk, and Miss Wilson twisted her ankle."

"It seems awfully trivial," Hope said, "what with everything else you've got to deal with. But it is uncomfortable. And if you could tape it for me . . ."

"I'd be delighted," Lewine said.

And he was not exaggerating. To be able to deal with a manageable medical problem was something of a relief. He was a little surprised to realize that he would actually have welcomed a broken arm, a simple appendectomy, or, best of all, a nice, normal delivery.

He crossed the room to the steel trolley table and picked up a roll of wide adhesive tape and a pair of scissors. He turned back to the young woman, smiled, and apologized, "This is a fairly impromptu arrangement, but I think we can work out something. If you'll sit on the edge of the desk and let me have that chair, it ought to work out right."

Donovan helped her to the desk. Lewine examined the ankle, turning and probing to be sure no major damage had been done. Then he taped it, deftly and efficiently.

"Thank you," Hope said, when he was done. "That feels much better."

"Dr. Lewine?" Donovan said. "May I ask you a question?"

"By all means."

"If we're so contagious that we've got to be quarantined, how is it that all of you military people have taken off those protective suits you were wearing when I saw you last night?"

It was just like one of those cigarette commercials that Lewine remembered seeing, not recently but a few years back. There had been an assortment of strange types observing that the first puff was all right but the second puff was like straw. The illusion of normal life as a doctor, the taping of an ankle, and the relaxing, afterward, with a cigarette. . . . It was all shattered now. In an instant that doctor-patient relationship was gone. They were adversaries. Not even his adversaries, but Major Robertson's. Or the army's.

He took another puff of the cigarette, not for the cigarette but for the time in which to remember what the official line was. "A good question," he said, still stalling, and trying also to maintain a continuity of tone and mood. "We have a new vaccine. It's still experimental, but for an emergency like this, we decided to try it. It protects against a whole range of viruses. If there'd been more tests on it so that we knew more about side effects, we'd have given it to you people . . . the two of you, and the four others, who haven't been hit by the disease."

"Who are the others?" Hope asked intently.

"Let me see," Lewine said. He leaned toward his desk and reached for a manila folder. He riffled through the papers, found the list, and read off the names: "Mrs. Ryle, Carl Jaspers, James Ishida, and Charles Pierce."

"And that's all?" Hope asked. "Out of the whole town?"

"That's it, I'm afraid."

"How long will the quarantine last?" Donovan asked. "Have you any idea?"

"No. That will depend on the lab results. Once we've isolated the virus and know what it is, we'll know how to protect against it. You can understand that we don't want to let this thing loose on the whole state. The whole country."

"But Hope here isn't sick. Hasn't been sick," Paul persisted.

"If we knew what the incubation period was, then we could be sure of that, couldn't we?"

He had done it rather well, he thought. It all sounded fairly plausible—except, of course, for that business of that universal virus immunization. That was sheer Ray Bradbury. But, as Deap had assured them, most people know nothing at all about biology and medicine.

That was the thought in Lewine's mind—he was to think of it later as a kind of reverse ESP, or, less fancifully, as a hunch, an emotional awareness of something that was awry—when Paul said, "If you don't mind, there are one or two things that still puzzle me. As a biology teacher, I'm curious about something you said a moment ago. . . ."

Lewine was no longer paying attention. He didn't have to. He knew perfectly well what the question would be. A biology teacher, for God's sake! He sat there, waiting for Paul to finish his sentence, not knowing what he would say in answer, not having the faintest idea of what attitude to strike. But then he was saved by the wonderful, improbable appearance of an orderly's head through the curtain.

"Excuse me, Captain," the man said, "but the Major would like to see you."

Hope eased herself off the desk, favoring her sore ankle. "We'd better go," she said.

But then Major Robertson's head appeared in the opening of the curtain. "Oh, there you are," the major said, looking from Hope to Paul and back to Hope again. "I'll be with you in just a moment." And then, to Lewine, he said, "Norm?" and, with a slight motion of his head, beckoned.

Lewine left the office area. He and Robertson moved away a few steps after closing the curtain.

"What's up?" Lewine asked.

"I am. They just woke me. How is our surgical patient?"

"No sweat," Lewine said. "Those boys are certainly crack shots. Or lucky. It could have been a mess. But it was just a flesh wound."

Robertson inclined his head slightly toward the office area behind the curtain. "What do they want?" he asked.

"Them? She twisted her ankle. She wanted it taped."

"Twisted her ankle? Where?"

"Between the foot and the shin," Lewine answered.

"Oh for Christ's sake! I meant where in town did she twist her ankle. Where was she?"

"I don't know," Lewine said. He tried to keep the irritation he felt out of his voice. "I guess they went for a walk. Yeah, that must have been it. She said she'd soaked it in the stream."

At first Lewine had taken all this suspiciousness as a harmless piece of army absurdity, but now it was increasingly irksome. So was the business of telling lies, spouting obvious nonsense to people who turned out to be biology teachers. He did not like playing detective, either. They were doctors, not cops. Or, anyway, he was.

"Okay," Robertson said. "Now, fill me in. What's happened in the last six hours?"

Lewine told him what had been happening. The death count was now fifteen. . . .

He turned, intending to point out specific cases to Robertson, but as he did so, he noticed, through the slight opening in the curtain, that the girl had moved from the desk to the steel trolley table. Still talking to Robertson, giving him a rundown of the cases on the critical list, he observed with a kind of disinterested fascination as the girl's hand picked up an object from the table. Apparently—he wasn't quite sure of this, couldn't quite see—she tucked whatever it was into her hip pocket.

He finished the rundown. "I have the papers in the office."

"No, that's all right. I'll see them later on. Let me get these two out of my hair."

Lewine followed the major back into the office. He had no idea what to expect. He supposed that it would be some kind of inquisition about why they had been walking near the stream. Or had the major noticed her taking whatever it was? He didn't think so, but . . .

"I understand you wanted to see me," Robertson began.

Hope was in the chair near the desk. Paul was lounging against the side of the desk, half sitting, half leaning against it.

The major sat down behind the desk. Lewine went over to stand near the steel trolley table. He listened as Hope explained to the major that she wanted to call her aunt's chest specialist in Salt Lake City. He had not noticed it before—he had not been looking for it before —but he realized that she was turning on a kind of actresslike charm. The smile, the inflections, the attitude of the body, the whole thing. . . .

But it did not work. Robertson was coolly affable, entirely amiable but entirely impervious. He made up some cock-and-bull story about wavelength priorities on the military radio telephones, shared time with other military installations, and all manner of barely plausible invention. And then, surprising Lewine a little, Robertson promised that during the night the call would go through. He wrote down the name and phone number of the doctor in Salt Lake City.

While they were talking, Lewine had been staring at the service table. It was like a child's game where you had to remember and write down as many items as possible after only a brief glimpse. But this game, this trying to remember only one object that had been removed, was more difficult. If only he were not so tired, so groggy. If only he had . . .

And then he remembered. Of course! There was a physician's sample card of Dexedrine. He glanced at Hope and, by moving a half step to the left, was able to see through the upright slats of the back of her chair, the outline of the card in her hip pocket. Yes, it was the Dexedrine. But why? She didn't look like one of those people who used amphetamines for fun. It made no sense.

"When was it that you hurt your ankle, Miss Wilson?" the major was asking.

"Oh, about an hour ago, I guess," she answered. "We'd gone for a walk to get away from all this for a little while."

"Good idea," Robertson said. "I wish I could do that myself. Was there . . . anything unusual that you noticed?"

The major turned suddenly and fixed Paul with a basilisk stare.

"Unusual?" Paul asked. "What do you mean?"

"Unusual. Out of the ordinary," Robertson said, pushing hard.

"You remember, Paul," Hope volunteered. "The scream. We heard a scream, or what sounded like one. Paul wanted to go and investigate," she said to the ma-

171

jor, "but he didn't want to leave me with my ankle."

Lewine realized that he should have made the connection himself. Of course, they would have both happened at about the same time. Why hadn't he thought of that? But then, why should he have thought of it?

"What was it?" Paul asked. "What happened?"

"That's what I wanted to explain to you," Robertson said, leaning forward in his chair. "We don't know yet just what this disease is. But I'm afraid we're finding out some unpleasant things about it. It seems that there are certain kinds of mental involvement, a result of the high fever, perhaps."

"What do you mean?" Paul asked.

"Well, to be blunt about it, people—some people anyway—seem to go a little psychotic. Delusionary. Paranoid. It may go away after a time, after the effects of the fever have passed. But of course we don't know that, yet, either. The scream you heard was that of a man who imagined he was being pursued by rats the size of dogs. They were so real to him that he got out of bed and ran."

"That's terrible," Hope said softly.

"I'm afraid it's not pleasant," Robertson agreed.

He stood up to terminate the interview, smiled, and waited as Paul and Hope thanked him, thanked Lewine, and then left the tent. Lewine sat down in the chair that Hope had vacated, and the major sat down behind the desk.

"You think they bought it?" Robertson asked.

"Bought what?" Lewine asked. "Bought which? The phone story sounded all right. But what will you tell them tomorrow?"

"It's August," Robertson replied. "The doctor is on vacation."

"Okay. Neat enough. But what was that business with the rats the size of dogs? Was there a point to that?"

"I wanted to find out whether they were just walking the way they said they were—in which case they would have admitted hearing that scream, as they did. Or whether they were up to something. If they had been, they would have denied hearing it. You think?"

"I don't know," Lewine said. "Maybe."

"And then I wanted to let them know about the mental part of it. There's no reason we can't use that. They're going to find out soon enough anyway. And in the meantime, it gives us one more weapon. They won't be able to trust anyone's judgment but ours. Not even their own."

The major leaned back in the chair. "Clever?" he asked, like a little boy who has brought home a good report card.

"Oh, yes. Very."

"Not that we need it. I mean, hell, it looks as if they're just going to screw their way through the whole business. Christ knows, I would. Now, what about the reports?"

Lewine handed him the folder.

"See you at dinner then," Robertson said, and left.

Lewine moved around and sat down in the chair behind the desk. He considered what he had done, or, really, not done. Had the major not been there, he might have said something to Hope, asking her what she was doing, why she wanted the pills. But the distasteful business of having to lie and of getting caught, and then having to listen to Robertson's shameless performance, had kept him from bringing it up. For that matter, he supposed he could have mentioned to Robertson that he had seen Hope take the pills. But Bill's deviousness, and his pride in his deviousness, had been so distasteful that Lewine had not wanted to tell him anything. Robertson would have leapt to all kinds of wild conclusions.

But why the hell *did* she want the pills? He promised himself he would ask her in the morning.

6:30 P.M., Eastern Daylight Time:

"Well, at least we agree this far," Colonel English said, tracing around and around a small circle with his forefinger on the corner of General Eastlake's desk. "What we need is time to operate, to keep as many options open as we can."

"All right," the general answered. "That far, yes."

"And the Public Health people have got to get off our backs. We've got enough to worry about without listening to Maxwell's nagging and his threats. . . ."

"What are you going to do? Shoot him?"

English looked at the general. He was used to this kind of joking—from generals, from secretaries, and even from presidents. It was their way of putting a little emotional distance between themselves and the unpleasant realities that the Defense Intelligence Agency so frequently had to face and to handle. And, yes, Eastlake was smiling. English returned the smile.

"Nothing quite so dramatic. But I think we can get to him."

"Do you? I'm not sure I want to do it that way," Eastlake said.

"What way, sir?"

"Blackmail."

"Blackmail? Good heavens!" He rolled his eyes upward. Eastlake laughed. Now, perhaps, he would listen for a few minutes.

"Maxwell is a doctor, but even more than that, Maxwell is an administrator. He's a bureaucrat! We can get to him by holding out the prospect of the one thing that any bureaucrat wants—more power."

"Go on."

"What might work is some suggestion that if he cooperates with us in this business, we'd back the idea of reorganizing the Armed Forces Epidemiological Board so that it came under Public Health."

"What?" Eastlake asked. "What are you talking about? That makes no sense!"

"Doesn't it? He'd have a chance—or he'd think he had a chance—at getting Detrick and Pine Bluff and the rest of it under his wing. More money, more doctors, more things to administer. . . ."

"That's giving an awful lot, isn't it?"

"If we give it, it's a lot."

"Would he believe it? Would he trust us?"

"I think he might. And I think he'd be right to trust us. If it goes bad . . . if it all blows up, then we'll have to do something dramatic. The President might transfer the whole program to Public Health—for appearance's sake, at least. It's a possibility."

"But that'd be disastrous!"

"Not if Public Health cooperates with us. It's a perfectly good front."

"And would they cooperate?"

"They'd have been cooperating already. They'd have been our partners in the Tarsus business! That's the beauty of it! It's a nice little whipsaw! We could dump it all, and still keep it."

"Maybe," Eastlake said. "Maybe. . . . It's tricky though. A certain degree of tact . . ."

"A great deal of tact. I thought we'd get Dr. Rebikoff to feel him out a little."

"Who's Rebikoff?"

"One of our psychiatrists. An old buddy of Maxwell's from medical school. A friend. . . . It'd all have to be informal and friendly."

"The friendlier the better," Eastlake agreed.

"I think it's worth a feeler."

"All right."

"If we blow this one, we'll need any help we can get to salvage what we can," English said.

"I agree. You'll let me know what he says?"

"We'll hear what he says at the next meeting. He might come on a little cooler, a little calmer. . . ."

"I hope so," the general said. "I do hope so."

"I'll go start Rebikoff then."

4:40 P.M., Mountain Daylight Time:

They had walked back to Hope's place together. Her ankle, now that it was taped, had given her much less trouble. Still, Paul had slowed his pace, forced himself to amble in order to accommodate her and, as he had realized, it had been a good thing indeed. The temptation to run had been all but irresistible. It was the feeling he had supposed that bank robbers, pickpockets, and other such types must feel, the urge to run like hell. Had they done so, those all-seeing eyes which he had imagined boring into his back, between the shoulder blades, would have had the final confirmation that they wanted.

When they were inside, after Hope had closed and locked the door, they were at last able to give expression to the feelings that had been seething under pressure all that time. Hope threw herself into a chair and slumped in a kind of silent sulking fury. Paul's rage was more outgoing. He paced the living room like a caged animal, whacking his palm over and over with a rolled magazine, punctuating his repeated, "Stupid! Stupid! Stupid! Shit!"

"You mean Major Robertson?" she asked.

"Him. Lewine. And me, too," Paul replied. "Mostly me. What a flaming ass I was."

"I'm not sure I agree," Hope countered. "I thought we carried it off pretty well."

"Oh, you were splendid. You were absolutely first-rate. That business at the end when Robertson was trying to test us and he asked whether we had heard anything. I just blanked. The clever bastard! But you were fine."

"And when were you not fine?" Hope asked.

"Before," he said, "before the Major came in. When we were talking to that ass Lewine. I had to go and shoot off my mouth. I had to tell him that I was a biology teacher."

"Well," Hope began, "you—"

"I was stupid! I was taking him seriously, I was behaving as if it were a real conversation, with real subjects and truth . . . that old stuff."

"You don't expect a doctor to lie to you," Hope said.

"No, you don't."

He stopped pacing, turned, and stood before her. Rolling the magazine now from palm to palm, as if in some surrealist way he were trying to unscrew it, he said, "That's the worst part of it. Those people come in here presumably to help us, and they're doctors. For them to be lying, for them to be shooting, for them to be holding us here as prisoners, to be our jailers . . . it's a goddamn outrage!"

"But why?" Hope asked. "Why are they doing this?"

"I wish I knew," Paul said. He tossed the magazine into a corner of the sofa and himself into the opposite corner. He sat there for a few moments, rubbing his chin and scowling, thinking. And then, moving his hand from his chin up to run through his black hair, he began to think aloud:

"We're cut off here. Nobody can leave. Nobody knows about us—nothing on radio or television. Ishida was healthy, was on Lewine's list as one of the well ones. So he couldn't have been paranoid or have had any of those mental problems. He must have been just trying to get out. And they shot him. They're not protecting themselves any more. . . . That universal virus immunization is crap. Just plain crap. If there were such a thing, they'd be able to prevent anything from the common cold to cancer. So they have to know what it is."

"Then why wouldn't they tell us?" she asked. "What disease would they want to keep secret?"

"One of theirs."

"One of theirs?"

"It has to be. It had crossed my mind before. . . . But I had rejected it. I mean, unless the President was lying to us, or something like that, they'd discontinued all those germ warfare tests. So it couldn't be Dugway. Or that's what I'd thought at first. But it *has* to be Dugway! Nothing else makes any sense. Why would they bring in a field hospital instead of just evacuating us to real hospitals? That's why my truck and the phones . . ."

"They're still doing those tests?"

"They've got to be! Maybe the President doesn't even know. Or maybe they're defensive tests. They still do defensive research, I think. I mean, the place is still there, they're still working. They're doing something!"

They sat there for a moment, not so much thinking as trying to summon up some emotional adjustment to what their intellects had already settled. It was a difficult leap to make. Paul found himself casting back over the past few years for any evidence that such a thing was even possible. And surprisingly, there was plenty. He remembered how, when the Air Force had lost those H-bombs off the coast of Spain, they had denied it for weeks. And of course there was the business about those thousands of sheep right here in Skull Valley. It had taken eight months before they had admitted that their nerve gas had been at fault. He remembered something about the United States government denying that chemical and biological weapons were being stockpiled in Germany. And then the Germans had admitted that those things were there a week or two later. And he remembered, too, the duplicity of the Department of Health, Education, and Welfare over the business of animal deformities and human sickness in Globe, Arizona, after the government had sprayed nearby Tonto National Forest with 2, 4, 5-T—one of the defoliants the army uses in Vietnam. Yes, it was possible all right, but, still, who would believe it?

And that was the immediate question facing him now.

And Hope, too. Whatever her thoughts had been, she had arrived at the same place now.

"Do we go together or separately?" she asked.

"I think our chances are better separately," he said. "Me tonight and you . . . Wait here two days, maybe three. If I don't get through, then you can try."

She moved in her chair, reached into the back pocket of her jeans, and pulled out the card with the six capsules encased in plastic bubbles. "I thought these would come in handy . . . whichever one of us went. I took them off the table in the office when Lewine went out to talk to the Major."

"They might be useful," Paul said.

"Except that . . . well, now I'm worried. What if he notices that they're gone?"

"With any luck, by the time he does notice, I'll be gone. Anyway, it's too late to worry about that. We've got enough to think about."

He summoned up a reassuring smile. She handed him the capsules.

8:40 P.M., Mountain Daylight Time:

Jackson did not want to play poker. The other guys in the old schoolhouse that they were using as a barracks had had the game going for a couple of hours, and it looked as though it would go on for a good while longer. Maybe as long as they stayed in Tarsus. There would be people dropping out to go on duty, but there would be others to take the vacant places. It was a way of keeping their minds off the green body bags and the boringness of the detail. A funny combination, that. Death was okay. It was part of a soldier's life. And boringness was a part of the army—maybe the main part. But death and boredom together were creepy. So they were playing cards. For more money than they could afford. And that was okay with Jackson. The thing to watch for, in another day or so, if the game kept on that long, would be the cheating, or the accusations of cheating, and then the fights. He'd have to cool the fighting before anyone got hurt. A thing like that looked bad on your record. You didn't want to lose your stripes because of a goddamn card game. Or lose the cushy assignment out here. . . .

Jackson lay on his cot, listening to the sounds of the game, the checks, the raises, the calls, the folds. . . . He liked the sound of it, the nervous rhythm of the calls. But he was in no shape to play poker, not this evening. He wasn't a kid any more, and money was money. These games could be expensive when you weren't paying attention, when you weren't concentrating, and he knew he was in no shape to concentrate. Not after that grave digging detail. It would have been less bad, somehow, if the grave had been for people. He could have stood that. What the hell, he was a pro. He was in for the twenty-year haul, and he was a pro. It was a matter of pride with him to be able to kill, dig a grave, risk his own life. . . . Any of the things that soldiers did. But this had got to him. It really had.

He lay on his bunk and, without seeming to move, eased the bottle from the ditty bag into his trousers. The advantage in being a sergeant was that they left you alone. Even on inspections, they'd take your word on your gear. So you could stow a pint of whiskey in case of need. . . . And he needed it, yessir! But he had to get the bottle from the ditty bag and get it out of the barracks without any of the others seeing him. A pint was no help to anyone if you had to share it around with six other guys. No help at all.

He got the bottle into his pants, and then got to his feet. Then it was easy. He just walked out as if he were going to take a leak, but walked on by the latrine and into the darkening scrub. Hoo-boy!

He unscrewed the cap from the traveler's-flask bottle and took a pull at the whiskey. He wasn't interested in getting drunk. All he wanted to do was to take the edge off a little, so that he could sleep. In the morning, he'd be okay. And then there'd be nothing to worry about.

It couldn't happen again, anyway. There were no dogs left in Tarsus.

9:00 P.M., Mountain Daylight Time:

The ham and red-eye gravy lay in Paul's stomach—or, no, it didn't just lie there, but flopped, contorted, changing itself whimsically, becoming at one moment a dumbbell, then a bookend, a heavy ashtray, and then a bocce ball, in which configuration it evidently found some satisfaction, for it remained there in that guise. Paul took a kind of masochistic interest in its progress as it wandered around the interior of his stomach, looking for an exit.

He had forced himself to eat it—to eat it all. The ham, and that terrible gravy, the mashed sweet potatoes, the lima beans, the salad, and two glasses of milk from the pitcher on the plain board table in the mess tent. He had not been able to get down the canned peaches and had not wanted to risk trying. By the end of the meal he had begun to recognize that each additional mouthful was risking all those that had so painfully gone before. He could lose it all. He had forced himself to eat partly because he knew it might be a good while before he had another meal of any kind. And then, too, he had been eager to demonstrate to Hope that his health was returning.

It had been an altogether absurd meal. Hope and Paul, off by themselves at the far end of one of the long tables, had been preposterously flirtatious. They had decided to extend her momentary charade of the afternoon and pretend to the foolishness of lovers, in the hope of gaining through that pretense a kind of invisibility. So they had whispered and laughed, made up private jokes, and indeed had all but convinced themselves. Paul, at least, had found the charade sufficiently distracting so that he was able to shake for a while the childish obsession that the officers in the tent could divine his thoughts, could look into his head and actually read the checklist—flashlight, canteen, knife, compass, radio, and, at Hope's insistence, her uncle's .38 Smith and Wesson special. The nervousness he had felt—and that Hope, no doubt, had shared—had enabled them to act out the parts they had written for themselves more or less convincingly. And having something to do, a pretense to maintain, had made it easier to get the food from the plate into his belly.

But now, lying on top of the bed in the guest room at Hope's place, trying to get an hour or two of comfortable sleep before setting out, he found that the excitement, the intensity of their mood at dinner, was still with him. It was hard to let go, to relax, to drop off. Of course, the weight in his stomach—it had turned now to a flatiron—was no help. And finally, beyond it all, was the prospect before him, which he was so strenuously trying to avoid brooding about. The thing was to fall into a deep, mindless sleep and then get up, and, at peak efficiency, go out there and just do it. Walk up the cut into the mountains and disappear.

Ishida had been crazy to try it in broad daylight, and blatantly down the center of town. Or maybe Ishida had simply failed to understand what he was up against, underestimating it—or in some wild way overestimating it, turning it into the internment camp of his childhood, so that he acted out of the kind of utter desperation that makes one function even without any prospect of success. For Paul the thing would be to succeed, to get out, to get through.

And be believed. That would be the hard part. Not that Arnie would dismiss out of hand anything that he, Paul, had to say. But who could he reasonably expect to accept the whole thing? Would even Marian have believed him? Yes, of course she would. But who else, who else in the whole world? The fact that there was now another piece that had fallen into place in the puzzle was less reassuring than it should have been. He suspected it was too neat, too easy. It was only in mystery stories that these clues presented themselves, two to a chapter, until at the end, in a British drawing room, the detective put it all together and pointed his long, elegantly manicured finger at the butler. But still, it had taken great restraint on his part not to react to the information that Mrs. Ryle had volunteered, coming over to their end of the table to ask Hope about her aunt and uncle. Hope had been drinking coffee and Paul had been toying with his second glass of milk, trying to get it down, when Mrs. Ryle had come up to them to blather commiseration, distress, puzzlement, hope, faith, amazement, gratitude . . . she tried on attitudes the way other women tried on hats. But she had left them with the great, gaudy, feather of fact. She had been away from Tarsus, shopping in Salt Lake City last Friday. And, blather blather, car trouble, blather blather, a ride home with Charlie Pierce, the trucker who had just come back from a haul to Cheyenne. It had clicked into place instantly. He had been out in the desert looking at lizards. And Hope—where had she been?

On their way back from the mess hall he had asked her, and she had told him about her ride on Friday, how she had had to kill the snake, and had had to hurry to get back for dinner.

It made sense. It made overwhelming sense, and Paul, trained as he was as a scientist, found himself dragging his heels, challenging, testing the hypothesis the way a suspicious tradesman used to bite coins. What kind of disease strikes an entire town in an hour's time? Even the Black Death had taken months to spread its infection, and it had not affected everyone. Yet the only ones unaffected here had all been out of town on Friday. It had to be, then, some kind of test, some experiment at Dugway, that had gone wrong and struck Tarsus directly.

The weight in his stomach had assumed the shape of

a bomb. He loosened his belt and shifted his position on the bed from flat on his back to a kind of fetal crouch and felt the pressure ease slightly.

The trouble was, you couldn't force yourself to sleep. You couldn't try. He looked at his watch and saw that it was a quarter past nine. Another hour or hour and a half and he would start. Already the twilight—artificially extended by daylight saving time—was rapidly dwindling. He had figured out—and Hope had agreed with him—that the best time to make his move would be between ten and eleven at night. It would be dark then, but there would still be some bustle among the soldiers, playing cards, relaxing, wandering from their barracks in the old schoolhouse to Smith's and back again. The very improbability of the hour weighed greatly in his favor. Who would go out to climb the mountain late at night? Not he, certainly, but he could go on up the cut and into the foothills. If he took it very slowly and very carefully, he could get far enough from the natural perimeter of the town so that at first light he could have a great head start, and would not risk being spotted trying to make his break then. At three or four in the morning it would be too quiet. Soldiers on guard duty would be suspicious then of any sound whatever. The price—a night on the ground—seemed cheap for the strategic advantage he would gain from it.

Paul felt quite good about the choice of when to make the move. And, actually, he felt rather hopeful about his chances. It was not just the ingeniousness of the choice of time, but the fact that they had got from the mouth of the tunnel back to the center of town, had got through that interview with Lewine and then with Robertson, without being challenged, and . . . the very fact that no one had, after all, been able to look into his head and see what he was thinking seemed in some primitive way reassuring.

He remembered the mess tent again, and the great wave of nausea when he had seen Lewine come in for dinner. Hope had leaned forward to ask him what the matter was, and he had whispered that Lewine was here. She had not looked around, and from her restraint, Paul had taken his cue. He had just sat there, feeling his stomach tighten, compressing all of that chewed food into this lump that had been bothering him ever since. In the event, Lewine had not drawn his sidearm, shouted orders, or, indeed, even taken much notice of them. He had not even ignored them, but had smiled and nodded before getting his food and sitting down with some other officers.

Hope and Paul had taken advantage of the fact that Lewine was eating to go for their medical checkup. They had avoided having to see Lewine again and face an extension of that delicate and risky interview of the afternoon. The medical check over, they had gone their separate ways. Hope had returned to her aunt and uncle's house while he had gone back to Mrs. Jenkins' house to change from sneakers to boots, to pick up his compass and his knife, and to put on his light V-necked lamb's-wool sweater underneath his shirt where it wouldn't be noticed in the still warm evening. He had puzzled over the problem of his safari jacket, which was waterproof and wonderfully fitted with pockets, and he had solved that by stuffing it in a paper bag and putting a six-pack of 3.2 beer over it. As it had turned out, he had not been challenged when he had gone strolling lazily up the road to Hope's house, but had anyone stopped him, the beer would have been almost a passport.

They had spent nearly an hour preparing for the venture. At the kitchen table, drinking the coffee she had made—a considerable improvement over the army's brew—they had gone over the topographical map and had filled the outsize pockets of his safari jacket with chocolate bars, dried fruit, bologna, and a hunk of hard cheddar. Then, at the last, she had brought out her uncle's gun, an ugly blue metal object that stained their manufactured mood of skylarking excursion. Up until then it had almost been fun, at least for a while. Hope had put the gun down on the kitchen table next to the small transistor radio, the card of amphetamines, and the bottle of aspirin he had brought from Mrs. Jenkins' house—and suddenly the fun had ended.

Hope had suggested that he should lie down and try to sleep, and he had agreed and had followed her to the guest room. He had sat down to unlace his boots while she had removed the bedspread and got an afghan from the cedar chest in the corner.

Remembering it now, remembering the way she looked when she had spread the afghan out for him, he felt a stirring of desire. But then, while the idea had crossed his mind, it had been merely an idea.

Perhaps if she had waited until later to bring out the gun with its faint whiff of gun oil, the smell of death clear and pure, something would have come of their being together in a bedroom, of their intimacy as conspirators, of their natural liking for each other. Now, after three-quarters of an hour of restless rest, he had begun to have regrets and to devise erotic scenarios. He could have got up from the chair and gone over to the bed while she was fluffing up the pillow. Even now, he realized that it would be possible for him to get up, to go back to the kitchen or the living room—or wherever she was—take her in his arms and . . .

But no such thing had happened or would happen. She had turned down the corner of the afghan and he had got up from the chair, walked the four steps to the bed beside which she still stood, and, without deliberation, without knowing quite what he was doing or what he intended, he had taken both her hands in his.

They had stood like that for a long time, not speaking, not even looking into each other's eyes but with their faces downcast, holding hands, tightly. Paul remembered that he had looked at the pillow and then raised his eyes to look at her. She had returned his gentle searching stare . . . but it had seemed too sad, too unutterably sad. And desperate. They had dropped hands.

186

"You'll need the sleep," she had said.

"Yes."

And then, before she had gone to turn off the light and close the door, leaving him to this fretful tossing, she had raised herself on tiptoes and kissed him, ever so lightly. It had been a nice expression of the possibility of the moment, a possibility that they had both seen and had declined for now.

And for his part, Paul was not dissatisfied. It would be an incentive, it would be something to come back to. The thought was pleasant enough to take his mind off that maverick lump in his stomach, off the incipient headache that had been with him now for two days, even off the perilous project before him. Indeed, off everything, for he drifted into a light slumber.

At any rate, it seemed only a moment later that Hope had returned and was standing over him beside the bed, a large mug of steaming coffee in her hand. Paul glanced at his watch. It was ten-fifteen. He raised himself on one elbow, took the coffee and sipped it.

"How do you feel?" she asked.

"All right. A little fuzzy, but not bad. What have you been doing?" he asked.

"Watching television. 'Tuesday Night at the Movies.' They're showing *Dr. No.* When I first saw it years ago, I thought it was terribly funny. It wasn't so funny tonight."

"Don't worry. There won't be any martinis and blondes in the mountains to distract me. And I don't have a script. I have no idea how it's going to come out. I don't even have a stunt man to do the hard parts."

He finished lacing his boots and tucked his shirt back into the back of his trousers. He picked up the sweater and put that on—over the shirt this time. And then he followed Hope to the kitchen for his jacket and the gear. He put the radio into one large flap pocket and stuck the gun into his belt.

"Well, that's it. I'm ready, I guess."

"This is . . . crazy," she said. "People—I mean real

people—don't do this kind of thing. It happens on television."

"I know," he said. "Sure it's crazy. But we're not the ones who are crazy. They are."

"The back door, this time?" she asked.

"Yes."

She went with him to the back door. They stared at each other.

"Luck," she said, forcing a smile.

"You, too," he said. "Take care of yourself." He turned as if to go, then caught himself, turned back to her, reached out his arms, and enfolded her in a rough embrace. He kissed her and she returned the kiss, pressing herself against him with the strength of defiance. Finally he released her and wordlessly turned away. He opened the door and stepped out into the darkness of a mild moonless night.

Paul crossed the back yard. He was able to make out, but only barely from the glow the house gave off, the darker shadow of an outdoor barbecue pit, that marked the end of the mowed, tended area, beyond which was higher scrub grass and occasional low bushes. Paul halted beside one of the bushes and waited for several minutes, allowing his eyes time to accustom themselves to the darkness. There was no moonlight, but there was a faint starshine, and after a while Paul was able to distinguish differences in the texture and intensity of the blackness. He did not look back. He did not want to contract his dilated pupils. He turned toward his right and set off into the thicker brush.

His progress was very slow, but then he felt no need at all to hurry. The object was to continue to advance steadily but above all silently. Each footstep was an experience with a shape—the tentative putting forward of the foot, the careful, slow exploration with the raised foot for purchase, the relaxation, and the final shifting of weight. He made it into a ritual. He did not want to get slovenly or careless; he did not want to make noise that would attract whatever sentry or sentries were posted. And the flashlight, of course, was out.

With this dreamlike, painstaking patience, he made his way up the cut behind the houses on the side of the road across from Smith's general store. It was very quiet. He could hear, even at this distance, occasional wisps of conversation floating out over the night to lose themselves in the thin mountain air. He checked his watch and the glowing dial told him that he had been going for twenty minutes. Walking in daylight on the road to the center of town, he could have covered the same distance in three. He was not discouraged, however; he felt on the contrary a great sense of confidence and even a touch of exhilaration and mastery.

He continued, concentrating on putting one foot in front of the other. He was well past Smith's by now and was skirting the settlement of trailers—now dark and deserted—clustered on their cement-block foundations above Smith's where the road began to narrow. Another hundred yards and it would dwindle into a mule track. He was walking just a shade faster now, but still carefully, still in the rhythm he had established at the beginning. But not with the same attention to each footstep, not with the same feeling of dread at the possibility of a misstep. And of course he made one.

The noise was not so loud as it seemed to him. Standing there, frozen, breathing slowly through his mouth, listening through his pounding heartbeat, he tried to reassure himself. A rabbit, a chipmunk could have made such a noise. Such noises had to be part of the normal night life of the woods. Still, it had sounded to him just slightly less than thunderous. And he stood for four, perhaps five minutes without moving, scarcely even breathing.

Each passing moment, however, brought with it a measure of reassurance. There were no answering noises —no challenges, no other footsteps, no discharge of weapons. He started to move, slowly again, even more slowly than at the beginning. That feeling of exhilaration he would postpone until he was well past the town and up in the mountains far enough to feel safe for the night.

He devised a kind of check for himself, stopping at every fifth step to wait for as long as it took to establish that there were no new noises in the night. It was at the fourth such check that he heard the sound. He thought at first that he had somehow got lost, that he was disoriented. The stream was supposed to be on the other side of the road. And he had not yet crossed the trail into which the road was about to dwindle. But still, the sound of rushing water was unmistakable. Then it stopped. And it was followed by footsteps.

It had been the sentry. One of the sentries, anyway. He had presumably taken a few steps away from his post to pee. Or perhaps he was making rounds and had simply stopped where he was. Paul waited until he could no longer hear the careless footfalls of the sentry through the underbrush. He felt an overwhelming temptation to run, as quickly as he could, up into the mountains and safety. He forced himself to be reasonable, to be intelligent, to wait. And then, as if punishing himself for his impatience, he took one careful step. Then another. And then another wait and a time of listening. There was no sound. There was only the barely discernible rustle of leaves above him in the night breeze.

Twenty minutes later he reached the place where the mule trail turned back upon itself, made its hairpin turn and went south again. Paul continued north. He went north for another twenty minutes. It was only then that he allowed himself to hold the flashlight pointed toward the ground and against his palm. The slope of the mountain was steeper now. The minuscule spill of light was enough to allow him to make his way a foot or two at a time. Then he would flash the light again for an instant and go another foot. It took him perhaps a quarter of an hour before he found what he was looking for—a large boulder with an overhanging dead tree. There was a kind of hollow between the dead tree and the boulder. He crawled into it, reached into his pocket, and, still exercising caution and trying not to make any noise by rustling papers, he allowed himself a piece of chocolate. He had made it this far; he would wait here until dawn.

Wednesday, August 12

Hope had been waiting for them. She had been up since first light, and she had been crouched on the sofa in the living room, peering through the ecru lace curtains, looking for signs of anything unusual, the movement of soldiers, or jeeps, or trucks, or, God forbid, an ambulance or a stretcher party. But she had also been waiting for them, for the emissaries from the field hospital. She had not discussed this with Paul. She had only thought of it after he had gone. But she was convinced, absolutely convinced, that the main function of those twice daily medical checks was simply to run a head count. And they would know soon enough that Paul was gone. There would be some leeway, she assumed, but not much. As it turned out, not much at all—for it was only a little after eight now and here they were, two of them, not quite marching, but not quite walking either, as they approached the front door. She ducked her head down so that the back of the sofa blocked her view—and theirs. She waited for the footsteps on the porch and then, an instant later, the ringing of the doorbell. She remained silent, motionless, forcing herself to wait until they rang a second time. Even then she waited. And then suddenly, she noticed that she was wearing her sneakers.

She had found the negligee, a foolish thing she had picked up in Mexico to cheer herself up, and she had put it on, tying the ribbons carefully at the throat. But the floor had been cold and she had put on the sneakers, too. Now, she had to remove the sneakers, and as she did so she called out, "Coming! Be there in a minute." She kicked off first one and then the other, and then checked in the mirror near the frosted glass side panels of the front door. The negligee looked fine, and the bare feet. But her hair was not right. It was too tidy. Out of habit she had run a comb through it when she had wakened. She messed it, running her fingers through it the wrong way and pulling a strand or two down over her face. She looked again. Fine. She looked like she had just rolled out of bed. And that was exactly the look she was aiming for. She opened the door partially and, through the aperture, greeted the two soldiers.

"Good morning, ma'am," one of them said.

"Morning," she said, faking a yawn.

"Sorry to bother you, ma'am, but it's after eight o'clock. You're supposed to report to the hospital."

"Oh, dear," she said. "Is it that late? I had no idea."

"I'm afraid it is, ma'am."

The other one cleared his throat, stared at his feet, and then said, "No offense, ma'am, but we've been down to Mrs. Jenkins' place to look for Mr. Donovan and he doesn't seem to be there. Don't think he's been there all night, either. Bed wasn't slept in. We were wondering . . . I mean, ah, the Major was wondering whether, er, that is . . ."

"But of course," Hope said, interrupting his stammer, "Mr. Donovan is here with me. He wasn't feeling well last night, and I didn't want to send him home." Coyly, she cast her eyes downward. "I'm afraid he's had a hard night. Would it be all right if we were to come by later? He's sound asleep now, and I'd just hate to wake him."

She smiled again, and now put those wisps of hair back, running her fingers through it as if to tidy it. "Suppose we came down later on in the morning? That'll be all right, wouldn't it? You could explain to the doctors for me?"

"Well, I don't know, ma'am. Our orders were . . ."

"Please," she interrupted, turning her blue eyes on him full force.

"Oh, hell, I guess so. What do you think, Jack?" he asked, turning to the other soldier.

"If you come in in an hour. Say, make it nine o'clock? I think they can hold still until then. Long as we know Mr. Donovan's here."

She blew them a kiss, said, "Thanks ever so much," smiled, and closed the door.

It had been cheap and absurd and silly. But it had worked. She had bought Paul another hour at least.

9:30 A.M., Mountain Daylight Time:

Paul was exhausted. It was not yet the heat of the day, but he was sweating like a pig. But do pigs sweat? No! His breath was labored and seared his lungs. His legs trembled. His headache had returned in full orchestration. He had begun to think of his body as an entity separate from himself, a kind of battered car he had borrowed and had to nurse along a difficult road.

He had been hurrying. Ever since first light he had been trying for distance and speed, counting on the first hours of the morning for his greatest energy and greatest opportunity. Until they discovered he was gone and until they started looking for him, he had to put as much distance between himself and Tarsus as possible. And he had not done badly, he thought. He had been moving steadily, setting himself half-hour goals and stretching those half-hours to forty-five minutes. He had crossed three sizable hills and had skirted one formidable mountain.

On the map, it looked to be about fifteen miles that he had to make due north through the mountains before cutting out to Tooele. Of course, that fifteen miles was a straight line, and in the mountains the cutting back

194

and forth and the progress up and down would at least double that, so he figured it as thirty miles through rough but traversable country. That was plan "A," and it assumed that the army's response to his disappearance would be conventional and limited to roadblocks and helicopters. Of course, he could not count on that. He would have to wait and see what they did. If the search proved to be more comprehensive, then he would not risk Tooele, but go on, cross the Oquirrh range, and head for Salt Lake City itself.

He was resting. He had allotted himself another five-minute break, and he had promised himself that this time he would have some of the chocolate and one of the pills. He had been reluctant to depend on the pills because he knew enough about them to understand that they were not the simple gifts of energy that most people assume. They were borrowings against the future, and the fatigue when the pill wore off would be even more profound than the energy and alertness it provided in the first place. With the touch of the illness that still lingered, more noticeably now after his four hours and a little bit of almost continual exertion, he was afraid that the terms of the loan would be even stiffer. And there were only six pills.

But he had little choice. The trembling of the muscles in his legs was a real problem. It was bad enough on the upgrades, and slowed him down; on the downgrades it was dangerous as he half-walked, half-lurched down these hills, grabbing tree trunks and low-hanging branches to steady himself and brake his rate of descent. He worried about falling, twisting his ankle—hell, even breaking his leg!—which would mean failure. He ate a chocolate bar, chewing carefully and forcing himself to swallow. There was a wave of nausea which subsided slowly. He popped one of the pills from its plastic bubble, put it in his mouth, and washed it down with a long swig from the canteen.

He sat there, checked his watch to see how much longer he could enjoy the luxury of rest, and then, to make use of the time, he took out his compass, took a reading, and established a configuration of the irregular horizon as his target.

He retied the laces of his right boot. They were rawhide and tended to slip. He was doing all right, he thought. If the army's efforts were minimal, if they were as covert and discreet in their search for him as he hoped they would be, then he thought he could make it. He would get up level with Tooele by nightfall and then cut east down into Rush Valley, cross the valley, and enter the town under the cover of night.

He untied the arms of the sweater that he had taken off at his second rest stop, fastened the canteen belt around his waist and retied the arms of the sweater over it. He buttoned his jacket. He had tried leaving it open, but it tended to catch on branches when he went through thick brush. He picked up the dead stick he had found, and, clenching his teeth with the effort, forced himself to his feet. Now that he had committed himself and swallowed the pill, he was impatient for the chemicals to take effect.

He began to walk, continuing to climb over the shoulder of the hill, and found it was not too bad going. He was able to snake his way through the larger bushes and take advantage of occasional open places in the scrubby timber. The nuisance of it was that his right foot was always an inch or two higher than his left and the muscles in his right thigh ached. His right thigh and the left side of his lower back. He had had a stitch there earlier, had decided to ignore it, and had been right. With the continuing exercise it had gone away. He promised himself that as soon as it was possible he would cross a mountain on the other shoulder so that his left foot would be higher.

He had just come through a fairly thick clump of Engelmann spruce, tall, foul-smelling trees, and he was about to enter a clearing of perhaps fifty yards across, when he heard the racket behind him and overhead. He stepped back, crouched at the base of one of the trees, and waited. The racket of the chopper grew louder. No, wait, there were two of them. He looked up through the thick canopy of the spruce foliage. Suddenly, over the crest of the hill, one of them appeared, one of those small, Plexiglas-bubble helicopters, perhaps a hundred and fifty feet above the treetops. It was close enough so that he could make out the white star clearly. It cut back and forth in a zigzag and then moved off to the west. A few moments later the other one came across from the northeast and passed almost directly over the spot at which Paul crouched. Obviously, the two 'copters were working as a team. How many other teams there were, he had no idea. What it meant to Paul was simple and practical. Instead of setting his own pace and his own rest periods he would have to adapt himself to their pattern. He waited until the noise of the second helicopter was fainter and then set out once more. He could not risk crossing the clearing now. He would skirt it. He would have to skirt them all.

12:30 P.M., Eastern Daylight Time:

It was absolutely too Balkan. And, at the same time, it was not Balkan enough. All this intrigue, all this duplicity, all this intricate maneuvering of high statecraft— and what did it work out to be? The same thing you'd tell somebody if you didn't want to go to a dance. You pretended to be sick. Not with this style, maybe, not in an ambulance going down through the middle of Washington, for God's sake, with announcements to the press. But those were just details, after all. And, having the ambulance to ride in, having the whole bit laid on, why not go the rest of the way with it? But, no, they didn't want to have a siren.

Without much hope of success, she turned to her

mother who was riding in the back of the ambulance in the jump seat, and she asked, once more, "Not even for a little while, mother?"

"No," her mother said severely. "They wouldn't use a siren for pneumonia. Not unless you were actually at death's door."

"Well, I'm supposed to be, aren't I?" Diana returned, petulantly.

"That's not necessary," her mother answered, smoothing the skirt of her Pucci shift. "It doesn't pay to overdo things in deceptions of this kind."

From the tone of it, Diana recoiled. It was another one of those damned embroidered sayings her mother was forever passing on to her. My God, what a bore! And yet she recognized that there was a certain sense in it. As she lay there on the ambulance stretcher, sweating in the muggy Washington heat—Jesus, but you'd think they'd air-condition these things—she considered the situation anew.

The main point, of course, was to protect daddy, to provide a cover for him. That's what they'd explained to her earlier that morning. If it got out that she wasn't sick, daddy's position would be compromised. That was the way they'd put it. What they'd meant was that he'd be embarrassed. For that matter, she might be embarrassed herself. After all, what would people think, what would it be more natural for them to think? They'd assume she'd got herself knocked up? No, probably not. And, realizing that, she realized that she felt a little bit disappointed.

It wasn't so much missing the dance at the club Friday night, or even that Jack would have to get someone else to crew for him on Sunday in the regatta—she could have accepted all that. But at least, in exchange, it would be nice to have the feeling that she was a participant, a central figure in the drama—whatever drama it was. She didn't even know. And didn't have to know. She was only a bit player with a walk-on part. And she didn't even get to walk, but was carried like so much

198

luggage. And then, afterward, she would not even be able to share it with her friends at Cathedral.

Well, all right, she could accept even that. But to miss even the minor, momentary fun of the siren! It was just too much!

On the other hand, maybe she could use it.

"The hospital is air-conditioned, isn't it?" Diana asked. "I mean, I'm melting."

"I believe so, dear. And you'll have a lovely room."

"I can't have *any* visitors?" Diana asked, rhetorically. "What am I going to do all day? Television is just lousy in the summer."

"You'll have a chance to get to those books on your summer reading list," her mother answered.

"Yech!"

"I thought we'd agreed that we would not make that sound any more," her mother said. "Really, dear!"

"Yes, mummy," Diana said. "I'm sorry."

She had explained that it wasn't a "sound" but a word from *Mad Magazine.* And what other comment was there to make about the prospect of five days or even a whole week locked away in a room in Walter Reed Hospital with *The House of the Seven Gables, The Education of Henry Adams,* and *The Federalist Papers?*

"At least may I have my records?" she asked.

"Yes, dear. I'll bring them over."

"All of them?"

"Well, no, not all. I'll choose some for you."

"Can I make a list? Can I choose?"

"Very well, dear," her mother said, sighing.

Diana thought for a while. She was not handling it right. The point was to make clear what an imposition this was on her, what a sacrifice this was for her. And she had to do it without being more of a nuisance than usual. It would be sympathy that she had to rely on. It was all such a bore. A perfectly straightforward bargain. But with parents, you had to work all these messy emotional angles.

It had already occurred to her that there was a simpler way. It could be done on a nice straightforward basis of simple blackmail. Her continuing silence about this hospital game in exchange for the coat. But that wouldn't work. Any suggestion of that kind and her parents would get all stuffy and noble, full of principle and bull.

"Do you think I'll get out in time to go and visit Aunt Mary on Nantucket?" she asked, quietly.

"I don't know," her mother said. "We'll see."

"Oh, mother. I've been looking forward to that all summer. I've been tutoring those kids, and . . ."

"I said we'll see," her mother said.

"We'll see means no," Diana said. "You know that."

"What I mean to say," her mother answered, "is that we can try. But it's out of our hands. It depends on your father, and on what the doctors say is believable. But if you can't go to Nantucket, we'll make it up to you some way. We'll take you to Nassau with us for Christmas."

Big deal, Diana thought. All those old, leathery people! And the only two weeks in the year when Washington wasn't absolute Dullsville.

"Nassau's no fun," she began. But then she caught herself and changed her tack. "And besides, that's your vacation. You and Daddy look forward to that every year. You don't want me tagging along."

"Why, Diana, sometimes I think you're actually a very thoughtful girl."

Diana was trying to gauge, trying to judge whether she had accumulated enough suffering points and enough virtue points to try to trade them in now. She was not quite sure, was still hesitating, when her mother provided the perfect opening.

"Don't worry, dear," she said. "We'll make it up to you somehow."

There was no thinking necessary now. It was pure reflex, the result of sixteen years of training in the art of manipulating parents. She broke into a smile, her best little-girl smile, and with the kind of diction her mother was forever encouraging, she struck: "Well, there *is* that coat. . . ."

Her mother sighed (bad), smiled (good), looked at her (suspense), and said, "Well, all right, we'll think about it."

She couldn't push it any further. But then, she didn't have to. Somehow, "We'll see" was negative, but "We'll think about it" was not. And the funny thing was that after all those years, her mother still hadn't figured that out.

She settled back on the stretcher. She would have to try to be a good girl now and not complain *too* much during the next few days. A little bit, of course, just enough to keep the extent of her sacrifice clear in her parents' minds. But not so much as to be a pain.

The ambulance swayed as it pulled off Embassy Row into the Walter Reed Army Hospital gate. A few minutes later, two orderlies were wheeling Diana Colebrooke, a perfectly healthy and perfectly happy girl, to a private room on the third floor.

2:00 P.M., Mountain Daylight Time:

General Wyatt made the introductions. Going around the room in the nearly random order in which the eight men had placed themselves, he identified each by name and function. To the general's immediate right was Captain Roy Phipps. "My aide," he explained. "Next to him is Special Agent Bert Carlson of the Salt Lake City office of the Federal Bureau of Investigation."

Carlson, a crew-cut fellow with shiny black shoes and a nicely weathered face, nodded slightly.

"Beside him is Captain John MacDonald of the Utah Highway Patrol."

The captain, in splendid high boots and natty uniform, raised a hand with the index finger extended.

201

"Chief Sid Conrad of the Tooele Police Department."

Chief Conrad shifted his cigar from one corner of his mouth to the other. "Right," he said.

"And then Captain Robert Sterling of the Salt Lake City Police Force. He's here to liase with us."

Captain Sterling, in civilian clothes, smiled. "I hope that's all it turns out to be," he said. The others laughed. Politely? Nervously? The general couldn't be sure. They would know that it was something big. This kind of manpower wasn't assembled to stop delinquents from smashing parking meters.

"Sheriff Hiram Sandor, Sheriff of Tooele County."

Sandor didn't look like a sheriff at all. More like a real estate broker or a high school principal. He looked around and said, "How do?" He was, the general knew, an elected official. It'd be hard to guess about him. He could be shrewd, tough, helpful—or utterly useless. "How do?" was not encouraging. But maybe it was his way of welcoming the rest of them to his office. Or asserting that it was, after all, *his* office. He sat behind the battered walnut desk, a squat, fiftyish man in Babbitt brown.

"And on my left, Lieutenant Colonel Fred DeLeo," the general said. "He's our security officer."

Neither of those statements was true. DeLeo was not a lieutenant colonel at all. He was a first lieutenant. And he was not the general's security officer. DeLeo had arrived that morning from Washington with an open brief from Colonel English. He was to be of any possible assistance. And one of the first things he had done had been to promote himself to lieutenant colonel and attach himself to the general as a special security officer. The second thing had been to suggest to General Wyatt a plausible story to tell the civilian authorities, a pretext for calling them in, a way of maneuvering.

Wyatt was uncomfortable about DeLeo. There was something ferretlike about him. The dark, Italian eyes, the peculiarly narrow head, the way the eyebrows would shoot up for no reason at all suggested to Wyatt a sour

202

alertness that was . . . well, ferretlike. Even without the normal suspicion that Wyatt felt about one of these wonder boys coming in from DIA to maneuver through the mess, he supposed it would have been difficult for him to warm to DeLeo.

DeLeo nodded slightly, modestly. Not attracting any attention to himself, of course. He didn't have to. All he had to do was sit there and watch the general dance to his tune. Sing the strange song he had composed that morning—or brought from Washington.

There had been no better tune, though, that Wyatt had been able to think of. And he had to admit that, in its way, this invention would get the job done, would probably work. It made no sense to reject help just because you didn't like the shape of a man's head. That was unprofessional. All right, so begin! And, military man that he was, he squared his shoulders, took a deep breath, and did as he had commanded himself to do.

"The reason we've asked you all to meet here this afternoon, gentlemen, is to help us with a very nasty sort of problem. I'm sure you are all aware of the kind of work that we're doing at Dugway, and what a great part that work plays in the security of our country. It is not pleasant to think about chemical and biological warfare, but it's even worse to have to face the prospect of that kind of warfare. What we're doing at Dugway is defensive research, which is one of the best kinds of insurance that we know against its ever happening. It's not only a way of saving lives in the event of that kind of war, but it also diminishes the likelihood of that kind of attack in the first place. Now, obviously, the security of the base is as tight as the security of any base in the world. We've tried to run the safest operation that it was humanly possible to devise. And until now, it's been a zero-defects security program. But we've had a leak."

He looked around the room. Except for Phipps and DeLeo, who already knew what he was going to say, they all reacted. And, as he could have predicted, Chief Conrad and Sheriff Sandor reacted most. Conrad dropped his cigar and had to lean over to pick it up. Sandor, who had been half lolling in his swivel chair— the only comfortable chair in the room—sat bolt upright.

"One can impose checks and double checks and triple checks only so far," Wyatt continued. "After that . . . well, no system is foolproof. I'm afraid I can't go into detail, even with you gentlemen. All of our work is classified, and most of it is top secret. All I can tell you is what I have to tell you—that a man has penetrated one of the Dugway labs, has taken some biological research samples, and has managed to get out of the base. How he did it, and how to prevent its happening again, is our problem. And we'll handle that. What I need your help for is that this man must be apprehended. What he is carrying is highly infectious. He, himself, may be contaminated. And for him to get through to a populated area could cause . . . well, I hate to think."

Immediately, the questions started. Like rifle fire, they came sputtering and ricocheting around the room. When did he break out? Does he have a car? Is he armed? What is he carrying?

As rapidly as he could, the general answered. He broke out yesterday. Did not have a car. Had gone into the Onaqui Mountains on foot. Was not known to be armed, but was not known not to be, either.

"And what is it that he's got with him? Or in him?" Sheriff Sandor asked again.

"I'm sorry, but I can't tell you that."

"But it's infectious."

"That's right."

"Can you tell us what disease it is?"

"It's a manufactured disease," DeLeo said. "We can't tell you anything about it except that it is highly contagious and that the kill rate is upwards of eighty percent."

"Jesus!" Sandor exclaimed.

"If I may continue, General?" DeLeo asked.

"Certainly," Wyatt said. They had agreed that the general would lead in and that DeLeo would pick it up and lead out from there. Wyatt listened while DeLeo delivered the rest of the scenario, placing the man in the Onaquis six miles north of Tarsus, where he had been spotted at dusk by one of the army helicopters. And immediately, there was another barrage of questions. What was the fellow's name? Was he a spy? A defector? A saboteur? What about Tarsus?

The last question had been Sheriff Sandor's.

"He was moving north, away from Tarsus when the helicopter spotted him. He might not have known that there was a town just a few miles to the south. Or he might have figured that that was where we'd expect him to go and then go the other way. We have a crew in there now, cutting that trailer rig that jackknifed on the Tarsus road. We were able to beef up that crew without causing any suspicion or alarm. We're quite sure he's going north, though. If he'd been heading for Tarsus, he'd have arrived there this morning, sometime. And we've got men fanned out north of the town. We'd have got him."

To the other questions, DeLeo gave evasive answers, as they had agreed he would. But now Wyatt was not so sure. After all, by refusing to say whether the fellow was a saboteur or a spy or a defector or not, the presumption was that he had to be one of those things. Especially when, at the end of the series of questions, DeLeo turned to Carlson, the FBI man, and asked him for the prints of the photograph. The FBI caught spies. They had the man's picture. The man had to be a spy!

DeLeo waited while Carlson passed around the wirephotos of Paul Donovan. They'd got the pictures that morning from the Boston office, which had taken the dedication picture of the *Tarboxer,* the Tarbox High School yearbook. General Wyatt looked at the copy that Carlson had put before him. The graininess of the wirephoto gave a shadowy look to the man's face. It didn't look at all like a yearbook picture, but like any post office flyer on a run-of-the-mill fugitive. Or maybe it was not so much the graininess but the fact that Carlson, the

205

FBI man, was passing out the prints. Or both together.

"This is a great help," Chief MacDonald was saying. "We can broadcast this, put it in the papers and on the television, and get the whole county turned out to look for him. . . ."

"Can you?" Sheriff Conrad asked. "If anyone catches him, it's a plague. And if we don't catch him, it's as bad, or worse. We've still got the threat of some kind of plague and a general panic too."

"Well, let's assume we don't make any public announcement. What do you suppose the chances are of our getting him with roadblocks and the helicopters and patrols of men from all the law-enforcement agencies through those mountains? I'd say only fair. Unless we can call on army personnel. Enough men in there, and we'd have a good chance. But still, there's the panic to consider. You send two or three hundred soldiers into the mountains, somebody's going to notice them. And a hundred more policemen. And roadblocks. And helicopters. People will notice that, all right."

"If I may make a suggestion, gentlemen?" DeLeo had let the ball bounce around. Now he was picking it up again. Wyatt watched the other men as DeLeo spoke, coming up with the second part of the scheme. The man with the bottle of bugs was for the ears of those in this room. The public story, DeLeo suggested, was that a dangerous mental patient had escaped from the State Asylum at Provo, had been apprehended, had overpowered his captors, killed one of them, and had taken off into the Onaquis.

"Not bad. Not bad at all," Sheriff Sandor said, squinting slightly. Under that Babbitt brown, he was, perhaps, a real sheriff. "That explains the manhunt, and that business about the killing keeps people the hell away from him."

"But then what?" MacDonald asked. "I mean, what do we do if we find him. We don't want to catch whatever it is. We don't want to go around spreading it ourselves."

206

"Never mind spreading it," Chief Conrad said, shifting his cigar again. "We just don't want to catch it, period."

"You have a suggestion about that, I assume?" MacDonald asked DeLeo, imperfectly hiding his distaste for the Tooele police chief's attitude.

"All we want is help in spotting him," DeLeo said. "Once we know where he is, we can take over and bring in our men in special CBW suits. . . ."

"CBW?" Chief Conrad asked.

"Chemical-Biological Warfare," DeLeo explained. "We can approach him safely enough. We shouldn't expect you to do that. All we want is word on where he is. Then we can bring in our men by 'copter and take over."

"Fair enough," Sheriff Conrad said.

Wyatt took a deep breath. It had worked. They had accepted it all, had gone along with it, and had come out to exactly where DeLeo or Colonel English or whatever team of schemers in Washington had worked this out expected. It was the best part of the whole operation. The business about the infectivity of whatever Donovan had could be used to keep these people away from the man. There would be no problem of a Highway Patrol trooper or a sheriff's deputy or even a plain Tooele patrolman finding Donovan and then listening to him, or turning him over to some district attorney who would listen to him. The lid stayed on, this way. It had worked, would work.

"But what if we can't call? What if there is some delay? What if he's armed? Or, hell, he doesn't even have to be armed. This guy is walking around with some damn disease. . . . It's like he was carrying a bomb around with him. It's like he was a bomb, himself. It's a hell of a risk for my men. And for all of the men involved."

"We appreciate that," DeLeo said.

"Well, that's right nice of you," the sheriff answered.

At this point, Captain Sterling of the Salt Lake City

police spoke up. "I don't know. Out here, maybe there's a chance that this'd work. But if he ever made it across the Oquirrh Mountains into Salt Lake, or even into the suburbs—Riverton, Midvale, Murray—it'd be a different ball game."

"What would you do in that case?" the sheriff asked the captain.

"I'd ask for authorization from the commissioner to give orders to shoot on sight."

"Do you need him alive?" MacDonald asked.

"Not really," DeLeo answered.

"But sir," Roy Phipps began, addressing the general.

Wyatt shook his head ever so slightly. He knew what Phipps meant. He shared Phipps's feeling. They hadn't talked about this part of it. DeLeo hadn't said a word about shooting on sight. Nor, so far as he was aware, had anyone. And the right thing for DeLeo to have done was—would have been—to pass that question to him, the general. What the hell was the point of being a general anyway, if chicken colonels who were really only lieutenants committed you to . . . to shoot-on-sight?

Sure, there was a kind of logic to it. It was the surest way to keep the lid on. It was as quiet as anyone could get. But this Donovan hadn't done anything. No, nor had anyone. It had been a freak of the weather. A sudden thundershower. And a shit-for-brains pilot. . . . But it was too late to worry about any of that now. Or any of this, either.

He looked down again at the grainy photograph. DeLeo was explaining how they could admit to having got the wrong man, and then, a day or two later, announce the capture of their fictitious lunatic. Those things happen.

Sure, they do, Wyatt thought. And then he realized that the meeting was breaking up. He had been sitting there, staring at the photograph, the photograph of a dead man.

He stood up. "Thank you, gentlemen. We're very

grateful to you. And of course, we stand ready to move any time."

He marched out of the room, leaving DeLeo to work out the communications details and the area assignments. That had been the point of the lieutenant colonel's rank he'd assigned himself. He was fucking well welcome to it.

8:50 P.M., Mountain Daylight Time:

Had it not been so desperately important, it would have been interesting for Paul to watch the sun set on this peculiar topographical configuration. The two ranges of mountains ran north and south, the Onaquis now behind him, and to the east, perhaps ten miles away across Rush Valley, the Oquirrh range. What one expected in any sensible sunset was for the east to darken and the west to retain a faint glow that tinged to crimson and then slipped around the spectrum to indigo before going black. Here, after the sun had sunk behind the Onaqui Mountains, the shadows had begun to creep from west to east. Across the valley, the tallest of the Oquirrh Mountains still caught some last rays of indirect light, but at their bases those mountains too were in deep shadow. The valley floor was in lighter gloom, and it was interesting to watch the two areas of shadow creeping to meet just west of the center of the valley.

Interesting and vital. He had planned it so that the tricky negotiation of Rush Valley would be in darkness. It would have been impossible in daylight—a man could be seen for miles. And it would be of some risk even in moonlight. The plan, then, had been for him to stop in the last safe hiding place of the Onaqui foothills, wait until darkness, and then, as fast as possible, rush eastward to try to reach the Oquirrhs not much later than moonrise at 1 A.M. That meant he had nine miles or so to cover in about four hours. There was no cover out there, nothing but sagebrush and occasional balls of tumbleweed. He would have to rely then on the darkness for cover and do it in those four hours. Barring unforeseen accidents he was sure he could make it. He was tired, bone-tired, and his body ached everywhere—partly from the exercise, and partly perhaps from the sickness. The nap he had managed to take for the last couple of hours on the stony ground had done its share, too, he was sure. He had needed it, could not have gone on without it, but he felt stiffer and rustier than the Tin Man.

He took another piece of the warm, greasy bologna—the heat of the day and the heat of his body had melted some of the fat, which made the slices glisten as if they had been sweating—but he forced himself to chew, to swallow, and then to eat a second piece. He was saving the cheese for breakfast. The bologna by then would not be edible. Only by thinking of the long pull at the canteen as a reward was he able to force himself to swallow the second part of the bologna. And then he drank the water. He had been able to refill the canteen from a small stream early in the afternoon.

He was feeling fairly well satisfied with himself. He had managed to avoid the repeated sweeps of the helicopters. He had left Tarsus almost twenty-four hours ago. In another twenty-four the journey would be finished. He checked his watch. It was a couple of minutes before nine. He looked out at the valley again. He could still make out fairly clearly the line of telegraph poles that marked the railroad track that ran down the center of the valley. He had decided to wait until five minutes had passed from the time that those telegraph poles were wholly obscure. He had some time to kill. He reached into the pocket of his safari jacket and took out the transistor radio. It would be good to hear a human voice. Even a commercial would be a pleasure.

He switched the radio on and turned the little dial on the side, trying to find a clear station. He overshot, edged the dial back the other way, and then listened.

Instantly he was excited, and, at the same time, furious with himself. Why had he not thought of it before? He had found a news program. He should have been checking those all day. Perhaps something had happened. Perhaps the secrecy had lifted. Perhaps somebody else had spilled the beans, or, now that he was gone, to save face, they had spilled the beans themselves. For all he knew, those helicopters out there were trying to find him simply to save him, to bring him back.

". . . mixed. Soybeans were higher, bellies were firm, wheat, cocoa, and greasy wool were down. Tomorrow sunny, high in the low nineties, low this evening in the sixties and, in the mountains, the upper fifties. Recapping the top stories of the hour: There is still no break in the most extensive manhunt in Utah in recent years. All available men of law-enforcement agencies are combing the countryside in the Tooele vicinity for the escaped mental patient. Captured early this morning, he overpowered and killed one of his guards and escaped into the Onaqui Mountains. Local, county, and state police are being joined by army helicopters in the search for the fugitive. This man is armed, violent, and extremely dangerous. Citizens are warned not to attempt to apprehend him, but to report his whereabouts to the nearest police station, sheriff's office, highway patrol barracks, or the FBI in Salt Lake City. This is the first time in twenty-two years that a shoot-on-sight order has been issued by the Colonel of the Highway Patrol. Repeating his description, the fugitive, Paul Donovan, is six feet, one inch tall, weighs a hundred and seventy pounds, has black hair and dark eyes, and is wearing outdoor sports clothes. . . ."

Paul stared at the radio as if it were some practical joke from a trick shop. For a moment he found it impossible to connect the name and description that the announcer had given with himself. An escaped mental patient? a maniac? a killer? what nonsense was this?

But, no, those filthy bastards! The Tooele region. The Onaqui Mountains. It was him they were after!

There were no limits to what those people could do. Or had done. Nobody would listen to him now. He was a lunatic. And . . . but then the other part sunk in, the part he had blocked out. He wouldn't even have the chance to rave. The order was out from the Highway Patrol to shoot on sight. He'd never heard of such a thing. And out here, in the West, where everyone had guns. . . . It was, if possible, even more insane than what they had done to Tarsus. He listened again as the announcer gave the time check, 9 P.M. That had been obviously one of those five-minutes-before-the-hour news spots. With luck, he could find another station that ran the news on the hour. Not that he was expecting to hear anything better, but he wanted to listen only to convince himself that he had heard what he had heard. And there might be more of it. Certainly he ought to know as much as they were telling. He fiddled with the dial, found another station, and heard it all over again. The only new detail was that the combined force of searchers was in excess of three hundred men. They did not say how many helicopters were involved.

He sat there, looking out over the rapidly darkening valley. The darkness did not seem so protective now. It was now as much of a shield for those three hundred pairs of eyes as it was for him. He could just barely make out those telegraph poles. He would move as soon as that five-minute news program was over.

Numbly he sat and listened as the announcer reported that Secretary of Defense, Jonathan Colebrooke, had cut short his Vietnam tour to return to Washington where his daughter, Diana, was gravely ill. The doctor's report from Walter Reed was that she had staph pneumonia, was not on the critical list, but was a sick girl. Paul shook his head at the disproportion of it. One sick brat and the Secretary of Defense flies halfway around the world. A whole sick town—hell, a dying town—and they send three hundred cops out with orders to shoot-on-sight. Him.

Maybe Hope had been right. They wouldn't—they couldn't possibly—issue a shoot-on-sight order for a woman. And if they did, nobody would shoot. And then, thinking about Hope, it struck him with fresh force all over again. He realized what it would mean to her when she heard one of these news broadcasts. He promised himself that if he got back, he would tell her that maybe she had been right.

If he ever got back . . . what were the chances now, he wondered? Tooele was out of the question. Salt Lake City? Not on foot. He'd never make it. And he couldn't risk hitchhiking. He couldn't even risk getting close enough to civilization now to steal a car. And that was assuming that somebody left the keys in the car. He had no idea which wires they were that those guys in the movies pulled and touched together. Every juvenile delinquent knew that, and he, a science teacher, didn't have the vaguest idea. He took the map out of his pocket, spread it out in front of him, and, with his nose perhaps four inches away from the paper, was just able to make out the details in the dying light. The other large names—all but one—looked like suburbs. But there, in large blue letters, was "Bingham Canyon." And, right next to it, "copper field." Between the two there was a tiny red square marking a Point of Interest, and an explanatory legend, "World's largest open pit copper mine." He thought about that for a moment. There would be tourists there, and the bustle and confusion of a huge copper mining operation. And the best part of it was that he could get to it through open country, away from highways, roads, houses, people, and policemen. And guns.

And once he got there? Well, he would have to make it up. But if there was any safety for him anywhere, he suspected that it would be in a crowd. They don't shoot into crowds. Even *they* don't do that.

He folded the map, put it back in his pocket, switched off the radio and put it away, and then looked out across the valley. He could not see the telegraph poles. Even knowing where they were, where to look, he could not work the trick by which memory turned into vision. He got up from the spruce needles, brushed his clothes off, sighed, and started to walk at a fast clip down the last seventy-five yards of the slope. At the bottom of the slope he paused, looked up at the sky, found the Little Dipper and the North Star, faced east, and started to walk.

8:45 P.M., Pacific Daylight Time:

There was a sharp rap at the door. General Eastlake had not been sleeping. He lay on the green leather couch in Major General Randolph Nickerson's office, his hat over his face, perfectly relaxed, resting.

"Come," he ordered through the hat.

He heard the door open. "General Nickerson's compliments, sir. His car is waiting for you. The Secretary's plane has acknowledged the message. It will be in the refueling area in two minutes."

It was Major Garrett, the O.D. General Eastlake recognized the voice by its slight Southern drawl. He was satisfied with Garrett. Like many Southerners, he talked slow but thought fast. General Nickerson had greeted him an hour before, when he had alighted from the F-105 that had flown him from Washington here to Bakersfield. The general had placed his office and the base at Eastlake's disposal, and then, with the tact and confidence of a senior officer who knows he has gone as high as he was likely to go, had had the good sense to disappear. Garrett had been available, attentive, but in no way intrusive. They had handled it all with satisfactory finesse.

Eastlake swung himself off the couch, stepped into

214

General Nickerson's washroom, splashed some cold water on his face, hesitated, borrowed Nickerson's comb and ran it through his slightly tousled hair. Then, on the way out, he picked up his hat from the couch, clapped it on his head, and marched out to the corridor where the major was waiting.

The major led the way out of the HQ building where the general's car was waiting, the motor running and the sergeant standing stiffly at attention beside the open rear door.

"Is there anything more I can do for you, General?" the major asked.

"Nope," he snapped. And then, realizing that the major had been offering simply to accompany him out to the Secretary's plane, and the offer had perhaps been prompted by the fact that he, Eastlake, had appeared without his aide—that the major was offering, in a way, to substitute—he softened his tone. He flashed his impressive smile at the major and added, "Just thank General Nickerson for me. I appreciate everything that he's done. Everything that both of you have done."

"It's been my pleasure, sir." Garrett saluted.

Eastlake returned the salute, dove in the back seat of the car, and moments later was speeding across the asphalt to the fueling area where Secretary Colebrooke's B-52 had just come to a halt at the center of a semicircle of waiting fuel trucks.

The driver pulled up close to the plane, and Eastlake sat back patiently to wait for the staircase to be wheeled up to the door. After the stairs were in place there seemed to be a few instants of confusion or delay. But presently the door swung open. And as it did so, Eastlake emerged from the car. He returned the driver's salute and strode quickly to the stairs, mounted them, and entered the aircraft.

"What the hell are you doing here, Edward?"

It was not exactly a hostile greeting. Secretary of Defense Jonathan Colebrooke had risen from the armchair in which he had been sitting and he was smiling. His tone was cordial, but still General Eastlake knew that the question was a serious one and it demanded a real answer.

"I thought it might save some time if I flew out here to meet you and used the flying time to Washington to fill you in on what's happened."

"Renchler know you're here?" Colebrooke asked wryly.

"I tried to get ahold of him," Eastlake answered blandly.

"But you ran out of dimes, eh?" Colebrooke laughed, and then, the joke over, he became serious again. "Sit down. Let's have it."

Eastlake sat down in one of the other armchairs—there were three chairs, a desk with a desk chair and a blue rug that had been laid on to provide the Secretary with creature comforts even on this hastily arranged flight.

It took fifteen minutes for General Eastlake to deliver his carefully impartial report. The Secretary sat and listened, asking no questions and taking no notes. Eastlake required no prompting, and the Secretary was famous for his grasp of detail. The plane had refueled, taxied, taken off, and reached cruising altitude by the time Eastlake was finished.

"I assume," Colebrooke said, "that the President has been informed?"

"Schleiman and McGrady have been at our meetings," Eastlake began.

"Yes, yes, I'm sure. That's not what I asked."

"The President has no official knowledge of this, sir."

Colebrooke said nothing but looked at Eastlake and raised one bushy black eyebrow.

"That's what Schleiman said he said," Eastlake explained.

"I see," Colebrooke said. He sighed, shook his head, and pulled his earlobe. "Tell me, where do you stand on this? I mean, it was Admiral Pennybaker who put Charlie up to calling me back from Saigon."

216

"To be honest with you, sir, I haven't taken a position. Not until now. At the beginning, I thought they just might get away with it, that it just might work. But it hasn't worked. It isn't working. And now that we've gone this far it's damned near impossible to go back and take the option we should have taken at the beginning."

"Option!" Colebrooke thundered. "Jesus Christ, option!"

"Sir?"

"Look, there's some poor son-of-a-bitch running around through the mountains down there, and you tell me there's a shoot-on-sight order out for him and all that means to you—to you general officers—is that we've picked the wrong option. We've got twenty-two dead civilians and the likelihood of having fifteen or twenty more, and you talk about options."

"Sir, there's not one of us who's happy about this situation."

"Damn it, nobody's expecting a celebration. What I want is somebody who's willing to take a little responsibility. What gets me, what really gets me, is that you guys have been sitting around having meetings and turning into robots. Instead of having an accumulation of experience and intelligence, you all wind up looking around the table and turning real problems into games. That's what I meant when I objected to *options*. If all that goddamn game theory really worked, you could retire and I could retire, and the President could go out and fish for marlin for weeks on end, and we could let the Rand Corporation run the world."

"All right, sir," Eastlake said, deliberately not looking down at his feet, but meeting Colebrooke's gaze, "what would you have done? Two days ago, I mean, when it first hit?"

"I could ask you the same question," Colebrooke replied. "If it had been up to you, I mean squarely, totally up to you—no President, no Jonathan Colebrooke, no Charlie Renchler, no Admiral Pennybaker—if it had been just your baby, what would you have done?"

"That's almost an impossible question to answer," Eastlake said. "I mean, now. Knowing what's happened. Knowing how it's been handled—and mishandled. I'm not sure I can give you an answer."

"Think about it for a minute. It's tough, I know, but without knowing what's happened since it first broke, what would you have done?"

Eastlake thought. And his thoughts were not so much about what had happened in Tarsus or even what had happened at the meetings in Washington, but about Jonathan Colebrooke, this curmudgeon of an industrial magnate who had come in, as all of them did, to direct the enormous defense establishment. Had all of that business about the dead civilians and the shoot-on-sight order been a real moral thrust or a feint, part of a one-two attack? If it was an attack, what could be the purpose? Who could be the target? The President was covered, the Secretary, if only because he had been in Vietnam at the time, was fairly well protected. It would be Wyatt, Norland, and himself, and maybe even Renchler, whose heads would roll. But that would happen anyway. The whole purpose of his flight out here to meet Colebrooke in L.A. and gain a beat on Pennybaker and on Renchler had been to try to work the situation, to try to find some safe ground. And of course, Colebrooke had smelled that out. All right, so the man was clever. But what did he want? He had taken—or pretended to take—a high moral tone about it. But to have announced at the beginning what had happened, that a town had been stricken, that the army had done it, and that it was one of the CBW weapons that had been the instrument—well, shit, that was crazy! It would be admitting that the President had lied. It would be a crippling blow to the program. And Colebrooke, an intelligent man, a shrewd operator, and, most important, a veteran of twenty years in the chemical business, the last eight of which had been as operating head of one of the largest chemical companies in the world . . . he knew how important this was.

218

Eastlake just didn't believe it, could not believe that the Secretary could come on at him like one of those liberal columnists. And he, Eastlake, could not be expected to sit there, listen to a two-minute Sunday school harangue, repent his sins—if they were sins—accept the call, and be cleansed.

"I think I'd have done . . ." he began. "Yes, I believe I'd have ordered exactly what we've done. With more safeguards, maybe, with a tighter lid. . . . But I'd have tried to keep it quiet." He looked at the Secretary, waiting for his reply. He had surprised himself. This was certainly not what he had flown across the country to tell the Secretary.

"Thank you, Edward. I appreciate your candor. It was a hard thing to say. And I think I understand your thinking. I believe I understand your motives. In fact, I think I share them. But I disagree with you about the means. We could have accomplished very nearly the same thing a lot more safely and a lot more easily by issuing a statement admitting it all at the beginning. We've never said we'd stop all testing and all research. I think that these tests were legitimate defensive research. Nothing wrong with it insofar as the President's announcement is concerned. And if we'd admitted that a freak storm and a faulty valve had caused the accident, we might have come out of it all right. An address to the nation on television, and the President could have turned all this into any ordinary disaster. Hell, if we'd have played it right, the public would have felt sorry for us. We'd have been the good guys."

It was an awful feeling. The stars on his shoulders, the fruit salad on his visor, the ribbons on his chest, were no help at all. He felt his ears tingle as they had not done since his days at the Point. Colebrooke had led him up the garden path. He would not show it, however. He was damned if he would show it.

"Then what do we do, sir?" he asked. "What do we do now? Shall I call off the manhunt? If you think that's the way to play it, if you think we can still play it that way . . . then we ought to let them know. We must be over Utah, now," Eastlake observed. "And down there, that guy is running. Or he was, half an hour before I boarded this plane, when I spoke with General Norland. If we moved fast, we could still make the announcement, beat him to it." He sat there, watching Colebrooke, watching the crafty ascetic face that was in profile now, looking out of the window and down into the blackness. Edward Eastlake waited for perhaps two minutes before he heard Colebrooke speak.

"Hell, Edward, it's gone too far now. What your meetings have done—what your decisions have done—is to destroy all *my* options. It's too late now."

Colebrooke had not turned his head. His elbow on the armrest and his chin cradled in his palm, he still stared down into the darkness of the Utah night. His tone had been—the expression on his face was still—resigned regret.

To his surprise, Eastlake found that he shared that regret.

10:35 P.M., Mountain Daylight Time:

He had crossed the railroad tracks—his first landmark —and, for that matter, the only landmark in the valley. For the rest of it, it would be dead reckoning, a matter of keeping the North Star over his left shoulder and aiming for the Oquirrhs which, sooner or later, would appear before him. He knew they were there. It was just a matter of patience. Patience and endurance. To try to calculate it was no good, except as a way of passing the time, giving him something to think about as he crossed the valley. The preposterous enormity of the news from the radio had joined with the featureless blackness to make a situation more terrifying and more bleak than any nightmare he could remember.

There was a kind of comfort, however, in mathematics and measurement. The appalling spaces between the stars seemed somehow a little less appalling when one could assign numbers to them, when one could quantify them, tame them. And this valley, this interminable expanse of flat blackness, punctuated only by pointillist clumps of sagebrush, scrub grass, and aimless drifting tumbleweed, was no more than ten miles across. The railroad track had appeared to be nearly in the middle. Allowing for tricks of perspective, Paul figured it to be at least four miles from the starting point of his evening's journey. That left no more than six miles to go. Nine and a half paces, he knew, were fifty feet. That meant eighteen paces to a hundred feet. A hundred and eighty paces to a thousand feet, and a mile then would be one-hundred-eighty times five. Somewhere around nine hundred paces. Allowing for deviations to the left and right, call it a thousand. But, of course, that was what a mile was, *mille passus,* a thousand paces. Funny, he'd never figured that out before. He felt an absurd pride in having made the connection, and the satisfaction he took from the admittedly trivial intellectual exercise was even greater than the satisfaction and relief he had felt half an hour before when he had seen behind him the firefly lights of searchers in the Onaqui slopes he had quitted.

There had been, of course, a moment of concern. And then he had devised a plan to meet the possibility of their descent into the valley. He was not at all sure that it would work, had no idea whether in the end it would come to such a desperate necessity, but still he had felt a feeling of accomplishment in having figured out that, should they come into the valley with their flashlights, he would simply take out his own flashlight and pretend to be one of them.

It was unlikely, implausible, but better than nothing. And now, half an hour and a couple of miles later, it had receded into dreamlike memory and had faded as surely as those lights themselves had faded. He wasn't sure whether he had gone too far to be able to see the lights, or whether the searchers had moved to another slope. It didn't matter. The point—the only point—was that he was still moving. In another couple of hours he would have reached the Oquirrh foothills and would have earned a candy bar and sleep. In the morning he would tackle the new range.

He began to count, and allowed himself even the luxury of saying aloud every tenth number as his left foot reached fifty, then sixty, then seventy paces. He was intent upon the counting and did not hear—or heard and did not notice—the drone of the airplane engine overhead. Then, suddenly, he realized that this was not some transcontinental jet five or six miles up, but a prop plane flying fairly low over the valley. It could not be descending to land at the Salt Lake City airport. Not with the Oquirrh Mountains in the way. It was looking for him. But, no, that was impossible at night, in this darkness. Or was it impossible? They had all kinds of sophisticated techniques—infrared photography on those U-2s could spot a handkerchief from miles up in the air. Or it could be worked with body heat. But by the time they got that kind of delicate film developed he would have been long gone. Then why?

Maybe it had nothing to do with him at all. He tried to believe that, tried to convince himself that the plane was only that of some local rancher coming home after a big night on the town and following the line of railroad tracks in order to avoid the twin hazards of the mountains on either side of him. But, no, that didn't make any sense. Why would he be flying that low? And how could he see the tracks anyway? Almost as if in answer to that last, irrelevant question, the first magnesium flare exploded. The flash was blinding white. Paul looked away, his night vision ruined even after only a split-second exposure to the preternatural whiteness of the flare. And it had been at least two miles away.

Had they seen him? Could they see him? Curiously enough, the light did not cast any shadow. Of course not. He was on the ground and the angle was such that there would not be a shadow. But from up above? From a plane? He had no idea how visible he would be. A few seconds later a second flare exploded, further to the north. Was it one plane or two dropping flares? He couldn't tell yet.

Even one was bad enough. This was not the mountains, and there was no place to hide. There was nothing to use as cover. He thought for a moment, desperately, of trying to dig, but that was no good. It was simply an atavistic desire to hide. He began to run. He ran for a minute, perhaps a minute and a half, until his chest was aching, his throat burning, and his legs quivering. Even as he continued to run, he knew it was no good. He could not make the mountains and the blessed sanctuary of rocks, trees, and foliage at a dead run. He would drop with exhaustion still in the valley, still unprotected and naked to the probes of that terrible light. He forced himself to slow to a brisk walk. It was hopeless. The best he could do, the only thing he could think of—and it was pitiable and absurd—was the old idea of the Scout's pace. Fifty paces running and fifty paces walking. But even at that it would take him at least forty-five minutes.

The drone grew louder. Or drones—he could make out now that there were two of them. Almost simultaneously two more flares blossomed into light, this time a mile or so to the south. The chances of crouching down and using the sagebrush as cover were nil. Even if he had the time to harvest a pile large enough to cover himself with, it would be noticeable, would look peculiar. It was no good.

But, yes, it was. Not with sagebrush, but with the tumbleweed. Of course! He looked around, and in the afterglow of the two recent flares he was able to see a fairly large tumbleweed rolling erratically a few yards ahead of him in the night breeze. He urged himself forward and picked it up. It was like a giant cat's-paw. Prickly, but not intolerable. He arranged it around his shoulders, experimentally, and contrived to secure it by folding his arms within it. He pried off a chunk and covered his head with it. It wasn't much, but it was better than nothing. He hurried onward, still headed due east. It just might work, he thought. For the first time he allowed himself a glimmer of optimism and hope. After all, the valley was ten miles across and thirty miles long. There was a lot of territory for them to cover, and for all their brightness, the flares only lasted for a minute or two.

In an agonizing suspense he continued toward the east, no longer thinking, really, about getting to the mountains, but thinking of each footstep as an achievement. Distractedly, he thought of Channel swimmers and how, after a while, when France seemed an impossible dream, their only reality was dragging a heavy arm up and out to make yet another stroke and continue for yet another painful yard. It was like that, except that instead of swimming through water he was wading through the terrible light and the noise. If only they would shut up! Just shut up—and then it happened. The third flare was behind him by perhaps half a mile, but the fourth hit only a couple of hundred yards away.

His first instinct was to run; his second was to freeze —and to blame himself for having moved, for not having frozen at the very instant that the flare had gone off. But, then, tumbleweed moves. Did he dare to raise the tumbleweed, to crouch . . . no, he couldn't. There was nothing to do but stand there, waiting for the damn flare to die out and to whisper over and over, "Fuck you, you sons-of-bitches, you goddamn sons-of-bitches, fuck you, fuck you!"

After an eternity the flare burned out. Three, perhaps three and a half miles to the north, two more lit up the sky, but at such a distance that he had nothing to fear. With the tumbleweed still tucked around him, he began to move. At least for the moment he had survived. He felt giddy with the joy of it. He promised himself that he would never again step on ants now that he knew what they felt like as they scurried across endless expanses of open space—and, for all he knew, muttered over and over again, "Fuck you, fuck you, you bastards, you sons-of-bitches, fuck you. . . ."

Thursday, August 13

12:10 A.M., Mountain Daylight Time:

It wasn't so bad for Uncle William. At least he was unconscious. All he had to do was continue the labor of breathing, to maintain the heart's gesture—and it was only a gesture now—of rhythmic contractions as it pumped the blood around the burning body. He did not know that his wife had died eight hours before. He did not know that his friends and neighbors were dead and dying. He did not know that his country had done such an incredible, such an outrageous thing to him and to his townspeople. But, most of all, he did not have to sit there and watch—as Hope had been doing for most of the day and night. She had sat at the bedside, watching the pitiable tremors as the muscles mimicked health and liveliness. And as the hours had worn on, against her will affection and pity had worn thin, to reveal an ugly substratum of impatience. She knew that it was partly fatigue, and partly the terrible hopelessness and depression that she felt—and had felt ever since she had heard the news on the radio. Fatigue and hopelessness would do it. There came a point when one simply wanted to give up.

It was ironic, she supposed, that the occasion for her absolute despair had been the news about Paul, whom she had known so briefly. Her aunt and uncle, whom she had known and loved all her life, meant more to her. Surely they did. But the manner of Aunt Emily's death had been deceptive, for she had sickened and died as elderly people do. And sitting beside Uncle William, watching him hang on from moment to moment, she found that she could scarcely make the connection between Dugway and this illness. It was not any less savage or direct than the bullets that were waiting for Paul. But it seemed so natural. It was hard, therefore, to work up the same kind of rage. That would come later, she supposed. Now there was only the exhaustion, the impatience, and the guilt.

Gently she mopped the sweat from her uncle's face. She had been sitting in that chair by his bed for the past two hours. She decided she would have a drink of water and a cigarette. Then she would come back.

She got up and went back to the curtained-off office, which Dr. Bartlett had given her permission to use. She could have gone outside, either to the mess tent for coffee, or just to stand out in the night air, but that creepy guard would be standing there, trying to talk to her, trying to convince her what a nice guy he was—what nice guys they all were. That was *his* problem. She wanted nothing to do with him. Or with any of them.

She lit a cigarette, took a deep drag, and, as she expelled the smoke, blew the match out. It was brighter in the office than it was in the ward. A desk lamp burned as well as the overhead light that was bolted to one of the support pipes. She looked at the chair, the same kind of hard, uncomfortable chair she had been using out in the ward, and decided against it. Instead, she lay down on the floor, and soon she felt her muscles start to relax.

It felt surprisingly comfortable to lie there that way, and she was grateful to Dr. Bartlett for his offer of the use of the office. Certainly she would not have been able to do this with the guard watching her. Not that she blamed the guard particularly. His presence was Major Robertson's doing. Hope had expected even worse treatment than what she'd got. She supposed she had her aunt and uncle's condition to thank for the fact that she was still able to walk around in relative freedom. Had it not been for them, she would have had . . . house arrest? real arrest? She had no idea. She didn't even know what the limitations were to the power that Robertson had at his disposal. Or whether there were any limitations at all.

Certainly he had been furious enough. Hope had protested blandly enough that, although she and Paul had spent the night together, she had known nothing at all about his intentions to leave Tarsus. She had claimed that after the two soldiers had appeared at eight o'clock she had gone to make breakfast, intending to bring it to Paul and wake him with it. When she had finished making the breakfast, she had gone into the bedroom and found it empty. He had just gone, she said. She had no idea when or where. She had stuck to the story, and it was impossible for Robertson to *prove* that she was lying. But he knew, and she knew he knew. What that would mean for her in the next few days, Hope had no idea. She knew she was being watched, but she had not begun to speculate with any seriousness or to make any plans. She was holding all that in abeyance, partly because she had her bedside watch to maintain and partly because it seemed disloyal to Paul—as if he were already dead. Not that she had much hope, but if they did get him and she were left as the only one who knew what they had done, she would have to try something. To run? To stay here and just wait it out? She had no idea.

She reached out to flick the ash of the cigarette into the ashtray that she had put nearby, and, as she did so, she saw Dr. Lewine approaching the office area. She shifted to a sitting position. She did not want him to see her lying there on the floor, but neither did she want to get up for him.

"Miss Wilson," he said, with some surprise.

"Dr. Bartlett said I could use the office," Hope said. "But if I'm in your way, I'll leave."

"Not at all," he said. "But are you comfortable down there?"

"I've been sitting out in the ward," she said. "This is fine."

Dr. Lewine went around her and sat down at the chair behind the desk. From her position on the floor, Hope could not see his face, nor could he see hers. She waited, hoping that he would ignore her and let her ignore him. She would finish her cigarette and then leave. But after a few moments he broke the silence.

"I'm sorry about your aunt," he said.

"Really?" she asked dryly.

"Believe me, I wish there was something we could have done."

"I don't believe you," she retorted, "I don't believe any of you."

"*I* am not your enemy, Miss Wilson."

"Captor, then," she said.

"Look," he said. "Last evening when you were here with Paul Donovan, I saw you take those amphetamine pills. I've said nothing. I don't intend to say anything. Perhaps I should have. Perhaps if I'd reported what I had seen, Mr. Donovan might still be here alive and safe."

Hope got up from the floor and sat down in the chair in front of the desk so that she could look directly at Dr. Lewine.

"Why didn't you?" she asked suspiciously. "Why didn't you tell them?"

"Do you think I like this?" Lewine asked in return. "Do you think I'm happy about . . . what's happened?"

"Then why do you do it? Why do you cooperate?"

Lewine leaned forward, rested his elbows on the vinyl top, and said, "I've done nothing to be ashamed of. I'm a doctor, and I've been trying to help sick people. Medically, all that can be done is being done for the people here in Tarsus. Beyond that, I have no competence. I have no authority. I am as helpless as you are, perhaps even more helpless because I'm an officer in the army."

"Just obeying orders, Herr Kapitan?" she asked.

Lewine blanched. "Perhaps. So far, at least. But it isn't over yet."

"For Aunt Emily it's over. And for Uncle William it'll

be over soon. And for Paul, too, I'm afraid."

"That's what prompted me to speak to you," Lewine replied. "Whatever you told the Major, I know you helped Donovan. I know the two of you worked it out together. At least you had each other's confidence."

Hope said nothing. She was suspicious—as suspicious of his friendly approach as she had been of the major's belligerent directness. The good guy and the bad guy. She'd seen it before on every crummy television serial. She said nothing, waiting for him to continue.

"Look," he said, after a moment's pause. "I'm not trying to get you to admit anything to me. All I want from you is your promise that you won't try to do what Donovan did. It's no good. They'll catch you. The only thing to do is wait it out here. I won't tell anyone about the amphetamines if I can have your word."

She wished she could believe him. It would be nice if there were someone she could trust—even a little way —now that Paul was gone. But there was no way of testing Lewine's sincerity. Or was there?

"Will you tell me what's been happening? What the disease is? How did the town get sick?"

"If I do tell you, will you promise?"

"If you tell me the truth," she said.

Lewine took a deep breath and told her, "It was an accident. They were experimenting with a virus, and somehow it got loose. Some weather fluke."

"But I thought they'd stopped all that a long time ago," she said.

"No, not all."

"What virus?" she asked, after a moment's thought.

"Japanese encephalitis."

"When?"

"Last Friday afternoon."

She sat there for a moment considering what the doctor had told her. If it was true, he had certainly taken a great risk.

"Let me ask you . . ." she began.

"Please," he interrupted, "I shouldn't have told you

230

even this much. I can't tell you any more. For your sake. But you must believe me that right now they will go to any lengths to keep that information from getting out."

"But what can they do in a week, in two weeks, in a month?"

"That's what we have to wait to find out," Lewine said. "But I have your word?"

"Yes," she said, "you have my word."

There was nothing more to be said. She stubbed out her cigarette and went back out to the ward to resume her vigil at Uncle William's bedside. She sat there until three-thirty before she drifted off to sleep. When she woke up—only a few minutes later—he was dead.

9:15 A.M., Mountain Daylight Time:

In a way, Paul thought, it was perfectly incredible. The idea that all those people had been looking for him for all that time—more than twenty-four hours, now—and that he had managed to elude them! It was quite marvelous. And Paul felt a wonderful exhilaration. It had almost nothing to do with his own skill or craftiness or luck in having eluded the searchers. It was instead a feeling of wonder at the openness of the country. As an Easterner, he was accustomed to a kind of civilization that developed all the available land. His notion of the country was one based primarily on his experience of the Eastern seaboard which, with only a few more or less deliberate exceptions, was entirely urbanized and settled from Portland, Maine, down through Richmond. But out here there were expansive open spaces, there were places where the chances were that no man had ever been before. The Oquirrh Mountains were not especially rugged, they weren't the craggy, rock-faced, snow-capped peaks that were in themselves forbidding. It was just that out here, in the middle of Utah, there was so much space. Aside from a few rugged trails that a jeep might pass on during the hunting season, there were no evidences at all of human kind. And in this splendid openness that Paul had come to understand only by having to depend on it, there was clearly the origin of that rugged Western individualism, that pioneer spirit, that feeling of freedom that was so much a part of American myth. It was real. He was sharing it, riding on it, sustained by it. In a way he felt that he was only now taking out his emotional citizenship papers.

He was hurrying along, really traveling now despite the fact that physically he was drained. He had taken another pill, and he was able to feel its effect on his mood and on his pace as well. He seemed to fly over the rough terrain with the agility of a mountain goat. Not that it was a lark, not at all. He knew that sooner or later the helicopters would start again. He was counting on these early hours to try to get as close to Bingham as he could. For the first time he allowed himself the luxury of looking beyond his present situation and planning for the moment of supreme satisfaction that would come within a matter of hours now. He would place the call to Arnold Rosenthal, explain to him what had happened and what was happening, and then let Dr. Rosenthal take it from there.

It was odd, really, Paul thought. To him he was Arnie, a funny, earthy, likable guy who had volunteered last year to accompany Paul on Saturday field trips for the honors classes because the child psychiatrist had advised him to spend more time with his son, David, a bright, fat, sulky, sullen teen-ager. Arnie had come along, but had not spent much more time with David. Instead, he and Paul had become friends—such friends that Paul quickly forgot the man's fifteen years seniority, his reputation as one of the country's leading pathologists, and—most important now—his powerful position in the elite world of Boston medicine. It wasn't something that Paul had thought about much. And that had been one of the great things about their friendship.

They went out to the Great Salt Marsh and explored as equals, as passionate amateurs, and, quickly, as friends. There had never been any thought of what either could do for the other. To Paul, Arnie had never been one of those eager, fawning parents, and to Arnold, Paul had never been one of those young hotshots, looking for an appointment, a grant, some recognition. They had just been friends, had liked each other. After Marian had died, Arnie had waited a decent interval, and then, early in May, had invited Paul down to the Cape to watch the horseshoe crabs come in at the full moon to lay their eggs. They had sat there in the small Audubon cabin on Nauset Beach, drinking brandy and smoking Arnie's great cigars—Cuban cigars smuggled in not by amateurs but in a diplomatic pouch—and had got pleasantly smashed together. And seeing those crabs had been a helluva thing. There wasn't anything like it this side of Galápagos. The best part was that now, when he needed him, Paul felt sure he could call up and tell Arnie this wild thing, this absolutely incredible story and . . . he was falling. Damnit, he had not been paying attention. He was falling, had dislodged a rock, lost his footing, and . . . Ow! His wrist had banged against the corner of a tree.

He lost his balance, his footing, and was rolling now. It was taking such a goddamn long time. There was nothing to grab, no way to stop it. And it kept on—like Alice down the rabbit hole. And then . . . Oof! Ow! He had bounced off the trunk of a tree and ricocheted onto the face of a large boulder. His wrist was on fire, his ribs felt as if they were broken. And his face was on fire, too. He put his left hand to his face . . . oh, shit! There was blood. He felt cautiously and found the cut. It was oozing, but not serious. And the ribs? He could still breathe, but only shallow breaths. Maybe it would improve. And then he realized that the radio was in the pocket. That was the pain in his chest. He'd landed on the radio. Goddamn it! He reached into his pocket and was surprised and annoyed by an incredibly searing flash of pain in his left hand. It was his left wrist. What the hell had he done to it? Was it broken? He thought maybe so. Well, better a wrist than an ankle or a leg. He didn't have to walk on his hands.

With his right hand, he reached awkwardly into the pocket of the jacket and pulled out the radio. Somehow the radio seemed even more important than the wrist. He turned the switch. Nothing happened. He shook the radio and there was the sickening rattle of loose parts. Mindlessly, foolishly, he remembered the joke about the man who opened up a pocket watch to find a dead cockroach inside and then exclaimed, "Of course it doesn't work, the engineer croaked." He shook it again. There were no sounds coming from it except that rattle of loose parts. He flung it at the tree and watched with satisfaction as the Bakelite case shattered. He tried his chest again. He could breathe a little deeper, but after a certain point it still hurt. Was a rib broken? Cracked? Or had he just knocked the wind out of himself? Well, he'd see. But the wrist, and the cut face.

Suddenly the cut face seemed terribly ominous. He had been counting on coming into Bingham and passing himself off as a tourist. But having felt for the blood, and having found it, and having found as well the stubble from not having shaved now in thirty-six hours, he realized he'd look like some kind of wild man coming out of the mountains. He would indeed look like that hunted maniac. Of course, that was the point of all this shaving, this brushing of hair, this brushing of teeth. To show the world that you had a safe place to go, a place in which you could groom and look civilized. It was the badge by which we identified ourselves to one another as tame, as safe, as accepted and acceptable. It was the wild men who walked around like this, with hair and blood, desperate and disheveled.

But that was hardly the problem facing him now. The real problem now, still, was getting there. If he got to Bingham—no, *when* he got to Bingham—he would worry about his appearance. Right now he had to do something about the wrist. It hurt. It hurt like hell! Carefully, painfully, slowly, he untied the arms of the sweater that were knotted around his waist, and, with his teeth and his good right hand, contrived to retie them into a square knot. He put the arms of the sweater around his neck, and then, with his right hand, eased his left arm into the makeshift sling. He staggered to his feet, stood there for a moment swaying slightly but still erect. And that was no mean accomplishment. He could stand. And if he could stand, he could walk. He took another breath, just to the point where it began to hurt, and then another. He could stand and walk and breathe. He would get there.

9:25 A.M., Mountain Daylight Time:

It was, Sergeant Harrison thought, one helluva jerkass place to be. He'd been there, up in the firetower, since six in the morning, peering out at the green mountainside with the high-powered binoculars until he knew every tree, every twig, every last damn pine needle, in the three hundred and sixty degrees. It had warmed up some; it wasn't quite so damn cold as it had been. But on the other hand, it had got to be more and more boring. There was nothing. I mean, like nothing! The high point of his day so far had been a couple of minutes watching a peregrine falcon descend out of nowhere and kill a blue grouse. But for Christ's sake! There they were engaged in the biggest manhunt in twenty years, and he was out here in this wild sanctuary bird-watching.

He held the binoculars to his eyes, sweeping the slope to the north once more, and . . . but this time he thought he saw something. He adjusted the range of the binoculars slightly and saw that, yes, there was a man. And then, an instant later he was gone—having passed onto the other side of a tree trunk and around to a thicker clump of foliage.

Was that the guy? After all, you had to be damn sure on a thing like this. This was the first shoot-on-sight order in Harrison's time on the force. It was creepy. I mean, suppose you shot the wrong man, he thought, arguing with himself. Or, on the other hand, what if it was the right man, the real one? MacDonald had explained it at the morning lineup. Harrison knew that it was nothing so simple as an escaped maniac. This guy was out of Dugway, and he was contagious. They wouldn't even say with what disease—which didn't sound good. I mean, it wasn't athlete's foot. So, if that was the guy, if that was Donovan, and if he, Harrison, went down the ladder and went after him, what would happen? If he got him, fine. That is, if it was Donovan. And then he'd have to identify the damn body. And come down with plague? Cholera? Cancer, maybe? Who knew what the hell they did at Dugway? And that was assuming he got the bastard. For all they knew, he was armed. So it could be simpler than that. You could wind up with a bullet in your head. In a pig's ass he was going to go down there.

He'd put in fifteen good years on the Highway Patrol, and he'd been cited for bravery twice. But not dumbass bravery. You don't go looking for trouble. This kind of thing, this was crazy. It was the army's fucking fault, anyway. What were they doing, still messing around with that kind of stuff? Or, if they were going to do it, why didn't they do it in Alaska? Let the army go get him. On the other hand, he couldn't just do nothing. He checked his watch. Figure it would take him fifteen minutes to get down there and make a real try at it and then come back. Make it twenty. He'd wait twenty minutes and then call in and report a sighting, a possible, and let them take it from there. For shit's sake, four and a half more years and he was due to retire. He held the glasses up to his eyes and looked again at the spot where he had last seen the figure. There was nothing. Even if he did go down, if he did try, he'd have no idea where to go, which place to look. He wasn't even sure of the direction in which the guy had been moving. It would work out to this anyway.

Slowly he put the field glasses down. There was no sense in peering through them any more. It was just a matter of waiting until the minute hand of the watch had traversed the arc and then making the phone call. He'd do it right. He'd remember to breathe hard.

11:15 A.M., Mountain Daylight Time:

Suddenly it was there before him, the largest man-made hole in the world. It was impossible to judge the distance across the top because the scale of it was so crazy. Paul could look down into the huge terraced crater of the Kennicott Copper Works, Bingham Pit, and see trucks the size of Tootsie Toys, trucks that he knew to be exactly the same size as these monsters that rumbled by with their double tires a full five feet high. There was a muffled boom from across the hole and a puff of smoke. A chunk of the mountainside collapsed into rubble, but the scale was all oddly childlike. The steam shovel, the train on the tracks, the double trucks were all minuscule. The size of the excavation—in fact, eight miles across at the top—was not only staggering to the imagination, but even unnerving. Paul doubted his own perception, wondered how far the exhaustion, the pain, the effect of the pills, had carried him. It was, he knew, a great tourist attraction. But, having approached the lip of the excavation from the southwest, he was directly across from the small area in which tourists parked their cars, gaped, took their pictures, and then, satisfied, turned around to drive to the souvenir shop to buy their copper belts, plaques, and bracelets and pick up their free samples of copper ore.

It was going to be more difficult than he had supposed. Even the reassuring bustle of trucks, cars, and people provided no clear opening, no avenue of action.

He knew he looked too disheveled, too grubby, to pass for a tourist or even one of the laborers in the mine. Whatever he did would have to be stealthy, clandestine, inconspicuous. He stepped back into the trees and started to circle the huge dig, moving in a clockwise direction toward that point on the opposite rim where there seemed to be a concentration of buildings, people, and activity. He had no definite aim. In a vague way it occurred to him that if Bingham offered no reasonable opportunity, he might try to steal a car from one of those happy tourists, drive to a gas station where there was a phone booth, make his call, and then, abandoning the car, strike out. . . . But no, stealing a car was no good. They could broadcast a description of the car, the license plate. It was safer to try here.

Every hundred yards or so he cut back to his right, toward the open pit, and it was on one of those checks that he saw the shack. It was, in itself, unimpressive—a small, weathered wooden shack with a slanting tar-paper roof. It looked, in a way, like a glorified outhouse. What was interesting about it, however, was the intricate series of wires that led to it. Assuming that one of them was an electrical wire, then the others—or one of the others—had to be for a phone. It was, presumably, some kind of observation point, some control point—a foreman's shack, perhaps. Perched as it was on the lip of the excavation it commanded a view of nearly three-quarters of the immense spiral hole. Not all of it. No one point could see everything. So there had to be several of these. And in each there might be one man. And certainly there would be a phone. Connected just to other phones in the Kennicott operation? But surely there was some switchboard, some way of making an outside call. He decided to chance it, to try to find out.

There was a rough dirt service road leading from the main circular road that ran around the mine to the shack. Paul avoided this, crossed the main road well behind the shack, and then, as quietly as he could, forcing himself to walk naturally, as if he were approaching the

238

structure on business, he walked up to the rear of the building. There was a small window in the back, and, as he edged up to it and peered inside, he saw the back of a man in work clothes and a steel helmet. He was standing at a desk before a large window. There was a pair of binoculars in one hand and a telephone in the other.

There was another muffled boom—another one of those explosions—and the man hung up. This, then, was the time to move. But what move to make? It was simpler, in a way, with the broken wrist. There was no question about trying to overpower the man. There was no temptation to a fair and honorable fight. He could either try to explain—and that, he knew, was hopeless —or he could use the revolver. But use it how? As a threat, of course. But what if this man took the dare? Would he be able to shoot? He had no idea. After all, what was the life of one man compared to the lives and safety of all the people in Tarsus? But, then, by that logic, it was perfectly reasonable, in a way, for them to put out a shoot-on-sight order for him.

He was still thinking, still debating with himself and feeling angry with himself for having to debate, when the phone rang. He could hear it through the screened window of the shack. He peered through the window again as the man talked on the telephone. He watched as the man slammed the phone down, scratched the back of his neck, and then left the shack.

It was too good to be true. He watched as the man got into a truck, started the engine, threw it into gear, and roared down the service road to the main road, leaving a cloud of rising dust behind him.

As quickly as he could, he darted around the shack and went inside. He picked up the phone and heard the voice of a woman at some distant switchboard.

"Call, please."

"Area code 617, 432-0514."

"Is this company business?" she sing-songed.

He hesitated. He had no idea what the drill was. If he tried to fake it and said yes, then, for all he knew it would have to be approved by someone. But the question suggested that employees were allowed to make personal calls.

"No," he said.

"Name and department, please."

He looked down at the desk. Who was he supposed to be? He faked a coughing fit, as, cradling the phone to his ear, he used his one good hand to rummage through the papers on top of the desk and then to look in the wide center drawer.

From the looks of it, he seemed to be John Carr.

"Name and department," she repeated with a touch of impatience. "We have to know who to bill it to."

"John Carr. Traffic Control," he said.

He had no idea whether John Carr was the man whom he had seen in the shed or that man's boss. There was, anyway, a memo signed John Carr, Traffic Control, and it worked. For her reply had been, "Yes, Mr. Carr," and those wonderfully welcome words had then been followed by the even more wonderfully welcome sounds of dialing.

"Pathology Department, Dr. Rosenthal's office," a voice at the other end said.

It was like being connected with heaven. "Dr. Rosenthal, please," Paul said.

"Who's calling?"

He hesitated, and then said, "Paul Donovan."

Almost immediately, Rosenthal came on the wire. "Paul!" he said. "Didn't expect you back until next week."

"I'm not back."

"Oh? How is it out there? Having a good time? Interesting?"

"Listen, Arnie, just listen. I have something crazy to tell you, but I'm not crazy. You've got to believe me. I'm not crazy. Just listen."

"All right, I'm listening," Rosenthal said.

"There's a shoot-on-sight order out for me here. You

240

know I've been in Tarsus for the last three weeks. The whole town is sick. Sick and dying. And I think it's Dugway, something from Dugway that's done it. The army has moved in and bottled up the town. There was one guy who tried to get out, and they shot him. I got out a couple of days ago through the mountains, and they've been hunting me down with helicopters and flares at night, and I heard on the radio that they're calling me an escaped lunatic and murderer and there's a shoot-on-sight order out for me. They've brought a field hospital into Tarsus, and they're pretending that they're helping, but what they're really doing is keeping us from talking to anyone or getting help from anyone. There are no phones, there's no way in or out of the town. They won't tell us what the disease is, but they say it's a virus, and they tell us we're in quarantine. But when they came in they were wearing these protective suits with masks and everything. CBW suits they call them. But they took them off. It's headaches, fever, vomiting, funny faces, thick speech, and psychosis. The doctor in charge is named Robertson, a Major Robertson."

"Funny face?" Rosenthal interjected. "Thick speech?

"Sort of slack and bug-eyed. There've been—well, there'd been more than fifteen deaths when I left. There are only eighty-five, eighty-six people in the town. Arnie, you've got to help. Look, you believe me, don't you? I mean, damnit, you've got to believe me."

There was a silence for a moment, and then Rosenthal asked, "What's my son's middle name?"

"Ephraim," Paul replied. "You wanted it to be the first name, but your wife thought it sounded too foreign."

"Where did we buy the ducks?"

"At Mayo's. On the road to Nauset."

"Are you sick?"

"Well, I've had kind of a fever. But I just don't know any more. I've been . . . I've been traveling now for thirty-six hours. I think I've broken my wrist. I fell, in the mountains. I'm full of Dexedrine. I'm exhausted. But I'm not raving. I swear to God I'm not raving. I'm as sane as you are."

"All right," Rosenthal said. "I believe you. I don't mean to belittle, but I've heard worse things."

"What are you going to do?" Paul asked.

"Check it out. Make a little noise. See what happens. I can make noise."

"I know. That's what I've been counting on; that's what kept me alive for the last two days and nights."

"But if they're playing it this close, what are you going to do?"

"I don't know," Paul replied. "I've had only one goal for the last three days. All I've wanted to do is make this call and talk to you . . ."

And then he heard it, the sound of the truck.

"Listen, somebody's coming. I've got to go."

He hung up the telephone and went to the window. It was the man, Carr, or whatever his name was, returning.

Desperate, Paul returned to the desk. If he could find some piece of paper for the man to sign, something to legitimatize his presence there in the shack . . . But there was nothing that presented itself, except, curiously enough, a pint bottle of Old Forester. Puzzled, he picked it up, and then, realizing that he needed his hand, he thrust the whiskey into his pocket and reached to hold the gun. He did not draw it out of his belt, but kept his hand on the butt as the door opened and the man entered.

The man looked at him for a moment. "Who the hell are you?" he asked.

Paul said nothing.

"What are you doing here?" he asked.

And then, not even expecting it to work, and delighted by the sublime irrelevance of it, he said, "Me? I'm the father of twins! Mother and babies doin' fine!"

The man looked at him. "Oh, for Christ's sake," he said, "go sleep it off. Go on, get out of here. I have work to do."

242

"Twins!" Paul repeated, and he walked out the door of the shack, to the service road and the main road. He forced himself to walk fifty yards on the main road before cutting left and into the trees. Let it look like he had to go to take a leak.

1:30 P.M., Eastern Daylight Time:

Practical considerations first. Of course. Arnold Rosenthal, pathologist, scientist, pragmatist, found no difficulty whatever in devising an efficient methodology. He had already run over the possibilities and had decided that Tom Gargan in the Public Health Service in Washington would be the man to call. Gargan would listen to him and would be in the best position to find out what the hell was going on. And to do something about it? Well, if anything could be done, yes. Tom was a fighter and the Public Health Service was not without power.

Rosenthal had known Gargan for twenty years. They had interned together, taken an instant dislike to each other, but ended up respecting each other. And from that respect had grown a friendship that had lasted far longer than any of those casual connections one made for those peculiar and idiosyncratic reasons of first attraction. Gargan was a first-rate doctor and, just as important, a man of high principle. He had gone into public health out of the conviction that preventive medicine, ignored and underpaid as it was, could be of far greater benefit to mankind than any number of flashy heart surgeons, cigar-chomping obstetricians, tedious psychiatrists, and unctuous internists. Now, after all those years, Rosenthal thought of Gargan—as he was sure Gargan thought of him—with real affection and with complete trust.

So, Gargan would be the one to call. The question in Rosenthal's mind, however, was not about method. He knew whom to call and how to put it. Those were the simple things. What he was unsure about was whether to share with Tom, or even whether to admit to himself, the dank, chill familiarity of the suspicion he felt. On the table behind his desk, under its glass bell cover, stood the only personal object in Arnold Rosenthal's laboratory—his father's microscope. He never used it. It was not at all appropriate to the kind of research that Rosenthal was doing now, research involving the use of electron microscopy. That old microscope was all that had been salvaged from the wreck of his father's life. Like him, his father had sat in a laboratory, peering into that microscope at thin slices of tissues, unaware of that greater malignancy that was apparent to the naked eye if only he had turned to look out of the window and into the streets of Vienna.

No, no, he could not share any of that with Gargan. He would not even accept it himself. Certainly not yet. The thing to do was simply to start the inquiry and then see what happened. He picked up the phone and placed the call. While he was waiting for the connection to be made, he arrived at a compromise. It would do no harm to caution Tom that he should be careful. Could he ask Tom not to say who had told him? He could, but he wouldn't have to. He could trust Tom the way Paul had trusted him.

1:55 P.M., Eastern Daylight Time:

When Tom Gargan returned to his office he was smiling. Poor Arnie, he thought. You couldn't blame the guy. He had reason enough for an habitual nervousness. He had a first-rate mind, absolutely first-rate, but even so, he was forever seeing storm troopers under the bed. And for all of the nervousness and concern that Arnie had communicated—concern not for himself so much as for Tom—it had turned out to be a perfectly simple, straightforward, reasonable interview. The problem it-

244

self was serious. Indeed, it might well be enormous. If what Arnie had said was true, and if it was in fact some epidemic—well, that was a bad business, always. And if it had anything to do with Dugway, then it could be a real headache. Those nuts in the biological section had developed strains of diseases that resisted conventional therapy. Which was, after all, the point. That's what an enemy would be trying to do. And that was what the army would have to do, too, for defense. Still, it was crazy that they were running such a sloppy program with such dangerous toys to play with.

The hush-hush part of it was bothersome, too, but still he was confident that if there was an epidemic, bureaucratic rules would just have to be broken through, gotten around, somehow suspended. And his interview with Dr. Maxwell had suggested just that. Maxwell had been surprised, of course, but concerned and eager to check out the story. Gargan had no doubt but that Maxwell would be able to make a phone call or two to the Surgeon General, the Secretary of Defense, the President if need be, and find out what the hell was going on. And then it would be a matter of mobilizing, getting in there and controlling the thing, whatever it was. It would be a big thing to organize, but, in one way, the job would be easier if Arnie's fears were true, because they would know exactly the disease they were fighting, the strain, the limits of exposure, and the range of possible therapies.

What was infuriating was that the army had waited so long. All these facilities, all the manpower and equipment were no good if nobody put them to use. But that would be corrected now. Even as he had left Maxwell's office he had seen him reach for the phone. It would be a matter of another twenty minutes or half an hour— and then there would be some word. He looked forward in a way to being able to call Arnie back and reassure him.

For the moment, however, there was nothing to do but wait. He was waiting for Maxwell, and he was waiting, too, for his secretary, whom he had sent out for the sandwich he would have at his desk. He wanted to keep himself available, so that the moment Maxwell had some hard information they could begin to move. In a way, it was exhilarating. It could be brutal, hellishly strenuous, exhausting, but it was also exhilarating. He had never doubted his decision to go into Public Health. He still believed what he had believed as a young man—that preventions were better than cures—but the routine, the endless paper work, the interminable meetings, the soporific routine of the day-to-day administration of the public health programs were hardly dramatic.

He looked at his watch with some irritation. Where the hell was Jane? He was starving. And later he might not have time even to eat the sandwich. It would be a long grind. He decided that he would call home and warn Marge that things might be a little hectic for a time. Yes, that was a good idea—he might not even have an opportunity to call later on.

He picked up the phone and dialed his home number. Marge was out. Flossie answered the telephone. He left the message with the maid: "Tell Mrs. Gargan that something has come up and that I may be home late tonight. I'll try to get in touch with her later, but she's not to worry."

"Yassuh. I'll tell her."

"Thank you, Flossie," he said, and hung up.

As he replaced the phone on its cradle there was a knock at the door.

"Come on in, Jane, I'm starving."

The door opened. Instead of Jane, his devoted and efficient secretary, there were two men.

"Dr. Gargan?" one of them asked.

"Yes, that's right."

"May we come in? We're from the Defense Department."

"Sure," Gargan said. "Come on in. What can I do for you?"

They approached the desk, but did not sit down. "We'd like to talk to you, if we may, about this Tarsus business."

"Oh? You have some information for me?" Gargan asked.

Without replying to Gargan's question, the taller of the two men said, "We're as concerned about this thing as you are. We'd like to know where you got your information."

What difference does that make, Gargan thought. He was about to say it, to pronounce the words, when it came to him, with the intuitive certainty that was the result of a rough-and-tumble childhood on the streets of South Boston, that these were cops. No matter how they were dressed up, no matter what they called themselves, they were cops. He could smell it.

"If it's true about Tarsus, then it doesn't matter where I heard it," he said.

"Would you mind telling us, Doctor, if you have passed this information on to anyone beside Dr. Maxwell?"

"I don't see why I have to answer any of these questions," Gargan snapped. "Who the hell are you, anyway?"

"As I explained," the taller one said, "we're from the Defense Department." He reached into his jacket pocket, pulled out a leather wallet, flipped it open, and flashed an identification card and badge.

Gargan got up. "Before I answer any of your questions, I think I'd like to speak with Dr. Maxwell."

The other man, the shorter one, spoke for the first time. "That won't be necessary, Doctor. Dr. Maxwell knows we're here. I'm afraid you'll have to come with us."

"Come with you where?" Gargan asked. "Why should I?" What the hell was this? What annoyed him more than anything was how it would all look, how it would all sound to Arnie. And Arnie couldn't be right. That was just crazy.

"It's a little more complicated, Doctor, than I think you realize. If you'll come with us, then we can discuss it."

It was an amiable enough remark, but Gargan realized that the two men had not sat down and were standing—indeed they were looming—in front of him. He was slow to realize it, but the realization had finally dawned. These men had come to get him. They would, if necessary, use force. What could he do? Fight? Scream? Ridiculous! Nobody got kidnaped out of the Public Health Service. But even supposing the worst, then what? It would be a couple of hours of unpleasantness, and then, sooner or later, he would be able to get through to some superior, somebody high enough up so that he could talk reasonably.

"All right," he said.

The three men walked out together.

If he was not back in an hour or so, he knew that Jane would start to ask questions. As it was, she would be puzzled when she returned with his sandwich and his malted to find that he was gone. She would start to inquire. . . . The only thing that worried him was something that the shorter man had said, about Dr. Maxwell's knowing that they were there. Could that be true?

In silence they went down in the elevator and through the revolving doors into the bright August sun. There was a black sedan parked directly in front of the building with a third man at the wheel.

It was not by accident that they arranged it so that Gargan sat between them in the back seat as the car sped away from the curb.

3:00 P.M., Eastern Daylight Time:

This time it was Jonathan Colebrooke at the head of the table, and this time, Eastlake felt confident, there would be at least the possibility of some decisiveness. Renchler

248

had just been scared, had not been man enough to deal with it or even to see it clearly. But Colebrooke was another breed of cat.

For his own part, after a long night of Jack Daniels and self-examination, Eastlake had decided that in a way his behavior, his posture, his attitude had been entirely correct. After all, it was up to the civilians to establish policy. The men in uniform were there simply to carry out orders and to achieve results. But it was not their responsibility to decide what those orders were to be, and what results they wanted.

That flight of the night before hadn't worked out quite the way Eastlake had expected. But it hadn't worked out badly. After all, in the end, Colebrooke had not rescinded any orders, and therefore, at least for the while, had given his implied endorsement to what was happening. Sure, he hadn't *liked* it. But none of them liked it. There wasn't a man in the room who enjoyed any of this. Not even Colonel English. It was just that English was able to think in such coldly logical ways that people like Renchler and Pennybaker were put off. And Dr. Maxwell, was . . . well, he had sort of a right to be angry. It was not the kind of thing that Eastlake would have liked, either. A couple of goons come into your department and shanghai one of your men out from under you, and you've got a right to be annoyed.

"If I may ask one question," English was saying, "I wonder exactly what Dr. Maxwell expected me to do when he telephoned me. I had Gargan picked up, and I requested this meeting. Dr. Gargan, I hardly need say, is perfectly safe, entirely comfortable, and he has nothing to worry about. His temporary inconvenience, I admit and regret. But it seemed to me that in balance the security and the time were probably worth that inconvenience."

"But you could have just told me to tell him to keep his mouth closed. I'd have done that. And he'd have cooperated. . . ."

"I was reluctant to compromise your position, Dr.

249

Maxwell. And Dr. Gargan is perfectly safe. You have my word."

"And mine," Secretary Colebrooke said.

They had crossed the Potomac and driven into the Virginia countryside. Then the driver had touched a button and black shades had sprung up electrically on the windows of the rear part of the car, while a black plate of glass had come whirring up between the driver's seat and the rear seat. One-way mirror? Gargan had no idea. At any rate, he had been unable to tell where the car was going. It had continued to move, and apparently at a fairly brisk clip, for some time, twisting and turning, doubling back, and then redoubling. Or perhaps it was just that the route was on winding roads. But he rather doubted it. It was fairly clear that there was a deliberate effort being made to prevent his being able to find this place ever again.

Their destination turned out to be what looked like a plain, fieldstone farmhouse tucked away in . . . Virginia? Maryland? Not very far, at any rate, from Washington. And he had to admit it was a clever arrangement. From the outside, it looked perfectly harmless, perfectly natural. From the inside, it was a fortress. A prison. A combination of these, and perhaps more besides. The underground area alone was larger than what one would have supposed to be the house and the barn. The two men—Riley and Goran—had escorted him into a chamber that looked like a cell—a prisoner's cell or a monk's cell—closed the door, locked it, and left him there. Not a word. And after a couple of hours, they'd returned, introduced themselves, which was odd—but then they might have been making up the names, probably were —and started to talk.

Gargan had not answered, had not said a thing. But he'd been listening. You couldn't help listening. It was all too fantastic to tune out entirely. And, let's face it, frightening. "Look, Doctor, you're an intelligent fellow. You don't get through medical school, you don't work

your way up in the PHS without being an intelligent fel-
low. You know the score. You know what the possibili-
ties are. You could even write the prescriptions yourself,
and you know what they can do. But why make us go
to all that trouble? And why put yourself to all that
trouble? Wouldn't it be simpler just to tell us what we
want to know? Just tell us who it was that told you
about Tarsus. Nothing's going to happen to him. Or
them. But it's vitally important that we know who
knows about this. We're going to find out. One way or
another, we're going to find out. So why not save all the
trouble and nuisance and let us have it, huh?"

It was perfectly possible, Gargan thought, that they
could use chemicals, could actually inject him with
Pentothal or whatever compound of Pentothal was now
the fashion. And they might get Rosenthal's name that
way. But, on the other hand, it also was conceivable that
they were only bluffing, were only using that as a threat
to get the information out of him. After all, they hadn't
even rolled in the table, hadn't produced the vials and
the needles. They could, he was sure. But would they?
After all, he was an American citizen, a government
official, a doctor. . . . It would be tough for them, later.
He'd see to that. And they would know that, would have
to know it. Were they desperate enough to take that
kind of risk? Well, he would see.

Meanwhile, he would say nothing.

Schleiman was right, of course. The explanations
didn't change the fact that there was that shoot-on-sight
order out on the poor bastard. Colonel English had gone
through the whole story of how it had happened, how
the story of the intruder into Dugway had been fed out,
and how the meeting in Tooele had produced, in turn, a
new story about an escaped maniac. And he was careful
to stress that it had been the idea of the civilian authorities to issue the shoot-on-sight order.

"Which was, of course, perfectly convenient for your
purposes," Schleiman snapped.

"It was not entirely inconvenient for *our* purposes," English replied with impressive calm.

"I want it canceled," Colebrooke said.

"But—"

"We've got to do something, though," Renchler protested. He had his thinking cap on, that Renchler.

"Of course, there is that," English agreed. "But, with respect, there is still Tarsus. It exists. His claims, however wild they may seem, happen to be perfectly true. All he has to do is get someone to check them out. An attorney. A reporter. Anyone."

"It's Tarsus that we have to deal with, then. Not Donovan," Colebrooke said.

"I still say we've no choice. We make a clean breast of it," Pennybaker said. He sounded like Melvin Douglas, all honorable and admirable. It would not be his pill to swallow, though. It hadn't been the navy, after all.

"The Cuban story . . ." English began.

"Is no good any more. It's too late for that. And I don't like it. It escalates the risk."

"We've got to do something, though," Renchler protested. He had his thinking cap on, that Renchler. Really paying attention, he was.

"A disaster," Colonel English said.

"Of course it's a disaster," Pennybaker agreed.

"All we have to do is change the complexion of the disaster. Disguise the kind of disaster."

"And just how do you propose to do that?" Colebrooke asked.

They had come back. They had disappeared for a while, had left Gargan there to think it over. But they were back now. And they wanted an answer.

"I think you're bluffing," he said.

"We're not."

"All right. But I still think you're bluffing. And I'm calling your bluff."

"It will take a little time," Goran said. "We've got to go through channels for approval. But we're not bluff-

ing. We don't have to play games. Sooner or later, you're going to tell us."

"Look," Riley said, "make it easier for yourself. Make it easier for your friend. What if he tells some other people? He's got other friends, doesn't he? What if he mentions it to them? Give them a break, why don't you?"

"And what happens to us? What happens to me? And to the . . . the person or persons unknown from whom I heard this information?"

"Nothing."

"Then I can go?"

"After a while. Of course."

"How can I believe you?"

"What choice have you got?"

"I can choose not to talk. And I can continue to choose not to talk."

"For a while, maybe," Goran said.

"Let's go," Riley said. "Clearance must have come through by now."

"We'll be seeing you," Goran said.

Maybe they weren't bluffing. But even if they were, they could keep him here for as long as they wanted. If only he hadn't told Flossie to tell Marge not to worry! He wouldn't be missed for days. . . .

". . . what it comes down to in the end is that, despite all your fancy ideas about which story you're going to give out, what line you're going to take, what lie you're going to peddle, there's still a town there," Pennybaker was saying. "There are people. There are buildings. They exist."

"Yes, exactly," Colonel English answered. "That was the very thing I had in mind, myself. But what if there were no town?"

"I beg your pardon?" the Secretary said.

They leaned forward, all of them, to listen. Their moods were varied—from Pennybaker's belligerence through Maxwell's guilt, through Schleiman's annoyance, to his own curiosity—but they were all listening, and, Eastlake thought, ready for anything. He'd timed it wonderfully well, that English. They were damned near desperate for some way out of this mess.

"What if there were no town?"

4:00 P.M., Eastern Daylight Time:

All right, so it was four o'clock. Big deal! Rosenthal was annoyed with himself for the transparent childishness of the games he was playing. If Gargan hadn't called yet, it meant only that he hadn't yet found out anything, or that he was still checking, still confirming. How could he know, sitting up here in Boston, what Gargan was doing in Washington, what red tape there was, what delays there might be? It was not so alarming. There were any number of possible explanations for the fact that Gargan had not yet called back.

On the other hand, all these arguments were familiar now. Rosenthal had gone through the entire routine an hour before. The only difference was that then he had managed to talk himself out of his incipient alarm by the simple maneuver of postponement. He had promised himself that he would give Gargan another hour. He would not worry about it until four.

And now it was four. And nothing had happened. The phone had not rung. There had been no word. But that, in itself, did not mean anything. Rosenthal knew he was behaving like one of those crazies who went around trying to tell you that the world was going to end at noon on Thursday—just because they had figured out, through exactly such mental processes as these, that that was all they could stand. And, of course, the world did not end. It was not ending now. He had set no particular time with Gargan. That had not seemed appropriate or necessary. When Gargan knew something, he would call. As simple as that. It could be at 4:15, or 4:22. . . . But after five? Rosenthal doubted

254

it. After the offices in Washington started to close, there would be a decreasing likelihood of Tom's being able to find out anything.

It was silly to call, but then it was silly not to call. He had accomplished nothing all afternoon, had been unable to concentrate, unable to work. . . .

The hell with it! He picked up the phone and dialed. A few moments later, he was through the Public Health Service switchboard and waiting while Dr. Gargan's extension rang.

"Dr. Gargan, please," he said to the secretary who answered the phone.

"I'm afraid he's gone for the day," she replied. "Who is calling please?"

"Gone?"

"Yes, sir."

"When did he leave?"

"Around one. . . . Who is this please?"

Rosenthal hesitated. It was pure paranoia. Or was it? Where the hell was Tom? Checking out the Tarsus story, of course. But why not do that by phone? From his office.

"This is Dr. Arnold," he said, feeling a little foolish. "I called earlier and spoke with Dr. Gargan. He was to get back to me this afternoon. It's extremely important. Have you a number where he can be reached?"

"No, I'm sorry," she said. "I don't. He left suddenly, while I was out getting his lunch. When I came back, he was gone, and I was told he wouldn't be back for the rest of the day. Can I transfer you to Dr. Maxwell?"

"No, no," Rosenthal said. "It's only four o'clock. He may yet call me from wherever he is. But thank you."

"You're quite welcome."

Rosenthal hung up. He was a little surprised at his behavior. Dr. Arnold, indeed! It would be tough to explain that to Tom. Tom would rib him about that for years. On the other hand, it was peculiar, this business of Tom's leaving the office that way. He reviewed in his mind what the secretary had told him. She had gone out, not for her lunch but for his. To bring his lunch back to him. And he had gone? With no note, no message as to where he was going, where he could be reached? It was certainly abrupt. But what could have happened to him?

Rosenthal was able to devise a scenario that was not wholly implausible—Tom calling someone in the Surgeon General's office and being invited to come over for a meeting. It was not impossible, but neither was it wholly convincing. In sum, he did not entirely regret that he had made up a name for the secretary. The call, after all, had gone through a switchboard. What was distressing, what was appalling was that there should be a need—even an apparent need—to have to think in such terms.

He was still sure, or mostly sure anyway, that it would all make sense sooner or later and that it was just a matter of waiting until the explanations were forthcoming. What else was there for him to do? It had been Paul Donovan's voice on the phone. He was sure of that. But . . . people do have breakdowns. The strain of the past few months, the months after Marian's death, might have begun to take their toll now. If there was no disaster, no epidemic, there would be nothing for Gargan to find out about in Washington.

He picked up the telephone book, looked up the area code for Utah, and dialed 801-555-1212.

"Directory Assistance. What city please?"

"Tarsus," Rosenthal said.

"Yes, sir. What name please?"

What would there be in Tarsus? What would there have to be? The Tarsus Drug Store? The Tarsus Bar and Grill? The Tarsus . . .

"The United States Post Office."

He felt pleased with himself. Of course it would have to have a post office, and the post office would have to have a telephone. She gave him the number. He thanked her, depressed the button on the telephone, and then released it, got a dial tone, and dialed. He waited for the connection to be made. He was surprised to hear the noise of the phone ringing. But after two rings, there was an intercept. An operator came on the line.

"What number are you calling, please?"

Rosenthal repeated the number.

"I'm sorry that number is temporarily out of service."

Should he ask how long it had been out of service? When service was going to be restored? But what could she tell him? He knew more about it than she did.

"Thank you," he said.

Slowly, he replaced the receiver. The laboratory was air-conditioned. Rosenthal, nevertheless, was sweating.

He would remain calm. Above all, he would continue to think as dispassionately, as coolly, as logically as he could manage. Those tendencies that Gargan saw in him, he recognized himself. Of course they were there. And it was necessary sometimes to try to compensate for them. But now?

Assume for the moment that what Paul Donovan had told him on the phone was true, that Donovan was not raving, had not suffered some sort of nervous collapse, but was simply reporting accurately what had happened. And assume, for the sake of argument, that even the suggestion about Dugway was correct. In that case, they would try to hush it up. But how far would they go? Gargan's disappearance—if that was what it was—disturbed Rosenthal. And not in any generalized philosophical way, either. It was bad for him, for Arnold Rosenthal. He was, after all, the link.

But he was not willing to believe it, or not yet. Or, putting it another way, he had to be sure before he acted. He picked up the phone once more, dialed the Washington area code, consulted his vest-pocket address book, found Tom Gargan's home telephone number, and dialed it.

"Hello?"

"Marge?" Rosenthal asked. "This is Arnie. In Boston."

"Why, Arnie, how are you?" Marge asked. "It's been a long time."

He breathed a sigh of relief. She had not used his last name. There were any number of Arnies in Boston.

"Just fine," he said. "We're all fine. And you?"

"All right," she said. "We're fine. But Tom will be disappointed at missing your call. He's not home."

"Oh? I tried to get him at the office today. He wasn't there. I thought maybe he'd come home early."

"No, something has come up. He called when I was out shopping . . . I guess it must have been around one. He left a message about being home late. And then, later on in the afternoon, someone from the department called to ask me to pack Tom a bag. He's gone up to Alaska."

"Alaska?" Rosenthal repeated stupidly.

"There's some sort of epidemic broken out up there, I guess. He's gone up to Point Barrow. They're not sure when he'll be back. . . ."

Marge prattled on about what a nuisance it was for her, but how much Tom would enjoy being out in the field again. Rosenthal was not listening so much to what she was saying as he was listening to the occasional clicking sounds that had come onto the line.

"Was it Tom that called to tell you about Alaska?" Rosenthal asked.

"Why no. It was somebody else from the department. He said that Tom had already left on a Military Air Transport Service plane. Is it anything urgent? I could try to get hold of him for you. The office would know where he is."

"No, no. Nothing urgent. It's just that . . . I thought I'd be getting to Washington in a couple of weeks. It would be nice to get together."

"Wonderful. I hope we can. I hope Tom is back by then. When I hear from him, I'll tell him you called."

"Thank you," Rosenthal said. "Take care."

"Love to Clare," Marge said.

"Thank you. And she sends hers to you, I'm sure."

258

That would have narrowed it for them. There were any number of Arnolds in Boston, but Arnolds and Clares? Well, it would still take them a while.

What really disturbed him, though, was the other thing that Marge had said. Point Barrow? Tom Gargan was a specialist in urban preventive medicine. He was the last man in the world to pick to send to Point Barrow. Panama City, Beirut, Damascus, Bombay—any of those places would have been plausible. But Point Barrow? Besides, since his latest promotion, Tom was a desk man, a coordinator of units in the field, not a man to send out to inoculate Eskimos.

Rosenthal did not believe it, not for a moment. As a lie, it was stupid, clumsy. But governments, when they lie, seldom feel the need to do so intelligently. And Gargan, where was he? If not in Alaska, then where?

That did not bear too much thinking about. Rosenthal felt a pang of regret for his friend as he remembered a fragment of a conversation on this very subject. They had been sitting together, late one evening, in his house out in Tarbox. Rosenthal had been explaining how he never joined protest movements, nor signed petitions, nor made noise. How he tried to keep aloof from politics, tried to keep his nose clean. Gargan had shaken his head, had chuckled, and then had said all the right things, all the good things, about the responsibilities of scientists.

"No," Rosenthal had answered. "It is you who don't understand. It is not just a question of whether or not it can happen here. You don't believe it can happen here because you don't believe it can happen *anywhere*. Once you have seen it happen, once you know what it is, once you admit it as a real possibility, then you learn to be careful."

Tom had not agreed. Of course he had not. But these tendencies were always there, in all governments. Even Gargan had to admit to the existence of a blacklist of scientific researchers in the Department of Health, Education, and Welfare. To him, it was simply an anachronism, a leftover from the days of McCarthyism. To Rosenthal, it was a reminder of a continuing impulse in all bureaucracies, in all governments. And now Gargan was learning. It had taken him too long to learn. Like Rosenthal's own father.

Not that Rosenthal seriously believed that Gargan would be marched off to a gas chamber. By the time that sort of thing started to happen, it would be too late for everybody. It was mysterious disappearances, it was telephones that were out of operation, it was sinister clicking noises on telephone lines. . . . Things of this sort had been clues to those who were shrewd enough, alert enough, timid enough—or, in a way, brave enough—to recognize them. And it took a kind of bravery, after all. What you were risking was feeling like a fool. But then, on the other side, what you were risking was your life.

He swiveled his chair around, looked at the table behind him, and stared at his father's microscope. In the curve of the glass cover he could see his own face distorted in the reflection. The time had come to face the facts. Or, indeed, that time was past. For he realized that he had already made his decision.

He spent a few minutes longer than usual assembling papers for his briefcase. Then he locked the lab, went down to the parking lot, got into his car, and started to drive home. On an impulse he went a couple of blocks out of his way, taking the route that led through all the traffic of Harvard Square, so that he could stop at the newsstand at the Harvard Square MTA station.

Through the open window of the car he called to the newsman and asked if he had any Salt Lake City newspapers. The newsman went around the corner of the kiosk to the out-of-town rack and came back with a paper in his hand.

"Thirty-five cents," the man said.

Rosenthal rummaged through his pockets for change, found two quarters, and handed them over. With the cars behind him honking, Rosenthal told the news dealer to keep the change. He moved forward, turned to the right, and then took the next left to cut over to the Massachusetts Turnpike. The next time he caught a red light, he stopped and looked down at the paper on the seat beside him. And there it was, in black and white: MANHUNT CONTINUES FOR MAD KILLER. In a box just beneath the headline, there was a picture of Paul Donovan.

There was nothing hallucinatory about it. It was real, it was there, in front of him, on the front page of the Salt Lake City *Tribune*. Rosenthal was surprised at his own calm. All he felt was a pastel sadness. He had had a good life here, but all the time he had kept himself detached, kept himself light, kept his avenue of escape open. There was no more need now for any rationalizations about property values and investment opportunities in the Caribbean. The house on St. Andros, the $22,000 in the Royal Bank of the Bahamas, the carefully cultivated professional friendships in the hospital at Nassau. . . . He had not been wrong. He would tell the children it was a vacation, a spur-of-the-moment thing.

He turned onto the Massachusetts Turnpike, and drove, just under the speed limit, being careful. He thought of Tom Gargan and of Paul Donovan. He wished them well. God knew, he wished them well. But there was nothing he could do for either of them. He reached over to the newspaper on the seat beside him and turned it over so that Paul's face was no longer staring up at him, vulnerable and reproachful.

5 P.M., Mountain Daylight Time:

"It's very loud, mommy!"

"Yes, I know, dear. But it won't hurt you."

"It won't? You promise?"

"I promise, dear. It won't hurt you. It will land over

there, just like the last one, and people will get on, and then it will go up again. And you can watch it. It will go straight up."

"Are we going to ride one of those, mommy?"

"Yes, dear."

"Will it be fun?"

"Lots of fun," Hope said. "You'll be able to see way down—the whole town and all the mountains."

"The whole town! My house, too?"

"Yes, your house, too," Hope said.

She put her arm around Martha's shoulder. Martha shifted the doll from one arm to the other and, with her left hand, took Hope's hand. Martha's thumb was wet. She had been sucking it.

Dr. Lewine had explained it all to Hope, had told her how the effects of the fever coupled with the very real trauma of losing all five of her children had produced in Martha Pratt this incredible, pathetic reversion to childhood. She had fled to the safety of the life of a five-year-old. Five-year-olds do not have children, and therefore cannot lose them. Or, in a way, perhaps she was herself becoming the children she had lost. How long it would continue, Dr. Lewine could not say. But for the evacuation, he had asked Hope to look after Martha. It was a request Hope had been unable to refuse.

Hope was perfectly well aware that, for all the simplicity of the request, Dr. Lewine's motives in making it might be mixed, even devious. For all she knew he had heard the same report on the radio, and it was not inconceivable that he had come immediately to see her in order to prevent her from trying to make a break for it then and there. She could not be certain of this; she had no way of proving it. But still, it had worked out that way. Just a few moments after she had heard that the manhunt was over and that the mad killer had been captured, Dr. Lewine had knocked at her door. She had thought—anyway, had hoped—that he would have some word about Paul. If the manhunt was over, was Paul alive? Safe? Or dead? But he did not know. She had asked him, and he had sworn that he knew nothing. He had even promised to try to find out, if he could. What he had come about was Martha Pratt. He had explained to Hope that the town was being evacuated temporarily, that the entire population was being transferred to a military hospital at Dugway.

"How temporary?" Hope had asked.

"I don't know," he had replied. "I assume everyone will be back tomorrow afternoon. You're just supposed to take an overnight case and anything of particular value. I understand they're going to fumigate the town."

And then he had explained about Martha, hurt and helpless, and how she needed someone to stay close to her, to look after her, and, insofar as it was possible, to humor her. The orderlies would be too busy with the desperately sick patients during the trip.

Hope had hesitated, had wondered whether her original fears about Lewine might still be true, but she had given in. Whatever his motives, he had been telling the truth about Martha. She was truly pitiable. And if Hope was now saddled with a thirty-five-year-old child, the additional weight was hardly perceptible, for the emotional burden she had been carrying anyway—Uncle William, Aunt Emily, and then Paul!—was virtually flattening.

She had promised Paul she would wait a few days. She had not yet given up hope for him, not entirely. And as long as she had to wait, as long as she had to stay here, Martha Pratt was a distraction, even a help. At least Hope had the feeling of being useful to someone.

The huge transport helicopter chattered into life again and slowly rose from the cleared area near the field hospital. That was the last of the stretcher cases. Hope looked around at the pitifully small group of ambulatory patients and the even smaller number of healthy residents of Tarsus. The two groups together amounted to no more than twenty. The helicopter roared more loudly, lifted off, and angled away into the sky. Martha huddled against Hope, swaying slightly. As the helicopter receded, and the noise of its engines diminished, Hope heard Martha crooning to herself in a childlike, childish voice and to a strange dirge-like tune:

"I do not like thee, Dr. Fell
The reason why I cannot tell
But this I know, and know full well,
I do not like thee, Dr. Fell."

5:25 P.M., Mountain Daylight Time:

The arm hurt. It wasn't just the wrist any more, but the entire arm from the elbow to the fingertips. It throbbed in angry rhythm and it had swollen hideously. As much as possible Paul avoided even glancing at the aching weight slung in his sweater in front of his chest. What good was there in looking at it, anyway? There was nothing he could do to help it. The aspirin was all gone and had not helped—even four and five aspirins at a time. He thought of it as if it were not in fact part of his own body, but one more obstacle, one more enemy. It had swollen to more than twice the size of his right arm, and it lay there in its sling protesting when he tried to go too quickly, tormenting him when he accidentally jarred it, distracting him from the concentration that he needed to negotiate hills.

The cheese was gone now. He had forced himself to eat it in order to stave off for as long as possible the combination of hunger-faintness with exhaustion-faintness. There were a few dried apricots left in his pocket and there was one more chocolate bar, but he was saving those. He would need them later.

He trudged on, half-walking, half-staggering. Every now and then he caught himself and issued the old orders to his body to pick up the feet, not to drag, not to leave such an easily visible trail, and for three or four yards his body would obey. But then, exhausted to the point of mutiny, it would revert to its slovenly habits. And Paul would find himself taking its part in the running argument, explaining to himself that at least it was still moving, at least it was still performing. There was a kind of grim satisfaction he could take in that—and in the fact that he was still riding on the run of luck that had kept him from the eyes of all those searchers. There had been no helicopters for the last couple of hours. Paul wondered where they were. Had they shifted to a ground search? Were they searching in some other direction? Without the radio, he could only guess. But it was no good relying on optimistic guesses. No good relying too much on luck. Pick those damn feet up, he ordered again, and, again, for a few yards, anyway, the feet obeyed.

After he had left the shack at the Kennicott mine and had forced himself to walk nonchalantly down that road, he had darted into the woods. He had run until he was unable to run any more, until hoops of burning steel encircled his chest to blend with the pain of his ribs and his wrist. He had half fallen on the ground and had sat for several minutes considering the question of what to do, where to go, from there. Having made the telephone call, having got word through to Arnie, he had done what he had set out to do. Now he could begin to look out for himself and to think of getting the medical attention he needed for his broken wrist. But how? Where? He could not even surrender himself to the searchers, not with the shoot-on-sight order out for him! He could see it all too clearly: The demand that he raise his arms over his head, his difficulty extricating the wrist from the sling, and then the nervous young cop riddling his body with bullets.

To try to get to a hospital, or a doctor, would be every bit as suicidal. To continue on from Bingham toward Salt Lake City would be to do what they would assume he was trying to do. Without the radio, he had no idea what degree of panic had seized the populace.

265

For all he knew, there were householders sitting with shotguns in every living room. The thing to do, then, was the opposite of what the search parties would expect. The longer he was gone, the wider the circle that they would draw on their maps. Ironically, the safest direction to take would be back toward the center of that circle—back toward Tarsus!

Tarsus! Of course! It would be the last place they would look for him. And the closer he got back to Tarsus, the safer he would be. There would be doctors there for his wrist, and Hope was there, waiting for him, waiting to hear whether he had made it through to the outside world. He had sat there at the base of the large spruce, waiting for his breathing to return to normal and examining this new plan. The more he thought about it, the more sensible it appeared. Tarsus would be the only place where he could surrender, could give himself up and they would know that he was not an escaped maniac, a mad dog to be gunned down.

He had set out, then, heading south. Insofar as possible he would try to retrace his escape route. It had worked once and might work again. Of course he was weaker now, and with the broken wrist he moved more slowly. If necessary, he would depart from the original route. He would stay in the Oquirrh range until nightfall, and then, wherever he was, cut west, cross Rush Valley again, and, at sunup, turn south once more for the last leg, down the Onaquis to Tarsus.

He refused to consider the question of whether or not he could make it. He had to make it. It was as simple as that. And when he got there, he would claim to have wandered around in the mountains without getting anywhere. He was in such lousy shape that they might even believe him. Yes, that was what he would do. And then, when Rosenthal's efforts blew the lid off, the publicity and the outrage would be enough to protect him from any retaliation from the army.

Having made the decision, he staggered southward. He had been going for hours now, and he was exhausted. It was not the exhaustion itself that frightened him, but the temptation that grew out of that exhaustion, the temptation to take chances. It was with increasing difficulty that he had been forcing himself to go around clearings and not cut across them. He knew that to cut across an open space was dangerous, but, tired as he was, spent as he was, he found it difficult to care any more. He had been making bargains with himself, promising himself that the next rest would be longer, that if he found a suitable hiding place he might even quit for a few hours, wait until dusk and then cut west down to the floor of Rush Valley. He had not been much impressed by these promises. After all, what was the likelihood of finding any suitable shelter, any really safe hiding place? It would be, when he finally gave out and collapsed, another boulder, a log, another patch of rough ground.

On the other hand, there would be the whiskey. It was a weird thing to have done, unplanned and almost unintentional. But it had been a lucky thing, too. All day he had forced himself not to touch it, not to use it to dull the pain because it would dull his mind, dull his reflexes as well, and increase the chances of falling, of disaster. But when he stopped for the big rest, then he would have a slug of it. He knew that if he opened the bottle and allowed himself even a sip, the temptation for a second sip would be irresistible. And there would be a third. He couldn't risk it until he was settled in some relatively safe stopping place.

So intently was he thinking about it, looking forward to the taste of it and the wonderful burning feeling as the heat of it went down his throat, that he almost missed the brush-covered and nearly hidden entrance of another abandoned mine—very like the one in Tarsus. The fact that he had almost missed it was encouraging. He was not even annoyed at himself. If he had nearly missed it, perhaps others would. Surely, it would be invisible to helicopters. And it would be dry in there and protected from the wind. It was a great find. If he believed in signs, he would have believed that this was a sign. It was, anyway, a cheering thing to find, and his hope, that had been languishing for so long, flickered tentatively into life again.

He could rest there, and sleep. He could make it until nightfall in there. And then, rested, he would have a good chance of crossing the valley.

He quickened his pace and hurried to the mouth of the tunnel. There was a large sumac bush that had grown up in front of the opening, concealing the aged timbers that had been used to shore up the tunnel. Paul pushed the sumac bush aside, shifted his weight to take another step, and then froze.

It had been his pushing aside of that bush that had disturbed them. They had been quick to respond to the threatened intrusion, and it was the rattle that Paul heard, even before he saw them.

Then he saw them, two rattlesnakes sunning themselves in a small patch of sunlight at the entrance to the tunnel. They were moving, coiling; it would be only a matter of seconds, Paul knew, before they would strike. Trying to move as smoothly as possible—not abruptly, not jerkily—Paul retreated a half step as he reached for the revolver. Good. He had it. It was in his hand. And now the safety was off. He fired, emptying the gun at the two snakes.

He had not intended to fire all six bullets, but he had done it. The gun was empty. He stood there, looking at the snakes. One was dead, the other still twitching. Paul backed away. He would look for a rock, a stick, something to kill the other snake with. But, no, what if there were more snakes inside? He would not be able to see, and he had no bullets left. He would be safer out in the open. Cynically, calculatingly, he forced himself to continue. He might as well get whatever benefit there was from the rush of adrenalin. He pushed himself a hundred yards, and then, exhausted, he sank down onto the ground. He looked around. This would have to do. He opened the bottle of whiskey and drank.

Friday, August 14

9:15 P.M., Mountain Daylight Time;
11:15 P.M., Eastern Daylight Time:

Paul had wakened from his long, exhausted sleep into broad daylight. He had had to wait, then, until dusk before recrossing the Valley. He had dozed, picked a few berries, finished the whiskey, had dozed again, and now, as it grew dark, he was descending toward the floor of Rush Valley.

Diana Colebrooke was watching a Colgate commercial between segments of "Friday Night at the Movies," and she was no longer amused by the fact that Arthur Godfrey was apparently unable to pronounce "fluoride."

Thomas Edison was dead.

Mary Edison was dead.

General Wyatt was pouring himself a drink.

Captain Phipps had left the general some time earlier and was taking a hot shower before going to bed.

William Smith was dead.

Hiram Sandor was playing pinochle.

Colonel English was eating a jelly doughnut and drinking a cup of coffee, black, no sugar, in the duty room of DIA's safe house somewhere in Virginia.

Mrs. Jenkins was dead.

William James was dead.

Emily James was dead.

Hope Wilson was sitting in a barrackslike building on the Dugway Proving Ground watching Martha Pratt soothe the rag doll she carried in her arms.

Soriah, Joseph, Hiram, Moriah, and Peter Pratt were dead.

269

Charlie Renchler was in the Connecticut Avenue apartment of his mistress, Elaine, watching the same Colgate commercial on the same television channel, and trying to believe her reassurances that it was all right, that it happened to a lot of men, that it was just fatigue. . . .

Stuart Peterson was dead.

Jason Keefe was dead.

Viola McNamee was dead.

Walter Schleiman was sitting in the Thermasol steam bath that had been installed in the bathroom of his Georgetown house only two months before.

Allan Redman was dead.

Homer Suggs was dead.

Homer Suggs, Jr., was dead.

Sid Conrad was at the station house waiting for the alderman whose youngster had been arrested for fighting at the A & W.

Fred Collins was dead.

James Ishida was lying in a bed at Dugway, groggy with painkillers so that, from time to time, he forgot the wound in his leg, forgot where he was.

Oliver Sinclair was dead.

Mike McGrady was reading a book of poems called *A Short History of the Fur Trade*.

Norman Lewine was on his third double Scotch, unable to talk with Elinor about what happened, but equally unable to talk about anything else.

Adele Himber was dead.

Ted Webb was dead.

Marvin Dawes, confined to quarters, was playing another hand of solitaire. He already owed himself $37,-825.00 (at five dollars a card).

Sidney Foster was dead.

Emory Basford was dead.

Davis Harding was dead.

Bill Robertson was talking with Dr. Rebikoff, the psychiatrist, who had flown in from Washington that afternoon to consult on the victims of the epidemic.

Laura was nearly finished with a small rosebud of a crewelwork pillow she was working on while she waited for Robertson to come home.

Julius Gillette was dead.

John MacDonald was in the last frame of a game in which he was bowling better than he had ever bowled in his life, hoping to break 200.

John Gillespie was dead.

Robert Sterling was watching a baseball game the Police Athletic League of Salt Lake City had sponsored.

Paul Brown was dead.

Alice Brown was dead.

Sandra Brown was dead.

Carl Bender was dead.

Special Agent Carlson was filing his report and was pleased that the work of the manhunt would really rack up the overtime for the Salt Lake City office the way the Bureau liked.

Rollin Winston was lying in the barracks at Dugway, his face turned toward the wall. He had not spoken for thirty hours, and Dr. Bartlett, writing in his office in another building, a hundred yards away, was wondering, as his pen paused over Winston's name on the list, whether those centers in Winston's brain had been permanently damaged or not.

Sergeant Jackson was feeding bits of leftover beef to the guard dogs in the Dugway kennels.

Major Garrett was polishing rocks in the lapidary polisher his wife had got him for his birthday that spring.

General Norland was addressing a meeting of the League of Women Voters in Provo, explaining the way in which the army cooperated to make sure that the soldiers were able to vote.

Laine Peterson was dead.

Oswald Keyes was comatose, had been comatose for the past twelve hours, but was still alive.

Dr. Arnold Rosenthal, his wife, and his two sons were on a BWIA plane an hour and a little bit out of Logan Airport en route to Nassau.

Edward West was dead.

Nora West was dead.

Harris West was dead.

Beatrice Sugar was dead.

William Harrison was turning a pawn on the chess set he was making on the lathe in his basement.

Dr. Tom Gargan was pretending to sleep in the small cell in the DIA building in Virginia, but only pretending.

Jonathan Colebrooke was crossing the Potomac in a green Pontiac, his limousine having been deliberately left behind.

Chester Conklin was dead.

Harvey Skaggs was dead.

Bradford Shaw was dead.

Henrietta Bartlett was dead.

Peter Ungerer sat on the edge of his bed in the barracks clapping his hands together slowly, rhythmically, even though his hands stung with the clapping that he had been keeping up now for more than eighteen hours.

George Slattery was dead.

Joe Viorst was dead.

Mortimer Deap was listening to Hindemith on his stereo rig.

Admiral Pennybaker was drafting a letter to the President, a letter which he had been working on all evening, which explained what had happened in Tarsus and Washington, and which concluded with the resignation of his commission, but which was left undated and open.

Jordan Burdine was dead.

Jefferson Byron was dead.

Dr. Blake Maxwell was sleeping, the barbiturate he had allowed himself having by now taken effect.

Kenneth Shaw was dead.

Frank Johnson was dead.

John Forrest was dead.

272

Charles Beaconsfield was dead.

Lidia Beaconsfield was dead.

Eva Beaconsfield was dead.

Mitchel Farrington was dead.

Oliver Porton was dead.

Anthony Gillon was dead.

Robert Gold was dead.

Elizabeth Eades gasped, shuddered, gasped again, and then she died too.

Fred DeLeo, no longer wearing the insignia of a lieutenant colonel but bearing only the double chevrons of a corporal on his olive fatigues, had jumped down from the truck. The three others appeared to be privates. DeLeo had had no idea what their real rank was, who they were, or where they had come from. They had flown into Dugway that afternoon, bearing orders from Colonel English and accompanied by a large number of unmarked crates which they had, themselves, transferred from the C-47 to the two three-quarter-ton trucks. All DeLeo had known about them was what he had been able to gather from their manner, their attitude, their silence: They were pros.

DeLeo had stretched. It had felt good to be free of the confinement of the truck cab. In the same way, it had felt good to be free of the confinement of all that bureaucratic hesitation and principled perplexity. It was not that DeLeo despised these things. Indeed, he was aware of them and felt toward them a kind of tender nostalgia. It was just that the pace of the world was such, and the risks were such, that those things were luxuries now. In the second half of the twentieth century, political and moral niceties were paralyzing. The only questions DeLeo would admit to be relevant any more were: Were you right, or, anyway, less wrong than the other guys? And were you efficient?

There had been no doubts in DeLeo's mind that what they were about to do was, indeed, efficient. And, in the long run, he had been sure that it was the least wrong thing that they could do. As he had walked along the main—and the only—street of Tarsus, he had found it hard to believe that this absurd no-place place had seemed to all those bigwigs in Washington a serious counterbalance to the security and preparedness of the United States of America. Now that the population had been evacuated, the town's perspective was subtly altered. What was it, after all, except a collection of unsightly buildings huddled absurdly in the crotch of a mountain range at the site of a couple of played-out veins of silver? Who needed it? What was it good for? Nothing!

Similarly, the people, now that they had been removed from the town, were no longer a political unit, but another group of victims, of refugees, of displaced persons. It was regrettable, but this was the risk of business. The entire history of the twentieth century could be written as an account of the alterations and varieties of displaced persons that wars and political upheavals had produced. That it had to happen here was unfortunate, but still DeLeo believed the country had been lucky. As between the crash of a Mohawk plane with the loss of fifteen lives, and the crash of a Pan Am plane with the loss of 330, which would any sane man choose?

They had started unloading the boxes. The geologist had checked his charts in the lowering twilight, looked for a moment at the steeper of the two mountainsides, and had remarked, "No sweat. It'll go just the way we planned."

They had picked up the boxes, two men to a box, each one holding one of the rope handles, and started up the steeper east slope. It had been a tough climb with the weight of the boxes—better than eighty pounds each. It had taken a good twenty minutes to reach the outcropping of face rock the geologist had selected.

"This ought to do it," he had said.

The two technicians had remained. DeLeo and the geologist had gone back for the third box, and then for the fourth. It had taken an hour and a half to set the boxes in place.

"It ought to go just fine," one of the technicians had said.

"It's got to," DeLeo had said. "And completely."

"No fear," the geologist had answered.

The three men had stood there while the fourth one had set the antennas on the visible corners of the by now mostly buried boxes. Five minutes later they had reached the trucks, turned them around, and had driven out of the cut to a position of safety. They had stopped the trucks and DeLeo and the geologist had gotten out. They then had gone back to the other truck where the two technicians—the demolitions man and the radio man—had been adjusting the radio detonator.

"All rightee," the radio man now said. "Would you care to do the honors, sir?" he offered to DeLeo.

"No, that's all right. It's your baby."

"Yes, sir," he said.

He then removed the switch guard and pressed the red button.

Nothing happened. But then three, perhaps four seconds later, there was a low rumble, a tremor in the ground they were able to feel, even at this distance, and then a louder roar, higher, but still well within the bass register, as the thousands of tons of the face of the east mountain loosed and fell upon the town of Tarsus. Or what had been Tarsus.

It stopped, then resumed, stopped again, and then continued for another spasm.

"We've got the chain," the geologist said. "It worked."

They waited for twenty minutes and then drove back to what once had been Tarsus, what once had been the cut. DeLeo looked with satisfaction at the changed contour of the mountainside and the cut between the two mountains. It would take months to excavate that—if, indeed, anyone was going to bother. And if the local

pieties were so extravagant, what they would find would
be a fair sampling of the population of Tarsus, the bodies the other squad had taken from the temporary
morgue and had arranged in likely configurations around
the town.

It had been a strenuous couple of hours. Of course,
DeLeo thought, they could have done the same job in
twenty minutes with a tactical atomic device. But not
even Colonel English had the authority to issue one of
those. The President's personal authorization was necessary for anything nuclear—another one of those political, moral niceties of which DeLeo disapproved in his
ascetic, puritanical way. He disapproved of all such luxuries.

They turned the trucks around and headed out of
Tarsus, back to the main road, and then out across
Skull Valley to return to Dugway, where the plane that
had brought these three men was waiting to take them
away again.

11:55 P.M., Eastern Daylight Time:

The door opened. Gargan sat up on the cot in the five-
by-eight cell. A soldier in uniform stood in the doorway.

"Will you come with me, please, Dr. Gargan?" the
soldier asked.

"Where are we going?"

"To the duty room."

Gargan sat there for a moment, wondering whether to
ask any more questions, to refuse to move, to make a
nuisance of himself. . . . But, no, he decided, he would
save his energy for more important things. He was afraid
he would need it.

He got up and followed the soldier out of his cell,
down a long subterranean corridor, through a heavy
steel door, up a flight of stairs, along another corridor
in another direction, through a second steel door, and

then into the farmhouse itself. The soldier led the way to an improbably comfortable, denlike room. There were bookshelves, comfortable leather chairs, and, over the fireplace, an impressive elk's head. Gargan noticed that the windows were heavily draped.

From one of the outsized leather chairs, a figure arose. The man was dressed in civilian clothes, looked to be in his middle forties, and impressed Gargan as being trim, athletic, in excellent shape. He was smoking a small, black stogie.

"Dr. Gargan," the man said, "I apologize for disturbing you at this hour. I'm Richard English."

He extended his right hand, but Gargan declined to shake it. Gracefully, English converted the gesture to a wave with which he motioned Gargan to a chair.

"Won't you sit down?" he invited. "Would you like some coffee?"

Gargan hesitated. He had eaten nothing since breakfast. He had missed his lunch and had refused the dinner tray that they had offered him. Partly, he had been afraid of what might be in the food, and partly he had been using his refusal to eat as a weapon.

"I'm going to have some," English said. "I thought you'd like to join me."

"All right," Gargan said, and he sat down in the chair English had indicated for him. English nodded and the soldier disappeared to get the coffee.

"I must apologize for detaining you here this way," English said.

"When are you going to let me go? How long will this go on? When do I get out of here?"

"That's what I've come here to discuss with you," English replied. "My hope is that it can be arranged quite quickly. I'd like nothing better than to take you back to Washington with me tonight. But that, I'm afraid, depends on you."

"Oh? How so?"

They had tried the threats before, and now they would try the promises. The trouble was, though, that they might be as slow to keep any promise as they had been reluctant to carry out any threats. But then, Gargan reasoned, he had nothing to lose by listening.

"As you can imagine," English began, "this is a very awkward situation. For both of us. You have acquired certain information you are not supposed to have. We're responsible for making sure that information doesn't circulate. . . ."

"You mean about Tarsus?"

"Yes."

"So, it's true then."

"It would be foolish for me to confirm or deny whatever version of the story you may have picked up," English said, after a thoughtful puff on his stogie. "That would make our situation only more difficult. All I can tell you is that the security of the nation requires that we take certain measures—even strong measures—to ensure your silence. And all this was made clear to you in the discussions you had this afternoon. Yet you were unwilling either to give assurances that you would remain silent about this matter or to tell us what the source of your information was."

The soldier returned with a coffee pot and cups and saucers on a tray, which he set down on the low table between the two chairs.

"Help yourself," English offered.

Gargan poured himself a cup of coffee and then waited until English had poured a cup. He watched to see whether English took cream or sugar, both of which he wanted. But English took his coffee unsweetened and black. Then so would he. It was, at least, hot and strong. Better than nothing.

"Good," said English, after taking a sip. He set the coffee cup down on the table. "I'm not here to interrogate you or to threaten you. I just want to make clear what choices we have so that you can decide what you want to do. We'd like to take your word—that is, if you would be willing to give it—that you would remain silent. Unfortunately, the world has become a very complicated place, and the delicacy of the situation is such that we can't take anyone's word. The choices left are all fairly unpleasant.

"We could keep you here indefinitely," he went on, "but that would be increasingly awkward. Your disappearance would not be difficult to explain, but your reappearance after a month would be another matter. And after six months it would be all but impossible. The second possibility, then, is inadequate. The third possibility is much simpler—your death. An unfortunate accident at Point Barrow, which, by the way, is where your wife thinks you are at the moment, on legitimate department business. But your death would be unfortunate. You have a wife, a family, a useful and successful career. It would be a terrible waste. . . ."

For the first time, Gargan was afraid. It was not the melodramatic quality of the suggestion but, quite the opposite, the very matter-of-fact way in which English listed it.

"And then there is a fourth possibility," English continued, "and the one which I much prefer."

"And that is?" Gargan asked, trying to match the insouciance of his adversary.

English pulled an envelope out of his breast pocket and handed it to Gargan.

"If you were to tell us where you got your information, and if you were to sign this document, then I think it would be perfectly proper and safe for us to release you in the morning."

Gargan looked at the letter. It was a letter of confession admitting that he, Thomas F. Gargan, M.D., had accepted a bribe of ten thousand dollars from the Pelican Lake Development Corporation of Pelican Lake, South Carolina, to prevent official reporting of four cases of typhoid that had been caused by a contaminated water supply at their resort.

"I didn't do this," Gargan said.

"Of course you didn't. But with this letter and your signature, we'd have a way of assuring ourselves that there would be no indiscretion on your part."

"How do you know that I wouldn't repudiate it after I'd signed it?"

"If there were no other evidence," English speculated, "I suppose you could. But someone would wonder why there were two cash entries into your bank account at the time of this Pelican Lake incident. And of course, we can produce witnesses. Perjury, I'm afraid, is among the least of our sins."

Gargan thought for a moment, staring down at the sheet of paper in his lap. After a while, he looked at English. "Let me make a counterproposal."

"By all means. Please do."

"If I were to give you my assurance that I would keep quiet about this business, and if I were to give you my signature on that unspeakable paper, could we let it go at that? I mean, if you were to kill me, you still wouldn't know who my informant was. You'd be no better off that way than this way."

"It isn't that simple," English returned. "Your refusal to name your informant is disturbing in other ways. It suggests an uncooperative spirit. It suggests bad faith. As a practical matter, we already know about old Arnie. . . ."

It was all Gargan could do not to rattle the coffee cup against the saucer. *Did* they know? How could they have found out? But, on the other hand, how could they have guessed at the name, Arnie? Desperately stalling for time, playing dumb just for another instant, playing the string out to the last millimeter, Gargan looked at English as blankly as he could and asked, "Arnie? Arnie who?"

English smiled.

"I was hoping you'd tell us the last name," he said. "Not that it will take us terribly long. We have our methods. And we've found people with a lot less to go on than this. So it's just a matter of time."

Gargan relaxed. He was saved, for the moment anyway.

But it was just for the moment. He knew that English was not boasting idly, and he believed that it would be just as English had said—only a matter of time.

Then why not tell them? Why not cooperate? It would be so much simpler to take the easy way, to cop out. And the results would be nearly the same. Exactly the same? No, not quite. There would be a bad taste, a taste he would have to live with for the rest of his life.

It was outrageous. What they were doing was insupportable, indefensible, evil. He was damned if he would tell them.

And then he smiled, not because there was anything amusing in his situation, but because it struck him that, quite literally, that was what would happen. If he told them, he would be damned. And to find out in these circumstances and at this late hour that he still believed, that the Sisters had got to him after all . . . well, it was something to smile about.

English sighed. "All right, then," he said, "we'll give you some time to think about it."

How much time? But Gargan would not give English the satisfaction. He would not ask.

"Briggs!" English called.

The soldier returned and came to attention.

"Take him back," English ordered.

Gargan followed the soldier back to the subterranean cell.

11:00 P.M., Mountain Daylight Time:

Lewine sloshed more Scotch into the glass, topped it off with what was left of the split of club soda, and considered getting up to go into the kitchen and wrestle ice cubes out of the freezer compartment of the refrigerator. Screw it. He would drink it warm, *à l'anglaise*.

He was sitting in the living room, not so much watching television as using the television set as company. Elinor had gone to bed, partly irritated, partly hurt, partly frightened by his dull unresponsiveness. There was a commercial on the tube, something about an aftershave lotion. A Polynesian girl was saying that she was a sucker for lime. Lewine wondered whether it was the Scotch or whether he just had a dirty mind. She was leaning against the trunk of a palm tree. . . . A palm tree, for God's sake! And she was holding on to the trunk of it like . . . They had to be kidding. He suspected it was the Scotch, but it was the commercial, too. With enough whiskey, you could cut through things and see what it was all about with wonderful alcoholic simplicity.

He regretted the disappearance of the Polynesian girl. There would be half an hour of news, weather, and sports before the talk shows came on. He was looking forward to the talk shows. He would listen to them until he could not understand what they were talking about any more. And then he would crawl off to bed.

"Good evening, ladies and gentlemen, this is Dan Weaver with the news. . . ."

Lewine took another healthy belt of the lukewarm whiskey. His hand was still carrying the glass back down to the table when he realized what Weaver was saying. The hand froze in midair as he listened.

". . . was completely destroyed this evening by an avalanche. The tiny town of Tarsus, sixty-five miles southwest of Salt Lake City, was just a remnant of the prosperous mining community that had existed there in the twenties. The silver mines that once were the town's prosperity also carried the town's doom, for the opinion of experts is that a gas explosion of unknown origin must have triggered a tremor in a geologic structure that was weakened by the honeycomb of tunnels around the Tarsus cut. The entire face of the east mountain collapsed upon the town, burying Tarsus and all its inhabitants under thousands of tons of rock and rubble. We now switch you to our helicopter unit on the scene."

Lewine looked in shock and horror, suddenly sober, as a picture appeared on the screen before him. There, lit by searchlights on the helicopter, was what had once been Tarsus. His first thought was of the narrowness of his escape, of the escape of all of them from the avalanche. The avalanche? But of course it was no avalanche! *They* had done it. The bastards! That was why they had evacuated all those people, to get them out of the way so that they could blow up the town—just blast the whole town off the face of the earth. And they'd done it! He returned his shocked attention to the television set. The shrill voice screaming over the sound of the engine of the helicopter was saying that there were no survivors—not one. Between eighty and ninety people had perished in the rock fall, one of the worst disasters in the history of the state of Utah.

But they couldn't, they just couldn't do that. Couldn't do what? He had no idea what it was they intended to do. They had blown up the town; what were they going to do now with all those people? Kill them? Would they really do that? But what choice did they have now? If they could destroy the town, what would stop them from taking the next logical step?

Surprised to find it still in his hand, still six inches above the table, he put the glass down. Without even bothering to turn the television set off he left the room, left the house. He walked the block and a half that separated his house from Bill Robertson's. It would have been faster to drive, but he did not trust himself behind the wheel. He was too drunk for that. Too drunk and too angry. He could not believe that this was happening. Or, no, that this had happened. But there it was. He had seen it on television. What was staggering was not simply what they had done, but the way they had lied about it, the scale of the lie. Well, they would have to answer to him. And then it occurred to him that this was no idle threat. He knew the truth—he was one of the few who knew what had really happened. And he had had enough of lies. He had had it up to here.

Lewine strode up the walk and climbed the step to Robertson's front door. There were lights on in the house—not that it mattered. He rang the bell, waited a moment, and then rang it again, just as Laura was opening the door.

"Why, Norm," she said. She sighed. "I suppose you want to see Bill."

"Yes."

"I'll get him," she said, and she left him there, standing at the front door.

She had a right to be annoyed, he supposed, but that was just too bad.

A moment later, Robertson appeared in the doorway. He was wearing a bathrobe. His feet were bare. He was carrying a bowl of shredded wheat.

"For God's sake, Norm, what is it? Can't it wait 'til morning? I'm exhausted. And you are too."

"Where's Laura?" Lewine asked.

"She went upstairs to wait until I get rid of you."

"Okay. Why didn't you tell me? What the hell are you guys up to? I mean, what the hell is going on?"

"It wasn't my decision, Norm. It came from higher up. And what alternatives were there?"

"Don't give me any of that shit," Lewine said. "I mean, we blew up a town. *We* did. All of us. We all share responsibility in this. You and me."

"I don't see how."

"We're part of it. We're party to it."

"Well, that's the rules of the game," Robertson answered.

"Game? What game? Some son-of-a-bitching game! And what are they going to do with the people who are left? Shoot them? Gas them?"

"Nobody's going to hurt those people," Robertson said.

"Oh, thanks. Thanks a lot. I'm glad to have your assurance on that. It really makes me feel all warm and secure. The way the public feels warm and secure because the President told them we aren't going to engage in germ warfare any more."

"Now, Norm, I know you're upset. But try to get hold of yourself. This wasn't germ warfare. This was an accident. A research accident . . ."

"And all those people, are they any less dead? And the ones who are left . . . What *are* you going to do with them? You can't just let them go, can you?"

"We'll deal with them. I can't tell you yet how, but we'll deal with them."

Lewine was silent for a moment. It was the silence of despair, utter despair, but Robertson took it for an indication that some of Lewine's excitement had subsided.

"Come on in. Sit down, Norm," he invited.

Lewine followed Robertson into the living room and sat down in the chair nearest the door. Robertson sat down on the sofa, put his bowl of shredded wheat on the coffee table, and took a spoonful.

"Nobody likes any of this," he said, "and none of us is any happier about this than you are. But the stakes in this thing are enormous."

"Bill, there are lives at stake. And lives lost! What could be as enormous as that?"

"I know how you feel. But when Donovan escaped, he left us no choice. All along, we've done what we could. You were there. You know we saved as many of those people as we could. And we didn't save them just to kill them or lock them up forever. You've got to think about it the way I think about it. These decisions are too big for emotional reactions. They're too big for you and me to make by ourselves."

"Bill, I saw the television program. I saw the eleven o'clock news. There are some decisions too big for me not to make by myself."

"Look," Robertson said, "if Elinor were sick, or one of the kids, you wouldn't try to treat any of them by yourself. Your emotions would be involved, you wouldn't be able to think clearly or trust your own judgment. And on a thing like this, too, your emotions are involved. The guys who are working out the decisions on this are specialists. They're able to see clearly; they're able to understand the implications for everybody of what they're doing. And we have to trust them. Not only as doctors, but as officers. I can understand that you're upset. Hell, I am too. But in the morning, why don't you go talk to General Wyatt—before you do anything. There's not much I can tell you; I don't have any power. No authority. I just do what I'm told. That's all that you and I can do."

Lewine shook his head. "You're forgetting one thing, Bill. In a way, this is my case. I was called in to see Mary Edison, and I came to you on a consult. I'm the attending physician here, and I've got a responsibility that nobody else has."

"Mary is dead! You know that, Norm. What the hell?"

"Yes, I know. She's dead. And that's why I came to see you. To let you know that when you decide what you're going to do with those other survivors of Tarsus, you better include me with them."

Robertson was silent for a moment. Finally he spoke, "You've made yourself pretty clear. I could put you under arrest. But I'm not going to do that. Because I want you to think about this. As a friend, I'm asking you to."

"Asking me what? To think about it?"

"Yes. And not to do anything before talking to me again. You're tired, you're smashed, you've worked like a son-of-a-bitch. You deserve better than being thrown in the guardhouse for a hasty decision."

Lewine sat there, stunned. "Okay," he said. "I'll think about it."

"Good. Now go get some sleep," Robertson said.

Lewine got up, went to the door, and left Robertson's house. He did not say goodnight. He walked back to the sidewalk and then turned to look at the house. Inside, he supposed, Bill Robertson was eating his shredded wheat. It was incredible.

What Lewine did not know, however, what he had

not supposed, was that Robertson was on the phone this very moment, talking with the Security people, instructing them to put a watch on Lewine and a tap on his telephone.

Saturday, August 15

2:00 P.M., Mountain Daylight Time:

At first Paul thought he was lost. The approach had
seemed to him the right one, familiar, correct, but in his
weakened condition he supposed that he could have
made a mistake, could have misjudged distances. It had
to be wrong. He looked down, into the cut, furrowing
his brow in puzzlement as he stared at the lake. With
some difficulty, because he had to do it with only one
hand, he spread the map out on the ground and tried to
figure out where he was. It made no sense. There was
no lake anywhere in the area. For a lake simply to have
sprung up out of nothing made no sense. But the map
bore last year's copyright, and there had been no lake
for six miles in any direction.

He looked up from the map and studied the cut again.
It was familiar and not familiar. The face of the mountain to his left was entirely strange, but the other mountain, the one on the right, looked familiar. He walked on
another forty yards to look at it from a new angle, and
discovered the mule track. It looked like the right mule
track, the one that had gone down into the cut, widened,
and become the main street of Tarsus. But now it simply
descended from nowhere to halt abruptly at the shores
of this small, muddy lake. He looked south, beyond the
lake, beyond the huge pile of rock, tree trunks, and
branches, and then, in one terrible instant, he realized
that it was, indeed, a new lake. That pile of debris
blocking the stream was new. There were leaves still on
some of those trees. The leaves were still green. My

God! This was the place. This had been Tarsus.

He stared down, at first in blank disbelief, and then gradually the disbelief gave way to rage as he realized that *they* had done this. If only they had managed to catch him, to shoot him, then perhaps the town would have been saved. But because he had been lucky—or unlucky—enough to elude the searchers, they had elected to discredit him by erasing the town from the face of the earth. And the people? All of them? And Hope? He had not intended it, he had not even known about it, but unwittingly he had exchanged his life for all of theirs.

Had he been less exhausted, less famished, less in pain, he might have been able to cry. As it was, he could do nothing. He stood there, staring down into the cut, and then, like a sleepwalker, he started down the mule track. It took him ten minutes to descend to the point where the stream had backed up to form a lake, another ten minutes to scramble around the shore of the newly formed body of water, and then perhaps a quarter of an hour to negotiate the slope on the west face and climb around the rubble and debris that had buried the town.

On the other side of the artificial murrain he saw them: The cars, the station wagons, the pickup trucks of the sightseers who had come to see the disaster. From his vantage point well up on the west slope he was able to see the barricades that the police had set up and the two highway patrol cars still parked at the site to protect the curiosity seekers from going too far into the still unstable pile of rock and earth. It was, of course, ghoulish of them, but in another way, from his elevated angle of vantage, he was able to understand that in a blind, groping way they had come to visit a holy place. They were being cheated, of course. In insurance policies these things were described as "acts of God." Paul knew better; he knew that God had had nothing to do with it.

And then he considered the Highway Patrolmen again. It was perfectly possible, even probable, that they were there not only to protect the sightseers, but also to look for him. He was now the only survivor of Tarsus. He was the only man who knew.

But somehow it didn't seem all that important any more. He was too tired, too miserable, too guilty. He was just spent. He had no plan in mind, no grand strategy. But tactically, he knew what he had to do. It was almost a reflex now. He had to keep to the cover and get south of that barrier. And then he had to get out of these damn mountains. Even if they caught him. The worst they could do was shoot him. Maybe that wouldn't be so bad.

Slowly, painfully, as carefully as he could manage, he worked his way to the south, and then, well south of the barrier the Highway Patrol had set up, he descended into the cut. He came out behind Dr. Cooley's empty kennels. Cooley's house, at the mouth of the cut, was the only structure still standing—all that was left of Tarsus. To the left and behind, the gawkers were leaning over the barrier, staring at the disaster area and, no doubt, trying to imagine what it had been like in those last instants. He moved unnoticed toward the main road where more cars and trucks were parked. He crouched low on the shoulder of the road, rapidly checking to see whether anyone had been obliging enough to leave their keys in the ignition. But no one had. At the end of the road, however, there was a pickup truck with a tarp tossed loosely in the back. It would do, Paul thought, as well or even better. He looked about him, checked quickly to make sure that no one was watching, and then, with painful clumsiness, heaved himself up over the tailgate and onto the bed of the truck. He covered himself with the tarp and lay there, trying to keep his breathing quiet, feeling the beads of sweat drying on his neck and shoulders, and trying to decide what to do next. The truck, he hoped, would take him to a town. And then? He would try to call Arnie again. He would tell Arnie what had happened, what they had done now, and he would find out what Arnie had been able to accomplish—if anything.

And then? If he could find a hospital, if he could present himself at an emergency ward, he doubted whether they would come in and shoot him right there, in cold blood. The wrist was hurting now less than it had before, and although he was glad to be relieved of some of the pain, he was more frightened by the fact that the pain had diminished than he had been by the pain itself. At the best, the bones had started to knit, and would have to be rebroken and reset. At the worst, there was some irreversible damage that could mean the loss of the arm. So, he would call Arnie and then try to get help for the wrist. It wasn't much of a plan, but it was the best he could do.

He lay there for a while, and then held his breath as he heard the voices of two men approaching the truck.

"Well, I've seen it, but I still don't believe it," one of the voices said.

"They explained it on the television. It was all them mine tunnels that caused the avalanche. The whole mountain was weak. Leastways, that's how they figger it."

"I dunno. Mountain looks pretty solid to me."

"But, see, that's the thing of it. Mountains always *look* solid. . . ."

They got into the cab and started the motor. Paul was unable to hear them any further. They backed the truck off the shoulder, turned it around, and drove away. Paul had no idea where they were going, nor did he care much. Anywhere would do. He was mostly intent on keeping the arm from getting jounced by the bouncing and swaying of the old, nearly springless truck.

Perhaps twenty minutes later the truck turned sharply, slowed, and stopped. The motor died, but the two men did not get out. There was a smell of cheap frying oil in the air, at the same time both delicious and nauseating. He was considering whether to risk peeping out of the tarp to see where he was when the question was resolved for him by a bored female voice that asked, "What'll you have?" The men ordered hamburgers, french fries, and coffee. So, they were in some sort of drive-in. Which meant they had to be in a town—or near one. Very slowly, moving only a fraction of an inch at a time, he lifted a corner of the tarp. He could see nothing but the sky and the overhead roofing of the waitresses' runway of the drive-in hamburger joint. It was safe enough for him to raise his head and peep out over the side panels of the truck, but not safe enough for him to risk getting out of the truck. It was too open and there were too many people. He settled back, hoping his luck would be better at their next stop, and that that stop would be soon.

The two men were talking as they waited for their food. At first they discussed seepage problems in some excavation that they were working on. But then their talk reverted to Tarsus. Paul listened in morbid fascination, picking up bits and snatches and putting together the public version of what had happened. Apparently the story was that there had been a gas explosion that had triggered an avalanche. There would be no attempt to recover the bodies. The army's experts—of course, the *army's* experts—had determined that it would be not only impractical but unsafe to try to dig through the rockfall. The Governor had proclaimed the next day to be Tarsus Day, with flags to be flown at half-staff throughout the state and special prayers to be offered up in all the churches. The President himself had sent a message of condolence, and all the relatives of those who had died were to be flown in on the Governor's own plane for memorial services the following Sunday at the site of what had been Tarsus.

It was amazing, utterly fantastic. It was all so far-fetched, so utterly preposterous that it took Paul a moment to realize what it meant to him. Governors, Presidents—who would believe him now? He would be dismissed as a lunatic. And, for all of their talk about Tarsus and seepage, they had said nothing about the manhunt. Was that still on? Had it been merely that the "avalanche" had eclipsed the manhunt, or had they somehow or other called it off? Paul could not be sure. If only those two bastards would stop yammering and turn on the radio. Or stop chewing and start talking again.

Paul waited, heard a loud burp, and then one of the men speaking.

"All right, let's move it."

"Yeah. Wait, we need gas."

"All right."

The truck backed, turned, moved for fifty or seventy-five feet, and stopped.

And then, Paul's luck changed. One of the men went off in the direction of the men's room. The other waited to order a fill-up and then asked for a cigarette machine.

"Inside," the attendant told him.

The attendant set the hose, then called, "Coming," and walked over to another customer. The truck was unattended. Abandoning caution, Paul sat up, looked around, and then, seeing that the coast was clear, threw off the tarp and half-jumped, half-fell out of the pickup truck. The attendant heard the noise and looked around, but Paul was on the other side from the boy and the body of the truck concealed him. Paul backed off, and went around another larger truck, putting it between him and the attendant.

This truck, a large, square, vanlike vehicle painted white, bore the identification, "Tooele County Bookmobile." It, too, was unattended. And, better than that, when Paul tried the door he found it unlocked. He slipped in, closed the door behind him, and peered out the tiny high window. The truck could not possibly be left this way for very long. Whoever ran the Bookmobile would be coming back and taking it—where? Presumably to Tooele. It was Saturday, late in the afternoon, it would have to go back to Tooele. There would be a hospital there. And phones. That would do him nicely.

A woman emerged from the ladies' room carrying the key with its wooden plaque, which she returned to the gas station office. And then, seeing that she was approaching, Paul ducked down on the floor. He had to wait only a moment or two before he heard—and felt—the slamming of the cab door. The ignition whined and caught. The motor started. The Bookmobile started to move.

Now Paul was able to look out of the window and to see with some puzzlement that they were in Tooele, were driving through Tooele, were leaving Tooele. Where, then, was she going? Salt Lake City? That would be even better. It was hard to stand at the window as the truck swayed down the highway. He sat down on the floor, then stretched out, and even allowed himself to close his eyes. It was hot in the truck, and he was exhausted. He permitted himself the luxury of dozing. It wasn't a deep sleep, and he was aware all the time of the truck's motion. But he was grateful for the rest.

Twenty minutes later, maybe a little longer, Paul felt the truck slow, then stop. Cautiously he raised himself to the window. He expected to see a traffic light or a stop sign or some other indication that they were approaching Salt Lake City. Instead, to his horror, he saw a sign:

DUGWAY PROVING GROUND

ENTRANCE TO THIS FACILITY IMPLIES PERMISSION FOR SEARCH OF VEHICLE OR PERSON AT ANY TIME.

WARNING:
DANGEROUS INSTRUMENTALITIES
OF WAR TESTED HERE.

6:15 P.M., Mountain Daylight Time:

It was an oven, a traveling oven. That was crazy enough, but to be saved from one oven by another one —it was too much. The whole thing was degenerating into a sodden farce, as if the world itself were as exhausted, as groggy, as disgusted as Paul knew himself to be. For the Bookmobile to be heading not for Salt Lake City or any reasonable, probable, sensible farmhouse, but here to Dugway! That was already absurd. He had not been discovered because the librarian who evidently lived here on the base—Paul assumed that she would be the wife of one of the scientists or officers—was a familiar figure at the gate. So he had been smuggled inside and then left in the middle of one of the most secret installations in the United States. Not, of course, that it looked like anything. From what Paul could see there was a curved street of fake Tudor houses. It looked like Newton. Or Brookline. Even Tarbox.

So, having spent four days to get to a telephone and back, he had now, in less than an hour and without trying, violated the United States security establishment. And the problem of how to get out of Dugway seemed, at least at first, just as simple. All he had to do was wait here in the truck and in the morning she would leave. But then as he calculated, reconstructing these incredible past days, an ugly realization dawned on him: This was *Saturday* evening. The likelihood was that she would not be moving the truck until Monday morning. Which meant that he would have to stay in the truck not for twelve hours but for thirty-six. All right, one could do anything. If it was necessary, one could survive, one could endure, one could hang on even under the most preposterous circumstances. Had he not climbed mountain ranges and dodged flares and search parties for four days and got away with it? Could he not now sit in a truck for thirty-six hours and wait to be driven to safety?

No! It was sheer agony. The temperature in the truck, which was parked in the direct desert sunshine, was well over 100 degrees. He was perishing of thirst. There was no water and no way of getting to water—at least until after dark. And then it would be risky. Risky as hell. He had watched in absolute agony as a man two doors down the street had come out to water his lawn and bathe his collie. All that water, all that wonderful cool wet, gorgeous water being wasted on grass and a dog.

And, beside the heat and the thirst, there was his increasing concern for his wrist. It was less painful than it had been, and less numb, but the use of it had not come back at all. It had become a dead weight and he was unable to open and clench the fingers. He knew he needed medical attention, and needed it soon, at least if he was to maintain any hope of keeping the wrist and the hand. And to have that to worry about, to brood upon for thirty-six hours of heat and thirst, and hunger, too—no, it would be impossible.

He had accepted the impossibility of his situation and the necessity of some kind of action, however desperate that action would turn out to be. He had not allowed himself, however, to do anything rash. He would wait at least until it was dark, at least until he had a shadow of a chance. Beyond that he could not vouch for himself. Already he was flirting with the idea of opening the door of the Bookmobile, walking up to the first person he met and surrendering—to water, medical attention, cool sheets, and the wonderful oblivion of sleep. But he was not ready to do that, not yet. He wanted at least to make one more call to Arnie, to find out what had happened, what was going on. What had happened to Tarsus? Could they have just killed all those people? Before he did anything so irrevocable as give himself up, he had to have the answers to these questions.

So he would hang on, at least for a little while longer. And while he was thinking these thoughts, psyching himself up to help himself withstand the ordeal of the last hour and a half or so of the sun's heat hammering down on the metal roof of the truck—the sun set late that far west in the time zone—he saw the other oven.

It was a smaller van than the Bookmobile. It was gleaming silver, and on the roof, slanted, so as to display the tomato, cheese, and pepperoni, there was an enormous plastic pizza that rotated slowly while a sound-box device played the first four measures of "O Sole Mio" over and over again. The legend on the side of the truck in bright red letters proclaimed, "Pecos Pete's, Suh. Travellin' Oven."

He had got in in a truck. He could get out in another truck. What guard could, in a routine way, come in and search Pecos Pete's, Suh, Travellin' Oven without feeling like a perfect fool?

He peered out of the narrow window of the Bookmobile at the garish van, waiting for the pizza man to finish preparing the order and leave the truck to make the delivery. That was when he would make his move. He would go to the pizza truck, sneak into that, and . . . what if the guy saw him? What if the pizza man had another order on the base? What if there were no place to hide? With a pizza oven and a two-way radio in that tiny space it'd be crowded. And then, he remembered the gun. There were no bullets left, but then he wouldn't need them. Most people assume when you point a gun at them that it's loaded. And only a maniac would defend a truck full of tomato sauce and mozzarella cheese, a radio, an oven, and an ungodly machine that kept chiming "O Sole Mio" like a defective music box or a retarded parrot. With luck, he wouldn't even have to use the gun as a threat. But he felt good knowing that it was there.

A youngish-looking fellow in a white jacket and a white paper overseas cap emerged from the truck holding four flat square boxes in his arms. Paul watched as he went up the walk of one of the Tudor houses down the street and disappeared from the narrow range of vision the Bookmobile window afforded. He checked the other window. The water-waster had disappeared, too. It was as good a moment and as good a chance as he was likely to have. Not too quickly, not too slowly, but trying for what seemed to be a natural pace and a natural rhythm, Paul opened the Bookmobile door from the inside and stepped out into the late afternoon sunshine. He had never before realized what a difficult thing it was to approximate a normal rhythm, to manage consciously what you could do unconsciously at any other time. The temptation was enormous either to run, or to look around furtively and stand there, frozen, waiting for the cries that his stretched nerves knew had to come any instant. But he managed to put one foot in front of another, to move, to walk, not run, to his nearest Pecos Pete's, Suh, truck, a distance of perhaps three front lawns. Paul reached the truck and tried the handle of the right hand door. It would not be budged. He tried again, more amused than enraged by the pretentiousness of locking a pizza truck. The best olive oil! First-quality mozzarella cheese! The very best dough! But to suppose that thieves and highwaymen were after your pizza truck? It was ridiculous. But maybe not; it was probably kids that Pecos Pete's, Suh, had to worry about.

Paul walked around the truck and peered into the cab. It was not locked, but it was terribly small. There was no place to hide. And with the enormous front windshield, there was no place to crouch down below the dashboard. The pizza man would see him if he tried to wait in the cab and either cry out or flee.

Then he figured out what to do. He went to the back of the truck and stood there, shielded by the van itself from the line of the pizza man's approach. He would wait until the fellow was in the truck, and then, using the gun if necessary, inveigle himself aboard. The only difficulty was that he had to stand there in the street, feeling himself naked and exposed, waiting for Pecos Pete's return. What could be taking so long?

And then, realizing that there was nothing so natural in the world than to be standing here at the truck, waiting to buy a pizza, waiting to place an order himself, he relaxed. In an odd way, once he had realized this, his impatience disappeared entirely. Let Pecos Pete take as long as he wanted.

Paul stood there, relaxed, looking up and down the street. He noticed with a kind of benevolent interest a small boy in a baseball uniform, approaching on a bicycle.

6:55 P.M., Mountain Daylight Time:

Fred DeLeo listened attentively as Dr. Bartlett explained to him what the still wet X ray meant. The wrist would have to be rebroken, reset, and immobilized in a cast. DeLeo nodded, registered the information, but was thinking about other things.

It seemed, at least in some ways, to be a stroke of luck, a fantastically fortunate coincidence, a gift of fortune. But, no, it was nothing so elaborate as that. If anything, it was simply the law of averages, working itself out. Up until now, all of the breaks had gone the other way. The four days of Donovan's excursion had been as fluky as a run of thirty straight passes. That he had finally crapped out was not surprising. And the manner of it, while perhaps improbable and fortunate, was no more unlikely than any number of breaks that had gone the other way.

The big thing had been his selecting the Tooele Bookmobile without knowing that Mrs. Doane, the librarian, lived at Dugway with her husband, a master sergeant. It had been just luck that had brought Donovan within the Dugway perimeter. But it had been their security system itself that had actually found him. The boy had been only the instrument.

Not that Fred DeLeo was minimizing the accomplishments of Talbot Cates. He was a good kid, and had done the right thing, reporting to his father that there was a man without the required I.D. badge outside on the street near the pizza truck. But it was the system itself that had made the lad aware of the importance of I.D. badges—even more aware and interested than his elders, who tended to take them for granted. Talbot, having just turned ten a month before, had been wearing his badge with great pride as a token of his maturity. All personnel on the base over the age of ten were

299

issued badges of this kind. And so, it was not surprising after all that the youngster had doubled back on the bicycle to check.

Donovan's condition—the five-day growth of beard, the disheveled hair, the filthy clothes—would have been enough to arouse suspicion in anyone, but it had been the specific information about his lack of a security badge that had prompted Master Sergeant Cates to call Security. Three minutes later, Sergeant Jackson and two men had picked Donovan up.

DeLeo, who had been half listening to Bartlett, interrupted, and said, "Yes, a local is fine. We need to talk to him immediately."

"Well," Dr. Bartlett said, "I'll have him ready for you in about half an hour."

"No," DeLeo answered, "I'll talk to him while you work."

After all, why not? As those hippie types were fond of saying, let it all hang out. He had everything going for him—the surprise, Donovan's exhaustion, the shock of the medical treatment . . . after holding on for four days there would be an inevitable letting down of wariness, a relaxation of his guard. Donovan would not be able to help it. DeLeo knew that his best chance for finding out what he wanted to know was there to be taken.

He followed Bartlett into the small tile-walled room where Donovan sat on the examining table. He was stripped to the waist and his left arm was in a white canvas sling. The nurse had washed his face, but he was still in need of a shave. His ribs had been taped and there was a piece of white adhesive tape covering the cut on his forehead. To his right, at his good arm, there was a container of coffee. DeLeo waited while Bartlett explained to Donovan that the break in the wrist had begun to knit improperly and that it would have to be rebroken and reset. He would use only a local anesthetic. DeLeo observed with interest Donovan's apparently calm reaction.

Dr. Bartlett injected Donovan in the left shoulder

with the anesthetic. "It'll take a few minutes for it to take effect," he said.

"I'm in no hurry," Donovan answered. "I don't much see the point of it, anyway."

"Surely you want your wrist to heal properly?" Dr. Bartlett replied. "Don't you?"

"What for? The firing squad won't take an imperfect specimen?"

"Aren't you being a little dramatic?" DeLeo asked, speaking to Donovan for the first time.

Donovan looked up for a moment, glanced at DeLeo, and then let his gaze fall. "You think so? No, I thought I was being conservative. I mean, you're not going to take me back and bury me with the others at Tarsus. I'm the only survivor."

"But Mr. Donovan . . ." Dr. Bartlett began.

DeLeo cut in quickly, "Tarsus was unfortunate. What we are trying to do here is to contain that misfortune."

He saw Bartlett staring at him, and he crossed the room so that there was an instant when he stood between Donovan and Bartlett and was able, during the apparently random thoughtful pacing, to gesture to Bartlett with a finger on the lips and demand silence. Donovan, DeLeo was sure, had not seen him do this. Dr. Bartlett turned away as DeLeo faced Donovan on the examining table once again.

"Tell me, Mr. Donovan, where did you go on your . . . little trip?"

"Nowhere," Donovan replied dumbly. "I just staggered around in the mountains. I broke my wrist and then I tried to get back to Tarsus. I never knew where the hell I was."

"Really?"

He nodded to Dr. Bartlett, who came up to the examining table and palpated Donovan's wrist, forearm, and fingers, asking him, "Do you feel this? this? or this?"

Donovan shook his head in the negative.

"All right, then," Bartlett said, "if you'll lie back on the table. . . ."

DeLeo waited for Donovan to be prone on the table and for him to have a good glimpse of the large wooden mallet with which Dr. Bartlett was about to rebreak the wrist.

Before Bartlett began, DeLeo asked, "Do you want to try it again, Donovan? A little more truthfully this time. We know all about your call to Arnie."

Donovan half raised himself from the examining table and brushed Bartlett aside, "Where is he? What have you done with Dr. Rosenthal?"

"Mr. Donovan," DeLeo said reproachfully, "we're not monsters. Dr. Rosenthal is just fine. Whom else did you call on your trip? You know, you really were too clever for us, almost all the way."

"Crap," Paul said. "I wasn't clever, I was just lucky. And I was just lucky enough to make one goddamn phone call."

"Well, I shan't trouble you any further," DeLeo said. "Not now. Thank you, Dr. Bartlett," he said, and he left the examining room to go to the office across the hall where he could call Washington and tell them Arnie's last name. He had not quite closed the office door behind him when he heard the sharp clop of Dr. Bartlett's mallet.

7:40 P.M., Mountain Daylight Time:

Okay, he had it figured well enough. It made for a nice arty ending all right; the bit about the doctor fixing up the arm, shot from weird angles and with peculiar distorting lenses. And no sound track. Just silent, the way it had been in the examining room, the occasional clink of an instrument on a tray merely underscoring that silence. Bartlett had said not a word, and the nurse had been just as mute. They'd put the cast on with meticulous attentiveness, with commendable care. . . . And the next shot would be the courtyard with the gallows or

302

the firing-squad wall. Whatever. A nice, mordant, contemporary bit of business.

Paul had seen the movie, had lived through afternoons as Alan Ladd or James Stewart or Richard Widmark and had learned how it was. Or, no, he had been misled. Because in the movies there were the nice, clean cuts from the examining room to the courtyard with none of this flabby, tedious connective stuff in the middle. It was merely tiresome, something to be endured, for the guard, the same Sergeant Jackson the kid had called—one of the Tarsus gang, in fact—to take him along a corridor and up a flight of stairs. Corridors and stairs! They were boring enough in all those Antonioni movies! But to have to live the scene, and walk through the pointlessness of the shot. . . . But then, maybe pointlessness was the point. What else?

They were going to some holding place, of course. It would not be until dawn that they would do away with him. It was always at dawn, wasn't it? Another nice piece of clanging irony. The rays of the new day breaking on the scene of finality and hopelessness. Well, okay, if that was what the director—or the general—wanted, he would have to endure that too, one more night of . . . of what? Sleep? Come to think of it, he was tired enough. He could, in fact, sleep even though it was his last night on earth. He was sure he could sleep. And if there were a gallows in the morning, and if the hangman weren't brisk and lively enough, he could even fall asleep up on the gallows, standing up. . . .

The sergeant opened a locked double door. It was a security ward, apparently. Which was not the right style. It was supposed to be one of those old-fashioned doors with a peep hole in it. What did they call it? A Judas gate? Something like that. But okay, they could make it up if the set decorator was off somewhere on a drunk. Goddamned low-budget pictures! Goddamned low-budget life! What the hell style had there been to any of it anyway? What point? What purpose?

And then, after a long time fumbling with a formidable ring of keys, the sergeant got the door opened and he nodded Paul inside. And . . .

"Paul!"

It was darker inside. He couldn't adjust his eyes for a moment.

"Paul, it is you, isn't it? Paul?"

And then, when his sluggish reflexes opened the f-stop of his pupils to compensate for the change from the brightly lit corridor to this half-light of the ward, he saw her.

"Hope?"

"You're alive! I was sure . . ."

"I was sure *you* were . . ."

"Oh, my God!"

She ran to him and held him in her arms. He kissed her. "Oh, Hope! Oh, dear Hope!"

They kissed again. And only then did he look around the room. There were the others . . . Ishida, Martha Pratt, Mrs. Ryle. The handful that was left from Tarsus.

In a curious, giddy way, it struck Paul that only the most cornball director of the soupy thirties would have the nerve to try anything as sentimental as this. To find Hope, to find the rest of them. . . . It was the most far-fetched silver-screen hokum he had ever seen! But the tears of joy were running down his cheeks, and not just the way they had done in theaters for those inspirational last reel fade-outs, either. This was . . . It was real!

As if to confirm that incredible hypothesis, he reached again with his good arm and held Hope close to him.

Sunday, August 16

9:00 A.M., Eastern Daylight Time:

Dr. Alan Rebikoff, Dr. Blake Maxwell, and Colonel Richard English were seated in the informal area of Dr. Maxwell's office at the sofa and easy chairs that were across the room from the desk and the work area of the Director of PHS. They had coffee and sweet rolls before them on the low coffee table, and they were in a more cheerful, expansive mood, all of them, than at any time in the past several days.

They had reason to be cheerful, English thought. It was not, as it might well have been, a desperate skull session at the Pentagon. It was not an emergency session of EXCOM at the White House. It was just the three of them, a couple of Public Health Service doctors and a security officer meeting to iron out the last wrinkle in what had been the dirtiest bit of laundry to have come down the chute in a good long while.

Partly, their luck had changed. There was always a little bit of that operating—unknowable variables, the think-tank types called it. But whatever you wanted to call it, it had finally come round. And Donovan was safe and sound at Dugway. And Arnold Rosenthal, M.D., had been identified, traced to St. Andros, and checked through. He was hardly the courageous type who would give them any trouble. There was nothing left, nobody left, except the survivors of Tarsus. . . . And Dr. Rebikoff had come up with the answer to that one. Maxwell, the good, humanitarian, principled Dr. Maxwell, was willing to go along with Rebikoff's suggestion. Or, he was more than willing. He was, like any convert, even more enthusiastic than was appropriate. Colonel English was wryly amused. And relieved, too, for it would not be so bothersome now to disappoint Maxwell's ambitions.

For Rebikoff to come up with such a solution was perfectly acceptable. This was Rebikoff's field. It was what he did, without any particular delight in it—as a surgeon may cut without any particular delight in blood or pain. Rebikoff was a psychiatrist who had come into the defense establishment in 1951 to study the Korean brainwashing techniques to try to work out some countermeasures that could be incorporated into training procedures. He was a professional. Maxwell, the newcomer, was the enthusiast.

What Maxwell wanted was clear enough. Ever since the President's announcement about the end of our germ warfare program, the research establishment's future had been in doubt—and up for grabs. Maxwell was salivating—as surely as any of Pavlov's dogs—for the research facilities at Fort Detrick, Dugway, Pine Bluff, the Navy's Oakland labs, the Fort Greeley setup in Alaska. . . . And the $300 million annual research and development budget that had somehow been unaffected by the President's public announcement.

Like any Washington bureaucrat, Maxwell was trained to scratch any back if he could get his own back scratched in return. That his *volte-face* was too abrupt, that it involved the betrayal of his colleague, Dr. Gargan. . . . These things did not seem important to Maxwell. But to Colonel English they were depressing and irksome. The man was not reliable. He deserved, then, to be used, to be exploited and then discarded. Not yet, of course, but eventually, after the dust had settled. English had kept it open, kept it loose, because he knew you could never rely on anything, that situations change drastically from one moment to the next. As this one damn near had. If Donovan had been caught. . . . Or if he had got clear away. . . . Either way, it could have been bad news. The worst. But Donovan had called Dr. Chicken from the old country, and gone back to get himself dumped into Dugway! Of all places! And Rebikoff had hopped out to Utah and back, and by the time he was back and had formulated his little program, it was all possible, and more than possible. It was a piece of angel-food cake.

"There are three categories," Rebikoff said, "each of which requires a slightly different approach."

There was a crumb of sweet roll at the corner of his lip, and, somehow, that, in combination with the high-domed forehead and the florid complexion, made Rebikoff look like an aged baby. But there was nothing babyish about his categories. "The largest category is that of the incurables, and they present no problem at all. We simply institutionalize them in appropriate government installations where they will remain for the rest of their lives. In any case, this is what would happen to them. This is clear. The second category consists of that group—perhaps as few as nine, or perhaps as many as fourteen—that may be expected to show some marked improvement during the coming two years. These people are rather more complicated in the choices they offer us, but the nature of Japanese encephalitis is, in paradoxical ways, useful to us, or at least manipulable. Practically speaking, the feature of their condition which is most interesting is their disorientation. In various ways, they represent psychiatric *tabulae rasae,* and are rather like the blanks that brainwashing requires. They are entirely suggestible and manageable, and they would work quite well in the situation. We assign them new identities, create for them plausible histories, and institutionalize them in a more select group of hospitals where we connect them to the new reality we shall have created for them. The program of treatment would be not much different from that which they would be following, in any case. Psychotherapy of this kind is an attempt to reestablish connections to the real world. Normally, of course, it is their previous real world, but the connections are infinitely variable. And so is the reality."

"It can work?" Colonel English asked.

"If Alan says it can work," Maxwell said, "it can work."

"Assume for a moment that in one or two cases I am mistaken," Rebikoff said, beaming. Finally, he got around to wiping away that crumb from the corner of his mouth. Colonel English was sorry to see it gone.

"All right," he said. "Doesn't that blow the entire business?"

"Not at all," Rebikoff said. "These people are, after all, mental patients. No matter where they go, they will always carry with them their record of confinement and treatment, their old diagnosis of delusional paranoia, their case histories. . . . Who is going to believe an ex-mental patient's word against that of the United States Army, the Department of Defense, the Governor of Utah, the President of the United States? . . . Imagine it, for a moment."

"You see?" Maxwell prompted, but it was not necessary. Even without Maxwell's enthusiasm, English was able to appreciate it. It was all right. It would work! Of course, it would work. The Russians had been using it for years among their own people. And the fact that we didn't do that kind of thing here only made it easier to do when we had to do it.

"Okay," he said. "But what about your third category?"

"Yes, well they are the most difficult. Ethically, I mean. But there is no reason why the same kind of approach will not work even with those who are unaffected somehow by the incident at Tarsus. They too, placed in specially selected institutions, could be disconnected and then reconnected. . . . There are procedures that have been developed to a considerable degree of sophistication."

"Brainwashing," English said.

"If you wish, yes. But there are only six of them. And

their alternatives are permanent incarceration. Or worse."

"It's a military kind of decision," Maxwell volunteered. "The sacrifice of a few to save the many."

"And they would, in time, be able to lead relatively normal lives, with only a very slight impairment of function," Rebikoff added.

For three-tenths of a billion dollars a year, and the best set of laboratories in the world, you could talk yourself into a lot, English thought. But okay.

"I quite understand," he said. "And I agree with you entirely."

"Then we're home free," Maxwell said. "More coffee?"

"No, thanks, I'm fine," English replied. "But . . . uh, what about your colleague? Dr. Gargan."

"I don't know," Dr. Maxwell said. "I just don't know."

"He is our only real problem," Dr. Rebikoff said. "If we treat him as we have treated the others, we would be ruining his usefulness as a doctor. For good. It's a terrible thing."

"But if it is the only way, if it's necessary . . ." Maxwell began.

"There might be another way," English suggested.

"But there's nothing. There's nothing in his file. No lever, no handle. There's no way to force him."

"We could try to persuade him."

"What do you mean?" Maxwell asked, his eyes narrowing.

English paused for a moment, letting Maxwell imagine bamboo under the fingernails, the thumbscrews, the rack. . . . All that Vincent Price paraphernalia. Then he stuck the pin in the balloon. "Just that. Persuasion. I have in mind talking to Schleiman and letting Schleiman take it up with the President. If the President himself were to talk with Gargan, were to ask him to cooperate . . ."

"But what could the President say?" Maxwell asked.

"It doesn't matter. That's the advantage the President always enjoys. He can simply ask. With no reasons at all. And most of the time, people will do what he asks them. Wouldn't you?"

"It would depend," Maxwell said. "But I see what you mean."

"It's the father figure, you see," Rebikoff explained. "The President asks you to do something for the good of the country, and it all sounds very grand. But actually, it is Daddy, talking to you in a serious way, treating you almost as a grown-up. Almost! That's the art of it."

"I don't know," Maxwell said. "I'm afraid of it."

"It can't hurt to try," English said. "It could work. I mean, what else can he do now? It's a *fait accompli*. He can't undo . . . what's been done."

Rebikoff smiled. "That's it!" he exclaimed.

"What?" Maxwell asked.

"You just gave us the key. It can be arranged that Dr. Gargan could be made to see how important it is that nobody try to undo what has been done. These people, the survivors, do not exist officially. But they are still living and breathing. If he could be made to understand that the survivors are also hostages, that their physical survival depends upon his—er, ah—discretion . . ."

"Certainly that would work," Maxwell said. "You sure you won't have another cup?" he asked.

"Quite sure, thanks," Colonel English replied, as pleasantly as he could. "I've got these reports to get out right away. You understand."

He rose. They shook hands all around. Dr. Rebikoff and Dr. Maxwell were sitting down again to their coffee and their sweet rolls when Colonel English walked down the corridor and past the bank of elevators to the stairwell. There was one elevator running on Sunday morning, but he didn't want to wait. As quickly as possible, he wanted to get back outside and into the fresh air. He took the stairs two at a time.

310

10:10 P.M., Mountain Daylight Time:

Sergeant Jackson sat in Mama Cash's bar, the Chicken Coop, and even though his buttocks were perched firmly enough on the bar stool, he was hovering, and it was as if he were the subject of one of those mirror tricks by which his body only appeared to be resting upon the stool. He seemed to be motionless, but that was only seeming. There were all kinds of motions, violent movements, abrupt dartings and lungings going on, but because they were in contrary directions, none of them were at all apparent. Or, in the terms that Sergeant Jackson conceived it, he was like that old mule of the story, frozen motionless between the equidistant piles of hay and slowly starving to death.

No, it was not quite like that. Because he wasn't starving to death, after all. Sitting there, just as he was, without moving, without deciding anything, he was, in his way, deciding. For the choice was perfectly clear. He could get up and go with Marcy, go upstairs with her and lay her. . . . But he could just as easily not do that, just stay here and keep on ferrying old I. W. Harper from the bar to his lips, taking those quick little swallows, and it'd work out to the same thing. It'd get him to the exact same place, after all. The two roads only seemed to diverge, but Jackson knew that they met again after a while at that dark place where it wouldn't matter any more. If he laid Marcy, it would be as much for the oblivion that would follow the familiar spasm as for the spasm itself. And the old I. W. would get him to that same oblivion just as surely, but his lips and his throat would do the work instead of his tool. The taste of the whiskey was only of secondary interest, as the smell and feel of Marcy's body would be only of secondary interest. The thing was the wonderful darkness at the other end of it all. And even though Marcy was a pro, an unemotional and matter-of-fact hooker, it just didn't seem right to Jackson to use her body if there wasn't going to be any pleasure in it for either one of them. Insulting, really. The Harper would do just as well. And maybe better.

Of course, things had come to a pretty sorry state when a reasonably attractive girl sitting next to you didn't mean a damn thing, when you came out to the Chicken Coop not so much to come here as to get away from there, when you were so absolutely plumb down that you didn't even care which way you went out just so long as it was quick enough.

"Another one?" he offered.

"Not for me," Marcy said. "But you go ahead."

"I believe I will," he said, and poured another shot of the bourbon into his glass.

"Cheers," she said as he raised the glass.

He appreciated the way she sat there keeping him company. It was no huge thing, because it was quiet and there wasn't much else for her to be doing. But still it was nice of her to keep him company while he got himself drunk. What they used to call back home, *mannersable*. He hadn't heard that word in a long time. But it was the right word. It was real mannersable of her to set with him while he drank.

"Sometimes, a body gets to feel . . ." he began. It was his intention to work his way around to thanking her, to letting her know that he did appreciate her undemanding company and her presence.

"I know," she said.

That was nice, too. She might not know what it was that he was going to say, what he had been about to tell her, but in another way, she knew. She had been there, wherever it was. Nobody starts a sentence like "A body gets to feel . . ." without its ending in some kind of misery. And one kind was not unlike another. So, in her way, she did know.

"It isn't right," he said.

"I know," she said again.

And it was because he felt that she did know or at least that she would understand if he talked about it, or —at the very least, and at the bottom line—that she would pretend to understand even if she didn't, that he said anything at all. He hadn't intended to say a word about it. But between the I. W. Harper and the amiability of Marcy and the quietness of the Chicken Coop on a Sunday night, he talked a little bit, not so much getting to the heart of it, because he hadn't even figured it out that far, but poking it at the edges. At least that.

"I used to hunt," he said. "Back in West Virginia, I was a real good hunter. I'd get me rabbits and quail and even a deer now and then. And it isn't the killing that bothers me. I mean, it never did. I was killing to eat. And that's natural. I mean, all you have to do is run your tongue over your teeth and you can tell in a minute that those are meat-chewing teeth. We're supposed to eat meat. I mean, that's part of the plan of things. So it isn't the killing. It's . . . it's what you kill."

Marcy looked at him, didn't say anything, but then she didn't laugh or disagree. In fact, she nodded slowly. Sure, she knew. Because one kind of misery is much like another, and it must be, after all, a pretty goddamn miserable life a girl leads in a place like this, Jackson thought. So he went on. At least a little bit in from that edge.

"I mean, your dog, for instance. Nobody eats dogs. Or do they? I think in China they do, maybe. But those dogs are different. And anyway, they're Chinks. And they don't know shit about dogs. . . . Sorry."

"That's all right," Marcy said.

"But I mean, your hound, that's a special kind of thing. I know dogs used to be wild, like wolves and coyotes, but they ain't any more. It's like we made a deal with them, ages ago, that if they'd come and help us hunt, we'd take care of them. It's . . . well, I mean, I always liked my dogs. I had a blue-tick hound, once, and half of what I learned about hunting and the woods I learned from that hound. And I've been working with dogs all my life. I never thought of it before, really, but it's like . . . it's like we had a contract with dogs. You ever had a dog?"

"No."

"No? Never?"

"Not . . . my own dog. I was on a farm though, when I was a kid. And there was a dog there. Like a collie but smaller."

"A sheltie it must have been."

"It could sit up and shake hands. And it could play dead. Fred was its name. How about that for a dog's name, huh? Fred!"

"But that's it, don't you see?" Jackson said. "I mean we *name* dogs. Duke or Patches or . . . or Fred."

"Fred," she repeated, shaking her head slowly.

"But you don't kill dogs," Sergeant Jackson said. "You don't just . . . kill them."

"No," she said. "Who'd want to kill a dog?"

"You don't just kill them. And you don't. . . . You don't do it that way! It ain't right. It ain't!"

He was talking louder now, and Mama Cash had come in from the other room where she'd been watching television.

"What's all the noise?" she asked. "Trouble?"

"We're just talking," Marcy said. "He got upset."

"Damn right I got upset," Sergeant Jackson said. "And I'm not ashamed of it, neither. It was the worst damn thing I ever saw."

"You sure he hasn't been hitting the booze too heavy?" Mama Cash asked Marcy, as if Jackson weren't even there.

"He's just upset," she repeated.

And Mama Cash turned to leave, to go back to her program. After all, it was a quiet night. But because it was quiet, the entrance of the other man into the room with the bar in it made her pause. She turned to look back, and Jackson thought she was looking at him, still wondering whether he was drunk. And he wasn't. He knew he wasn't. He'd been drinking all right, but he wasn't drunk. And so, to explain it to her, to make her understand that he had a right to be upset, he went on with it, went back to it, for his own sake and for Marcy's too, because she'd stood up for him, and she'd told Mama Cash that it was just his being upset.

"Of course I'm upset," he said. "You would be too. It was awful. I mean, it was just bloody and awful! Worst thing I ever saw! Six dogs, all of them good hunting dogs, too, and all of them with their goddamn heads cut off! They done it to them, and they told me to dig a hole and bury them. Six of them!"

"What dogs? What are you talking about?"

It was the man who had come in. He had heard, and he was asking now. And it wasn't the kind of question or the kind of discussion that was likely to help business any. Men could behave in odd ways. A death in the family, and they'd come out to tomcat, some of them. But not dead dogs. Nobody was going to get horny over a bunch of dogs. Not anyone she wanted in the Chicken Coop, anyway.

"He's just had too much to drink, that's all," Mama Cash said. "You better go on back and sleep it off, soldier," she said to Sergeant Jackson.

"How do you sleep off a thing like that?" he asked. "I mean, have you ever seen a dog with its freaking head cut off? And I'm as tough as the next man, and maybe tougher."

"And drunker," Mama Cash said. "I've asked you nice, and now I'm telling you, soldier. . . ."

"No, no. I'm interested," the man who had come in said, partly to Mama Cash and partly to Sergeant Jackson. "Let him go on."

"But what kind of talk is that for a nice place?" Mama Cash wanted to know.

"We've all got our troubles, Mama," Marcy said.

"Yeah," Sergeant Jackson said. "She knows."

"What dogs?" the man asked.

"What business is it of yours?" Jackson wanted to know.

"None, really," the man said, smiling. He was a fellow in his late twenties, crewcut, big. "I just never heard of anything quite like it before. Dogs with their heads cut off! I mean. . . . That's pretty bad. And in a bar, you talk to guys, you listen to guys. You know how it is."

"Yeah, I know," Jackson said. He took up his glass and drained it. He'd talked enough, maybe, he thought. Maybe he'd better go on back to the base.

"Hell, I get sick to my stomach when I see a dog out on the highway that's been hit. . . ." the crewcut guy said.

"Who doesn't?" Jackson asked. "What the hell! That's only natural. That's normal! Nobody likes to. . . . But they cut the heads off these dogs. Every damn one in the kennel. Well, all right. But if they did that, they should have finished it off and gone the whole way with it. They could have buried them too. But. . . . Shit! What's the good of talking about it?"

Sergeant Jackson looked at Marcy and at Mama Cash, expecting that now they would really throw him out. Mama Cash didn't hold with language. But she didn't say a word.

Of course, Jackson did not see the man with the crewcut, couldn't see him because the man with the crewcut was behind him, also looking at Mama Cash, and signaling to her with his finger to his lips, asking for silence, or, more precisely, bidding for it with a sheaf of bills in the other hand.

"Sometimes it helps to get it off your chest," Mama Cash said, after a moment.

"You think? I have nightmares about it, I tell you. And I'm not the kind to have nightmares easy. I . . . I shot the Jap in the leg and it didn't bother me a bit. The whole fucking town was sick, and they were dying faster than you could wrap them in body bags, and that didn't get to me. No, but them dogs did."

"What town?" the crewcut fellow asked.

"Why, Tarsus, of course!"

Monday, August 17

8:00 P.M., Mountain Daylight Time:

Less than twenty-four hours had passed since Andy Herrin had given Sergeant Jackson the Minolta from the glove compartment of his car. At one moment he was convinced that he was onto something big, the biggest story of his career, and then, at the next, he was sure he was the victim of the wildest con job of the century. It was all an enormous snipe hunt, and he was out a good camera.

The camera had been his own idea. He had coaxed the story out of Jackson piece by piece, making all the sympathetic noises until Jackson had told so much that Herrin had been full of confidence, but that was the name of the game. One of them had been conning the other, and now he was not at all sure which had been the con man and which had been the mark. Still, each time he came around to it, it seemed most implausible that the sergeant could have made up such a thing just to put him on. The drunkenness, the rage, the whole maudlin recitation had seemed authentic at the time. And the fear afterwards, when the sergeant had realized how much he'd said. That had been real enough.

Herrin had thought of the business of the camera not so much to prove anything to himself but to be able to prove to others the authenticity of Jackson's story. The Minolta in the glove compartment had a partially exposed roll of film in it, and Herrin knew what the pictures were and when he had taken them. The first two frames of the roll were of his niece on the bus arriving home from Girl Scout camp the morning before. Any pictures that Jackson could get to prove his story would have to be pictures that he had taken after Sunday morning, August 16.

It had all seemed so likely, so clever, so certain the night before. Now he was worried that Jackson had been putting him on, or, more plausibly, that—even if the story were true—Jackson would prefer to risk Herrin's threat of making an inquiry at Dugway and citing Jackson as his source. There, too, Herrin thought he had been fantastically clever. The deal was that if Jackson cooperated, Herrin would keep Jackson's name out of it.

Herrin paced the living room of his small wood-frame house on the East Bench of Salt Lake City. He had everything ready in the darkroom. He had the folder of glossies that he had taken home from the television station where he worked as a cameraman. All he needed was one matching face, and he'd have it made. It was bigger than My Lai, and better—because this was right here in Utah, and not 12,000 miles away. After this it would be Washington or New York, or maybe London or Paris. . . . The big time!

It was frustrating that there was nothing he could do to speed up the sergeant's progress. He sat, stood, went to the window, returned to the chair, heard the motor of an automobile, went back to the window, saw a car drive by, pass the house, and disappear. Maybe the next car, or the one after that. He stood there and counted ten cars before he began to feel . . . foolish, discouraged, powerless, angry. All those things.

He fixed himself a drink. One little drink wouldn't matter. Would do him good, in fact. He'd be calmer, and could get ahold of himself. He was beginning to think, again, that it had been a hoax, a con, a fantastic finesse. Or . . . there were other ways to account for it, weren't there? Maybe the sergeant had drawn some extra duty. Maybe he had got caught with the camera, had been discovered trying to take those pictures of the survivors. If it was true, if what he'd been saying had been even partly true, the military wouldn't let him wander around with a camera, taking snapshots for his album. Of course, a clever enough photographer could work with a Minolta so that no one could tell he was taking pictures. But was the sergeant clever enough?

Or was he too clever? Thinking of the camera once again, Herrin was convinced that the sergeant had tricked him. After all, the story was fantastic. Things like that can't happen in this country. A thing like that just couldn't be kept secret. Too many people would have to know about it. Somebody—sooner or later—would have to talk.

It was after midnight before Herrin gave up and admitted that Sergeant Jackson would not ring the doorbell; opportunity would not knock; Paris, Rome, London would not call upon his services. He had drunk most of the bottle of Cutty Sark during the four hours he'd been waiting, and he was feeling sorry for himself for having been such a fool, was sorry about the camera.

He thought of going out to Tarsus to look, himself. He actually went to get the car keys from the little table near the front door, and . . . But no. He held the car keys in his hand. What did he expect to see out there in the middle of the night? And he was really too drunk to drive. In the morning, maybe.

He put the keys back. Then he started to get undressed to go to bed. A warm shower and bed. In the morning he would think what to do. Drive out there, or call the base. . . . Of course! He could do that any time. Now, even.

He dialed information, asked for the Dugway number, and called the base. He asked for Sergeant Jackson.

"Who is this calling, please?" the man at the Dugway switchboard asked.

"My name is Jones," Herrin said.

There was a pause. Then the voice said, "I'm sorry, Mr. Jones, there is no Sergeant Jackson on the base. Is there anyone else?"

"No, no thanks."

He hung up. So the guy hadn't even been at Dugway. He was just some soldier from some other base with that crazy cock-and-bull story. Maybe he wasn't even a soldier at all. Just some con artist dressed up in a soldier's suit who . . .

The hell with it. He turned out the lights in the living room and went to bed. Because of the whiskey he was able to fall rapidly into a deep sleep.

Almost as deep as the drugged slumber of Sergeant Jackson in the ward now with the other survivors at the Dugway Proving Ground.

HENRY SUTTON is the occasional pen name of David Slavitt, poet, playwright, novelist, and critic. Born in White Plains, New York, in 1935, he was educated at Phillips Academy, Andover; at Yale, where he was Scholar of the House and from which he graduated *magna cum laude;* and at Columbia, where he received his master's degree. In 1965, he resigned from *Newsweek,* where he had been the motion-picture critic, set out for Cape Cod, and set up on his own to write full time. With the signal successes of THE EXHIBITIONIST and THE VOYEUR, he has become an *enfant terrible* of the American novel; but with ROCHELLE OR VIRTUE REWARDED, with FEEL FREE, and with DAY SAILING, his serious reputation is growing solidly. VECTOR may represent a confluence of the two currents of his career.

THE ANDROMEDA STRAIN

by Michael Crichton

This is the breathtaking story of "Project Wildfire"—
the crash mobilization of the nation's highest scientific
and medical resources—when an unmanned research
satellite returns to earth lethally contaminated.

Four American scientists, chosen in advance for their
experimental achievements, are summoned under conditions of total news blackout to Wildfire's secret laboratory five stories beneath the Nevada desert. There
they work against the threat of a worldwide epidemic
to find an antidote to the unknown microorganism that
has wiped out all but two inhabitants of a small Arizona
town. "Terrifying . . . one of the most important novels
of the year."—*Library Journal*

A DELL BOOK $1.25

The
new
novel
by
the
author
of
The
Manchurian
Candidate

MILE HIGH

by Richard Condon

Mile High is the story of Edward Courance West, the man who invented Prohibition and amassed billions of dollars by exploiting it. The novel begins in Ireland, moves to New York and Washington, shifts to Sicily, then to the capitals of Europe. Edward Courance West's interests are everywhere: in Middle Eastern oil fields, in industries, properties, skyscrapers, banks and governments almost everywhere across the globe. **Mile High** is fiction on a grand scale.

A Dell Book $1.25

If you cannot obtain copies of this title from your local bookseller, just send the price (plus 15c per copy for handling and postage) to Dell Books, Post Office Box 1000, Pinebrook, N.J. 07058. No postage or handling charge is required on any order of five or more books.

26 Weeks on the New York Times Bestseller List!
"Terrifying, suspenseful, mind shattering."
Washington Post

DELIVERANCE

by James Dickey

This novel, by one of America's finest poets, is a tale of violent adventure and inner discovery. Four men embark on a canoe trip down a wild section of a river in the heartland of today's South. When two of the group are attacked viciously and perversely by mountaineers, a mildly adventurous canoe trip explodes into a gruesome nightmare of horror and murder.

"The limit of dramatic tension . . . a novel that will curl your toes!"   *The New York Times*

Soon to be a major movie.

A DELL BOOK $1.25

If you cannot obtain copies of this title from your local bookseller, just send the price (plus 15c per copy for handling and postage) to Dell Books, Post Office Box 1000, Pinebrook, N. J. 07058. No postage or handling charge is required on any order of five or more books.

How many of these Dell bestsellers have you read?

DELL Bestseller List

1. **SUCH GOOD FRIENDS** by Lois Gould $1.25

2. **THE SENSUOUS WOMAN** by "J" $1.25

3. **DELIVERANCE** by James Dickey $1.25

4. **BALL FOUR** by Jim Bouton $1.25

5. **MARY QUEEN OF SCOTS** by Antonia Fraser $1.50

6. **GOING ALL THE WAY** by Dan Wakefield $1.25

7. **THE ANDERSON TAPES** by Lawrence Sanders $1.25

8. **DOCTORS AND WIVES** by Benjamin Siegel $1.25

9. **THE DOCTOR'S QUICK WEIGHT LOSS DIET** by Irwin Maxwell Stillman, M.D. and Samm Sinclair Baker   95c

10. **PLEASE TOUCH** by Jane Howard $1.25

11. **MILE HIGH** by Richard Condon $1.25

12. **THE TERRITORIAL IMPERATIVE** by Robert Ardrey $1.25

13. **THE ANDROMEDA STRAIN** by Michael Crichton $1.25

14. **THE POSEIDON ADVENTURE** by Paul Gallico $1.25

15. **THE $20,000,000 HONEYMOON** by Fred Sparks   95c

If you cannot obtain copies of these titles at your local bookseller, just send the price (plus 15c per copy for handling and postage) to Dell Books, Post Office Box 1000, Pinebrook, N. J. 07058. No postage or handling charge is required on any order of five or more books.